A THOUSAND PAINTED HOURS

OTHER TITLES BY BARBARA O'NEAL

The Last Letter of Rachel Ellsworth

Memories of the Lost

The Starfish Sisters

This Place of Wonder

Write My Name Across the Sky

The Lost Girls of Devon

When We Believed in Mermaids

The Art of Inheriting Secrets

The Lost Recipe for Happiness

The Secret of Everything

How to Bake a Perfect Life

The Garden of Happy Endings

The All You Can Dream Buffet

No Place Like Home

A Piece of Heaven

The Goddesses of Kitchen Avenue

Lady Luck's Map of Vegas

The Scent of Hours

PRAISE FOR *A THOUSAND PAINTED HOURS*

"A lush and colorful look at the first half of the twentieth century—and the colonial politics that played out as world wars raged—through the eyes of a British artist born in India who longs, during the Blitz in London, to return to the town that holds her heart in the foothills of the Himalayas. Those hungry for epistolary novels will enjoy Barbara O'Neal's *A Thousand Painted Hours*, written largely in letters of love, regret, and duty that span continents and decades."

—Kristin Harmel, *New York Times* bestselling author

"From the forested hills of India to the bomb-scarred streets of London to the searing heat of Cairo, *A Thousand Painted Hours* is a colorful, transportive, and heartrending novel. In a sweeping tale of friendship and love through the ages, O'Neal grabs her readers by the heart and doesn't let go. Not to be missed!"

—Heather Webb, *USA Today* bestselling author of *The Hope Keeper*

A THOUSAND PAINTED HOURS

A NOVEL

BARBARA O'NEAL

LAKE UNION PUBLISHING

This is a work of fiction. Names, characters, organizations, places, events, and incidents are either products of the author's imagination or are used fictitiously. Otherwise, any resemblance to actual persons, living or dead, is purely coincidental.

Published by Lake Union Publishing, Seattle

www.apub.com

EU product safety contact:
Amazon Media EU S. à r.l.
38, avenue John F. Kennedy, L-1855 Luxembourg
amazonpublishing-gpsr@amazon.com

ISBN-13: 9781662514968 (hardcover)
ISBN-13: 9781662514975 (paperback)
ISBN-13: 9781662514982 (digital)

Cover design by Joanne O'Neill
Cover image: © CR Shelare, © kentarcajuan, © silviasprints / Getty;
© provectors / Adobe Stock

Printed in the United States of America
First edition

With deepest love and thanks to the generous writer and thinker Sonali Dev. I am so honored and grateful to call you a friend.

PROLOGUE

London, 1940

You will think this a story of the war. *The* war, as if it is the only one, when this century has been so filled with them.

It is not about war. It is about the opposite.

My story begins with cyanide tablets.

A DINNER PARTY WITH CYANIDE

September 6–7, 1940
London

—1—

The night before the bombs started falling was hot in London. Blackout curtains forced us to keep the French doors closed, though some of us went out to breathe between courses, shaking our clothing away from our skin. Pale roses climbed the wall, perfuming the air with unseemly innocence.

After a dessert of rosewater sponge, Jonathan, a man with the slim hands of a pianist, held up a tiny glass bottle. "These are cyanide tablets," he said. "I have one for each of us."

"Cyanide!" Reed exclaimed.

"Yes." Jonathan passed the basket of bottles. "In case."

The diners, eight of us, silently selected a bottle, as if there would be some difference to one or the other. A Bach cello symphony played on the gramophone, as bittersweet as the moment. When the basket came to me, I paused. "It's come to this?"

"Hitler will invade," Nina said. "What then?"

Paris had fallen just months before, once thought impossible. I looked at my old friend's sober face, the first friend I'd made upon arriving in England from India, furious and lost, at the age of fifteen. A parade of images marched through my mind: my golden childhood in India, running wild in the hills; the halcyon years of dancing and kissing and drinking wine in London when my father's inheritance brought us all back to England. I thought of that picnic on the beach in Brighton when we were all so young and whole and completely unaware of what was about to happen, that last summer before the war.

The other war.

I looked at my husband, survivor of that last war, the husband who mostly hated me, my enemy and one of the central pillars of my life.

But not the only one.

I took a glass bottle from the basket and passed it on.

~

After the party, we traveled home late, Peter a bit too far in his cups to drive. I navigated the dark, quiet streets carefully. The blackout made driving an exercise in madness, and we should have walked, but Peter wouldn't hear of it—his gout made walking painful, and I was not completely heartless. I gripped the steering wheel so hard my hands sweated, and crept along like an ancient snail.

The vial with cyanide was tucked into an inside pocket of my coat, but Peter held his up. "Do you suppose anyone will use these?"

"I hope we never need them." My mind ran through the potential horrors, Nazis overtaking London as they had Paris. It still made my skin ache to think of it, my friends and all the beautiful streets in that city I'd grown to love, overrun by tanks and trucks. The idea of German soldiers dictating our lives the same way made my stomach hurt, but would I give in to suicide? "It's terrible to think about."

"We need one for your mother," he said, tucking the bottle back in his coat pocket to free his hands to light a cigarette. "We couldn't very well leave her to the Nazis."

"Please don't smoke," I protested. "It gives me a headache in the car."

He blinked and tucked the cigarette in his mouth, then smirkingly lit it and blew the smoke toward the roof. I steeled my face to show nothing, hands on the wheel. Below the surface, fury battered the underside of my skin, tried to force its way out of my body.

"My mother would not take poison," I said calmly. And of course, she was the reason I could not, and the reason I remained in my marriage. Peter and I were no more or less unhappy than many of our peers. Our generation had been marked by chaos from the beginning, and now would face more. It was difficult to keep up a sense of optimism.

"I wouldn't, either," he said. "Sounds hideous." Relenting, he cracked the window, and we rode the rest of the way in silence, parking the Austin on the street in front of our town house. Blackout shades prevented any light from leaking through the windows, but I knew my mother would be reading on the second floor, and I'd left a lamp on in my studio.

"I'm going to check on Mother," I said. "Good night."

He gave me a sardonic salute, standing on the sidewalk to smoke the rest of his cigarette, cupping his hand to hide the red tip. I walked upstairs and found my mother tucked into her bed, a lamp close by to illuminate her book. Spectacles slid down her nose, and her luxurious hair was thinning and laced with silver, but all her life she'd been a great beauty, and that remained true. Illness had whittled away only the superfluous, lending her cheekbones and jaw a feline grace, making her large blue eyes all the more compelling. "Hello, darling," she said. "How was the evening?"

"Amusing enough." I sat on her bed. "They're a witty lot."

She nodded. A faint yellow cast marked her skin, and her hands were cold. "How are you tonight?" I asked. "Do you need anything?"

"No, thank you. Betty brought me my ginger tonic before she went to bed."

"And how are you?" I repeated, smoothing my hand on her wrist.

"Well enough," she said, glancing away. She was seventy and suffering liver disease from a recurrent malaria infection she'd suffered from since my childhood. Ill health had plagued her repeatedly since, but this last round seemed far worse.

Always my mother, she patted my hand and put her book aside with a smile that did not mask the pain around her mouth. "I was only waiting up to say good night. Go paint now. I'll see what you've done in the morning."

I kissed her forehead and turned off the light, tucking her in as she'd so often tucked me, then headed upstairs to my sanctuary, the studio that had been part of the bargain I'd agreed to when I finally gave in to Peter's wish for me to come home. It was a wide-open space beneath the eaves, an attic meant for storage, but perfect for my purposes. It was too hot in summer, too cold in winter, but in the daytime, I could look out over the treetops of Bloomsbury.

Within, the floors were spattered with decades of paint, and canvases leaned against the wall. It was startling to see the reduced number—I'd sent more than two dozen to Helen Bonhome, a friend from art school who lived in the north, where we hoped they'd be safe from bombing. I was in the process of finding places for the rest.

A bubble of worry burst in my diaphragm as I imagined any of them going up in flames. The work of my life. I flipped through some of my earliest oils, the courtyard in Nainital with the laburnum tree, a portrait of my friend Gurdaya when she was still young. I paused at the rendering of the maharani and my mother taking tea in a sunlit room, the light shining behind them, highlighting the crowns of their heads, the edges of their hands, shining through the delicate china of the cup my mother held. I'd once been offered a small fortune for this particular work, but as with so many others, I found it difficult to let it go.

Foolishness. Especially now.

I wrapped myself in an oversize cardigan, opened my sketchbook, and found my peace in drawing the faces around the dinner table this evening, and the roses hanging in ghostly beauty in the garden. Art, as I'd learned so many times, could distract me from the harshest pain.

I remembered sketching the receding skyline of Bombay the day we left it.

LEAVING INDIA

1911

—2—

I was born in India, where my father had been in the ICS, the Indian Civil Service. When I was fifteen, his elder brother, the Earl of Herewich, died suddenly of a spleen injury sustained on a hunt, and my father was abruptly summoned home to take up his title.

It was the worst news I could have heard. I had never known any home but Nainital, and I loved it—the forests and the mountains and the lake, my friends and my collection of little animals.

I protested. I wailed. I begged.

There was no negotiating. We were leaving India, immediately.

It took two weeks to travel to Bombay from Nainital, in the foothills of northern India, then a week to await the ship. Every minute of it I burned with resistance.

And yet, here we stood on the stern of the great liner, watching Bombay slip away below the horizon. Parts of my body felt as if they were tearing away from me, my veins turning to fragile glass, my lungs as thin as rice paper.

My mother stood behind me, her hands cold on my shoulders. I did not turn to see if she was weeping, but I certainly was. Every thread of my life was being severed—the sight of the mountains rising in the distance, parakeets and monkeys, the sound of a treepie crying out, laburnum trees dripping their yellow flowers like long hair from their branches, the scent of my ayah's sari, the courtyard on summer evenings, the air alive with insects and stars.

And of course, Tanveer, mixed into every single second of it. I could not speak his name for fear my mother would hear more than she should in my tone, but it was he that I would most mourn, even as I was furious with him.

When land had disappeared and there was only sea everywhere around us, my mother shook herself. "All right, then," she said. "That's done. Shall we find some tea?"

I held my arms around my ribs. "I will stay here."

"My dear, it will serve no good to cling to what must be left behind."

"Perhaps not," I said, and then could think of nothing else to add.

She stroked my hair. "We shall return one day, you and I."

I did not reply, and she left me standing alone against the rail, wind blowing my shawl up around me, rustling my skirts. In my pocket was his letter, but I dared not take it out in such gusts. I fingered the edges, imagining that I could feel his words against my skin, words he'd written in the Urdu script, which we had learned first as a challenge, then later to hide the words of our communication. His father spoke and wrote four languages, but had not bothered with the written script of Urdu. My mother had some skill with Hindustani, even some Persian, but she could not write Urdu. It had become our secret code.

I did not need to read the words, for I had memorized every paragraph.

> My life, we knew this day would come, that our paths would come to this place of parting, that I would go on to my duties and you would go to yours in another world. It grieves me more than I expected. I am sensible and clear sighted, but my heart seems not to recognize the presence of reason. It only wants what it wants, to hold you always, to have you as my own. I cannot bear the idea of a husband for you that is not me, nor a wife for me that is not you. It is a great tragedy.

And yet, we are dutiful. We must each serve the lives we were born to live.

I do not think it wise for us to continue to write to each other. It will only sear my soul each time I see your words, but know that I am always your love, until the stars no longer shine.

Tanveer

I did not wish to be sensible, nor accept my fate so passively. I did not want to leave my beloved India for a landscape unknown to me—and to my mother, for she, too, had been born and raised on the subcontinent.

Two months before, my father's inheritance had made him an earl, thus elevating our status in the world remarkably. The British community at Nainital had been entirely aflutter at the news, fussing suddenly over the new countess, whom they'd always slightly shunned for doing things her own way, befriending locals like the maharani, studying methods of medicine they did not approve of (though I noticed they leaned on her when they wanted help with some recalcitrant stomach problem or sore feet).

Of course, they never entirely shut her out because she owned the thing in a woman that cannot be ignored—a great and impossible beauty, with wide blue eyes, perfect red lips, and exquisite dark hair. I'd heard all manner of gossip about my mother, that she was the secret daughter of a sultan, that she was the love child of English royalty, even one that said she'd been found in the forest and was therefore an orphan of uncertain parentage.

In truth, she was the daughter of a Welsh couple who'd taken the road to India as a way to escape the brutality of their home village. Her father had been a minor bureaucrat in Lucknow, and they had indeed raised their status, and thus their daughter's, in the world. She had not been my father's social equal, but beauty will level the field in such matters.

Mother dismissed every bit of gossip, holding no grudge. "People make up stories when they do not have enough to keep themselves occupied."

Nor did she take her beauty seriously. She was far more occupied with her passion for healing, for the vagaries of the human body, with caring for the poor.

My father adored her. I do not think he ever understood, his entire life, what grand surprise of fortune had landed him such a beautiful wife, and one who was not foolish or empty headed, or driven by social climbing. He, too, was a man who did not fit well with his peers, a second son left to his own devices who liked reading rather too much, and desperately wanted—against all odds—to serve the people he was charged with leading. He no more wanted the title and lands he'd inherited in England than my mother wanted to move, but what choice did he have? One did not turn down an earldom.

So now we sailed to England, and I wept for the loss of all I knew.

October 10, 1911
Aboard the SS Peregrine
[In Urdu]

Tanveer,
I do not know how to address you, so I shall lead only with your name.

You said we should not write, and I will not do so again after this, but I have one more thing to share with you.

Tonight was another interminable dinner, at which I had to perform my role of the earl's daughter in front of an audience of unspeakable sycophants. They do not care about me or even really my father, but only his position. Six months ago, they thought him beneath them, and now, they can't crowd closely enough.

I escaped to the deck and the cold seafaring dark. The darkness at sea is an encompassing, unbroken blackness, no distant lights from windows or the village or an inconsiderate moon, only the vastness of night, lit with uncountable numbers of stars.

So vast, Tanveer! Endless, endless swathes of stars, large and small, white and red and blue, all the way to the horizon, in all directions. I have never seen such a thing!

And there above me was Venus, shining so brightly I could see her glow reflected on the sea.

I could not help thinking how much you would have loved it, how much I wished you were standing there with me, looking up. You would have told me what the constellations were. I know some of them, al-Jabbār and Thāt al-Kursī, of course, but never so many as you do.

It made me feel less bereft, bathing in the light of Venus, knowing you might at that very moment be seeing her, too. It shrank the distance between us, somehow.

I won't write again, but I thought you would want to hear about the stars over the ocean. I painted them for you, but it is a poor imitation of the reality.

Be well,

Elsie

[Enclosed watercolor of the night sky and Venus]

—3—

London, 1940

The first bombs fell on September 7. We'd been bracing for weeks, but perhaps in the way of every person who has known comfort and is loath to let it go, we kept believing that the war would remain distant, far away from us.

We were setting the table for tea when the sirens went off. I looked at Mother, and then at Peter. We'd had a number of false alarms. Was this one real? Betty, our housekeeper, ran through the door from the kitchen, wringing a towel through her hands. "What do we do?" she cried.

I headed to the back door to look out, and the sky was clear. I could hear no engines over the sound of the sirens, but that didn't mean there weren't any.

Peter said beside me, pointing, "There."

On the horizon was a sprinkling of what looked like birds. I felt my blood drain through my body, leaving me shivery and frightened. I froze until Peter took my arm and gently directed me toward the cellar door.

Mother nudged Betty ahead of her. "All is well, my dear. We've prepared." She waved her hand at Peter and me, and we followed her through the kitchen. "Elsie, bring the biscuits. Peter, that pitcher of water."

Before we reached the stairs, the first bombs whistled through the air, the sound piercing, terrifying, and we instinctively looked toward the sky, holding our breath, counting as with lightning. A boom sounded, and another, and another. The walls shook. I ducked instinctively.

Behind me, Peter roared, "Down to the cellar!"

Dust shook from the rafters as we clattered down the steps, diving into the shelter Peter had painstakingly built over the past three months, larger than an Anderson shelter, making more space for all of us. I was grateful as we took our places around the little table Mother had ordered brought down weeks ago. We sat on the old sofa, draped with blankets, and she sat in the chair that had once graced our house in Nainital, so many years before. A bag of knitting awaited. "There, now," she said, raising her voice to be heard above the noise, the sirens going on and on, along with the irregular whistling and thudding of bombs.

Betty shivered, arms clasped around herself. "I didn't know it would be so loud," she said.

I grabbed a shawl from the back of the sofa and flung it over her shoulders. "Never mind," I said. "Let's have some biscuits. We mustn't waste the sugar, now, should we?"

Only Peter paced, back and forth, back and forth. His face was the color of snow, and I felt pity. He'd known terrible suffering in the last war, taken prisoner in North Africa. "Bloody bombs," he muttered.

"Language, please," Mother said. "Come, sit and have a biscuit, Peter. The sugar will do you good."

The sirens slowed, and I took a breath, reaching for a biscuit. "Are these lemon—?"

A loud whistle, sounding as if it were right over our heads, sailed down, down, down, and an explosion much closer than any other we'd heard made the windows rattle. Dirt shook down on our heads. Betty yelped.

"Oh, dear." Mother met my eye. Smoothly, to create distraction, she said, "Elsie, do you remember when the tiger threatened the village?"

TIGERS AND STARS

1906
Nainital, India

—4—

We had moved to Nainital, in the hill country, from Lucknow, mainly for my mother's health. The cooler mountain air was thought to ease her bouts of malaria. My father remained in Lucknow and visited for a few months each summer, but we stayed. I loved the forests, the cooler air, the lake, the mountains hanging in a ragged curtain across the horizon.

The summer I was ten, a tiger had been plaguing the area, stealing goats and small livestock. A farmer reported his dogs gone, and everyone fretted that a child would be carried off next. Reports of a wild man-eater in the east had come to us, and many feared she had made her way over the mountains.

My father, spitting tobacco off his tongue, called that notion poppycock. "It is not a magical beast. It would never travel so far."

I found the idea of a tiger thrilling. From my high window, I peered into the forest, hoping to glimpse her. She would stalk to the end of the garden on her giant paws, then pause and look up to see me, her compatriot of spirit. Our eyes would lock, and I would peer deeply into her gold irises for long moments before she gave a roar and trotted back into the trees.

The adults were less romantic. As a result of the threat, we were confined to the courtyards, so I sat in the heat with my ayah, sketching the laburnum tree. I was ten, one of only a handful of English children in the village my age. The others had all been sent away to England for school.

I must have sketched a great many other things before that day—I had always had a pencil in my hand—but my mother had given me a grand new sketchbook for my birthday. The pages were heavy, bound in leather, complete with a little strap and buckle to keep it closed.

The house was built in the Indian fashion, with verandas and a large courtyard in the middle. Benches and fountains filled the sunny space, and at the center was the great tree in full, cascading flower.

I sat on a bench in the slender shade of the courtyard. My ankles and feet were warmed by sunshine, my stockings and shoes discarded to one side. Before me, the tree bloomed yellow against the blue of the sky. The sight so excited my heart that I spent two hours trying to capture it—the shape of the tree trunk, the arch itself, and the tumble of flowers like sunlight hanging in the air. I had begun to grow frustrated as the heat rose, and might have torn it out of the book and flung it away had not my ayah come by and exclaimed loudly in Hindustani, "So beautiful!"

She loved me more than anyone, so it wasn't a surprise. Still, I accepted her praise with a warm flush of pleasure, and carried the book inside to show my mother. She sat in the open-air parlor, drinking tea with another woman I had not seen before. The other woman was delicately lovely, with large dark eyes and a smooth tan complexion framed by her gold tissue scarf.

"Elsie," my mother cried. "I was about to send for you. This is the maharani of Talwarpur, and these are her children, Tanveer and Gurdaya. They have just come to Nainital, and will be our neighbors, just down the road."

Until then, I had not seen the children, who sat in poorly hidden boredom on a settee nearby the open doors to the courtyard. The girl was a little older than me, I thought, already getting long legged. Her black hair was tied back in a braid, the same as mine, and she viewed me with a haughty gaze, beneath her notice.

In contrast, her brother jumped to his feet. He was nowhere near as compelling as his sister. His nose was prominent, his brows quite heavy, but his eyes were friendlier than hers. He peered at the drawing I carried. "Did you draw this?" he exclaimed.

"Who else?" I said, but instead of taking offense, he smiled.

"Let me see, Elsie," my mother said, and I gave it up to her.

She took her time, and I moved from foot to foot, worried that I would not please her, that she would give me the most desultory of smiles and hand it back to me as she so often did, but today she said quietly, "Elsie, this is quite the best thing you've done so far. Well done, you."

"May I?" asked the maharani.

I nodded. She, too, gave grave consideration to my creation, then handed it back to me. "It is lovely, my dear."

"Elsie," my mother said, "take the children to the playroom, and you may have your lunch there."

"I'd rather stay," the girl said. "I've brought my embroidery."

"All right," her mother said, and then to my mother: "She dislikes children's games."

"I was such a girl myself."

I led Tanveer to the playroom, another room off the same courtyard, but because it seemed so plainly watched, I'd discovered the servants and adults paid me no mind here, amid the games and toys. A breeze lifted the curtains, cooling the space, and the open doors looked toward the mountains towering in the distance.

Tanveer kept his hands behind his back as he inspected the space. He wore a white tunic over loose trousers, his hair gathered in a knot on top of his head and covered with a thin cloth, as was the custom for such boy children.

"I hope you are not a bossy boy," I said.

A smile flashed over his face, transforming his sober expression. "I hope *you* are not as bossy as my sister."

It made me laugh. "How old are you?"

"Ten."

"So am I! I just had my birthday."

"Why aren't you in England?"

"My mother refused to send me."

He measured me, hands still tucked behind him, like a little old man. "It is unusual."

I sat at the low table, scattered with paper and drawing utensils. "I'm glad. I don't want to leave India." He continued to stand, surveying the room, the windows, the tools. "Sit down. Do you like to draw?"

He sat across from me, his hands flat on the table, as he considered the tools. "I have, at times, yes."

It was a serious answer, very precise, and I inclined my head. "Are you a prince if you're the maharani's son?"

"I am a prince, but not heir," he said, again so specific. "My brother will be maharaja."

"Do you ride on elephants?"

"Sometimes." He pulled a sheet of paper toward him, and picked up a small block of charcoal. A silver bracelet on his right wrist clacked against the table, an adornment I had often noticed Sikh men wore. "Do you always ask so many questions?"

"Yes." I grinned. "And I often get into trouble over it. My father says I am too nosy by half."

On the paper, he drew a curve, and then a small tube, and feet, and then a big tube, and ears.

"An elephant!" I cried.

"This is Noor Baba," he said, adding a blanket over the creature's back and then ears. "He is a very good elephant."

"I like your drawing."

"Thank you." He raised his head and gave me a much less impish smile. This one was small and quiet, shining in his dark eyes.

I thought perhaps we could be friends.

"Have you heard about the tiger?" Tanveer asked, taking a new sheet of paper.

"Who hasn't?" It was all the adults spoke of, servants in whispers, parents and visitors in voices that hummed with fear and excitement. "I heard it dragged off a goat yesterday."

"It stole a girl from a village in the mountains!"

"A girl! How old of a girl?" I thought of the tiger in my imagination, golden eyed, sleek.

"I don't know. Not very old. Her mother came to see my father, weeping and weeping."

"Why?"

He looked up. "Why did she weep?"

"No, why did she come to see your father? What could he do once the tiger had taken her?"

"She wanted justice. She wants the tiger dead, the hide given to her as compensation."

I recoiled. "Dead! But tigers do what tigers do!"

"Yes, but once they get a taste for humans, they won't stop hunting them."

Tears sprang to my eyes. "I can't bear the idea of it being hunted."

He sobered, his great dark eyes shining. "Nor I, to be honest." He touched his chest. "I hope he eludes the hunters."

"Me, too." I turned to a fresh page. "Let's draw tigers, shall we?"

So we did. It was more challenging than I expected, and I started over a few times, my mind snagging on the stripes, the orange of the body, the long tail. Tanveer instead drew a face, the ears and whiskers and eyes, staring right out of the page.

"That's good," I said. "Show me how!"

"I only drew my cat, and then made it bigger like a tiger."

"You have a cat? What is its name?"

"He is Shera," Tanveer said with a smile. "That is the Punjabi word for *tiger*."

I laughed, delighted. "Is he orange?"

"He is!"

"I would love to have a cat of my own." On a fresh page, I copied the shape of the tiger Tanveer had drawn, working with the fatter cheeks, the strong nose.

"There are always kittens. I shall bring you one if you like."

"Oh, yes! I would like that very much."

"Would you like to see how to write *tiger* in three ways? I am learning scripts."

"Yes!"

He wrote them out. "Shair," he said, "which is Urdu." The letters ran right to left like a vine. "Shera in Punjabi." It was a word like little houses, left to right. "And this is Sanskrit, vyāghra."

"How do you know so many languages?"

"I only know this word in all of them. I am given lessons in all of them, so I might be well versed in my father's palace."

"But you are not the crown prince?"

His smile flashed, showing a dimple in his right cheek. "True, but one must be prepared."

"Teach me!"

"I will show you Urdu."

The letters were nothing like English, but I carefully copied them, loving the shape of the script, the tails and accents. "Do you know the whole alphabet?"

"No. But I can show you the ones I do know."

—5—

The tiger shaped our every move for months. Reports of its size and ferocity filtered back to us, more and more alarming. It was the biggest tiger that had been seen in a decade! The biggest seen in fifty years! None larger had been spotted since the British had arrived! Who knew what exaggerations were actually true.

What was known was that it had developed a taste for humans. First the girl, then a boy and his father from the forest when they were collecting figs. Their bag was abandoned, and only a blood smear, along with a hat and a single sandal left behind on the dry dirt showed where their bodies had been.

Adults shushed each other when we children were listening, or rather, when they knew we listened. That summer, Tanveer and I, and sometimes even Gurdaya, became adept at lurking around the edges of a gathering, imagining we were tigers stalking the ladies in their finery, the fat men with their cigars. We heard plenty.

Because our mothers had become fast friends, working on some project for the poor that we didn't care about in the slightest, we were often together, and the nearness of our houses gave us easy access. The friendship between the maharani and Mother was not common, but it had been born of Mother's healing arts. She was often called to any number of duties among the women of the community, low and high, but she had developed a reputation for treating an Indian of any caste.

The maharani had heard of my mother's talents with back pain, and had found some relief with her.

So the children became friends, too, sharing stories to terrify each other, playing games in the courtyards and pretending to be masters of the forest, with Tanveer's cat and an old black dog, my pet birds—two parakeets and a mynah I was attempting to teach how to speak—and an orphaned baby monkey that my father had rescued.

I loved the cat wildly, her purr and long whiskers, her soft orange fur unlike any of the fur of the dogs my father kept for hunting. Because of the birds, my mother counseled me that I should not bring a cat home, so I loved when I could curl up with Shera. She liked to come with us to the playroom and up to the roof. Once, she trotted into the room and proudly dropped a rat at my feet. When I bolted, terrified, Tanveer laughed. "It is a gift. She likes you!"

The cat helped me understand the body of the tiger. I drew Shera over and over, and then more drawings of the tiger. I was obsessed with her.

Every story, exaggerated or not, fueled my imagination. I drew a thousand tigers, and tiger paws, and tiger snouts. I found illustrations in storybooks to copy, tracing them out carefully, refining my knowledge. Tigers had a broad nose, with eyes tilted upward. Their paws were white, with claws marking each toe. It was a challenge to learn the structure of the nose, with odd compartments, until we studied Tanveer's cat and mastered the triangle shape.

The maharaja's summer residence was only a short distance from our house, both located in the hills to avail the inhabitants of the cooler temperatures up high, but when we traveled to and fro that spring, an army of servants traveled with us, all of them armed and watchful. A sepoy—an Indian solider serving with the British—few miles distant had seen the beast and reported it to be gigantic.

Just before the monsoons, there was to be a gathering of politicians and wives at the maharaja's residence. My father would attend, along with many other officials and a handful of princes. To the east, the state of Bengal had been divided, and the experiment was rocky. Of course, we children cared little for politics, and all I wanted was to play with my friends. I carried with me a satchel loaded with paints and sketchbooks and plums plucked from our trees, something to share as I'd been taught. As we traveled, I peered hard into the trees to see if I might catch a glimpse of the tiger, slinking through the shadows.

But we arrived without incident. Tanveer and Gurdaya met us at the door, and we children wheeled away to their playroom. In her own world, Gurdaya was far more friendly.

"I brought my paints and pencils," I said.

"We have those things," Gurdaya retorted. "Do you think us poor?"

"Gudiya," Tanveer said, his nickname for her. "She's only being kind, to share." He turned his smile on me. "Isn't that right?"

"Yes," I said. "I also brought plums, but perhaps you have them as well."

Gurdaya snatched a plum. "My favorite!" She sank her teeth into the flesh, swirling around in happiness. The light from the window caught in the thin tissue of her scarf, across the planes of her face.

I smoothed my hand over my sketchbook and picked up a pencil, struck by some magic in her spin, her braid flying out sideways, the scarf lifting in delicate purple light. Her face intrigued me, the angles and the planes and the softness of her lips. I tried to show it in spare lines, a curve, a sharp mark for her nose, the sidelong angle of her eye.

It wasn't what I hoped. I missed some essential something, but by then she had collapsed near the table, legs akimbo. "Is that me?"

"I'll do better," I said, abjectly embarrassed at the poor attempt.

"Nonsense," Tanveer said. "You've caught her movement. How did you do that?"

I shook my head. I didn't know how to say it in words—something had blazed through my imagination for a moment, the light and her limbs and hair, and I felt it in my hands.

"I like it," Gurdaya said.

"Thank you."

~

That night, Tanveer led the three of us up to the roof after dark. The sky stretched like darkest blue velvet overhead, scattered with glittering stars. "My father is a student of astronomy," he said. "I asked his permission to show you his telescope, as it is a dark night, and we shall be able to see a great deal."

"Aren't all nights dark?"

Gurdaya snorted.

Tanveer touched my shoulder, ever so lightly, as if to shift my attention his way. "A dark sky is a moonless night." He gestured toward the darkness above us. "Do you know what you see here?"

I shook my head. "Only stars."

He drew a finger along a spray of white. "That is Akash Ganga, or what you know as the Milky Way. It is made of millions and millions of stars."

"A river of stars," I said.

His smile flashed. "Yes. And there is Jupiter, the largest planet in the galaxy."

"I do know the solar system."

"Good." He pointed again. "Mars is that little star, and Saturn. Venus is the brightest one, there, sparkling."

"Can you see them through the glass?"

"Yes." He showed me how to position my eye. "It is easier if you don't press your eye right into it, but hold your head a little away."

I struggled to see anything, and frustration rose in my chest. Frowning, I lifted my head, and looked again with my bare eyes, then back through. Nothing. I shook my head. "I cannot see anything."

"Let me adjust it," he said, and bent in, tapping the scope a little, a little, a little. His kurta was pale in the darkness. "There," he said, and backed away. "Carefully."

Moving with extreme caution, I held my eye just a little away from the viewfinder, and to my delight, there was a round ball of shining light. "I see it!"

"That," he said with some satisfaction, "is Venus."

I stood up, beaming. "How magical!"

He grabbed my arm suddenly, his grip tight, and pressed a finger to his lips. With his free hand, he pointed out toward the garden below, a stretch of manicured grass surrounded with encroaching oak and chestnut trees.

And there, walking stealthily around the edge of the perimeter, was the tiger. In my excitement, I covered my mouth to avoid making a sound.

We stood motionless, but below, the tiger paused as if she sensed us. One paw hung in the air, her tail high, only visible because of the white stripes. I was transfixed by her size, the sense of power emanating from her muscles and stance. She paused only for a few seconds, then walked into the trees.

He was gripping my arm so tightly I felt indentations. He let go. "Sorry, but—" His face reflected my wonder, his eyes shining. "Can you believe it?"

I let the wonder and magic well up through me, spill over. I could think of nothing to express the gilded delight, but already I was thinking of how to draw her, the way she melded with the shadows, her stripes echoing the bright and dark shape of the night and the trees.

"We must tell someone!" Gurdaya said.

"No!" Tanveer said, catching his sister before she fled. "This is her world—we are the intruders."

"I don't want to die because a tiger has eaten me!" She shook off his grip, and made for the door.

"Gudiya," I said. "What if you were the tiger, hungry and needing to feed your children?"

It was a last-ditch plea, but it seemed to sway her. She glanced over the wall, to the darkness. "All right. But if she attacks another person, we must tell them we saw her."

"Yes," Tanveer said, and gave me a conspiratorial glance.

"I am going to read," she said. "Do not follow me."

"Do you swear you will not tell?" Tanveer asked.

"I will not tell," she said, and was gone.

He looked at me, and I at him. We were almost exactly the same height, eye to eye. "She will not tell, not now," he said. "And when the tiger kills again, it will be too late."

"When? Do you think she will?"

"Of course," he said, ever clear eyed. "We are simply prey, after all."

Worry rose like a miasma, blotting out my joy. "But won't we then be responsible for those deaths?"

"No," he said firmly. "She has a right to live in her world, even if we don't like what she does."

I shivered. "She is so beautiful. I want to go downstairs and paint her before I forget."

"Yes," he agreed. "The stars will be here another night."

As we turned away, I looked over my shoulder. What if she did kill someone else? How would I feel?

I didn't know.

—6—

Not long after we spied the tiger in the trees, she attacked a woman doing laundry at the river and dragged her into the forest. Her husband found her empty sari on the banks, and tracked a trail of blood into the forest, where it disappeared. Her body was not found.

A party of villagers arrived at the maharaja's palace, demanding the tiger be hunted. My father was invited.

It was distantly horrifying that it had killed another person, but the tiger was a hundred times more real. I'd seen her. When I heard, I marched to my father's study, where he was preparing himself. I said, "You can't kill the tiger!"

"Don't be ridiculous, Elsie," he said. "It's killing people. You could very well be next. Would you want that?"

"No!" I thought of what Tanveer had said. "But it's her land. She was here first."

"Progress has brought us here now." He dropped his booted foot to the floor, shook down his trouser leg. "God gave man dominion over the beasts, and at times they must be subdued."

He stood and made to pass by, but I grabbed his arm. "No, please, Father! I saw her. She's so beautiful."

"Many beautiful things must die," he said more gently. "This tiger will not halt until she's brought down. How many people would you agree were enough to trade for her death, hmm? Twenty, fifty? There's a tiger to the east who has killed hundreds. Would that be cause enough?"

I wept, pulling on his arm, aware that I was out of control, but unable to rein myself in. It seemed so brutal to hunt her. "No, please, don't!"

"Enough," he said, and yanked away harshly. "When you grow up, you'll understand that nature must be subdued."

He left me collapsed in a heap on the floor, unsubdued and unwilling to be.

~

The maharaja, along with other ICS members, formed a party with my father, and the maharani brought Tanveer and Gurdaya to our villa to wait. The children gathered in the nursery, quiet in our games but taking comfort in each other's company.

"When do you begin school?" Gurdaya asked. The hunt didn't bother her, and she was plainly attempting to distract her brother and me.

"Not long. I think in September."

"As will I," Tanveer said, shading the stripes of the tiger on his page. Unable to bear drawing the tiger, I focused on sketching his hands against the page. He had long fingers and oval nails. The angle of thumb to wrist was quite elegant, and I tried to decide why.

I looked up. "Will you go to the Diocesan Boys School?"

"No, I must travel to Ajmer."

"Boarding school?"

"Of course."

I stared at him, gutted a second time in two days. "When will you be back?"

"At the winter holidays."

"But that's months from now!"

"I will be in school with you here," Gurdaya said.

I looked at her, and swallowed the searing disappointment in my chest. "That will be nice." But I looked back to Tanveer, head bent over his paper. I'd grown used to his easy company. Gurdaya was pricklier, harder to please, and I didn't always know how to meet her mercurial moods.

He looked up and must have caught something in my expression. "It will be all right," he said. "You shall see."

Later, Gurdaya deserted us to sit with the women. Tanveer and I escaped to the grand lawn behind the villa and set up a game of bowls. The air was quite still, sunlight so bright its weight scorched the grass. Cicadas whirred in the trees, off and on, off and on, and the mountains were so washed out, they seemed as if they'd been watercolored against the horizon. I could not think of anything but the tiger fleeing from the hunt, and then of Tanveer leaving for school, just as my brother had several years ago. My chest ached, but to be a good sport, I desultorily hit the balls, taking my turn and watching as he took his.

"Well done," I said, pulling my braid off my neck to let air get to it.

"Not really," he replied. "You hardly played."

"It's hot."

He gestured toward the grove of trees nearby the back wall, where a collection of chairs sat in the shade. The adults often sat there in the cool of the evening. "You should have lemonade and a snack."

I nodded. It was often the case when my mood fell—I forgot to eat, forgot to drink. A servant named Champa polished a soup tureen just inside the door, and Tanveer spoke to her in Hindustani. She bowed and hurried away.

We settled, and in the shade, the temperature was not so exhausting. A breeze swept over us. His gaze fixed on the horizon, his mouth sober.

"I shall miss you," I said. "I did not know you would be leaving."

He bumped his sandaled foot against mine. "Will you send me drawings?"

"Yes, if you will write back." I frowned. "My brother never writes back, ever. I have only ever had one letter from him in all this time. He barely writes to Mother."

"Do you miss him, your brother? I never hear you speak of him."

I shrugged. "Not as much as I did. It seems a very long time since he left for school." The servant returned with a tray holding a pitcher of lemonade, a bowl of small apples, dal vadas, and a hefty slice of cake.

"Cake," Tanveer cried. "Your cook makes the best coconut cake in the world."

"He sent it to you, I'm quite sure." I disliked the cloying taste of coconut very much. I poured glasses of lemonade and took a deep drink, feeling the cooling sensation all through my throat and belly. I sighed in relief.

Next to me, Tanveer dug into the cake with great intent, pausing to wash it down. "I will write."

I nodded. It wouldn't be the same, but it was better than nothing.

I watched him finish eating, carefully scraping up the very last bits of icing from the plate. "Do you like school?"

"Yes," he said. "I get lonely because it's far from home, but I like my studies. Do you?"

"Sometimes. Not maths, but history and literature please me. Poetry, art, all those lady things."

He grinned. "You like astronomy."

Warmed, I smiled back. Then paused and blurted out, "I shall hate when you go to school! I have not had a real friend before, Tanveer."

"Nor have I."

"That must not be true," I said. "You have your sister, your many cousins."

"Not the same as this," he said, moving his finger to indicate our bodies.

"Truly?"

He pressed a hand to his heart. "Truly. Perhaps we have been friends in other lives, and in some part of ourselves, we remember."

I was not unfamiliar with the concept of rebirth. It permeated the cultures around us, but I had never considered that perhaps *I* might have had other lives. It opened something in my heart, giving spaciousness to my thoughts.

Narrowing my eyes against the bright light, I tried to imagine our friendship in some other time, perhaps in some other land, like Egypt. "Perhaps we built the Pyramids."

"You are a girl!"

"Perhaps I was a boy in another life, and you were a girl." My spirits lifted, and I leaned forward, apple in hand. "Perhaps we were both girls, or both boys!"

He frowned. "I do not think I was ever a girl."

"Why not? If people can be oxen or birds, why not boys or girls?"

His scowl deepened. "I have not been a girl."

I laughed at him, but when he didn't soften, I allowed his myth. Chewing another apple, I thought to myself that men never wanted to be women, but I wanted—deeply—to be a man. To have that power, that choice. "I don't like being a girl," I said.

It surprised him. "Why?"

"Why don't you want to be one?"

"Because girls—" His forehead beetled. "Because."

"Because everyone tells girls what to do!"

He measured me for a long moment. "That is the way of things."

"Why?" I said back to him.

"Because you are small and weak and need protection."

I snorted. "Your sister doesn't need protection from anyone." And when I saw his recognition that I was right—Gurdaya was a fierce girl, and her father indulged her, to a point—I said clearly, "Neither do I. I am your equal, Tanveer Singh, and you know that's true."

He continued to look at me, the waters of his dark eyes roiling with his thoughts, light and dark. At last, he took a breath. "I fear I must admit you are correct."

I laughed. "That is why we are friends!"

~

It took them three days to track the tiger down. By the time the party returned, grimy and still half drunk on both Scotch and bloodlust, it was twilight. We saw them from the roof, the motley group with the body of the tiger strapped to a long wagon. I cried out, seeing her, and Tanveer gripped my hand. We shared a moment of deepest grief, both of our faces streaming with tears.

"We should go down and pay our respects," he said.

"I cannot bear it."

He said, "She died. We can manage to bear witness."

Nodding, I followed him down. By the time we reached the yard, others had poured out of the palace, eager to see the slain tiger. Tanveer and I ducked between them until we stood by the wagon.

She was so much larger than I had imagined, her paws the size of my entire belly, her nose as long as the body of Tanveer's cat. Her golden eyes stared sightlessly out at us. A terrible pain rose in my chest, through my throat, and poured through my eyes, a stream of hot tears that did nothing to ease the sorrow of her loss. I looked at Tanveer, and his jaw was set hard against his tears, tears he dared not shed in this company, but he looked at me, and gave a faint nod.

I looked back, took her in, tried to truly see her, this creature of infinite beauty, her fur thick and even more orange than I had imagined, the stripes clearly defined. A wound on her chest showed the death mark, and I hoped she had died quickly and without pain.

"May we touch her?" Tanveer asked.

My father nodded. We moved as a unit and each of us placed a hand on her head. Her ear was soft and flexible, the whiskers long and magnificent. Tanveer tilted his head, feeling under her jaw, around her nose. "She is just like a cat."

One of the hunters snorted. "A cat that would eat you like a mouse, tearing you bit by bit."

I shuddered, looking at her big yellowed teeth. I stroked her shoulder, realizing that my fantasy of her seeing me and letting me be was only that, a fantasy. She would have eaten me, too, and that seemed both terrifying and fair. It had been her world and we invaded it. Surely she was right to kill invaders? "I'm sorry," I whispered, then kissed her and fled to a hidden place in the garden where I could weep my sorrow out properly.

Tanveer found me there a little while later. I had worn myself out sobbing, and rested my face on my arms at the small table. He touched my shoulder, and I looked up. He was silently weeping, and I stood up to embrace him, letting him cry on my shoulder, taking comfort in our shared despair. "She was so beautiful," he said.

"She was," I agreed.

"We shall never forget her."

"Never."

A PHONE CALL FROM AFAR

September 7–8, 1940
London

—7—

The story of the tiger distracted us for a time, but after an hour, I lost steam. The teapot had run dry, and we'd eaten all the biscuits. We fell silent, listening to the world beyond our little room. Whistling, distant booms, the rattle of guns and engines overhead.

Mother relentlessly knitted. Betty sniffled. Peter paced the very small area available to him, raising the tension in the room. He could hardly settle. His hands were shaking. My pity was laced with fear—his demons could make him violent and cruel. The presence of my mother ordinarily kept his temper in check, but these were extraordinary circumstances.

"I need a smoke," he growled.

"Peter," my mother said mildly. "It will no doubt be over soon. Just wait. Surely a cigarette isn't worth dying for."

He grunted, recommenced his pacing. Four steps to the far wall, four steps back.

Again.

For another hour, we huddled together, Betty curled against me, her body tensing every time we heard the whistle of a falling bomb and waited, waited, waited for it to land. The sound of the explosion let us know how far or near it was. Most of them farther. One or two nearby, the noise rattling the window glass, sending showers of dirt over our heads.

Mother brushed it from her shoulders. "We'll need to cover the ceiling with cloth, I suppose."

Just after six, the sustained song of the all-clear siren rang. Betty spoke for all of us when she patted her bosom and stood up eagerly. "I need the loo something fierce."

My mother laughed, holding out a hand so Betty could help her up. "Indeed."

Peter was already to the top of the stairs, and by the time I brought up the rear, he was nowhere to be seen.

"Betty," I said, "perhaps we shall have sandwiches for our supper? Is there any bacon left this week?"

"Not a bit," she said. "I have some tomatoes from the garden, and can fry some potatoes."

"That sounds just right," Mother said. She reached for the wall to take a breath. The ordeal had exhausted her.

"Come," I said, catching her by the waist. "Let's go sit while we wait."

She didn't protest, leaning on me as we made our way down the corridor. "I loved remembering the tiger," I said in an upbeat tone.

"The summer we met the Singh family." She settled in her chair. "Quite notable in your life, certainly."

I deflected. "I'll fetch a cup of tea."

"Leave the sugar for someone else," she said, but she sank against the chintz of the chair with a weary sigh, closing her eyes.

Betty sliced potatoes at the table, appearing to be fully restored. I said, "I'm going to make a pot of tea for Mother."

She nodded, gesturing toward the box that held our ration.

The kettle was hot on the stove, the fire low but warm in the grate. What would happen if a bomb fell on the house? I wondered, but it was plain once I considered. The gas lines would break in the bombing, and there would be an explosion.

"Will you fetch a handful of parsley, Miss Elsie?"

"Of course." I opened the back door, to head out to the garden. "Oh, my!" I cried. "Look! Betty, come look!"

She rushed over, knife in hand, and we stared agape at the southern horizon. Great billows of black smoke clouded the sky, and all around the clouds was a deep-orange glaze. "I reckon they've bombed the docks," I said, and although we'd known it was likely coming, it was hard to adjust the mind to the reality.

Her family lived on the East End. "Do you want to go?" I asked. "Make sure your family is well?"

Tears welled in her eyes, and she nodded. "I would, please. I'll make the dinner and then go on, if that's all right."

"Heavens, no. I'll manage."

She yanked off her apron, dropped the knife on the table with a clatter, and raced down the corridor. Her coat was on a hook near the door, and I followed her out, to see the aftermath from this angle. It was much calmer here, people in the streets returning from the Tube station, full of chatter and worry, comparing notes. A car made its way down the street. Nothing appeared to be hit or on fire, but then we were a long way from the docks.

Mrs. Newsom, from two doors down, stopped at the foot of our steps. Her hat was askew, but her jacket was as tidy as ever. "Everyone all right in there, Elsie?"

"Yes, thank you. Do you need anything?"

She raised a hand as she walked on. Betty hurried away to the bus stop. Would buses run as normal? Would she be able to get through? I thought to call out to her, but she was too far away to hear. If a bus did not come, she would soon return.

I saw no sign of Peter. He'd likely made a beeline for the pub, and would be working his way into an obliterating drunk. Well, he could make his way home on his own tonight. I needed to tend to my mother.

By the time I brought the tea, she'd fallen asleep. I left it at her elbow and went back to the kitchen, turning on the radio for company. The announcer's voice came through, a comforting ordinariness, and I found calm in slicing the robust potatoes.

Toward the end of the last war, when food had grown scarce in London, I'd retreated to our deserted family estate in Herewich, and learned how to grow a victory garden. But that had been twenty years before and I hardly remembered any of it. Luckily, Betty had been raised in the country. She ordered the local man to build beds and dig them deep, augmenting with eggshells and coffee and other mysterious additions until we had the mix she pronounced ready. The two of us pitched in to do the planting, while Mother had sat with us in the cool of the garden, enjoying the fresh air. It had proved a soothing way to spend our time, digging and weeding, keeping anxiety at bay over the encroaching march of the Nazis, the air battles overhead, the heavy threat of bombings.

Awake too early over worry, I'd come outside and pull weeds and tuck up a tendril of beans, pluck snails from the tomatoes. In the evenings, when dark thoughts of what might happen crept in to haunt me—how would I keep my mother safe? What would happen to all of us?—I puttered again. A weed, a handful of snails, a carrot, and I could breathe again.

While the potatoes fried, I stepped out the open back door to gather the parsley Betty had asked for. Clouds of smoke still billowed against the horizon, but it was otherwise a mild evening, the drama over for the day. From the earth seeped the reassuring scent of fecund summer. I pinched parsley between my fingers, and the sharp green fragrance brought back that other summer when I had not been alone, when the war had taken so much, but delivered a blessing I could almost not grasp.

Closing my eyes to inhale it all, earth and herbs and carrots and the onset of evening, I was filled with longing. The story of the tiger had called up my yearning for India, the smell of it, the feel of it enfolding me. I wished for a forest that might hold a tiger, for a market alive with color and animals and bells, for elephants, for bowls of spice in many shapes and colors.

And as ever, I longed for the company of Tanveer, for his perceptive gaze, and gentle teasing, his questing mind and far-reaching ideas.

Standing there below the smoky sky that promised another long, exhausting war, I ached for a different life, one where we might have been able to live our days as husband and wife, and raise a family, and be happy.

But that was not the life we were given.

Alone in the garden, a wave of deep loneliness moved through me.

Abruptly, the air-raid sirens bleated their warning of incoming airplanes. I jerked in alarm, dropping the herbs, and looked up, fear bolting through my chest. I ran for the house, pulled the potatoes off the burner on my way through to Mother, who stirred awake at the noise. "Do you think it's an error?"

"I don't know. It does seem odd that they would come back, doesn't it? Surely they'd have to refuel?"

The sirens continued, up and down, up and down. Through the back door, I saw nothing amiss. "We can wait a little." The stairs to the basement were close enough.

And then, on the horizon, I saw them. Lines of birds, so many birds.

But not birds, of course. Planes. "We need to go down," I said. I closed the back door, and I helped Mother hobble back down the cellar stairs to the little couch and her basket of knitting. "I hope Betty's made it home all right," I said.

"Where's Peter?" Mother asked.

"The pub, no doubt." I shrugged. I deeply hoped he would stay there. "It's just us now."

"Poor Peter," she said, taking up her needles. "His nerves have never been well, have they?"

"No." He was better when he didn't drink, and he'd left it alone for quite a long time, but had taken up the habit again when the Nazis invaded Paris. It could make him unstable and volatile, a complication we truly did not need at the moment.

Somewhere not far away a bomb exploded, and I yelped, covering my head instinctively. Some deeply uncharitable part of me hoped it was the pub, but of course, that would mean harm to people I genuinely liked, rather than just the one I wished to escape.

~

In the close cellar shelter, the waiting was both tedious and horrific. I dozed at some point, the screen of my dreams flashing memories I would have gladly left behind, the look of the lamplit windows the night we heard that my best friend Nina's brother had died in the Battle of the Somme; the searing cry that was torn from her throat.

In another flash, I saw myself on the train from Lucknow to Bombay, bound for the ship that would carry me back to England and the husband I did not want, weeping every tear that had ever been mine to own, knowing I could not shed one more once I arrived. The porter brought me chai, milky and sweet, and a towel to absorb my tears—

In another, I swam with Gurdaya and Tanveer, all of us wickedly diving into the lake with abandon. Flash . . . an orphaned tiger cub. Flash . . . arriving at last on a dark, misty day at Herewich Manor, the skies gray, the stone house gray, my heart gray with loss. Flash . . . that same house, those same stones, golden with summer, and a kiss so deep and wild I would have happily died.

I shook myself awake. On the sofa, my mother dozed, and I was grateful that she could rest at all. The room was silent, but outside were sirens, the whistling of bombs, far away explosions. How many planes had the Germans sent? How many more could possibly be coming? Surely they would eventually run out of bombs or fuel or the pilots would need to sleep.

I made myself seek out happy memories—the weekend at Nina's when we were all so young and happy, so wildly unaware of what was about to befall Europe. I saw myself, dancing with Rocky and Jonathan, and Peter, so handsome, younger than me but so earnest.

But when I fell asleep, it was the darkness that came back. Peter coming home from war hollow eyed and unmoored. The hospital at Brighton. The sight of Tanveer there, broken and so desperately unwell.

A howl rose from my gut. *Stop, stop, stop!*

I sat up straight. How did people bear living entire lives? My mother was seventy. I was forty-four, and I couldn't imagine how I could carry another twenty or thirty years' worth of memories and sorrows and disappointments. Perhaps it would be a relief if the Germans killed us all.

You will paint.

I took a breath, steadied as ever in the work. That was always the thing, the one thing.

I would paint.

Taking refuge in my practice, I took up my sketchbook and captured my mother's hands, long and beautiful even as age gave them depth in veins and marks. How often she had been my model! How many times I had drawn and painted her, to the point that the bones of her face, the tilt of one ear, the changing shape of her mouth were as familiar to me as my own. Now, I sketched her too-thin body beneath a blanket, her stockinged feet, her face in slight detail. Her frailty showed in the sharpness of shoulder and jaw. Little stars of injury marred her hands and cheeks, marks of her failing liver.

This, too, roused melancholy. Impatient with myself I turned the page. Nothing was ever solved by wallowing.

Outside, the bombs whistled and fell. My shoulders braced for the explosions—boom, boom, boom—but they were not as close as the previous group. I uncapped my pen, settled into myself, began to write. Another ritual—a letter to Tanveer.

How long had I been writing letters with my old friend? More than twenty-five, close to thirty. In recent years, we'd written less, as I struggled deeply with the circumstances of my life and he grappled with the changes sweeping India.

As he'd always known it would be, his life was filled with the responsibilities of his position as a leader, a husband, and a father. Those duties lent a reserve to his letters now, as was appropriate. It was never cold—we had shared too much of our lives, our interests and passions woven tightly in a fabric that had been made over decades, but I sometimes longed for the depth of intimacy that had once bonded us.

I wished to be able to speak with him tonight, to have one of our long rambling conversations that wandered easily between memory and politics, astronomy and books, hope and darkness. A conversation with him might help ease this sense of despair.

Instead, I imagined Tanveer standing on his rooftop with his father's telescope. I felt myself standing there, next to him in the warm, dry night, and telling him, *I am so afraid.*

He would straighten, his long fingers swiveling the eyepiece to offer it to me. *Look,* he would say. *How small we are. How fast we disappear.*

September 7 (perhaps September 8, for it is nearly morning), 1940
London

Dear Tanveer,
[In Urdu]: One small beauty: My mother is asleep on the sofa we've moved to the basement, her elegant hands folded, a loose lock of hair trailing over her cheekbone. Her skin is translucent, like opals, and I am grateful to look her tonight, right now.

[In English]: I write this from our fortified cellar, where we have taken shelter from the bombs falling all over London. You will already have heard that the Germans have taken their revenge for Berlin. They have been dropping bombs on London for hours and hours, a relentless barrage of whistles and explosions that are hard to describe—although I suppose you know these sounds all too well.

I fear what I will find when we emerge—if we emerge.

I heard an owl the other night in the garden. It hooted overhead somewhere, then swept down and captured some small hapless being and flew away. What will happen to the owls in such an onslaught? The squirrels, the cats, the humans who didn't know it was all going to be over for them *tonight*?

It's all so wasteful. That's what I think about, the utter mess of it. War wastes lives, but also everything else. It lays to waste homes and perfectly good streets that have to then be rebuilt, and parks that have been standing for years and years. What will be left when all the shouting and fighting is over? Where will the homeless live? What will be left of London, Paris, Berlin? How long will it take to smooth the fields and repopulate them with wheat and sheep?

To tell you the truth, Tanveer, some part of me was so very sure that it would never come to this, even as I've already witnessed one war and all the catastrophe it unleashed, even as Paris fell. I had hoped that England might emerge unscathed. The heart bends toward hope, I suppose, or at least mine does.

My heart hoped that something would clog the war machine, this destructive monster mowing everything down in front of it, before it got here. Even after the Germans bombed the ports to the south, the aerodromes, the various targets that one would expect to see destroyed.

I ask you, what point is there to all of this? When it's all done, what will be left of Europe, of England? Wasn't it enough to destroy a generation once before?

Never mind.

Let me think of something happier. We told the story of when the tiger first came the village tonight, how she terrified us all. I was so sure that if I met her in person, we would be friends, as if she were a creature in a fairy story. How I wish I could capture that sense of possibility tonight, that wonder.

Tell me what transpires in your world. How does India fare these days? How is your family? Give my love to Channan and Kirandeep.

Your friend always,

Elsie

—8—

The all clear sounded at 4:00 a.m. I helped Mother upstairs, and looked for Peter, but he was nowhere to be found. I tumbled into my bed and fell into a hard sleep.

It was the ringing phone that awakened me. Electricity zapped my nerves as I rushed down the stairs, worrying who might be hurt or need help or have news. My brain ran through a litany of people I worried about, but mainly Betty, who must not be here if the phone went unanswered.

I snatched the receiver at seven or eight rings. "Hello?"

The line sounded staticky, and it was a moment before a voice came through. "Elsie, is that you?" The tone was tinny and far away, but I knew it instantly.

"Tanveer!" I sank into the chair by the phone table, pressing the earpiece harder to my head as if to clear the line. "How in the world are you calling? Where are you?"

"I am in Delhi, and it was complicated." His voice, so rich and particularly accented, filled my ear, my head, sent relief cascading through my body. "I couldn't bear not knowing if you were safe."

"I am safe. Mother is safe."

"I have been so worried. The reports have been terrible."

I imagined him sitting in a telegraph office, dressed in a loose, fashionable suit, wearing good shoes—his city clothes. The visual settled the thready beat of my heart, calmed me enough that I could take a deep, long breath. "It *was* terrible," I said. "It just went on and on and on. They didn't sound the all clear until nearly four."

Silence fell between us, echoing down the line. A twist of the connection made his reply staccato, and I couldn't decipher it. "I didn't understand that. Can you hear me?"

"Yes." The word came through as if he were sitting right next to me, and the next phrase was so clear I could hear the raw worry. "Please keep speaking."

"The cellar held up well. We drank tea."

He chuckled, as I'd hoped. "Tea cures all." And then, in Hindustani, he said, "I was so afraid you would be killed. It was—" The line swallowed the words.

"I wrote you a letter," I said in the same language.

"Will you write me every day, so I know that—" *you are still alive.*

"*Ha*, yes," I said, softly. "Will you write to me, too? It will give me something to look forward to in all the madness."

"Every day," he promised. His voice deepened in sorrow. "They'll destroy the whole of Europe this time."

Tears rose in my throat as I thought of the letter I'd written. "It is unbearable."

"No," he said, clearly. "It is bearable. You will bear it, and you will live. Do you understand?"

I took a breath. "I promise. You should be grateful Kirandeep is too young to fight."

"I would never allow it."

I smiled, thinking of how he'd defied his own father in the first war. A decision that changed both of our lives. "He is too young."

"A blessing."

For another long moment, we listened to the space connecting us. "You should hang up," I said in English. "Every second will cost a million pounds."

"I should." I heard his breath, in, then out. "I am so relieved that you are still here. There."

Tears sprang to my eyes. "Look for Venus tonight."

A short pause. "I shall." And then: "Write. Every day. Do not miss. Swear."

"I swear."

I heard the click of him ending the call, but I listened to the silence a moment longer. I thought of him sitting with his long fingers resting on the receiver, far away in Delhi.

Still connected.

ONE SMALL BEAUTY

1907
Nainital

—9—

Tanveer left for school, but as he promised, he wrote many letters. He always included a joke or a riddle or a story about a book he was reading.

Until I met him, I'd considered myself the most accomplished reader I knew. He was even more avid than I, and bested me by reading in several languages—the English we shared, but also his family's Punjabi, and the courtly language of Farsi, and of course Hindi and Urdu, which were spoken mainly the same under the umbrella of Hindustani, but were written entirely differently.

When he first revealed this to me, on a rainy winter holiday afternoon when our mothers had taken refuge in their friendship, I narrowed my eyes.

"How can they sound the same and be written so differently?"

He shrugged. "Who knows?" He took paper from the stack I used for drawing. "Do you want to learn?"

"Speaking or writing?"

"Both," he said, as if it were obvious. "Writing words brings a different understanding, wouldn't you agree?"

"I suppose." It sounded like a lot of trouble. "Maybe I'd rather just draw."

"Suit yourself." But he began to write out script on the page, and the flowing look of it piqued my interest.

"It isn't like English letters at all."

"No." He pushed the pencil and paper toward me. "Try it."

And while he might be entranced by the words, the elegance of the script itself, the beauty of it, captured me so I could not resist.

A few weeks after he returned to school, I received a letter written almost entirely in Urdu. He opened with *Dear Elsie, I have news.* Then the rest was in Urdu.

It was a challenge I couldn't resist. It took me two days to decipher his simple paragraph, another week to compose a few words in return. "Tigers live in the forest."

He was so delighted by my return letter, he sent another. I asked my mother to find a textbook for me, so I could study, and she did.

And so we began our long history of writing letters in Urdu.

February 3, 1907
Ajmer

Dear Elsie,

I will write about one small beauty in Urdu so you can practice.

[In Urdu]: Today a pair of birds built a nest in the tree outside my window.

[In English]: We have been studying the making of maps. I think you would like making an old map, with a dragon at the middle, like the old-world explorers. This year, we have studied Magellan, who sailed the world and discovered places that had not been found before. I asked my teacher why they were discovered if people already lived there, but he did not answer me.

I do admire Magellan for being the first explorer to sail around the world. Not that he was able to complete it himself, of course, but his expedition was the first to complete it. Have you studied the explorers yet?

I am also learning to play polo, which I quite like. We are also marching in formation. I like the sound of our feet in unison.

Your friend,

Tanveer

March 10, 1907
Nainital

Dear Tanveer,

[In Urdu]: I put a red flower in a vase.

[In English]: There! I will not tell you how long it took. I do love the look of the letters on the paper.

I study explorers. My favorite is Magellan. I have also been reading stories about Alice in Wonderland. I have art classes. The teacher is good.

The explorers' lives are exciting. It would have been terrifying to sail across a vast ocean with no idea of what was beyond it. I have drawn you a map with a dragon. I hope you like it.

Write soon,

Elsie

[Enclosed map]

March 29, 1907
Ajmer

Dear Elsie,

[In Urdu]: One small beauty is that I found a sarus crane feather.

[In English]: Thank you for the map. It was quite good. My friend thought you must be a grown-up.

I have broken my arm, and not playing polo, but falling from a wall laughing. Is that the silliest thing you ever heard? My friend is a good joke teller, and I laughed so hard that I slipped off the wall and cracked the bones in my wrist. I acquired a cast in the infirmary. It is very heavy! I have to wear it for two months. At least it is on my left arm so I can still write to you.

Your friend,
Tanveer

Nainital
May 1, 1907

Dear Tanveer,
[In Urdu]: One small beauty is the cat who sat with me while Mother shopped.

[In English]: Thank you for the feather! I drew it for you. I'm sorry you broke your arm. I expect you will be home soon. We shall all have a picnic!

Your friend,
Elsie
[Enclosed drawing of a feather]

—10—

The summers became the best time of year. The three of us, Gurdaya, Tanveer, and I, convinced our mothers that Nainital was safe and intriguing for children, and we would watch out for each other. The freedom was not common, and it did not happen all at once, but an incident at a time, a picnic, then another time a hike. Because our fathers were always away on various matters of business and our mothers approved and had few others to socialize with in the hill station, we slid beneath their attention.

We pretended to be explorers, sighting strange flora and fauna, giving things nonsense names. Gurdaya liked using pretend Latin names to make us laugh. She and I had become better friends in Tanveer's absence. She was a year older than me, but I had been pushed into higher forms when I arrived, so we shared a handful of classes, one of which was Latin. I despised it, but she was as clever as her brother with languages. She named trees *Barkius grumpii* and *Stickius cratchii* and *Sneezia allergica*. Tanveer liked climbing to the top of a hill and declaring all he saw to belong to the Land of Maharaja Tanveer Singh.

"You are not the heir," Gurdaya said disdainfully.

He retorted, "And there are no trees named *Barkius grumpii*."

Her comment made me pause. "Is a maharaja the same as a king?"

They both looked at me as if I'd lost all my brains. "What else?"

I frowned, choosing words carefully. "Well, it seems there are rather a lot of maharajas, while in England there is only one queen, and she is queen of all the lands, including the empress of India, yes?"

"And?"

"If there are so many maharajas, how can any of them be really kings? Aren't they more like dukes and suchlike?"

Gurdaya snorted, but Tanveer held up a hand to still her. "It is a good question, Elsie, and complicated. It was not always this way, one country under an empress. We had our own lands, each of us, some quite large, some very small, only a village, but each one is ruled by its own maharaja or raj."

"Does your father rule a large country or a small one?"

"It is smallish. Only a small city, a few villages, and much desert."

"But we are still royalty," Gurdaya said. "And very rich."

Tanveer snorted. "We are hardly rich."

"Still royal."

I gave her the eye. "Perhaps, then, I am too ordinary and poor for you."

She laughed, and leaned hard into my shoulder. "Your father is the younger son of an earl, so you're hardly ordinary."

"How do you even know that about my father?"

She blinked. "I know the status of everyone."

It would never occur to me to collect such information, but it impressed me nonetheless.

On those hot summer days, I brought along my sketchbook and logged hours drawing the leaves and flowers and tree bark we encountered. I hardly knew the names of any of them, while often the two of them knew the names in several languages, a fact that amazed me and challenged me. They switched between them all the time, arguing in Punjabi, melding a mix of Hindustani and English for casual conversation, telling jokes in English. My Hindustani was improving, but I could understand more than I could speak. The Punjabi was their own.

My gift to the group was a sense of adventure, as I was the least fearful. It was my suggestion to hike the trails in the forest, keeping a compass in hand at Tanveer's insistence. Gurdaya made sure we had lunch and water.

One of our great discoveries was a small pond, hidden away in the forest. It was fed by a waterfall, and flowed out the other side, so it stayed fresh and cool, even at midday when the sun poured down like molten gold. The first time we came upon it, we were hot and tired from the hike. "We shall have our picnic here!" Gurdaya declared.

"I'm going wading." I sat on the ground and tugged off my shoes and socks. Sweat itched down my back and across my chest. The air felt good against my hot toes. Wading into the water was instantly cooling. In delight, I called back, "You must try!"

Tanveer was already wading in beside me, his pants rolled up to his knees. He kicked water at me. It hit my back with a shocking splash, and I turned around with a shriek. "Not fair!"

I kicked water back at him, and he laughed. In moments, we were soaked, my dress and pinafore and chemise, Tanveer's kurta. Gurdaya sat on the blanket she'd unpacked, legs stretched out in front of her. "You shall never get dry."

Tanveer gave me wicked look, one I interpreted exactly. We moved as a unit, dashing toward Gurdaya and grabbing each of her arms. She screeched and yanked back, but together we were too much for her. We dragged her to the pond, and we all fell in with a great splash, sending water high in the blue sky. Furiously, she pulled free. "I hate you both!" she cried, trying to wade out with her tunic clinging to her legs.

"Wait!" I said, catching her arm. "Notice how it feels!"

She halted in water to her hips. The end of her braid floated on the water. I could see she was about to cry and was trying not to. "It is not the same for me as it is for you!"

I looked at Tanveer. He moved toward his sister. "Gudiya, we will be dry by the time we return. No one shall be the wiser."

She slapped at her tunic. "How?"

He skimmed off his tunic, leaving him standing in an undergarment that clung to his thin chest. "We shall lay our clothes in the sunshine."

"I am not a boy!"

"But you are not a big girl yet, either," he said.

She wavered. Even though she was older, she often deferred to his advice.

To encourage her, I turned and offered the ties of my pinafore to him. When I was free, I tugged it off, leaving me in my thin muslin dress. I shed it, too, and stood in my shift and drawers. Covered well enough. "We are siblings!" I said. "And come, once we spread out our clothes, we can swim."

"I don't know how."

"I do," Tanveer said. "I'll teach you."

Gurdaya could hardly resist after that. She waded to shore and spread her tunic on a wide, flat rock in the sunshine. She wore a shift below, as I did. I spread my dress beside hers on a shrub, and Tanveer shed his tunic and pajamas, leaving him standing in shorts that showed his long thin legs. Free, we splashed into the pond.

It was one of the most wonderful things I ever felt, floating in that water, sun hot on my head, moving easily. Tanveer showed us how to move our arms and legs. Gurdaya took to it quickly, skimming across the top of the pond like a dragonfly, her arms strong. I was less coordinated, but Tanveer was patient, correcting me and practicing beside me until it clicked.

"Oh!" I said at last, and propelled myself like a puppy through the water, splashing loudly but happily.

Tanveer laughed.

By the time we stopped, starving and weary, we had grown comfortable. Gurdaya took down her braid to let the sun work its magic, and Tanveer unwound the bun on the top of his head, spreading it out across his shoulders. It was much longer than I expected. I unwove my braid and combed my fingers through the heavy mass. I fancied that we could be mistaken as siblings, given our dark hair, our long limbs.

We gobbled strawberries and cold ham, jam puffs and tinned cheese biscuits, drinking great gulps of lemonade in between.

"We are being very wicked," Gurdaya said, but she said it with her legs crossed, her hair falling around her body, and seemed mostly unconcerned.

"No," I said. "We only swam."

"In our underclothes!"

"With our siblings!"

"We are not your siblings," she countered.

"But Tanveer is yours." I bit into a strawberry. "And I do not think you are concerned with what *my* parents will say."

"Oh, what do I care?" She fell backward on the blanket, her shins bare to the sun, and closed her eyes. I glanced at Tanveer and he grinned.

"Next time, we shall prepare."

"Next time!" I echoed.

"I hope so, don't you?"

"Yes."

And so it became our secret, the three of us. We learned to swim, and grew strong and brown in the sun. My father growled that I was going native, but my mother shushed him. "Let her be a child."

It only lasted one summer. By the next, Gurdaya had developed breasts and a figure and was under the hawkish eye of her ayah, for she would be a fine prize on the bridal market. All of us would grow up far too quickly, our freedom curtailed.

But the taste of it could not be erased.

BREAD, VINEGAR, AND RUNNER BEANS

1940
London

—11—

After my phone call with Tanveer, I washed and dressed, pulling my hair under a scarf. My growling stomach insisted on breakfast. Betty had not returned, which gave me a twinge of worry, but considering how long the bombing had gone on, who knew what things might get in her way—broken streets, debris, things I didn't even know to consider. If she didn't appear midday, I'd telephone the drugstore near her sister's flat.

Meantime, I put the kettle on, then went around opening the curtains and shades to allow the day in. It was odd to see the ordinary September light, gloomy but oblivious to the events of the night before. Across the way, purple-and-yellow asters bloomed in profusion in Mrs. Ball's garden, as always.

There was no sign of Peter yet, but I worried even less about him. He had nine lives and a canny ability to get through anything.

The quest for breakfast was a bit thin—the dregs of our tea ration, which I'd save for mother, a half a loaf of bread, some jam. No meat and, of course, no eggs, though Nina had brought some hens to town from her country house, and there soon would be.

Betty managed the shopping and the ration coupons, and Mondays were her shopping day, so I'd have to make do with what I could find until tomorrow. The potato from last night would offer a substantial base. I picked some peas and new lettuces, then inside, I shredded carrots and potatoes and mixed them with the lettuces, sprinkling the whole with vinegar we'd made the week before from a starter Betty had thought to maintain. With a cup of very hot water to drink, it was plenty, and filled the hole in my stomach.

My mother would need more nutrition than this, however. She was much too thin as it was. Looking through the drawers, I found the ration books and tucked them into my handbag. I wouldn't be gone long, but in case Peter returned before I did, I hid the tea and the last of the sugar so I could serve it to Mother when she awakened.

Outdoors, the neighborhood looked as it always did, which was strangely unsettling. I saw no rubble, but the sky was covered in a yellow haze, the evidence of fires still burning. As I rounded the corner toward the fish market, I saw the queue was half the block, and my hope of getting something decent plummeted. "Have you heard what he has?" I asked the woman in front of me.

She shook her head. "As long as it isn't that awful dogfish from last week."

I nodded in sympathy, but I would have taken it.

As I reached the counter nearly a half hour later, Mr. Foley asked, "Where's Betty today?" His thick wiry brows ruffled together, like two caterpillars. "She didn't—?"

"No, no," I said. "She went to check on her family between sirens and hasn't returned yet."

"Hope she's all right." He passed me a white wrapped package. "I saved her this bit for dinner."

Relief flooded through me. I didn't care what it was—fish could give my mother some genuine sustenance. "I'm grateful. I'll have her check in with you as soon as I hear from her."

On the way home, I stopped in the pub to ask after Peter, but although he'd been there last night as I expected, he'd left at midnight and not returned.

"He left in the middle of the bombing?" I asked.

George shrugged, a gesture I could interpret easily enough—he'd left drunk and likely belligerent, and no one would have bothered to stop him. I couldn't see how the noise of the bombing would have helped his shell shock, and imagined a terrified dog running mindlessly through a thunderstorm.

There was no help for it. Outside on the pavement, I stood still for a moment, struck by a shaft of sunlight on my face. It seemed so strange it should shine at all.

But weather didn't care. It continued on in its usual way, just as the stars would shine tonight. Through everything.

~

At home, I settled the meager shopping, and went upstairs to my studio. I opened the windows to create some cross drafts and set to work cataloging the paintings that remained. The ones I'd had shipped up to Helen's were more recent, explorations of portraiture and color that I thought were my best pieces. She only had space for so many, and now I had to sort the rest.

I'd been painting for nearly thirty years, more if I counted the youthful work before I started art school. The sketchbooks were stacked on shelves by the wall, not valuable but as meaningful to me as the diary of another woman. Those pages, year after year, had captured my world a day, a drawing, a watercolor at a time. It would grieve me to lose them. Perhaps they, too, should be boxed up and taken somewhere safe, along with the rest of the paintings.

But where? The family estate no longer belonged to us; after my brother's untimely death, it had passed to a distant cousin, a loss I grieved still to this day, especially when I had been living at Herewich at the time and could easily have cared for it myself.

But of course a mere woman could not inherit. It had placed both my mother and me in dire straits.

Shaking off the memory, unwilling to linger on yet one more thing I could not change, I considered other possibilities for the safekeeping of the paintings. Obviously, they could not stay *here*. I wondered if Nina would consider asking her brother to store them at their family estate, Clystmere Hall. Perhaps later I could walk over to see her, make sure they'd fared all right.

I spent an hour sorting by era. There were the school pieces, when I was trying on styles and sorting out my own voice. Nothing much would be lost if they went up in a fiery bomb. The others fell into several eras, the work I'd done at the Slade School of Fine Art and then during the last war, both in London and, after, at Herewich. Most were evenly divided between small domestic scenes and portraits, though I had certainly done my share of landscapes.

There was also a group from our travels to Egypt when Peter had been with the diplomatic corps in the twenties. This was the work that had made my reputation and solidified the themes and palettes that expressed my vision most thoroughly. They covered a spectrum of subjects, women and servants and merchants for the most part, centered in their worlds in ordinary ways. I had few of them in my possession, only those I couldn't bear to sell, like the portrait of my mother and the maharani, and a flower seller in the market in Egypt, her feet dirty, her smile easy as another woman bent over to tell her a secret. Light fell on her wares, on her toes, across the crown of her head. The painting of my mother and the maharani grew out of that time, my skill finally catching up to my vision after decades of work.

I would take them all to Clystmere if Nina was amenable.

The final group were paintings I'd been working on for the past few years. Landscapes of India and Egypt, with a less saturated palette, flatter depth, experiments I hadn't quite worked out. And portraits of women, nudes in natural light, in ordinary tasks—bathing, dressing—but not young or fecund or objects of desire. They were simply women in their bodies, ordinary, no longer particularly young, some aging or unwell, with sometimes sagging breasts and flattened buttocks or a wealth of flesh in ripples and rolls.

When I'd first learned to draw bodies, I had used my own in a full-length mirror in my bedroom. It was deliciously scandalous to lock my door and disrobe, and use the natural light pouring in through my French doors to trace the shape of legs, hips, breasts (such as they were), my neck, my arms. I drew my body from a hundred angles, but it was a challenge to get poses correct. I asked Gurdaya to help me, and, to my great delight and surprise, she did. My sketchbooks are filled with her lush body, her softer hips and thighs. She proved a great model, taking poses so I could learn how the body moved, bent, creased.

Downstairs, a door slammed.

Betty!

I clattered down the stairs to see if she was all right. Instead, it was Peter. His hair and clothing were disheveled, and he swayed unsteadily. When he raised his eyes to look at me, I recognized the haunted expression.

I met him at the foot of the stairs. No matter what he had done or how he had behaved, my pity rose when he was in this dejected, lost state. "There you are," I said. "Are you all right? Have you eaten?"

He shook his head. "Not hungry."

"All right." I gently took his arm. "Let's get you to bed then, shall we? Careful now."

Up close, he smelled of gin and cigarettes and something acrid I couldn't quite place. "Did you go to a shelter?"

He nodded. "Russell Square station."

"I'm glad you were safe. We worried."

We made it to his bedroom in a lurching, uneven walk. He fell on the bed, and I unlaced his shoes, stripped off his socks. It was an old routine, forged over the decades of his off-and-on drinking. "Come now," I said gently. "Sit up, and let me take off your jacket."

He obliged. I removed the coat and then unbuttoned his shirt, and took that, too, leaving him in his undershirt. "Lie down, dear," I said.

But he clasped my hips suddenly, burying his face in my abdomen. "I am so sorry, Elsie. I'm a wreck of a man. You deserved so much better."

I patted his upper back. This, too, was part of his pattern, the sudden wretchedness. "You did not deserve your portion, Peter. Let me get you an aspirin and some water. Things will look better when you've slept."

As he fell into bed and closed his eyes, I covered him. The blackout shades kept it dark, but in the gloom, I was pierced by the look of him, his eyes sinking into hollows the color of pencil lead, weary lines of strain thinning out his cheeks.

Guilt touched me, and sorrow, and anger, all rolled together in one thread I'd carried heavily for twenty years. Once, he'd been so full of light.

A LATE SUMMER PARTY

1912
England

—12—

When we arrived in England, I found out I had cousins. So many cousins! Everyone wanted to meet the family of the new earl, so all through that first year we were invited to garden parties and dinner parties and balls and weekends at one country house or another. It was a bewildering and exotic whirl, and if the rituals seemed odd to me, I was delighted by the new wardrobe which my brother insisted was de rigueur. I found myself draped in whisper-thin silks and elegantly beaded bodices, wearing shoes with T-straps and little kitten heels. The ensembles made me feel beautiful.

Which was lucky, as the manners and customs here seemed impenetrable. The local girls had all known each other from the time they were children and didn't allow room for me to settle in. Mostly I didn't mind their cuts and sharp snickers, and found them thoroughly awful, but I'd been used to the closeness of friends I'd enjoyed in Nainital, and the lack made me lonely.

At a garden party at a manor house, a particularly horrid knot of girls had trapped me into a silly little revelation of something I couldn't know. When I realized the trick, I flushed with fury and my temper rose so dangerously that I stormed away into the shade beneath an enormous spreading oak. There, I let myself weep in my fury, wishing I could just go home. "I hate this place!" I cried aloud.

"Oh, dear," said a young woman. I hadn't seen her sitting on a bench on the path. "Is it so terrible?"

I straightened, hurriedly sluicing tears from my cheeks. "I'm sorry. I didn't see you."

"It's all right." She stood. "Come, sit with me. Don't worry about those awful girls. They're all ninnies, angling for the right husband and afraid you'll capture someone they want."

This woman was a bit older than I, perhaps twenty to my sixteen. She had very dark hair smoothed back from her heart-shaped face. Large blue eyes dominated her features. "I'm Nina," she said. "I believe we're second cousins, through my mother and your father."

I sank next to her. "I suppose you know I'm Elsie, then."

"Yes. Tell me what you hate about this fair land." Her eyes twinkled. "Is it the rose gardens, the wide lawns, the beautiful summer skies?"

I laughed. "Of course I like those things. And my new frocks." I smoothed my skirt, took a breath. "I miss India, that's all. It's the only place I've ever known. This is quite a change."

"Tell me, darling," she drawled, "what is one thing you miss the most?"

A dozen things tumbled through my mind—the sound of music, the marketplace, the mountains holding down the entire horizon, Tanveer, monkeys, Gurdaya, the way the light fell into blue hues at evening. "I was free there," I said at last. "Here, I am the earl's daughter, and everyone wants me to be someone I don't know how to be."

"Hmm." She regarded me silently. "It isn't only that, you know, suddenly finding yourself in a position you had not prepared for. You're a young woman now, and eligible, and they wish us to behave in a certain manner."

"To find a husband!" I exclaimed. "I do not want a husband!"

She laughed, and the sound was as delicate as her features, a sound I did not realize until later that she had cultivated as carefully as she'd cultivated everything else about her persona, to hide her secret in plain sight. "Certainly an understandable sentiment, but hardly practical." She raised one arched dark brow. "The trick is to find a husband who will not limit you too terribly."

"No," I said. "I'm going to be married to my art. Husbands, families, all those things will distract me."

"An artist!" she cried. "How marvelous! You must meet my friend Rocky. He's not here today, but I shall write to him immediately."

Her kindness suddenly made me suspicious. I narrowed my eyes. "Why are you being friendly?"

Her grin flashed. "Good. Be wary of everyone in this world, my little doe." She reached up and brushed a lock of hair from my face. "I like your fire. It's so refreshing."

A young man emerged from the patch of forest nearby. "Hullo!" he called. A red-and-white dog trotted alongside him.

"Peter!" Nina called. "Come, meet my cousin."

He was tall and graceful, with a thatch of blond hair, and the regular, pleasing features I'd come to expect from this lot. His eyes brightened when he looked at me. "How do you do?"

"Very well, thank you."

"Elsie is the new Earl of Herewich's daughter." She gestured toward him. "Peter is the third son of a marquess, so he'll be looking at a life as a barrister."

He didn't seem to mind the rib. "Not a barrister, darling. My grandmother has left me a fortune, you know." He winked. "We wouldn't want our new friend to think I'm poor."

I smiled.

Nina jumped up. "Luncheon will be served soon. You must both come sit with me."

Peter offered his arm as we headed back to the house. For the first time, I felt I might not wither away in despair in this new land.

MINT TEA WITH NINA

1940
London

—13—

With both Mother and Peter napping, Betty still missing, I grew restless. The air was charged, as if the molecules of dust freed by the bombings had been magnetized. Walking had always been one of the ways I could shake out any mood, so I donned a hat and gathered a small offering of vegetables and one of the pears I'd found, then headed over to Nina's.

Jonathan and Nina's city dwelling was much larger than ours, taking up an entire corner of a block near Bedford Square. Built of white stone in the 1790s, it showed the wealth of its owners in the details of stone carvings and wide marble steps. I patted the lion on my way by, as I always did, and rang the bell.

Sassy, her housekeeper and cook, answered, looking weary. "Afternoon, Miss," she said. "Mistress is in the garden. You can go right through."

"Thanks." I gave her the cloth bag full of vegetables. "Maybe you'll find this useful. I'll take the pear to Nina."

"She'll like that."

Inside, the rooms were as elegantly undisturbed as ever. The parquet floors gleamed, the Turkish rugs precisely in place. A vase of late roses and dahlias bloomed on the square table of the sitting room. Light, golden with so much dust, poured through generous windows, the blackout curtains shoved behind the velvet draperies. Such order gave me a sense of peace, and I found myself exhaling.

Nina lounged on a chair on the patio, a large brimmed hat shading her face and torso. "Hello, you," I said, coming out the French doors. Had it only been two nights ago that we'd had dinner around the table there? I offered her the pear and sat down sideways on the bench beneath the shade of an enormous catalpa tree.

"Oh, what a beauty!" She held the fruit in her palm, admiring it. The fat bottom half blushed reddish pink, the narrower top shading from yellow to green. "Let me call Sassy to bring me a knife and we can share it."

"No, I had one. But—" I scrambled in the satchel I carried everywhere for my sketchbook and pencil. "But hold there for a moment if you would."

She chuckled, but held her palm steady so I could capture the visual—her lean palm and elegant fingertips, the slightly misshapen pear. It was quick, gestural.

"Done," I said. "Thank you."

"Always." She examined my face. "How did you fare? Did the cellar hold up all right?"

"Yes, but I fear my mother will not navigate the steps well over time. How was it here? Was Jon home?"

"No, they all stayed to strategize." She relished the pear, one bite at a time. "He's still there, actually. He rang briefly, but of course the navy is on full alert." Jon, too frail from the last war to serve in combat for this one, had risen in naval circles for his brilliant strategic mind. "Was Peter home?"

"For the first round."

She allowed me the dignity of leaving it there. "Perhaps work will ease his nerves as time goes by."

"Perhaps."

Sassy brought out a pitcher of mint tea, leaves floating appealingly in the jug. "'Tisn't sweet," she said apologetically, "but cooling on a summer day."

"We drank mint tea in India," I said. "Very wise of you, Sassy."

She nodded and shuffled off.

I sipped the tea, and despite the lack of sugar, it transported me to a day on the veranda, rocking with my mother and the maharani, looking out toward the mountains, lost in a haze of sunshine and heat. I sighed. "I have been terribly nostalgic this summer."

"Yes, so have I." She waved a fly off her skirt. "When the air-raid sirens were going off, I kept remembering the summer we spent in the country, right before the war. I don't know why I was thinking of it then." Gazing into the distance, into the past, she said, "We had no idea what was coming, did we?"

"Thank God. Our innocence made us very happy."

"Innocence?" She laughed. "Not a single one of us were innocents. Rather an orgy all summer as I remember it."

I laughed, too. "Ignorance, then." I thought of the swimming pool, and the lake, and the long dinners, and Tanveer, as free as I'd ever known him, laughing with my friends, telling jokes. Rocky had adored him, of course, and they struck up a clever duel over one long weekend. "We were so young and drunk on love, all of us. Maybe that's why you're remembering it."

She shook her head, sobering. "I'm afraid, Elsie. It's been coming all summer, but I just don't know how to do this, another war, more losses."

I reached for her hand. Her fingers were cold. "Of course you are afraid. Who wouldn't be?"

She gazed into the flower garden, looking so ordinary. "Do you think the Nazis will invade?"

"I have no idea. But even if they do, it isn't happening today. Maybe that's the only way to bear any of this, one day a time."

"Not today," she said, smiling wanly.

To distract her a little, I said, "Tanveer called this morning."

"From India! How did he manage that?"

"Who knows?" I thought of his voice in my ear, urging me to stay alive. To write letters. "I told him that I didn't know how I could bear it all again, and he said, and I quote, 'You will bear it.' And we will, Nina. We're strong."

She sighed. "*You're* strong. I'm spoiled."

I laughed. "True." I paused. "One thing I must manage now is what to do with the rest of my paintings. I wonder if I might store them at Clystmere Hall, or even Greylake. Will your brother mind, do you think?"

"Of course not. I'm sure he'd be delighted."

"It's a bit more out of the way, and I'd feel safer. I don't know what will happen in London."

She shifted, her legs beneath her on the flagstones. "No, you must let me manage it all. They're your children. You must send them to the country. I'll speak with Father and arrange for transport."

Having a task to manage energized her. "Thank you."

She tapped her index fingers together on the side of her glass. Condensation beaded on the surface splashed ever so slightly. "Do you think we made a mistake, not having human children?"

I looked away, throat tight. "I did try."

"I know." She touched my knee. "And really, how much worse would it be to think of them in the war, or getting bombed somewhere, or taken prisoner, or God forbid, becoming Nazis if we're invaded?"

"Some things don't bear thinking about." Carefully, I sipped the mint tea, thinking of Tanveer and Gurdaya and me, unsupervised and wild in Nainital. How happy we'd been! "Whatever made you think of that?"

"Your paintings—which will be your legacy. I don't have one."

"Of course you do. You have your big, beautiful life, and your lovers and your friends."

"It isn't the same. What has my life meant at all? Frivolity, all of it."

It was unlike her to be so introspective, and I paused to take it seriously. Her eyes seemed doubly enormous in her thin face. I moved from my chair to sit next to her, settling my body against hers, thigh to thigh, shoulder to shoulder, and looped an arm around her. For long moments, I could not imagine what might lift her spirits in any meaningful way.

"At least we have survived," I said at last, thinking of Rocky and my brother. Grayson. So many others. "I think about Rocky almost every day. How much light he brought into the world. How happy he made all of us."

"There's never been anyone else like him."

"There's never been anyone like you, either, my darling Nina. I cannot even imagine how my life would have unfolded without you."

She leaned into me. "Don't mind me. I just feel so tired."

"Perhaps you should visit your father in person, get out of London."

"Mmm. Jonathan is in need of my support just now."

"Are you speaking of me, wife?" Jonathan said from the doorway. "I'm not a frail old man, you know."

But he did walk with a cane, the legacy of his war injuries, and his neck bore a pink scar from those terrible days. Still, he was a handsome man, sleek and aristocratic. He dropped a kiss on Nina's head and one on mine. "How are you, Elsie? Your mother get through the night all right?"

"She did, thank you."

"Good, good." He sat in the seat I'd vacated. "I'm only here for a bath and a bit of a lie down."

Nina asked, "Shall I have Sassy prepare some dinner?"

"No, we're eating well enough at headquarters." He was in charge of transporting troops, both in and out of England, and of course could not talk about it at all. "Have you heard from Peter?" he asked at last.

"He spent the night in a shelter," I said. "I left him sleeping."

"It's all hands on deck, if you could relay that to him."

"Of course."

He stood, slapping his hands against his thighs. "I'll leave you, ladies. Do take care." He limped with his cane toward the staircase.

Nina said, "He is terribly good to me."

"You're very good to him as well," I said. "He's been able to live as himself always."

"Thank you, my dear friend. I think I shall keep him company in the bath if you don't mind. I'll ring you when I've spoken with father."

"Wonderful." I kissed her cheek as I stood. "We've weathered everything before this, my darling. We'll get through this, too."

Her smile was thin. "You're my inspiration, Elsie. Always so brave. You and your prince."

I nodded and let myself out. Brave was not the word I would have used, I thought, fixing my hat to my head. It was more that I'd been swept along. Both of us had.

A PALACE IN THE DESERT

1911
India

—14—

The spring of the year I was fifteen, our family traveled to the desert to visit the maharaja. My father had even been invited to participate in some gathering of influential Indian princes, military notables, and various forward-thinking Englishmen. I didn't pay much attention to the reason—I was beside myself that I would finally see the actual palace Gurdaya and Tanveer had so often told me about. Their summer dwelling was Victorian, like most of the Nainital residences, but the Talwarpur Palace had been built in the Mughal tradition, with towers and courtyards, and I longed to see it for myself.

Magically, we were met by a gathering of elephants at the dusty train station, which was thrilling in itself. They had painted legs and trunks, and their backs were draped with embroidered silks in bright colors, and they even had bells on their ankles that chimed as they bowed down to allow us to climb aboard their backs. My mother and I rode together, high up in the air, with a view over the grassy fields and the river running along the road. I spied a village, where women in bright saris came out to watch us pass. I waved at a pair of girls close to my age, and they burst into grins and waved back happily.

It was hot, much hotter than it had been in Nainital, which, of course, was what had drawn both the maharani and my mother to the cool slopes of the lakeside town. A ripple of worry crossed my heart—would my mother be all right here?

The palace appeared suddenly when we climbed the slope of the hill. It rose imposingly in archways and towers, the color of the desert itself, pale rosy yellow. A shiver ran through me. "It's beautiful!" I cried.

My mother squeezed my arm.

A gathering of servants helped us off the elephants in a courtyard shaded by neem trees. A large fountain cooled the air with both sound and water, tree branches casting fingers and angles of shadow across the space. Flowers climbed the walls in dazzling hues of pink and peach, and pots of fragrant blossoms filled the air with fragrance.

The maharaja, fully adorned in ceremonial dress and draped in jewels of enormous size, rubies and emeralds and diamonds on his turban and around his neck and on his fingers, met my father and his group with a cheerful welcome, observing ceremony I cared nothing for. Instead, I patted the sketchbook in my deep pocket, imagining how I'd capture this splendor, and the dazzlement of the courtyard, the splashes of color, the winding shape of the vines, the alluring arches and tiles. I loved the repetition of pattern and shape, the elegant complements of color, blue to green to yellow, with a splash of red here and there, a tiny line of black. What a time I would have sketching here! I was quite glad I'd brought my watercolors.

Now *this* was a true palace.

I was so absorbed that I did not see Gurdaya and Tanveer approach until they were right in front of me. And when I saw them, I halted, stunned to silence for a moment.

The Tanveer I'd seen at Christmas looked nothing like this boy, who had sprouted five inches. His face had shifted, too, in some subtle way, his cheekbones and chin catching up to his always aggressive nose, his brows thickening over the same large deep eyes.

He was not exactly handsome, but the changes wrought in his face made him compelling. Magnetic to look at. I stared, trying to define what it was.

"I know," he said, acknowledging my stare. "I cannot get used to it, either. I bump my head a hundred times a day."

He sounded just the same, my own Tanveer, and it eased something in my chest. "You look so different!" I said, and found I could after all look him in the eye. The sparkle was there, the place I could rest.

"It was my turn, I suppose."

The previous year, the changes had been in my person—not height but shape, a girl out of a tomboy, with more hips than I wanted, and the promise of my mother's figure, which caused more attention than I wished. I'd learned in the intervening months to drape my body to make it appear straight, boyish.

"Welcome," Gurdaya said, coming forward to greet me. She was dressed more formally than I'd seen before, with jewels around her neck and hanging from her ears. Heavy bracelets ringed her wrists, and her hair was covered in fine gauze, embroidered with flowers along the edges. All of it showcased her beauty, the turquoise of her scarf bringing out the rosy richness of her complexion, her fingers long and graceful, the shimmer of hair at her face a deep black. "I've missed you!"

"Me, too!" I said, embracing her lightly. "How beautiful you are!"

She glanced toward the officials and princes milling around one another. "Like a lamb ready for the oven."

I squeezed her arm. "Not yet."

She gave me a small smile. "Not yet."

Tanveer offered me his arm. I reached for it, such an ordinary moment, but our eyes met, and I suddenly smelled something immensely delightful—forest and earth and something cool—that swept through my body and pooled in my belly. I wanted, all at once, to touch his face, his mouth. I thought of kissing him.

Kissing him.

It could not have lasted more than a second or two, but I saw it strike him, too. The knowledge that things were different.

And then we looked away. We didn't speak, but marched as we were meant to do, into the courtyard with the other youths. I was aware of his body next to mine, his ribs against the back of my hand, his leg moving beneath the fabric of his trousers.

The ceremonial moment passed, and he let go. I joined the side of the English while he took his place on the side of the princes. I dared not look for him, but pressed a hand to my stomach, trying to quell the strange sensation. If he was no longer my friend, I could not bear the world, and yet this seemed to change everything.

It was many long moments before I looked back toward him, and saw him staring my way with the same aggrieved recognition.

Something had changed. Something wonderful and horrible.

~

Hours later, he found me. "You must come. I have something to show you."

For a moment, I hesitated, a little wary with this new Tanveer. "What is it?"

"A surprise." His grin, so familiar, flashed. The strangeness dissipated, and it was only my friend standing there in a plain white tunic and pajamas, his eyes glittering with excitement. "Very well."

"Cover your head." He gave me a thin peach scarf, embroidered in white along the edges. "It's very hot today, and you are unused to it."

So I did as I was told, and out in the sun, I was glad of the head covering. I wished for looser dress. Although my outfit was not the fussy layers I'd seen on many other English females today, I still wore too many layers for the climate. I felt my face getting hot. What could I get away with discarding after this?

In the deep shadows of the hallways it was cooler. I followed Tanveer through a maze of turns, passing beneath archways and doorways leading mysterious places, and minor courtyards. Everywhere servants swept the tiles or watered a pot of bougainvillea or stood sentinel over some unknown thing or another, all of them bowing deeply as we passed. "You have many more servants here than in Nainital," I whispered.

He merely shrugged. "It is my father's palace."

His father, the maharaja, who was royal in a way I had not quite perceived before. It made me feel suddenly uncomfortable, for Tanveer, too, was royal, while I was not. Seeing this world through that filter, I saw the wealth gleaming in every detail. The inlaid walls and well-tended fountains; the armies of servants, even Gurdaya's jewels and the maharani's emeralds.

"What?" Tanveer said. "You've gone very quiet."

"I did not quite understand how high ranking your father is." I looked up at him, and it was so odd to look up! "And you, I suppose."

He gave a little shake of his head. "He is but a nine-gun salute. Our lands are small."

"In comparison," I said with a lift of a brow.

"True." He smiled. "But I am still myself, Elsie. And you are the granddaughter of an earl."

Which was true but seemed quite immaterial, considering. "My father is a second son, and a bureaucrat."

"And I am a second son, so unimportant. Even more so now that my father has taken yet another wife. Soon there will be a tribe of sons running through the palace." He already had a passel of siblings from a collection of mistresses.

"Well," I said, "When you put it like that, I suppose neither of us matters at all."

He laughed at my droll humor, and we continued our long trek through the palace. Up one direction, then down another, through a courtyard where a fountain poured water into a blue pool. My greedy eyes filled up on all of it, on bright winding vines, on trees in pots casting lacy shadows on the ground, on elaborate tile work. I paused to run my fingers over a post inlaid with triangular mirrors. "It's enchanting. Like an illustration in *A Thousand and One Nights*."

He looked around, nodding. "So it is. Will you draw?"

I rolled my eyes. "Of course."

"Good. I think you will draw this, too." He gestured toward a less splendid hallway, and we left the enclosure of the bright walls for a wooden door that led down a shaded path to an area of outbuildings. In the distance, I saw stables, and an elephant splashing in a shaded pool. "This way."

We walked down a dusty path lined with yellowed grasses, and finally to another outbuilding surrounded by a high wooden fence. Tanveer opened the gated door, and I followed, blinking in the dimness. He secured the door behind us. I stood still, waiting for my eyes to adjust. The room was cool, with windows cut high in the walls. A half door led to the fenced area, and sun poured through, spilling on the dirt floor. It smelled of hay and dust and something I couldn't quite name.

He was already approaching with a creature in his arms, which at first I thought was a puppy.

"Meet my new cat," he said, "Chhoti Billi."

The shape resolved itself, a round soft ball of orange and white, with long whiskers. His left front paw was half gone, a bandaged stump. I gasped. "A tiger cub! How did you find him?"

"Her." He hefted her weight into my arms, and the cub made a mewling noise, turning her head toward me. "She was orphaned in a hunt, and her paw was mangled by a trap. My father brought her to me."

My entire being glowed with the sandbag weight of her warmth. I bent my head to kiss her, and she rubbed upward against my chin. Instantly smitten, I plopped down right where I was so I could settle her on my lap. Her fur was soft, baggy on her muscles, and she leaned on me easily, titling up her golden eyes to look at me. "Oh, Tanveer, she's so beautiful!"

He rubbed her ears and chin, and she closed her eyes, just like a house cat. "I kept her in my room for a while, and then this room was prepared. Eventually, when she's healed, she'll have a home in an enclosure we're building, outside, so she can hunt and sun and all those things, but she'll be safe."

"Does she purr?"

"No, but she chases balls, and anything on a stick, and she likes to sit in boxes." He pointed to a wooden box in the corner.

I cooed to her, rubbing her body, winding her soft ears through my fingers, touching her broad nose in wonder. She liked that, and rubbed hard against my knuckles, making me laugh. "I wish I'd brought my sketchbook down."

"You can come back." He glanced toward the door. "No one comes here until I tell them to." He looked at me. "Only me. And now you."

All at once, the strange thing between us awakened again. I could not look away from his reassembled and remarkable face, a vivid rustling in my throat, my torso, even my thighs. Embarrassed, blushing, I looked down, my gaze falling on the bright kara around his wrist, and the shape of his oval nails.

Silence hung between us, as alive as the dust motes wafting around each other in the bars of sunlight. I was afraid to look at him again, completely unsure how I should respond, if there had been some other thing implied in his words that I both wanted to hear and did not want to hear.

The tiger playfully clutched my hand and bit it with tiny teeth, and I squeaked, yanking my hand out of her mouth. The tiger, unafraid, reached out and grabbed me back, wrapping one white-tipped paw around my wrist and slamming her lower paws against my forearm like a bunny.

I laughed, and next to me, so did Tanveer. I hazarded a glance at him, and he was grinning at the baby, tugging her ear, and all at once, it was again the most precious face I had ever known. As if he felt it, he looked up, and, pierced, I looked down again.

"Elsie."

I swallowed. "I can hardly look you. Something changed. It's scaring me."

He took my hand, which he must have done a hundred times before, but the feeling of his skin against mine sent a current through my bones. "I shall hate it if you are afraid of me. Imagine if it were reversed."

At that, I did look up. "That would be terrible."

"It is new," he said quietly, and lifted a hand to my face. His fingers burned a tattoo over my cheek, brushed across the corner of my eye. "Is this all right?"

"Yes." I could barely breathe.

And then, the tiger attacked my arm a little more forcefully, and I yelped. Tanveer swept her out of my lap, and we tumbled sideways into the soft hay, face to face. So close. Not quite touching, but only the smallest space between us. I smelled his skin, and again, it made me dizzy. "I never noticed how wonderful you smell."

"I thought you might be wearing perfume." He stroked my hair, my ear. I found my gaze on the sooty thickness of his lashes, the angle of his eyebrow.

Then I was snared in the depth of his dark eyes, and I tumbled into the moment, feeling as if our spirits traveled between us, mine to him, his to mine. I touched his jaw, some distant part of my brain mixing paint to capture the shimmer of light over his irises, the pure white of his sclera, the faint rose in the brown of his jaw, the red ocher of his full lips, cut precisely.

It might almost have been enough to just lie there. I felt suspended, alight. His hand moved on my neck, my shoulder, and then we acted as a single entity, and our lips met.

His mouth was so soft! So full! I made a little sound, and we moved closer, his arms coming around my shoulders, mine around his back, so that it was not only our lips touching, but chests and bellies and thighs.

We kissed slowly, with wonder, pausing once to open our eyes and look—so closely—into each other's eyes, and then we dipped again, opening each to the other, and it was an entirely different sort of kiss. Intoxicating, delicate, exploratory.

After a time, a long time or a short one, I had no way of knowing, we paused, catching our breath. "I have never kissed anyone before," I said.

"Nor I." He smiled. "I quite like it."

I laughed. "Me, too."

"We should return before they wonder where we are."

I suddenly thought of what my father would do if he saw me lying there kissing Tanveer. What *his* father might do. "Yes. We might get into terrible trouble."

He stood, brushing dust from his sleeves, then offered a hand to help me up. I brushed at my skirt, and smoothed my hair. "Anything amiss?"

Taking a small bit of straw from my hair, he said, "Turn around."

I did so. He brushed the back of my skirt, and tucked a tendril of hair into my bun. "There."

I turned back slowly, wishing we could stay here in the cool room with the tiger cub and the silence and kiss all day.

He said, holding my hand, "I feel as if I didn't know what it felt like to be alive before this. As if the world was gray, and I didn't know that it had color."

I laughed in startled recognition. "Yes!" But then I frowned, aware that I was missing a piece of our connection, something that might be lost now under the weight of desire. "It scares me to think we are so changed. What if this ruins our friendship, Tanveer? I don't think I can stand a world where I've lost my best friend."

"Nor I." He held up his hand, offering his little finger. "Let's swear it, then. I swear you shall always be my best friend, Elsie Turner."

"And I swear you shall always be mine, Tanveer Singh."

~

The maharaja's birthday celebration was held that evening in the great hall, set with banquet tables groaning with food, free-flowing drink, and dancers.

I wove along the edge of the crowd, sketching. Mother had not allowed a new dress, saying I'd barely worn the one she'd had made for the school fete, which was true. But it was bland, meant for school, and dreadfully dull in this landscape of glittering scarves and jewel-encrusted bodices and brocaded saris. The Indian women, Sikh and Hindu, wore bracelets and earrings and nose rings and heavy collars made of rubies and emeralds and pearls. Their eyes were ringed with kohl, their lips bright with paan.

The men were no less spectacular. The maharaja wore a necklace with an enormous teardrop sapphire at the center, and alternating pearls and diamonds in a star shape. And while the Muslim women were hidden behind screens, the men were lavishly dressed, too.

I sketched as much as I could—the groaning tables of food, rajma and dal, mutton korma with almonds, piles of rotis, naan and puris and rice, towers of jalebis dripping with syrup. I was deeply fond of petha, here sprinkled with rosewater and pistachios, and devoured it as well as sketched it.

Around the courtyard I went, drawing portraits of the laughing men, the swords some of them wore, the turbans adorned with strings of jewels and brooches. I sketched women covering their mouths with the edge of their scarves when they laughed, sketched their heads leaning together to whisper or gossip, sketched the children playing hide and seek amid the draperies and their mother's skirts.

The maharaja had taken his third wife, a haughty beauty with enormous black eyes, who could not have been much older than Gurdaya. I was appalled when I heard, but the maharani, Tanveer's mother, only laughed. "Darling child," she said, stroking my hair, "I was his second wife, and it is no hardship for me. Rather pity her."

I sketched the new wife, too, and she did not appear to be particularly happy. Like Gurdaya, who sat beside her, she looked weighed down with jewelry and bangles, expression hidden behind a mask of calm.

Also seated at their table was Surinder, Tanveer's older brother, and the prince who would one day inherit the title and lands. I'd never seen him before, and he did not at all have the same look as his siblings, for his mother had died at his birth. He had none of Tanveer and Gurdaya's elegant shape, but rather a harsh, squat form and a nose I struggled to capture, finding it lumpish and purple. His eyes were small and sharp, revealing his cleverness, upon which Tanveer had often commented.

Officials and other princes deferred to him, and he ate vigorously. One day, I thought, he would be very fat.

It was a strange and intriguing world. I slipped through the crowd practically invisible with my bland dress and schoolgirl hair, eavesdropping. I could make out some Punjabi and a great deal of Hindi, of course, but there were other languages I didn't know. Arabic, perhaps, or Persian. The speakers all thought themselves protected by the ignorance of a British girl, so I listened avidly, pretending ignorance, drawing a pair of shoes while two women gossiped about a woman who had behaved badly, and sketching the head table while a trio of men spoke seriously about politics. I didn't know all the players or even what they meant, but it made me feel like a clever spy that they'd never dream I could understand them.

Tanveer, clad in a silvery tunic brocaded with an elaborate pattern of vines, sat beside his sister, listening intently to an old man to his right. I wondered if the man was a relative. He had the look of a seer, with a long white beard and a rich velvet tunic. I tucked myself near a thick drapery to draw them both, first the old man, and then Tanveer. As I followed the line of his arm to the table, his shoulder to his neck, up to his jaw and face, my skin rustled with memory. He never looked my way, so I was able to layer in details I already knew by heart—the shape of his eyes to his eyebrows, the high intelligent forehead, his mouth. Had it always been so rich looking, or was that new?

An old croaky voice said at my elbow in lilting English. "Turn the page, girl."

Startled, I did exactly that, hiding the portrait so she could not see it, and smoothed the new page as if to start again. My eye fell on Gurdaya, and I loved drawing her, so I began shaping her on the page, wondering how I would mix that exact shade of green from her scarf.

"Hmm," the woman said. She was ancient, with hooded eyes like a hawk and a nose even bigger than that, and even a pointed chin with a wart on it, like a drawing of a witch from a fairy tale. It startled me.

I didn't believe in witches, but the resemblance made me wary. "She's a beauty, but she will suffer."

"She's my friend."

Her dark eyes turned on me. "You will also suffer. Beware."

I turned and ran from her, darting behind the curtain, weaving around the edges of the women, and plunked down next to my mother, my heart racing.

"Whatever is the matter?" Mother asked.

"A strange old woman gave me a bad fortune."

The maharani laughed. "The crone gives everyone a bad fortune, until you pay her for a good one."

I glared across the room, and there she was, staring back at me. I didn't think she wanted money. I feared she might have seen something true.

~

It was much later that Tanveer and Gurdaya found me. Gurdaya had shed her jewels, and eagerly took my hand. "You must see the stars from the desert!" I allowed her to tug me along to a set of stairs so old their centers were worn away into little half-moons.

"Careful," Tanveer said when my slick shoes slipped on the stone. "Take off your shoes."

We stopped en mass, and as I squatted to take off my shoes, I looked at their feet to see why they weren't struggling. Both of them wore soft leather slippers. Gurdaya said, "I shall bring you a pair tomorrow."

We climbed and climbed and climbed—three stories? Four?—until we reached a short corridor that opened onto a flat roof surrounded by a stone wall. We tumbled into the small area, where a telescope was set up with a pair of chairs and a small table.

Tanveer flung out his arms as if he'd prepared the sky himself. "Look!"

The sky was enormous here, stretching horizon to horizon in a vast blackness that made me vaguely dizzy. An ocean of stars filled the canvas, bright and sharp, small and red, scatters and clusters and knots, some in swirls of haze, some in piercing points shining alone. I lifted my hands to my face, turning in a circle to look in all directions. "Oh!"

Tanveer stood close beside me. "Now think," he said quietly. "There is nothing above us at all, only air and sky. Nothing between us and that star, right there. If we had a vehicle, we could simply fly there."

My sense of wonder deepened. "What would we find, do you think?"

Gurdaya joined us. "Perhaps there is a place where elephants rule, and humans are made beasts of burden." She was as fond of elephants as Tanveer was of tigers and cats.

"What could humans do for elephants?" he asked. "I do not see how we would be useful to them."

"Maybe they would have no use for us," she allowed, "but I would very much like to see a world where they reigned."

"Mmm." I peered into the river of the Milky Way. "What if there were roads between worlds, and people moved between the planets the way we move from country to country?"

"On sky ships!" Tanveer exclaimed.

"I would find a planet where precious jewels were like rocks on the beach," Gurdaya said, and then lowered her chin to laugh and give me a wide-eyed grin. "Imagine that! A beach littered with rubies and emeralds!"

I had never seen a true beach, but imagined the shores of Nainital lake glinting with colored gemstones. "That would be beautiful." I wondered if I could paint the vision for her.

"You have so many jewels already," Tanveer said. "Why do you need more?"

"I don't *need* them," she retorted. "We are imagining what might be beautiful."

"What would you want to find, Tanveer?" I asked.

He folded his arms, gazing off toward the horizon. "I am not sure. The places would not be the same as our world, would they? Maybe some planets have more than one sun or ten moons." He gave me a sidelong glance. "How about you?"

In that little twinkle, I felt something living reach out and whisper over my cheek. As if he'd stepped closer, I was aware again of the fragrance of him, the faint sandalwood scent of soap, the oil he used in his hair. And something more, something deeper. For a moment, I closed my eyes, letting the pleasantness fill me, and imagined an evening sky with ten moons. "Do you think the moons would all rise at the same time? Or in a row?"

"In an arch, some brighter than others, perhaps."

An invisible hand in my mind painted this vision. "Maybe the sky is not so blue, but some other color."

"Pink!" Gurdaya said. "Yellow!"

I laughed. "That sounds beautiful."

"It isn't only about beauty, though," Tanveer said. "What sort of people would live in those worlds? Do you remember when we read Flammarion? He speculated there could be many societies."

It was one of my favorites of the books he'd challenged me to read, full of speculation on the flexibility of time, and the soul's travels away from earth. Tanveer had liked the astronomy portions more, but we talked about it for weeks. "It seems logical," I said. "There are so many societies on our world."

Tanveer nodded. "If you could travel between worlds, there would likely be treaties. And almost certainly conquerors."

"Why, though? Why not imagine cooperation, and peace? Maybe war gets left behind."

"I have difficulty imagining how that would happen."

I gave a little huff. "Perhaps it isn't a terribly efficient way to solve conflict, with blood and death and destruction."

He tucked his hands behind his back and turned my way. "And what instead?"

"How do humans who don't want to kill each other navigate problems? We do not kill each other at the first disagreement, do we? Our fathers are not in agreement over politics, but they sit down to discuss answers to their problems and conflicts."

"True, but they are only two men."

Gurdaya sighed. "You two are so boring. I am going to my room."

We fell silent as she departed. Tanveer stepped slightly closer so that our hands brushed. After we'd been standing there alone for a long moment, he turned that hand and took mine. We walked to the wall and looked over the edge. Far below, light spilled from the room where everyone danced and feasted. A few people milled around the enclosed garden. We looked down on them, weaving our fingers together. I felt his body next to mine, as if he were a star exerting gravity over the planet of me.

I noticed people far below looking up toward us, and pulled him into the shadows. In no part of my body or mind or soul or heart was there a single moment of caution. I fell against the wall, and he followed laughing softly, pressing his body against mine. A soft wash of light touched the angle of his cheek, his forehead, the straight line of his nose, and I absorbed all of it as if I'd never seen his face at all. I raised a hand and touched his cheekbone, the edge of his eye, his nose.

In return, he touched my hair, my ear, the line of my neck, his fingers leaving a trail like a comet. In a quiet voice he said, "I have been waiting since last summer for this."

"What? Why didn't you say?"

A rueful smile touched his mouth. "Would you have wished for this then?"

I had to be honest. "No."

"You had to catch up."

"What if I never had?"

He shrugged. "We would have continued as we always have, as we always will."

A slight darkness rippled through the silvery moments, the recognition that the future—

"Do not think of it," he said, and kissed me. I kissed him back, greedily, our bodies melting together. I could feel his shoulders and the muscles in his back, and he ran his hands over my waist, and lower. There was no thought, only sensation, in the places where our forms met and our hands, and our mouths, but all through my limbs, too, and my belly.

I pulled away, panting. "I am quite . . . this is . . ."

He flung himself away to put his back against the wall beside me. "Yes. As am I."

"I did not know that anything could feel that way."

"Nor I." He laughed helplessly.

"I know we should not," I said.

"Oh, no," he said, and rolled toward me, kissed me again. "There will be a time that our lives will take us somewhere else, to other things, but we have now. It can be our secret thing, like writing in Urdu. No one needs to know."

I pressed upward toward his mouth. "It will be our secret."

He pulled away again, taking a breath. "We shall have to be quite aware of our faces when we are with our mothers. I do not worry about my father, or yours, but our mothers will scent a thing without our knowing."

The words landed with a thud of truth. "Yes, you are right." I paused and pursed my lips exaggeratedly. "When I see you, I will think of smoked fish."

He laughed. "And I will imagine an unshorn old ewe."

I slapped his arm. "Horrible."

"Effective."

I nodded. "We should go back, so no one suspects anything."

"Suspects what?" he said. "I brought you up to see the telescope, as I've done before."

"Of course."

"Wait," he murmured, capturing my hand. "One more." My skin rippled, and I leaned in, lingering in the galaxy of his being before reluctantly pulling away. I followed, alight.

A small worry whispered through me—now that this had bloomed between us, how could I ever live without it?

A SUMMER OF OUR OWN

1911

—15—

The maharani, Tanveer, and Gurdaya returned to Nainital with our party to take up residence for the hot months. We played cards and drank chai and made up word games.

Tanveer and I became split beings—the selves we had been as children, all the days we had been together over years, best of friends, sparring intellectually and rambling through the forest like little animals, and the new selves we had discovered, the parts of us that had blended with our kisses in the tiger shed, and only wove more tightly together with each moment we spent in secret, exploring this new and dazzling thing.

It was not as easy to escape alone together as it had been. My mother only allowed the three of us to go together, and blocked any suggestion of Tanveer and me on our own. It wasn't seemly, and I did know the eyes of the village always watched us.

But we found ways. When the three of us hiked up to the pond, we waited until Gurdaya napped and slipped away into the trees, where we kissed ourselves into a fever. My skin felt as if it would melt right off my bones, and my fingers were greedy for the feeling of his body, the muscles along his shoulders, the tensity of his slim waist. We slid and twisted around each other until we had to halt or burn to cinders.

The rest of the time, when we played games with our mothers, when we all ate together in the hot evenings, telling stories, we were only ourselves, our secret connection hidden and humming at a frequency only we could hear.

In the hottest days of August, a summer virus swept through the village. It was not fatal, but entire households were stricken, servants and families alike. For a time, the maharani's household servants held strong, and Tanveer and I were pressed into delivery service, carrying jugs of soup to leave on the doorsteps of households laid low by the virus.

Including both of our own, in the end. Gurdaya and our mothers fell ill, and our servants. Tanveer and I kept up our deliveries, fetching food from the market to bring to the sick, making sure water jugs were filled, that the cool breezes could be captured.

In the still of the afternoon one day, we sat in the courtyard beneath the shade of the laburnum tree, tossing rocks in a desultory contest to see who could hit a crack in the pavement. "It's so hot," I whined, pushing hair off my head. "I wish we could escape to the pond."

Tanveer straightened, hands on his thighs as he looked around to the empty grounds. "Who will know?"

I widened my eyes. "Is it terribly wicked, do you think?"

"Terribly." A tiny smile belied the word.

"Then we must. Let's pack a picnic."

We filled a basket with a flask of lemonade, bread and butter, the last of a batch of shortbread baked before this Great Summer Flu of 1911, and a pile of apricots. I donned a hat to protect my face, and we set off in the heat.

We barely talked until we made it into the trees. As we dived under the shade, we talked about the book we were currently reading together, *Silas Marner*. "I suggest we read in Urdu next," Tanveer said.

"I am not proficient enough," I protested.

"It will be good for you," he said with a grin. "It will give us much to discuss in our letters."

A pain threaded between my ribs. I tried to keep my voice neutral. "When do you return to school?"

He reached for my hand, laced his fingers in mine. "Three weeks' time."

I leaned into him momentarily. "I shall hate it."

"As will I."

"No," I said, straightening. "You'll be engrossed in your studies and polo and your friends."

He met my smile with one of his own. "I shall. But I will also miss you terribly."

I took a breath. "I'm weary of the things I study in school—I can read on my own, and study languages, and study history because I find it interesting." I swung our hands. "I wish I enjoyed classwork as much as you do."

"But your path is clear."

We had to pause speaking for a bit as the trail traveled uphill for a long stretch. We picked our way through tree roots and over rocks. Overhead, birds called and shouted. A breeze stirred the leaves around us. "What is my path?" I asked at the top of the hill.

"You're a painter," he said with a quizzical shift of his brows. "Of course."

A swell of longing moved through me, a life of canvases and exploration, something freer than I could see from here. "If I were a man, perhaps. I do not see how it is my path as a female."

"Don't you?" He regarded me calmly, his posture as straight as it had been since we were children, the square shoulders of a person who knew what he was about. "What else could it be?"

A thousand things rose in me, visions of the future bending and swirling—a painter, a mother, a wife, *his* wife, perhaps, which would not be impossible, only difficult. "A mother?" I said quietly. "A wife?" For no reason I could name, tears stung the back of my eyes, and I looked away to hide my emotion.

"And only that? Leave painting behind forever?"

"No! Both, all."

He measured me for a long moment, and I felt suddenly ridiculous. I regretted coming here with him, regretted the foolishness of my longings, regretted how stupid I had been to spin a possible future with Tanveer. I did not realize I'd been doing so, but it humiliated me that the thought had not even crossed his mind.

I flung his hand away and marched into the forest, breathing hard as the shadows moved over my head. I could not halt the tears that streamed down my cheeks, but I would not let him see.

My ears roared with my foolishness. At the pond, I halted, breathing hard. It had been several seasons since we'd come here. The beauty caught me, the glimmering water, the green and yellow ripples over the surface, the sound of the waterfall tumbling into it. All I wanted was to dive in.

I kicked off my shoes and sat down on a rock to peel away my stockings, reveling in the cool air on my toes, then shed the top layer of my clothing, a light muslin dress, and without looking at him, waded into the cool water. When it reached my hips, I plunged in wearing my shift, gasping at the immersion of cold, the fingers through my scalp. I broke the surface and looked back toward the shore. He stood on the bank.

"Shall I stay here?"

I shook my head, and watched as he placed the basket on the ground, and took off his sandals and his tunic, then his thin undershirt, and the layers covering his hair, which was tied high on his head.

He was no longer a boy, and his torso was defined by the muscles he built riding and playing polo, his shoulders strong and round, his belly lean. Clad in his shorts, he moved to the water and waded in, our eyes engaged every second of the journey.

He dived and surfaced near me. For long moments, we treaded water face to face. My foot brushed his shin. His hand brushed my arm. "Why are you so angry with me?" he asked.

"Not angry. Embarrassed."

"What? Why?"

I moved until I could set my feet against the bottom of the pool. Sunlight warmed the top of my head, caught like stars in his eyelashes. "All I want is to look at your face forever."

He swam closer. "That would never be enough for you."

"How can you possibly know that?"

His smile was tender. "Because I know *you*."

I looked away, again feeling tears rise in my eyes.

"Elsie." He touched my outer arm. "What is it?"

"It's so humiliating that you have not even considered the possibility of a future for us. I have fallen in love and thought you had, too"—the tears poured from my eyes, tripling, *quadrupling* my humiliation—"and I find that I'm a foolish caricature of a swooning miss."

"Is that what you think?" He captured me when I would have fled again, catching my legs with a hooked knee, my shoulders with his arm. Our chests met, and I still refused to look up, aching with emotions roaring through me like the waterfall behind us. And yet, his body was warm, his palm hard on my neck and ear. "Look at me," he said very quietly.

When I raised my eyes, he wiped my tears with his fingers. "You are my life," he said in Hindustani. "I love you, and you are the other half of me. Never doubt that." His head moved slowly. "But marriage between us would be a terrible punishment for you."

"I don't believe that." I lifted my arms, pressing myself into him. "It would not be a punishment because I would be married to you, who knows me, who would be my equal, and would allow me to be your equal."

He closed his eyes. "That is a dream, Elsie."

I pushed him away from me. "You are so . . . arrogant!" I splashed away, struggling for the words. "You are not my father, or yours, and you are as young as me, so what makes you think you have the answers?"

"I do not think I have all the answers," he said, hands on his hips. "I only know *this.* I will not subject you to the life I see the women in my world living." He shook his head, fierce. "Do you think you could be happy dressing for court and managing the affairs of the women? You would hate it." His eyes were suddenly too bright, his voice raw as he continued, "Do not think it is because I would not give all I am to make it so. I can barely countenance the dream, it is so painful to know we cannot achieve it. But Elsie, you are my soul. I vow it."

In his words I heard his truth, and I swam toward him, wrapping my arms and then my legs around him as I kissed him. "I know," I whispered, tasting his lips, pressing kisses to his cheeks, his chin. I spoke in Hindustani, to please him, "You are my soul. My world. My heart."

He wrapped me in his embrace, hard, and we kissed as if the act would hold the sun in its orbit, deep, deep, our bodies aching to become one thing.

Which we found a way to do, backing out of the water, shedding the last of the garments between us, until we were skin to skin, sliding and tangling, hands and lips exploring, and it was exactly why we had come here, to be alone and explore each other completely. When he was over me, in me, he grasped my face, and I held his gaze, and so in the oldest way we became one flesh, at least for a little while. I had seen his face a thousand ways, but forever I would remember the expression when we had finished and he paused, still buried in my body, and whispered in Urdu, "Tum merī jān, merī zindagī ho." *You are my soul, my life.*

I clutched him close to me. In the same language, I said, "Hamesha. Hamesha." *Always. Always.*

~

After a time, we pulled undergarments over us, but wove our legs back together while we ate, replete and starving. He offered a bit of biscuit, and I gobbled it with my lips, making both of us laugh, and we could not help dipping into a kiss, over and over. I tasted sugar on his lips, and licked it playfully. He captured me in return and kissed me deeply.

"Are you all right?" he asked, biting a fat apricot.

"Yes." I inclined my head. "Are you?"

He grinned. "Yes."

I said slowly, "I do fear that we shall injure each other somehow with all this."

"As do I. You are where I feel most myself. Without our connection, I should feel unmoored."

"How will we preserve it?"

For a long moment, he looked out toward the water, and I wondered what he saw there. Then he looked at me and took my hand. "I shall always do my best to help you be happy," he said at last, and pressed a kiss into my palm, as if for safekeeping. "If you vow the same, we will take care of each other forever, and always be—what we are, no matter what else happens."

"Our own sacred invention," I said. "Not siblings, not just friends, not *only* lovers. I vow it, too." I pressed a kiss to his palm.

"True friends are one soul in two bodies."

"Yes." I leaned in to kiss him, lingering in the taste of sweetness on his lips, refusing to imagine a time in the far distant future when I would not be able to indulge my longings so easily.

Unfortunately, it was much sooner than either of us knew.

AN EMPTY CUP IN THE SUNSHINE

September 1940
London

—16—

September 12, 1940
London
[In Urdu]

Dear Tanveer,
You are right to suggest that my letters will be censored less if I write in Urdu. Although I am somewhat rusty (is that right?), it is good for me to have something to focus on.

It's terrible here. The Dark One has bragged that invasion is imminent, and it's hard not to believe it could be true. So many bombs every night! Endless, loud, designed to unnerve and demoralize us. It's working. We're all afraid, wincing at the sirens, ducking at every noise. I haven't slept in a week. Mother and Peter seem to be able to sleep in the daytime, but I find I cannot let down my guard. I lie there and listen intently for any small thing that might alert me to danger.

Betty is missing. I sent her to see her family after the early round of bombs on the first night, and she has not returned. That was almost a week ago. I fear she might have been killed, but I cannot seem to get through to anyone who might know. The number I ordinarily ring goes unanswered. I've twice thought I should make my way over there to see if I can find her, but that would mean leaving Mother alone for too long. Peter is in one of his states, and unreliable. I rush out to get rations when I can, but else, I stay here. Waiting for the next bomb, or the invasion, or whatever awful thing might be coming.

It makes me furious. Furious! Did our generation not give enough to war already? How many women never had the pleasure of a home or a husband because so many young men were wiped off the earth? And I know it matters less to you, but how many of the great old piles were abandoned or left to crumble when there was no one to inherit, or if there was, no funds to keep them up? It seems a terrible loss, just as the crumbling of palaces in India are a terrible loss, the stories they hold disappearing like the stories the dead soldiers will never live.

England will be the last of Europe to fall to the Nazis, and I fear we cannot hold them off forever. I constantly think of how to plan in case of invasion. What will we eat? How many resources will they take for themselves? My cellar is stocked with carrots and onions and various other root vegetables, and the larder is filled with jars and jars of lentils, chickpeas, and white beans. I am hoping to find some chicks. Nina has a few in her garden, and the eggs are a boon.

We shall not starve if they leave the food to us, but what if they take it for themselves? How will I care for my mother?

It's impossible to know. For now, I live day to day, hoping that dreadful thing will not occur. The government and RAF and navy are determined to hold them off, and perhaps I'm an ostrich, but I cannot live in that place of terror every single day. One prepares, then lets go. I must live in this day, where they have not yet invaded.

One small beauty: a painting I made of a little scene in the kitchen one morning, an empty cup in a puddle of sunshine, the garden a hint beyond.

The moment was the beauty. Stillness and quiet amid the madness. And painting was the beauty as well, making something in defiance of the darkness, recognizing that there are, even now, moments of peace.

Give my love to Channan. Tell Gurdaya I eagerly await the next installment in her story.

Elsie

—17—

Once the bombing began, the Germans proved relentless. Night after night, we hurried down to the cellar, making do until the all clear, which was many hours later. No one could sleep. Our tempers grew short.

Every night, the sirens. The drone of planes, circling, circling, the anti-aircraft guns, and the threatening, nerve-racking whistle of a falling bomb. Explosions, two or three at a time, close in, and farther away. Most nights, the attacks lasted nearly until morning.

It was utterly exhausting.

Such a disruption was bound to take a toll on anyone's health, but it starkly undermined Mother's already fragile state. After two weeks of it, she was thin as a needle, unwilling to eat much of anything.

In the meantime, cooking and the procuring of rations fell to me. I'd never gone with Betty to various shops and had to learn, one by one, where she'd purchased fruit and meat and flour and tea, since rations could only be used at the shops where she'd registered. We spent a lean week or so before I managed to restore the rations for all of us, a week during which I brewed vegetable broths and milky bread puddings sweetened with pears that suddenly arrived from the country. Plums were ripe, too, and apples to give us some sweetness.

I spent one hot afternoon making apple butter from a bounty Nina shared from Greylake Cottage. The skill made me grateful again for the time I'd spent at Herewich at the end of the last war. I'd learned many useful skills that I'd not made much use of since, picking fruit, growing vegetables, preserving. I'd also learned to darn, and to wear my brother's trousers, a style I'd kept after the war. Skirts were impractical in a world of so many chores, and I'd worn an overall in the studio for decades.

But no matter what I conjured up for her, sweet or thin or easy, Mother barely consumed enough to keep a kitten alive. She picked at everything, trying to pretend she was eating, but I wasn't so easily dissuaded. One way or another, I'd find a way to pique her appetite.

Both of us enjoyed the curries and meats and gravies I'd grown up eating, and in anticipation of embargo and lack, I'd purchased spices in bulk a year before—cumin and coriander and curry leaves, cinnamon and nutmeg. To that end, I cooked rice and lentils to make khichdi, sending the aroma through the house. Peter was drawn by it when he came in from some errand, likely guzzling gin in some pub, even though it was barely noon.

"That smells marvelous," he said, tossing a packet of mail on the table. His skin was dull and greasy.

Eyeing him, I shook my head. "Perhaps you should give your body a rest from alcohol, Peter. You're looking a bit wan."

"It's the only thing getting me through." He slumped at the table and lit a cigarette.

I coughed. "Please take that into the garden. It does my mother's health no good."

He mouthed the butt and flipped through the letters on the table, ignoring me. "A letter from the prince," he said.

I didn't bother to look at him. This was an old song, worn from many plays.

He exhaled long, the blue smoke filling the kitchen, canceling the fragrance of my dal.

"Peter," I said sharply. "Please. I'm cooking. Leave me be."

He tossed the letter at me, dangerously close to the open flame, and sauntered outside. I snatched the envelope, pinching the flame on the edge. Looking after Peter, I wondered for the thousandth time how I might have helped him avoid the bitterness that had so ruined him. I'd gone into the marriage with the best of intentions, but in the end, we'd done each other no favors.

Which paved the road to hell for both of us.

I opened Tanveer's letter.

September 17, 1940
Talwarpur Palace
[In Urdu]

Dear Elsie,
Every day, the radio tells us of new bombings in London. We all worry constantly for your safety. Channan prays for you daily.

Instead of asking you to carry our fears, I will instead offer you a better view than the one you currently must endure. We are somewhat insulated from the war here, far away as we are, although many of the men in the village have volunteered to fight in Europe and elsewhere. I argued most virulently against their sacrifice, but colonialism has planted a twisted patriotism in too many hearts, and a young man wants only to prove himself in battle. It will be a grievous waste of our best, who will be needed to continue the fight for independence, but I can only do what is mine to do.

And once, I, too, was a young man, eager to raise my sword in battle—but in that case, I was fighting for the promise we were given, that if we traded our bodies on those battlefields, Britain would at last grant our freedom.

If I consider it for more than a moment, I am angry again, and that anger is better made a pointed tool. The importance of politics here on this home front remain foremost in my thoughts, for there is a great deal of talk of Muslim homeland, and I fear the repercussions of that on Sikhs in the Punjab.

Channan is more frail than usual. She suffered a bout of influenza last month, and has recovered, but the onslaught of terrible news around the world dismays her deeply, to the point that I have insisted she must not listen to the radio, but instead play her recordings, the ragas and operas of which she is so fond. It has always been her hope that she could see the opera in Paris, and I think she grieves the loss of that dream, for who knows when it will again be possible? I fear she will not last the war, but her loss will be deeply sorrowful for Kirandeep. He adores his mother, and he is the light in her life. Without him, she would have left this plane long ago.

Kirandeep is becoming a vigorous athlete like my brother was. He loves polo and games of all sorts, and he has strong leadership qualities, including an ability to listen, which my father never did. He's quite good with the tigers, the injured and ancient ones we care for on the estate, and I am glad to know they matter to him as much as they do to me.

I painted this watercolor not long ago, thinking of you. I hope you enjoy it. The body of cats has always been a conundrum, but I believe my mastery of human form is better.

I shall close now, but promise me you will try to stay safe. Keep writing, my friend. If I'm able, I will call again.

Your friend,

Tanveer

[Enclosed watercolor of Channan and a ginger cat by a window]

[Enclosed photo of Kirandeep in polo clothes. He has his father's big nose.]

I read it twice, taking courage in the shape of his handwriting, the homey painting of Channan, the ease of a life still ordinary, far away from here. I tucked it away in my pocket, and made Mother a tray. She would like the photo and little drawings. "Peter," I called out the door, "I've left you a bowl on the table. You must eat."

He ignored me.

When I carried the tray upstairs, I found Mother's window open to the day. The room smelled fresh and herbal, with omnipresent undertones of smoke.

Mother sat in her bed jacket, her hair in a long braid over her shoulder. She set her small tome aside as I entered, mustering a smile. "That smells quite wonderful, Elsie. Have you made me a curry?"

"Not quite so rich as that," I said, settling the tray over her lap. "A thin dal to tempt you. I wish there were lemons, but I tucked some mint into the water for interest."

"Sit with me, Elsie."

I settled in the chair I'd dragged to her bedside, finding myself in a patch of sunlight falling through the window. It glowed yellow on the hem of my cotton trousers, and across the bare arch of my foot. My brain offered possibilities to mix the color—chrome yellow tinted with white, naples yellow for the shadows, cinnabar and blue mixed for the darkest shades. "How are you feeling now that you've slept?" She had been unable to make it down to the basement last night, so we'd sheltered in the sitting room instead. The blitz had gone until the wee hours.

"Well enough," she said, her standard answer. "The water is delicious."

"I've had a letter from Tanveer," I said. "They are desperately worried about us, of course."

"No doubt. How is Channan? Has she found relief from the tinctures I sent?"

"I do not know about the tinctures, but I shall ask. She has not been well, and mourns her chance to see the Paris Opera."

She touched her fingers to her chest. "Perhaps after the war."

After the war. If anything was left. If any of *us* were left. "Shall I read to you?"

"No, let's just talk, shall we?" She managed the tiniest bite of khichdi, dabbed her lips. "That's lovely, Elsie. I've been dreaming of India so often of late."

"Maybe it was telling the story of the tiger."

"Mmm." She took another infinitesimally small bite, but I was cheered. "I think it's just rising out of some forgotten place. I always thought I would return."

"You went to America instead."

"Yes." A delicate smile lit her features. "And I would choose it again."

"Even though it ended so sadly?"

"Oh, it wasn't that sad," she said. "I enjoyed Lawrence's company for ten years, and I'm quite sure the time in the desert extended my life."

"I am grateful." I smoothed the edge of her bedcover. "What have you been remembering about India?"

"So many things," she said quietly. "The sound of monkeys, and how mischievous and awful they are. And elephants, the poor things. And Nihal's coconut cake!" She closed her eyes momentarily. "Perfection."

I wondered if I could find coconut, save enough sugar and flour for a small cake. Nina would give me the eggs. "My favorite was kaju balls."

"I remember." Her hands had gone idle.

"Can you manage a few more bites, Mother? You've barely eaten enough for a flea these past few weeks."

She looked at me. "I'm dying, sweet girl."

"What? No! You're just weak with all the interrupted nights."

Her smile was kind, and she held out a hand for mine, which I gave. "The interruptions are hastening the end, but we both know this has been coming for quite some time. My liver is failing, darling."

Tears sprang to my eyes. "I don't want you to die."

"I know. But it comes to us all."

"Not yet, though." I shook my head. "I'll find some things to tempt your appetite, and perhaps we should move the bed to the sitting room so the travel time to the cellar isn't so long."

She gazed at me for a long moment. "All right."

I bent over and kissed her forehead. "Not yet," I said, and pulled back to look into her blue eyes. "Please."

Lifting my hand to kiss my knuckles, she nodded. "Why don't you paint, my dear? I think it would be good for you."

"Yes, all right." I pointed to the tray. "Will you have a few more bites?"

"I'll try."

~

When she'd managed a bit more lunch, I allowed her to shoo me out, and took the tray downstairs. I saw no sign of Peter in the garden, but he'd eaten, so I washed up the dishes and headed back up the stairs.

The studio held the scent of herbs and smoke from the bombings as well, but the fresh air was good anyway. In the breeze, I wrapped an apron around my body and went to my easel, where I was working from memory on an iteration of an Egyptian woman selling vegetables. Her expression was hostile beneath her dull-blue hijab, one knee tucked under her skirts. The rendition of the vegetables was too acute, I saw now, and began to smooth out details, leaving impressions of bananas and dates, the suggestion of carrots, the harsh sun burning down on her head, on the wall behind her, the cobblestone street.

Peter had been stationed in Cairo on his first diplomatic assignment. We'd only been married a short time, and had not yet become entangled in the betrayals that would unravel whatever fabric we might have woven.

The post delighted me. I loved being back in a world that while not India, struck some of the same places in my soul. We explored the wonders of the ancients, and I painted the Pyramids, those magnificent and magical monuments. We traveled on the Nile, and tried rather earnestly for a child. I was not in love with Peter, but a child would have given me hope, a sense of purpose. Perhaps it would have healed Peter as well.

The child never arrived, but I found my voice as a painter in the workaday women of the souks and bazaars, in the builders and laundresses, in the bright, hot light and flat colors of midday. Something in my art that had been dulled by the losses of the Great War came alive, and I'd found myself painting with wild intensity. I painted small things, domestic moments, women's work and women's hands and women's point of view.

And I painted faces. Each face I encountered I found myself weighing for whether I was creating a fantasy or giving life to an actual human woman.

They proved to be quite popular works, and I traveled between London and Cairo regularly, showing in a gallery that sold a great deal of my paintings. I found, too, a gallery in Cairo. For the first time, my work was celebrated, and I reveled in it.

My sketchbooks, from those years and all the others, were stacked on shelves I'd had built for that purpose, each labeled with the year. I left the painting and searched out the original sketches, taking down the books from the mid-1920s, all of them thick and bursting, held together with string. I unwrapped one, and leafed through it to find the record of our trip down the Nile, the open desert with the bright blue sky. I'd struggled deeply with finding my voice in art school, and in Cairo, I'd found some magic.

On a lower shelf were the first notebooks I'd kept when I was a girl. I reached for them, looking this time for the endless, endless iterations of tigers we'd drawn that summer, and then to a later set, sketches of the maharaja's palace, both the dazzlement of the tile work and courtyards and the surprise and sadness of the crumbling rooms where pale-winged griffon vultures nested.

And last, the swimming hole that had become so sacred to us.

A DEATH IN ENGLAND

August 1911
Nainital, India

—18—

My father arrived unexpectedly from Lucknow late on a Thursday evening. I saw him from my bedroom window, but he asked immediately for my mother. They were cloistered away until supper, which was laid in the courtyard to take advantage of the breezes from the hills. As happened in late August, there was a hint of the coming season beneath the heat of the day, nothing so overt as a chill, but a crispness in the corners, a whisper of cool along the flat tiles. I'd been out sketching with Gurdaya most of the day and arrived at the table famished.

Mother had not yet fully recovered from a recent malarial flare. Her skin held a pale-blue undertone, and at the neckline of her dress, her collarbone stood out too boldly. I kissed her head as I passed. "I'm glad to see you at the table tonight."

My father said, "Have you been as ill as that?"

"I am much better," Mother said, waving a hand. "You know the heat sometimes wears on me."

"Indeed. All the better—"

Mother interrupted. "All in good time," she said. "Elsie, have you been sketching?"

I stabbed a chunk of melon. "Gurdaya and I walked to the lake." I pulled my book from my deep pocket and flipped through to show a drawing of a red-billed magpie in all its drama. "The birds are beginning to migrate, so we saw quite a few things. We saw stilts, too."

"Such an eager naturalist," my father said. "I was the same as a boy."

"Were you?" He rarely shared anything about his life. "Did you like birds?"

"Indeed." He gestured for his plate to be filled with roast mutton. "My favorites were the swans and ducks. There are a lot of ducks at Herewich."

"The estate where you grew up?" The melon barely dented my thirst, and I drank water greedily. "I've seen a painting of it."

"Yes, it's quite beautiful, and old, for England, anyway. It was built in 1532."

"That's old," I agreed, "but not as old as the maharaja's palace."

"It's far older than the palace." He looked at my mother, and I suddenly felt a warning.

"Elsie," Mother said. "Your father has had some news."

I looked at him, feeling the pit of my stomach give way.

He cleared his throat. "My brother, the earl, has been killed in a hunting accident."

"Oh no! Father, I am so very sorry."

"Yes, well. The second part of the news is that I am now the Earl of Herewich."

"That's good news, isn't it?"

My mother said, "We shall be returning to England forthwith, Elsie."

The words made no sense. "What?"

"I've booked passage from Bombay on the third of October," my father said. "That will give us time to pack both houses and wrap up our business here in India. My replacement will need to be trained, and I'd not like to leave that for some imbecile who understands nothing of the delicacies of the position."

My mother patted his arm approvingly.

I continued to stare at him. What language was he even speaking? What was he talking about? "Leave India?" I said at last. "I don't want to leave India. This is my home."

"I know it will be a challenge," my mother said, "but it's time."

Something in her gentle gaze made me think she knew my secret, that she was relieved that we would be leaving. "You've never lived in England!" I cried. "This is your home, too."

"India is trying to kill your mother," Father said. "The climate in England will be so much better."

A howl whirled around my spine, gathering power until it tore from my throat. "No!" I cried. "No. I won't go. I will not leave my friends and the landscape and—everything." I stood up, and my knees caught the seat of my chair, sending it backward. The violence of my move knocked the table, too, and a glass of wine spilled red over the flowers and vines of the tablecloth. "I won't."

"Sit down," my father said, as close to a shout as he ever came.

It startled me enough that I took the seat a servant had righted.

"You *will* be going to England with us, your parents. And you will learn to live the English way, as befits the daughter of an earl. Do you understand me?"

I glared at him, my eyes filled with tears. I could not speak.

"Do you understand?" he repeated, steely, his eyes boring through my body.

"Yes," I whispered, tears spilling down my face. "May I be excused?"

"Elsie," my mother said.

But I fled.

~

An hour later, Mother came to my room. I was flung over the bed, exhausted from weeping, and she sank down beside me. "I know it seems terrible now," she said in her soothing voice, "but you will come to see how well it works out in time. You'll love England."

I shook my head. "I don't want to."

"I know." She stroked my hair. "I was once fifteen, you know." I heard her smile. "Things feel enormous, but that doesn't mean that they *are* enormous."

"That helps ever so," I said sarcastically. "Why don't you just tell me I'm being a foolish child? That will ease my sorrow."

"I knew you would be desperately upset, Elsie, but in truth, there is no place for you here. Your friends are royals and soon will take their own path, leaving you behind. What then? Will you marry some boorish INC officer? Some middling bureaucrat who wants you only because you're pretty and will make him shine?"

"No! That sounds terrible."

"What then? Here, in India? What?"

I plucked at a loose thread on my coverlet, taking a savage pleasure in the way it ruched the fabric. "I don't know. Surely there is a way to study art? To make a life here without marrying some awful person?"

"Perhaps." She took a breath. "I have allowed you a great deal of freedom, my dear. I was loath to constrain your mightiness." She paused. "But I fear that was not in your best interest. For all that I wish it to be true, this world is not an easy place for women." A glimmer of tears gathered at the corners of her eyes, and it pierced me as nothing else could have. "As a girl, you have some freedom, but as a woman, you must be strategic."

I sat up. "That is not fair."

"No," she agreed. "It is not fair."

Fresh tears welled in my eyes. "So how will it be any better in England? I only trade a boring officer for boring country Englishman. How is that better? At least here, I'd be in the landscape that I love."

She looked away, as if considering her words, then back to my face. "If you stay here, your soul will be shredded by all that you want to be, and all that you are not." She took my hand. "In England, you will have some modest standing, and therefore some measure of power. In England, I will have more ability to sway your father to what you wish, not what he wishes."

I held her gaze, and felt a fool that I thought she had not noticed my liaison with Tanveer. I blushed, thinking that she imagined I wanted to be his wife, when I clearly knew I would not. But in some small part of me, had I not been thinking there was a way around the roadblock, the dire future he predicted, that she now also predicted? "I don't want to be anyone's wife," I said, fiercely, leaving the truth unsaid: *if I cannot be Tanveer's wife.* "I want to paint."

"I know." She smiled. "In England, perhaps you might study art. And in a few years' time, perhaps you'll be less opposed to marriage."

I scowled. "I doubt it."

"Hmm. Well, I daresay that between now and that possible day, you'll learn much more about the ways of the world than you know now and perhaps will change your mind."

Seeing that I would not escape my fate of leaving India, I closed my eyes, letting grief fill my being. "I can't bear it," I said.

Mother allowed me to collapse against her. "You can," she said. "And you shall."

—19—

Tanveer appeared at the door to the former playroom, now my studio, the next morning. He halted in the doorway, the sun behind him casting his figure into silhouette—and I could not even stand for the fresh grief that washed over me.

"Is it true?" he said. "You are going to England?"

"Yes," I whispered. "In two months' time."

He sat beside me on the wide windowsill. "This is terrible news."

I nodded, airless. It seemed impossible. "What will we do?"

He pressed the back of his hand to my thigh, and I dropped my hand to let him enfold it. The steel of his kara rested against my inner wrist. The contact gave me a focus, his warm palm, the hard bracelet. "We shall write letters, hundreds of them." He nudged me with his elbow. "Thousands."

I smiled reluctantly, as he meant me to. "Thousands?"

"Hundreds of thousands."

"I will miss you desperately."

"I am here now."

I looked at his face, which had become even more dear, and lingered on each detail. The wings of his brows, the thick sooty sweep of his lashes, the shape of his mouth. I had drawn him hundreds of times, drawn his face and parts of his face, his eyes, his nose, the sweep of his hair from his temple, the bend of his lips. I'd sketched his hands and throat, his wrists and toes, dusty from sandals. I'd drawn his figure in motion, riding a horse or throwing a rock, or bent over a book. I could not imagine how I would even live without the sustenance of his presence.

As I gazed at him, I saw tears spring to his eyes. "I shall miss you like the moon."

His tears gave me tears, and if we had been elsewhere, I would have kissed him, but we could not. Not here.

"Meet me at our place," he said, meaning the pond.

"When?"

"In an hour." His expression grew serious. "My father is sending me to school a week early because he's traveling that way. We leave tomorrow."

"No!" My heart squeezed so hard in despair that I thought it might stop entirely.

He traced the edge of my inner wrist. "I suspect that they know our secret."

I thought of my mother's warning that I would not have the life here that I had spun in my mind. "I fear you are correct."

"An hour, then," he said. "I will be waiting."

~

It was early afternoon, and hot. I waited until everyone was napping, then slid out the kitchen door and ran for the path to the woods. I'd never traversed it on my own, but after so many visits over the years, I knew the way intimately. By the time I made it to the pond, I was sweaty and disheveled. Tanveer was there already. He held out a hand, and I closed the distance between us, leaning my head on his chest, his hands on my back. "Let's not spend this short time grieving, Elsie. For today, for these hours, we shall forget everything, and swim, and make love, and eat together."

"Yes, one small beauty."

"Ours," he said.

I turned to let him unfasten my buttons, and slid out of my shift. He shed his turban and tunic and trousers, even his undergarments. It made me dizzy to see him so completely, and my fingers itched. "Is it terrible that I want to draw you like that?"

He stretched his arm out to the sides, offering himself. "I am yours, to do with as you will." He inclined his head. "I do wish you would join me."

So I shed the last of my undergarments, too, and stood in the sunshine as God made me. "I am not thinking of drawing you," he said with a faint roughness.

"Let's swim." I dashed into the water, wanting to wash away the sweat of the walk.

He dived in beside me, and with clean, sharp strokes, moved across the pond to the waterfall. He bobbed beside it, brown shoulders gleaming in the sunshine. An explosion of joy burst through my entire being, filling my veins and organs and bones with light—that I was alive in this moment, with Tanveer, and the sky of India over us, and this body of water where we had learned to swim. I glowed with the feeling, and pressed every detail I could gather into my soul, and then I swam to him and flowed around him, chest to breasts, and legs and arms, my hair and his teasing our skin.

He maneuvered me into the cold stream of the waterfall. I gasped and screeched, then wrestled him into it, laughing. We circled and swam, and then, as a single being, swarmed toward the beach and the cloth he'd spread out on the sand, and there in the sunshine, we tangled again, and explored, and touched every inch of skin, buttocks and bellies and thighs. We explored with our hands and our mouths until we had gathered as many moments as we could, and lay in sated silence, side by side, skin to skin. "As long as my feet carry my body through this world," he said in Hindustani, a language so much more romantic than English, "I will love you entirely."

I looked into the depth of his eyes, feeling our souls meld. "We are woven together now, light and dark, hope and sorrow," I said in my own language. "I will love you until my last breath."

We were so young, so fierce, so deeply in love. Is any love truer than first love?

Back down the mountain, we hid in the trees, kissing once more and once more, weeping in disbelief that it had come to this, that we would not meet again for who knew how long. "Write to me," he said.

"I shall." I pressed my tender lips to his, breathed in the scent of his skin one last time. A jagged tear burst through my chest. "When will we see each other again?"

"I don't know. We cannot depend on it, Elsie. Our lives are splitting now. You will go to England, and I will stay here, and this is what we will have."

I heard the truth of his words, and grief ripped through me. "I hate this," I said. "That someday this will be some faraway memory."

He kissed my forehead. "Never faded."

In the distance, someone shouted, and we broke apart. Holding hands, we looked toward the voice, then back to each other. Tears shimmered in his eyes, and flowed freely down my cheeks. In Hindustani he said, "My life, I love you always."

In the same language, I said, "You are my heart, my soul, my sun." And then I turned and ran, afraid I could never find the courage if I didn't move.

I didn't look back.

The day before we left for Bombay, his letter was delivered, the one I tucked into my pocket and carried onto the ship.

My life, he'd written, *we knew this day would come, that our paths would come to this place of parting, that I would go on to my duties and you would go to yours in another world. It grieves me more than I expected. I am sensible and clear sighted, but my heart seems not to recognize the presence of reason. It only wants what it wants, to hold you always, to have you as my own. I cannot bear the idea of a husband for you that is not me, nor a wife for me that is not you. It is a great tragedy. And yet, we are dutiful. We must each serve the lives we were born to live. I do not think it wise for us to continue to write to each other. It will only sear my soul each time I see your words, but know that I am always your love, until the stars no longer shine. Tanveer.*

THE REFUGEE IN THE GARDEN

Autumn 1940
London

—20—

September 25, 1940
Talwarpur Palace
[In Urdu]

Dear Elsie,

Your letters take longer to arrive than they did in the past, which is to be expected. I've just read the letter in which you feared invasion and were planning to find chicks for eggs.

I hope by now you have found that Betty is healthy and well. I hope you have found hens. I pray there will be no invasion. For all my criticisms, the British are a stalwart lot, and I cannot see how Churchill would countenance an invasion of London.

I wish most desperately that you had been able to flee back here to Talwarpur before it was impossible to escape. Or even not here, but somewhere safer.

Although what land is safe now? Each day I think the news cannot be worse, and each day it is.

Your painting stirred a memory of when you painted the flowers at Herewich so long ago. What a rich pocket of peace those days were! Did we know how precious they were? I hope we did.

Here is a small beauty from my life: Last night I went to the roof to study the stars through my telescope. It was a clear, dry night, and I felt I could see into the farthest reaches of the universe. At such times, the petty dramas and sorrows of humankind seem very small, and I find reassurance in that vastness of space, and time, and the uncountable multitudes of stars.

All my best,

Tanveer

—21—

One dark, dry day, I swept the front walk, the steps, and porch of the dust that seemed to collect everywhere. In the air hung a taste of soot, and the cloudy sky held an orangish tinge. The climbing roses that wound round the balustrade drooped from dust. I tapped the leaves and late blooms to allow them some air, taking pleasure in the glow of pink, the sweet scent released.

Peter had pulled himself together once more and took himself to work most days. Like Jonathan, he worked in the foreign office. He was not allowed to speak of the work, of course, but it made him less fragile, and although I knew he was often desperately hungover when he went in, he managed well enough. It was unlikely he was the only one—it was a hard-drinking lot, and the only crime was letting anyone else know you could barely stand for the headache.

Snipping a few of the roses to take up to Mother, I was about to return to make tea when a voice said, "That's a fool's errand if I ever saw one."

I whirled, and there stood Betty in her blue work dress, her hair wrapped in a chintz turban, as ever. "Betty!" I cried, and hurried down the steps, just barely halting before I flung my arms around her. Instead, I grabbed her hands. "Oh, my goodness. Are you all right? I've been so worried."

"Well, it was a palaver, that's sure," she said. "Let's get inside and have a cuppa, and I'll fill you in."

We made the tea, and then carried it upstairs so mother could hear the story, too. Taking center stage in a chair in the sunlight, she settled in. "So, there I was, heading home on the bus when the second siren rang out. The bus driver wasn't about to stop, even though we were all shouting at him, until a bomb fell right on the street in front of us!"

The passengers had poured out of the bus, scattering to whatever place they felt safe, but Betty didn't know where she was. The building that had been hit was set afire, expelling a pair of young lads who ran, yelling at her, "C'mon, lady. Shelter down the way."

She took refuge in the shelter with hundreds of others. "The bombing lasted all night. I never slept a wink." She reached out and touched Mother's arm. "How d'you fare, sweet? Can you manage them stairs?"

"No," I said, just as Mother said, "If I must."

Mother waved a hand. "Tell us the rest, Betty. I'm enthralled, and so happy you're here with us!"

Betty unwound the rest of the tale. The next morning, she'd emerged to find a different world, one of tumbled walls and shattered glass. It was hard to even understand where she was, but she made her way to an Underground station and rode a train to her family's neighborhood. "But I couldn't find my sister, and the building was gone, nothing but a tumble of dirt." She patted her chest. "I hardly knew what to do with myself, and I was hungry as a wolf, and just stood there for an age, until one of the neighbors saw me, Mrs. Foster, and took me in for a cuppa and some toast."

"How terrible," Mother said.

"'Twas," she agreed. "Took me two days to find Sarah in a shelter, and then we had to get her resettled before I could come back. I'm sorry I didn't ring you, but I never found a working line."

"I'm just glad you're safe," I said. "Can you stay?"

“What else would I do? This is my place!”

I reached for her hand. “I’ve missed you terribly.”

“There, there.” She stood. “I reckon I should get our supper on. What have you collected this week?” When I would have hopped up, she waved me back. “I’ll work it out myself. You sit here with your mother.”

—22—

It was such a relief to have Betty back. A few days later, she brought tea and toast for Mother and then set off on her daily rounds. Her purpose was mainly to gather any produce that might have come up from the southern orchards, but she really wanted to check on the neighborhood, make sure everyone was safely back home. She gathered information along with rations of sugar, coffee, and the odd rabbit or chunk of kidney.

Bombs had fallen all night, and Mother went to sleep after breakfast. I covered her tenderly. The doctor called in to see her every week, but he was terribly busy with injuries from the nightly attacks, and Mother talked him out of coming more often.

Later, I would nap, but the morning was cool and misty, blanketing the world with a kind obscurity. The bombs last night had fallen far from us, making up for the two nights in a row this week that they'd battered the area, leaving gaping holes like broken teeth in the rows of houses a few blocks away, and breaking a waterline that flooded the basements of many of our neighbors before it could be staunched.

This morning was quiet. Clad in a worn woolen sweater and the corduroy trousers I favored, I headed out to the garden. The nights were growing colder, finishing off the more tender vegetables, but the late peas were still vigorous. I plucked a small basketful, along with some late lettuce and more runner beans. The carrots and potatoes could stay in the ground as long as it didn't freeze, so I left them alone. Depending on what Betty brought back this afternoon, we could have a stew or a soup, something to last a few days.

Kneeling in the dirt, I bought a handful of thyme to my nose and inhaled the scent deeply. Overhead, a robin sang as if life was exactly as it always had been. And in this moment, it was. I sat back on my heels and let the moment weave through my overwrought muscles and bones and mind.

As if drawn by my quieted soul, a cat peeked through the hedge. "Hello," I said. "I don't remember seeing you before."

She trotted out of her hiding place, letting out little *mewp*s as she hurried toward me. Her fur was calico, patches of orange and black and tan over her face, and when she came closer, I saw that she was quite wet. "Poor darling," I said, holding out my hand. Boldly, she bumped into me, an almost frantic energy about her. She mewed again, looked hard at me with green eyes, and turned a circle under my hand. "What do you need, sweet?"

Another urgent mew, her tail whipping around. She was quite young and thin. "Do you want to come in for a bowl of milk, little girl?"

She dashed away, paused at the hedge to look over her shoulder, and disappeared.

I would get her something to eat and leave it on the step. In a little while. For the moment, I was in no hurry to get back to the grind of daily life. My mother was asleep. Breakfast would wait. The robin twittered, and I heard another, some distance away, answer.

The cat appeared again, this time with a kitten in her mouth, a kitten she trotted right over to drop in my lap. Walking backward for a moment, she stared into my face, earnestly communicating her desire for me to care for it. "I've got her, love," I said, picking it up. The poor thing was only a couple of weeks old, wet and cold like her mother. I tucked her into my shirt next to my skin.

The cat dashed away, and I knew to expect her return. She made three more trips, depositing a kitten each time, for a total of four. I tucked them all into my shirt, where I felt them wiggling as they warmed. I couldn't tell if they were all warming and moving, but some of them were.

When she deposited the last one in my lap, I tucked it into my shirt and waited, but she sat down. "Is that all of them, then?"

She mewed quietly. As if in response, the babies moved against my body, making tiny noises of their own. I stood, carefully holding them in place. "Let's get them into the warmth, then, shall we? And something for you to eat, poor darling."

She followed me up the steps and into the kitchen. I wondered if she knew a different kitchen, one that had been bombed or, judging by the wet, flooded. As she wove back and forth, watching and mewing cautions, I found a basket, lined it with a clutch of old kitchen towels, and placed it near the stove.

"Will this do?" I asked, and took a kitten from my shirt, a yellow-and-black one that would probably look like her mother, and set it into the nest. Mama leaped into the basket and began cleaning her baby vigorously. It protested loudly enough that I thought it was probably fine. I relocated the others one by one, a black one that was bigger, and noisy, a tiger orange that made me think of Shera, mewing and shaky, but eager to latch when I set it down. The final was colder and not moving much. Clearly the runt, it was small and scrawny, also black with white socks and nose. "Come on, little one," I said, rubbing it gently. "You were cold, but it's warm now."

No response. I brought it up to my neck, and started to hum a lullaby I remembered from my ayah. I held my other hand close to the stove and let it get warmer, then cupped the baby and kept singing. In a moment, it moved ever so faintly. I kept it up until I felt its body had lost the cold.

Finally, I settled the runt into place amid his siblings, close to a teat. Still unresponsive. I pushed his mouth against the nipple, moving him back and forth. I thought it had failed. Mother gazed at me anxiously.

And runt baby latched. “Hoorah!” I said quietly. “Look. All of them made it safely inside.” I stroked her back, which was still damp. With another kitchen towel, I rubbed her dry. “What a good mama you are!”

I filled a shallow dish with milk and offered it, remembering that Tanveer had said cats did not thrive on milk as the only part of their diet, but needed meat all the time. I didn’t know what we had to feed her. In the icebox, I found some fish soup, and turned to offer it, but she was already yelping, kittens left in a tumble, as she scrambled to beg.

“There you are, sweetheart.” I watched her eat, feeling a sense of hope. “What shall we call you, hmm?” It should be something honoring her bravery.

“I know,” I said, stroking her back as she ate, “I’ll call you Bastet,” an Egyptian goddess.

She ignored me. I sat on the floor with her, happy when she returned to her kittens, warm in their basket next to the stove. It made me remember the kittens at Herewich Manor, the first winter we arrived in England.

A COLD, WET, MISERABLE COUNTRY

Autumn and Winter 1911
Herewich Manor, England

—23—

The first few weeks in England did not endear me to the place. Everything about it was wrong, opposite, empty. My brother, for whom I'd longed forever, was no longer the boy I remembered, but a crisply dressed man with a marbled accent and a way of looking down on everything I liked or wanted or was.

"You're turning out to be quite pretty," he allowed one evening when it was only the family at dinner. We dined at home alone quite often, as my father had been poorly on the journey over, his lungs giving him trouble, and it had not appreciably improved in the cold, damp weather. My mother made potions of ginger and turmeric, which he dutifully drank. "You should be presented to court this summer."

"No one does that anymore," I said.

"Says the expert in English manners."

I scowled.

"You'll need a good match, Elsie," he said.

"Why must it be me? Why not you?"

"I shall. First let's get you settled, and then I shall seek a bride."

Mother said mildly, "Leave her alone, William. She's only fifteen. There's plenty of time."

"Fifteen is winsome," he said, inclining his head with a faint smile.

I glared at him. "I don't know that I ever wish to marry." I stabbed a slice of roast beef and sawed it mightily. "If I marry, I shan't paint."

"Painting will not contribute to our fortunes," Will said.

"How do you know? Perhaps I will prove to be a generational genius."

He snorted. "I've seen your work, and while I'll allow you've a fine eye, I hardly think you'll make your fortune. The little orientalist things you're doing have been out of style for years."

"I'm not an Orientalist," I cried. "My paintings are tribute, born of my true love of the home I had to leave."

"Call it what you will," he said. "That does not alter the need our family faces for you to marry."

"Father," I said. "Will you please intervene? He is not the head of this household."

He huffed, and took a long swallow of water. "William, the matter can be tabled for a year or so, surely. Let the girl sow her wild oats. In my experience, a girl finds her way to marriage soon enough."

I barely resisted sticking out my tongue, even though it would be childish and therefore lend weight to my cause—I was too young for marriage.

Mother said, "Perhaps you wouldn't mind meeting other people your age, Elsie. We've been invited to a number of fetes." She raised one perfectly arched brow. "We could get some frocks made in London, so you'd feel at home with the new crowd."

I knew what she was doing—smoothing the waters between siblings, and dangling the delight of new frocks in front of my greedy eyes. I had discovered my clothing to be quite horrifically out of fashion. "I wouldn't mind."

"Wonderful. We'll make a week of it."

"Excellent," William said. "I've been invited to a country house party three weeks hence. You may tag along, and I'll introduce you to the right set."

I blinked at his snobbery, thinking with a sudden ache of the mixed English and Indian company I'd kept in Nainital. But I would go along with the plan if it meant I could have my own wishes.

—24—

November 3, 1911
Mayo College, Ajmer
[In Urdu]

Dear Elsie,

I offer my regrets that you did not know how to address me, for that was my fault in attempting to end our correspondence. I introduced the awkwardness between us when there has never been anything but purest trust.

Truth.

Let us keep to that truth now. More letters between us are a kind of madness, but I was so overjoyed to see your words that I cannot hold to my resolve. Please write to me. I will write back. Surely there is no temptation in words on a page, when we are parted by thousands of miles!

Thank you for sharing that vision of Venus shining on the sea. I could picture it so clearly, the fresh breeze and nose-biting cold, the sky stretching above, so vast and full of stars, and only the two of us, apart from the world.

I would that it were so.

Truth. In truth, Elsie, your absence has leeched my world of all color. I taste no salt in the food, or sugar in my chai, essential things that make each day fine and good. Everything reminds me of you—the lake, the kittens, a tangle of flowers, my own sketchbook, filled with things you taught me, even if I am a poor artist at best.

At least now I may think of Venus, and imagine you raising your hand to her as I am, and, thus, will we be connected for a moment.

I have returned to school and will devote myself to my studies. I am most engaged with maths and discussions of economics, but I have also found a friend here, Sunil, who shares my love of literature. We find ways to discuss books most deeply. We are reading a novel of the Sannyasi Rebellion, which some say was the beginning of Indian independence. Sunil believes as I do that the time will be coming in our lifetimes, sooner rather than later, that India shrugs off the yoke of the British and we make our own way into the future. I suppose by attending my studies of economics and systems (along with the British way of doing everything), I will be more thoroughly prepared, much as I would love to study only astronomy and poetry. I can take those up on my own. In this moment in history, there are more pressing questions. How will India become her own nation? How can that best be accomplished?

Which is what our fathers discussed endlessly, I suppose. Will your father still support such ideas, or will he settle into becoming a bastion of English gentry?

And now you, too, are one of that number, *Lady* Elsie. How will that change you, I wonder? Because of course it must.

I hope it does not, at least very little. I pray you remain as fierce and independently minded as you ever have been. Your soul holds a great light.

Perhaps one day, while gazing at Venus, I will discover some new star. If I do, I will name her for you. Will that make up for my harsh first letter?

And at last, this—we can continue our poetry study and translations as easily here as in person. I have enclosed an Urdu ghazal for you to translate. Do not be afraid! It is quite simple.

Now I am off to post this and hope for a letter in return. Our paths have split in different directions, but it feels too much to ask that we not be able to continue the conversation of our minds.

Be well, ham-nawā,

Your own Tanveer

PS: One small beauty: watching a chestnut mare frolic in her pen, mane dancing the long light of afternoon.

[Enclosed Urdu poem]

December 12, 1911
Herewich Manor, England
[In Urdu]

Dear Tanveer,
When I saw your handwriting, and felt the solid weight of your letter, I was filled with such gratitude

and relief that I wept. I can bear leaving India (just), but not if I am also required to sever our connection.

How well I understand the feeling of dullness you describe, that sense of lack—no salt, so sugar, no sun in the sky, not even the comfort of a peacock's cry. Nothing but cold and wet, the skies endlessly weeping, not in the way of a monsoon, but just a constant, wearying rain.

There is not even the smell of spice from the kitchens, for we are now truly relegated to English meals. I've never seen my father so happy at the table, but Mother and I are not. I've promised to gather recipes to replicate the Anglo-Indian dishes we enjoyed, but for now I shall subsist on dull grains and colorless vegetables, boiled half to death.

Tanveer, truly—thank you for writing. Your letter gave me such a moment of joy, it was as if the sun itself had broken through the gray and poured gold into my heart. I have drawn the moment for you. It is only me, and my paints in the window of my room, looking east to India, hoping to smell its fragrance on the wind.

One small joy: Mother has consented to my enrolling in the Slade School of Fine Art when I am old enough, which allows women.

My father does not yet know, but I have decided that I shall not marry, and will put at the center of my life the only other love I can bear—this work, my painting. A husband will only take it from me.

Of course, my brother (never to be called Willie anymore, only Will, and he now prefers the full William) has been plotting a wedding for me for years, thinking to shore up with a brilliant marriage the rather thin fortunes that accompany my father's title.

The boy who caught frogs and came home with muddy feet is long gone, buried beneath a proper British education, unlike his sister with her wretched accent, which I wickedly make worse for his benefit. Mother implores me not to tease, but I see her lips twitching. She loves him so and is wildly overjoyed to be back in his company. Because I love *her*, I don't begrudge her this small comfort.

Here is my drawing. Send me something that smells of sunlight.

Tell me more of your reading and your thoughts of Indian independence. Do you think it will happen in the next decade or two? A worthy subject of study. I remember my father bemoaning a strike on English goods at some point. Was that the division of Bengal? The details are lost to me—but I suppose children have no context for politics.

In honor of our truth, I will tell you that I *also* fear I will become some other person here, that somehow the weight of clouds and expectations and pressure will conspire to quench the fire that has fueled me to this point and I will become some limp imitation of myself. What if I am sugared down to a wife who only cares for parties? The lure of the ease in that life is tempting at times.

I hope you will help me hold fast to myself.

In hopes of sunlight and good friendship,

Elsie

PS I have attempted a translation, poor though it may be. I've included a sonnet from the bard himself to challenge you to capture the cadence in Urdu.

[Enclosed drawing of Elsie with her paints looking toward the horizon]

SKETCHES AT DAWN

Autumn 1940
London

—25—

We enjoyed a few nights of quiet in October, all of us getting a solid night of sleep several days in a row. On this dark, rainy afternoon, I felt clearheaded and even mildly optimistic—maybe the Nazis would continue to be stymied by the dark, stormy nights—and Mother sat up in bed, her cheeks pink. I read to her most days. She'd asked me to find things set in India, and after discovering we could not tolerate the arrogance of Kipling, no matter how good his descriptions, I found a much-thumbed copy of *A Passage to India* at the lending library. Both of us were enjoying the trip down memory lane, and, although Nainital had not been much like Chandrapore, the writing was excellent and the divisions between British and locals were familiar.

The kittens frolicked over the bed, little balls of wild happiness, all still clumsy with too-long claws getting caught in the cloth of her blanket, shrieking their little hearts out when they were caught. Mother patiently freed one, then another, and they often curled up in various hollows of her body, for Bastet had firmly decided she was the finest human in the household and draped over her belly at every opportunity, purring.

"Never mind that I'm the one who feeds you, young traitor," I said, stroking her multicolored back. She purred happily, but didn't move. Tanveer had told me once that purring was a healing sound, like chanting or singing. If Bastet could pour healing into my mother's failing system, I would help her purr all day.

I read for a little longer, then settled the book in my lap. "How did you and the maharani become friends, anyway? Wasn't that social suicide?"

"Oh, Elsie, what did I care about the club and all the gossip? So many of those women were bored to tears, and I had things to do."

"But wasn't it odd from her side, too?"

Her long white hand slid down Bastet's spine. "It might have been, but we found common ground in our interest in women's health, and in truth, her husband had begun to court his third wife, so he found some peace in her taking up residence here." She blinked. "I mean Nainital." Her smile was thin. "I find it all blending together of late. The maharani and Nainital and Herewich, and Santa Fe and London."

"So many adventures."

"Not like yours. The Pyramids and the Buddhas of Bamiyan. India in the twenties, when everything was changing so quickly. It must have been so exciting."

"I was far away from all that, really." The piercing layers of the time I spent in India in the twenties were secret even from my mother. How desperately I had wished to stay there. It had been, in part, my mother's need that drew me back to England, and Peter, and all that I had come to loathe.

"Channan was on bed rest," I continued, "and I spent most of my time with her. And I painted a great deal." I glanced up to one large canvas that had emerged from that period, both saturated and soft, a hazy painting of our old house in Nainital rendered with an almost abstract eye. Three children played on the steps while two women took tea in the shade. All of us.

She made a sharp move, as if stabbed, and cried out softly. I leapt to my feet, but she waved me down. "A stitch," she said, pressing her hand to the spot. "Nothing more."

"Would you like some tea?"

"No, just read to me a little more, will you?"

I picked up the book to do just that when a clatter came from below, and then leaping footsteps on the stairs. Peter appeared in the doorway, looking cheerful and flushed, carrying a bag. "I bring gifts! A beef rump roast big enough for an army, and"—he drew out a flat dish I could smell five feet away—"an apple pie. An actual apple pie, not a mock one."

"Oh, Peter, how miraculous!" my mother cried.

"How on earth . . . ?" I asked.

"Ask me no questions, I'll tell you no lies, my dear."

"Ah."

"I must return to headquarters, so I'll take this down to Betty, shall I?"

"Surely, you'll be back to share it with us?" Mother asked. She'd always been very fond of Peter.

I rose. "I'll come down with you."

On the landing, I paused. "Are you well?"

"Yes, wife, I am. It's a tonic to try to thwart the bastards. I think we might have turned a corner at last. They lost so many planes on the fifteenth."

I nodded, not quite convinced. He could be mercurial, but I saw that his eyes were clear, and he smelled of aftershave rather than gin.

A new love interest perhaps? He'd ever been given to crushes on beautiful young women, mostly to worship from afar, as he had done with me until we married. "All right, then. Thank you for the roast. Mother has not been at all well."

"I know." He started down the stairs, then turned. "Jonathan said to remind you of the party on Friday evening. Seven p.m."

"Ah." That was where the black-market goods had come from. "I shall have to see how Mother is doing."

"Surely she'll be all right with Betty for the evening? You know she'd want you to get out."

"I worry there will be a raid, and they'll be here alone."

He rested a hand on the banister. "We cannot allow the Nazis to keep us from living our lives, Elsie. Otherwise, we're already dead."

The thought of a party did lift my spirits. "All right. Will you meet me there?"

"Let's go together, shall we? Will you wear the blue dress?"

His mood was so much improved that, for a moment, I searched his face, feeling a sense of warning. He had at times been dangerously unstable, but to be fair, that was a long time in the past.

Perhaps his nerves were adjusting to the reality of the bombings, just as we all were.

"Of course," I said finally. "I'll ring Nina and find out what I might bring." Wartime shortages made it acceptable to ask. At any other time she would never have tolerated such a question. She had been known for her talents as a hostess, and she'd been quite clever about bringing together our circle of bohemians and eccentrics.

Without her, I would never have found Rocky.

A SUMMER WEEKEND

Summer 1913
Kent, England

—26—

The fashion that summer of 1913 was very much for the country house getaway. Everyone trooped out to one estate or another and stayed for three days, playing croquet on the lawn, drinking cocktails in the late afternoons, dashing off to swim if it was warm enough. The swimming was the only activity that saved these weekends for me. I'd learned to swim in India and had never lost my taste for it, nor for the evening walks that framed my days.

In this one thing, I liked England better than India. Here, everyone indulged in long walks that looped through gardens, and woods, and over fields, for miles and miles. The mild weather made it possible. On those long treks, I discovered new beauties, the surprise of a sudden mist in a thick forest, a shaft of sunlight illuminating a single flower. I began to fall in love with the rich gardens surrounding every great house, the softer palettes of lilac and rose, white and pale green.

But nothing pleased me so much as the swimming. We swam in ponds and lakes, and even sometimes a sleepy river, though this made my mother quite nervous. We swam in clever pools designed to look like grottos, surrounded with ferns and rocks and topless mermaids spouting water from their lips. Whenever a country house had a pool, I awakened early to swim.

In late August, I was invited to a Saturday-to-Monday party at cousin Nina's house, or rather her father's estate. For the first time, the guests were all youthful, no one much over twenty-five or so. I also didn't see many of the nemesis faces who so plagued me elsewhere.

Nina herself met me at the door, slipping her arm through mine. "There you are, darling! I've been so looking forward to seeing you. I think you'll be much happier here with my friends than you have been. Let's get you settled and go for a swim."

The house was sprawling, luxurious. It made me think of Talwarpur Palace, although of course it was entirely different in style. Still, one could see peacocks on the wallpaper and carpets woven in oriental patterns. "What is your family's connection to India?" I asked.

"My grandfather was some muckety-muck back in the seventies."

"You've never been?"

"God, no. Why would I?"

At my expression, she seemed to remember. "Oh, I am sorry. You miss it, don't you?"

I nodded.

"Never mind. Here's your room, and I'll meet you down at the pool in an hour, shall we say?"

"Yes."

I didn't travel with a lady's maid—my brother, watching pennies, said it was unnecessary because all the big houses would have them, and everyone would forgive me since I'd come so recently from India. I protested that we'd had dozens of servants in India, servants who'd always done everything for me. I hardly knew how to pack, to unpack, to prepare my clothing for travel and then dressing. "Some of my frocks have two dozen buttons down the back!"

He waved away my concerns. A girl would be loaned to me for the duration. "The cost of servants is dear in England," he said, and glanced over his shoulder to make sure no one could overhear. "The coffers of Herewich are hardly overflowing, my dear."

"Then why all these new frocks? I had plenty."

He gave me a pitying smile. "The clothing you brought from India was entirely unsuitable. You must look the earl's daughter, Elsie, to attract the right husband."

I clamped my mouth closed. He had no power to force me to marry. There was no point to arguing with him. But a wave of worry sent ripples through my body, like a pebble into a pond. My mother had influenced my father and brother to allow me to attend art school, but how far would her reach extend? Would she stand with me against marriage? I hadn't discussed it with her.

Perhaps I wouldn't. For now.

But for today, I was free, and in the company of my bohemian cousin. My trunk had been delivered, and as William had predicted, someone had cared for my things, the dinner dresses and the day dresses hung neatly, everything else settled in drawers.

The room was well appointed, the walls hung with landscapes rendered in a style popular a hundred years before. I stepped close to admire one of a rolling landscape dotted with sheep, a single black one making a focal point. Nicely done.

My fingers itched for a paintbrush or a pencil. Perhaps there would be a little time over the weekend to sketch the landscape. I'd spied a pond with willow trees bending into it, and the patterns on the water clamored for my attention.

I had not yet heard from the Slade School of Fine Art, and the new term would open in just a month. Would they allow me to study? The possibility swelled through me, vague images of easels and classrooms and the smell of turpentine rolling across my imagination.

Without art school, life looked bleak. Parties and dinners and introductions to the right people until I was successfully married off. The narrowness of that path compressed my lungs.

Have faith, I told myself. Why would I be given such a hunger to create art if I were not meant to fulfill it?

I changed into a swimming costume and made my way to the pool, drawn by the sound of laughter. It sounded robust, not at all faked, as so many of these parties had seemed. I emerged through French doors to an area rocked to resemble a cliff face, with a round pool at the base. Water poured out in little fountains from the mouths of mermaids and cherubs and a wicked Pan, peeing.

Lightly clad young bodies, tanned and glistening, adorned the chairs and sluiced through the water. My eye caught on a young man swimming, his arms and back splendid with power. A willowy young woman lazed on a chaise, her shoulders showing through a diaphanous drape over a silk suit. Nearby her, a shirtless young man rubbed oil on his broad chest.

Everyone, *everyone* seemed unconcerned, splashing and dozing in half nudity beneath the warm sun.

I wanted to paint them all.

The youth in the pool swept himself up to the side, lifting his arms to smooth his hair from his forehead. "Hello!" he cried. "You must be Elsie. Nina's spoken of nothing else."

He was quite dazzling—fit and tall, his eyes a piercing blue that seemed almost unreal. "I'm Rocky."

"Hello."

Nina joined us, an enormous hat protecting her very fair skin. "Wonderful, you've met! Rocky is a student at the Slade, and I told him you were going to join him in the autumn."

"I hope so."

"Darling, you'll be fine," Nina said, herding us over to a collection of lounges half in the sun, half in the shade. "Having all that time in India, you can likely tolerate the sun, can't you, Elsie? I can't bear it at all." She waved to a footman in livery who looked red faced in his uniform. "Bring us cocktails, Tom, will you?"

"Elsie," Rocky said, lighting a cigarette, "tell me all about your art. Every word."

A young man, dark haired and too thin, sat down very close to Rocky. "Every word," he echoed, leaning bare arm to bare arm into Rocky.

"Don't mind David," Rocky said, pushing a lock of hair from the boy's forehead. "He's jealous of everyone."

A buzz of heat burned up through my neck, to my ears, as I realized what he meant. I was not ignorant of men who preferred other men, but the preference had never been so public.

Nina gave one of her tinkling laughs. "Elsie, have we shocked you?"

For a moment, I didn't reply, taking in the small gathering, the long legs, the skin, the sense of relaxed expectations. "*Surprise* is perhaps a better word," I said. "But I welcome surprises."

"Here, here," Rocky said, smiling at me. "Now, tell us about your art. Do you paint?"

So I told him about painting India, and humans, and my desire to get better. "It's all I've wanted," I said in conclusion. "What about yours?"

Rocky inhaled his cigarette, then exhaled, pressing a palm to his lover's thigh. "My mother took me to Italy when I was ten," he said. "Her grand tour, I suppose. I fell under the spell of the great sculptors."

"What material do you prefer?"

He laughed. "Marble, of course, but as a student, I make do." He tossed away his cigarette and stood. "Do you swim?"

"Oh, yes."

"Then let's leave David and Nina to their gossip."

~

That evening, the supper was served with the same ceremony as the others I'd attended, but the attendees were much more vigorous in opinions and discussion. The woman to my right was the one who'd worn the diaphanous bathing costume. Dressed now in an evening frock, her dark hair swept off her long neck, I saw that she was an Anglo-Indian, strikingly beautiful, as everyone seemed to be in this crowd. Her name was Diana, and she told me her husband was a lord who didn't mind her bohemian friends as long as she decorated his arm when he so required it. "I expect I'll have to give it up when I bear a child, but that's a trouble for another day."

On my left was Peter, whom I'd met at the other party with Nina. He was a charming conversationalist, drawing me out about things he must have known I could talk about easily. "Tell me, Elsie," he said, sipping wine. "Have you truly never been to England before now?"

"No. My mother refused to send me to school here."

"How extraordinary. Everyone is talking about her, you know, and you."

"Something new to gossip about," I said dismissively. "We'll be old news soon enough."

He inclined his head. "I doubt that. Two such great beauties are rare in any moment."

I smiled. "Thank you. But I know my mother is like a jewel in the night sky. I'm only a pale echo."

"Hardly," he said, but gracefully let me retreat. "Are you sorry you've not been here before?"

"Oh, no! Not at all. I was quite brokenhearted when we had to leave."

Across the table, a man in his mid-twenties said, "Really? I thought everyone wanted to escape India." He sipped wine. "Whatever could you have loved so? I visited in my teens and found it dreadfully hot."

I felt the eyes of others on me, guests wondering who I was to be invited into the enclave, and I was anxious to make the right reply. Rocky caught my eye, and it reminded me to be myself. What other person could I be? "I did not want to escape. I loved it all—the light, the sound of the birds, the customs and cultures of so many different kinds of people, all mingling."

"What cultures?" Rocky asked. "I know so little."

Tanveer rose in my mind, tall and good humored, his hair hidden behind an exquisitely wrapped turban. "Sikhs and Muslims and Hindus, and others, too." I spoke to Rocky directly. "At the market, you might hear four or five languages." I thought of that market, the faces I missed, and my throat felt tight. "In contrast, England seems very . . ." I couldn't think of a word that didn't carry some tinge of offense.

"Homogenous?" Rocky supplied.

Gratefully, I smiled. "Yes. Exactly."

"Is homogenous a bad thing?" Peter asked. "It would seem to provide a bit of stability in a world that isn't terribly reliable."

He seemed a little out of place in this crowd, more earnest than bohemian, and I wondered how he'd come to be associated with Nina. Were they related? "Not bad," I said, taking his question seriously. I needed to be less judgmental of the people I met here. "Just less . . . interesting . . . I suppose."

"I see."

"What about you, Peter?" I asked. "What fascinates you?"

He considered, chasing peas with his knife and fork. "If I were given my choice, I'd rather like to build things."

"Oh! What things?"

"Homes," he said. "Not this heavy, Baroque grandness, but . . . less. Have you been to Paris? I quite love the Art Nouveau style, those natural lines and shapes."

"I don't know anything about that," I said. "Tell me more."

He shook his head. "It will never be more than a hobby, I'm afraid. I'll be a bureaucrat in the government, no doubt, or perhaps in the foreign service."

"Oh, do not give in so easily! Surely there is a path toward a respectable career in architecture."

"Not if your father is the Marquess of Guildford," Diana said with a snort.

I glanced at her, then back to Peter. "I have talked my mother into letting me study art for two years. Perhaps your father would give such a window?"

His smile was sad. "I highly doubt it. But thank you for your enthusiasm."

A clutch of worry squeezed my gut. Would I, too, be forced to give in to what was expected of me?

I vowed I would not.

~

The morning after the dinner party, I awakened just before dawn, tugged from sleep by a dream of tigers. For long moments, I lay still, blinking in the soft twilight of early morning, trying to capture the last shreds of the dream, but they dissolved, leaving behind only a sense of yearning.

Birds sang outside. I got up to open the window. Soft, humid air carried a scent of greenery along with the melody of birds I couldn't name. One tiny creature whistled exuberantly, the sound much larger than its tiny body. It lifted my spirits, and I stretched hard, feeling the energy in my limbs, a need to walk. Just beyond the edge of the lawns, I could see a small lake, shimmering pale lavender in the subdued light.

I washed quickly and donned sensible short boots and a skirt and blouse, and carried my bag of sketchbook and paints out to the newly breaking day.

Outside, my feet made a dark-green path through the dew. I lifted my head to the landscape, taking in the willows bowing over a little stream, and a row of tall rhododendrons bloomed in pink and white and purple. Trees as wide around as a wagon stood guard as they must have done for centuries. Birds twittered and chirped and sailed through the branches. I chose a slender path leading through a copse of trees, stepping into shadows that smelled of hummus and growth and little beings, and thought suddenly of the fairy stories my mother had read to me when I was small. This was their landscape, these deeply rooted trees, the little holes in the trunks, the tiny ferns and wildflowers scattering color and scent throughout the space. I paused, turning in a circle, and felt a well of happiness that had been missing in my heart for many months. Perhaps this was what English people missed when they went to India, this greenery and softness.

Through the branches, I saw the first fingers of sunlight cracking the horizon, and hurried so I could see it break over the lake. It wasn't far, and I came out of the trees to see the dance of light just beginning on the water. I also saw that I wasn't the first person up after all—a strong swimmer cut through the water, their clothes left in a pile on the ground.

Would they mind me disturbing their solitary swim? Better to apologize than ask permission.

I scooped a cupful of lake water for my paints, then sat on a flat rock and propped my sketchbook on my knees. The light was the main thing, and it would change quickly, so I focused there first, catching the glimmer of pinkish-yellow dawn on the leaves and the edges of the water. The water itself took on waves of light as the swimmer cut through, creating a triangle of ripples, first out, then back, the light moving like the folds in fine satin, light and dark in easy waves.

It was only as the figure came close that I recognized Rocky. He stood in water up to his waist, smoothing his hair from his chiseled face. "Hello!" he called.

I waved back.

"I'm afraid I'm out here in nothing but the skin God gave me. You'll want to look away."

I turned a page quickly, and sketched the rounds of his shoulders, his lean arms and flat belly. "Must I?"

He laughed. "I think you know my tastes are not for ladies."

"All the better," I returned. "Less scandalous, isn't it?"

"Scandal has no place here. Shall I just—" He waved toward the shore.

"Please." Some boldness made me say, "Slowly, if you would."

He laughed, and accommodated my request. I hurriedly sketched his body, strong legs and nipped waist, hairy calves, the suggestion of his genitals. On the shore, he waited, but I could see gooseflesh rising on his body. "Good, thank you!" I cried.

He wrapped himself in a blanket and carried his clothes over. "Let me see."

Without modesty, I showed him the sketches, coming out of the water, and then standing on the shore. "Well done, you." He wiped his face with the blanket. "Have you drawn male bodies before?"

I thought of the stolen moments in Nainital, the dangerous sketches I kept hidden. But to this fellow artist, I felt I could admit the truth. "Yes."

"Elsie, you surprise me! But I'm glad. It can be difficult to find models. Probably more so for women. At the Slade, you'll be able to draw both men and women." He grinned. "The sex bits are covered. You'll have to use your imagination."

"Better than nothing." I sketched his bare foot, the high arch and long toes. "No matter. I look forward to it more than I can say."

"It's quite wonderful, being there," he said. "You shall adore it." His stomach growled, and he hopped to his feet. "Are you going to stay and sketch, or will you come back and have breakfast with me?"

I allowed him to pull me to my feet. "I'll join you."

"Wonderful. No one else will be about until ten."

"Do you have any of your sketches with you? I'd love to see your work."

"I do not, but"—his eyebrows rose mischievously—"I suspect I know a willing model or two. Would you like that?"

I wavered. "Other guests?"

"Yes." Something in the depth of his glittery expression challenged me. Was I a bohemian, or not?

Two choices faced me—the life my father and brother had laid out for me, or the life I wanted, which would be entirely built from unconventional choices. The decision was easy. "Yes," I said. "I would love that."

His smile was small, but highly rewarding. I didn't think I'd often met a man so beautiful as Rocky, but his beauty lit nothing in my heart. My desire was left behind, in India. Perhaps I would never feel such a shimmer again.

The thought made me feel terribly sad.

—27—

September 30, 1940
Talwarpur Palace

Dearest Elsie,
[In Urdu]: One beautiful thing today is the music I can hear from my balcony, where I write this letter. I do not know who plays, but it is a sweet raga lifting into the morning. I am grateful for this moment of peace, knowing it is rare in this world today.

[In English]: Your letter arrived riddled with holes from the censor, but I gather you went into the city to see what you could see. You might write in Urdu to avoid this trouble (or will even that work?). I welcome the drawings, and Channan is delighted with hers. She takes the tonic faithfully, and some days she indeed seems to have more strength, but she remains bedridden and quite frail. In truth, the injuries of her youth weakened her long ago. I suspect it is only her love of Kirandeep that has allowed her to linger so long.

She tells me to say that she has a wonderful view from that bed, over the plains of Talwarpur and a sky full of clouds drawing themselves in new ways every hour. She wishes she could draw so she could show you. I've told her I would buy her a camera, but she refuses.

Kirandeep is away at school, and has not shown much inclination to write home. Unlike his father, he is not a studious lad, but a vigorous one who loves athletic activities and charging through the world to eat it all alive. He is a boy who vividly enjoys the company of his fellows, and I encourage that.

We have taken in a new tiger, found half starved (near Nainital, actually) from a terrible infection in her mouth. By her teeth, she is quite old, so she will not enter the general population, but stay in the local park where she can be fed and tended more gently, though still have a sense of freedom. She was quite savage in pain, but once her bad teeth were pulled, she became much more approachable. Soon she will be given the run of the small park.

So you see, even in the midst of darkness, there is hope.

Do not despair, jaanu. Wars end. The earth will turn. Yours is only to endure, and you will do that by painting and tending to the people you love. I've enclosed a pressed sword lily for you to remember your beloved land, and the people here who love you. I shall try to manage another telephone call when I go to Delhi in a month's time.

Dost-e-Azīz, dearest friend,

Tanveer

[Enclosed one pressed sword lily]

October 8, 1940
London

Dear Tanveer,
[In Urdu]: One small beauty is a pot of red geraniums blooming in a puddle of sunshine amid a pile of dust and bricks.

[In English]: I've found a little cat. Or rather, she found me, with four of her tiny kittens. She must have been living in a nearby basement that was flooded when the water main shattered a few nights ago. I've named her Bastet, and settled her in Mother's room. The lot of them have lifted her spirits magically, and she's been able to come downstairs most days, and enjoys tea with Betty and me most afternoons in the sitting room. We no longer take shelter in the cellar—after the first two weeks, she was too weak to manage the steps during raids, and of course the public shelters are too far for her.

So we camp in the sitting room, pretending we are safe. I cannot imagine that anything would protect us from a hit, not even in the cellar. But what is one to do? We must make the best of it.

I admit the cellar had begun to make me feel panicky. I don't fear dying, but I am terrified by the idea of being buried alive in a pile of rubble, unable to move. At least at street level, I feel we would be found quickly.

Such thoughts!

We see little of Peter, for, of course, he works. I will not bother to write with what as it will be censored. You know the gist of it.

Feeling restless, I took myself out today. It's impossible to know what is happening from the radio or newspapers, of course—it's all so understated. I took my sketchbook and my watercolors out to see what might be what.

Our little corner of London has only been modestly injured, and tends to be a patchwork of blocks alternating like a chessboard, this one with a crater in the middle of the street, and a trio of houses crumbled more or less completely, with a tumble of bricks piled up to one side. A shimmer of powdered glass glazes everything, sparkling on tree leaves and the iron railing standing guard around an unmarred home. Cross over one street and one would never know there was a war at all—children play in the street, and a dog barks from behind a fence, and a last stand of roses blooms around a cheerful doorway.

As I traveled toward the city, the damage became more apparent. Entire blocks have gone missing, and the storefronts show the damage. It is eerily deserted, empty in a way I have never seen here. Very little foot traffic, and there is a grime of soot and ash and dust on every surface, making all gray, beneath gray skies. My heels crunched over the pavements, and I feel heartbroken that London might never recover. I know you will tell me it has been built on the backs of the world, and, of course, you will be right, but I will still mourn the loss of each beautiful old building.

The bombings are relentless, going on for hours and hours and hours every night. It's meant to break us down, and I fear it shall. We are terrified, hungry, and desperately short on sleep. It has been thirty-two nights!

And honestly, it is so distressing to see the wreck of it all. Why do we still solve problems of nations by flinging the bodies of young men into the void, by blasting entire cities of homes to pieces, and the little shops we shall miss always? I so mourn the bakery we lost last week—she made the cleverest little twists of bread, and it's gone forever now. Nothing left of it but a pile of debris.

I am mindful that Mother and Betty need me to hold steady, so I do not let myself descend into my fear and anger unless I pour it out to you here. I made kheer for mother a few days ago, saving up the sugar from my tea (and the unused portion of Peter's). We had saffron in the spice safe, and a handful of nuts. Betty is wonderfully resourceful about tracking down the source of fresh harvests, and she found the almonds when they first arrived.

And of course, my art gives me calm. Bearing witness to all of it in my sketchbook, the erased bakery, the empty streets, the surprisingly upsetting sight of a tree burned free of her leaves.

As ever, give my love to Channan. I've drawn her this little vignette of the yellow trees around Russell Square.

Be well, mere ham-nafas. Your letters are a lifeline, as they have been so often. I was remembering the challenge you gave me to examine my "Orientalism" when I struggled so that first year at Slade. How we sparred that winter over complicated ideas of colonialism and women and freedom. Do you remember?

Ever yours,

Elsie

[Enclosed sketch of the park, charcoal drawings of the geranium blooming amid the debris]

PAINT AND OTHER BRUISES

1913
London

—28—

November 1913
London

Dear Tanveer,

[In Urdu]: One small beauty is the smell of oil paint on my fingers. The texture is so rich and vibrant! I feel I have discovered an entirely new world.

[In English]: Despite my joy in the paint, I am struggling in some of my classes, and today, I have had the most horrible day. A few days ago, we turned in our projects, and I felt I had done well—I worked most diligently on a portrait of a vegetable wallah in Nainital, and I was pleased with it, though it could have done with more time. The green of his tunic, the glare of his eyes, his heavy mustache.

But to my dismay, my professor hated it. Or perhaps didn't hate, but even worse—he *disdained* it. He went on at length about my "Orientalist" style, my unsophisticated palette, even my "quaint" subject. It was all I could do not to burst into tears right there.

Of course I did not. We're learning to be tough, to say thank you for the feedback, even if it's terrible. Naturally, Helen, the pet of every single teacher in the place, was praised to the heavens for her portrait of an old man and his pigeons. Her palette is all soft browns and golds, and I do quite admire it, but it isn't the only palette to be had. The world is not only one kind of light.

I am crushed, and I fear that I'm only a dilettante.

This is the second time I've been criticized for using an "Orientalist" style. Honestly, I don't see my work that way at all. Orientalism makes a fairy tale of the people and landscapes of India (and other places). I am painting what I saw, what I knew, the true faces of the chai wallah at the bazaar with his missing front tooth; the girls walking to school with their heads together, the library and the bakery and the tiger. (Oh, how they hated the tiger series, and I was devastated because I thought I'd done very well. How much did we practice?)

It appears I have overestimated the extent of my talent, and I do not know what my life will be if I am not a painter. Perhaps I am only meant for the vapid life my brother has plotted out for me, a socialite giving teas and balls and vying for the attention of duchesses.

I'm sorry not to add more cheerful notes to this. What am I even doing in this cold, wet, miserable place with all these cold, judgmental people? Am I a fraud, Tanveer? Tell me the truth.

Your friend,

Elsie

January 1914
Talwarpur Palace

Dear Elsie,

[In Urdu]: One small beauty—a boy walking with his tiny sister down the rows of vegetables at the market. He was so gentle with her, laughing when she picked up an aubergine or potato.

[In English]: Of course you are not a fraud, and by now I am sure you have somewhat recovered from the blow of the criticism.

You do not yet know who you are as a painter. That will take time to develop. Perhaps your taste for painting the images you remember of India will grow, or perhaps over time it will fade, but your worth as a painter does not come from outside validation. It must come from you. You know this, but you are feeling lost because they are not fawning over you the way everyone always has.

Which sounds unkind, and I do not mean it so. Give it time. Win them over with your great capacity to learn.

I have other news. Gurdaya is to be married next month to a raja of great wealth from near Amritsar. She is very unhappy that she will have to go so far away, but my father has had enough of her protestations and rejections of suitors, and he has put his foot down. The marriage will be advantageous for both families. He is unfortunately a bit older, and a widow twice over, but has not yet produced an heir. That will be Gurdaya's task, it appears.

Seeing her unhappiness, I cannot help but think it does no favors to allow girls to be educated when they must marry anyway. How can she be happy now? Would it not be easier for her to have been left to the ordinary amusements of women, knowing she would have to serve in capacity of wife and mother?

It grieves me on her behalf. I am quite sure she would love a letter from you.

Your friend,

Tanveer

January 1914
London
[In Urdu]

Tanveer, I have sometimes known you to be dense over the rights and wishes of women, but I cannot believe you would actually say Gurdaya would have been better off if she had not been allowed an education. Do you think her mind would be less, a mind at least as facile and bright as your own, if not more so (and you will argue, but I think you know it's true)? It is a tragedy, an actual living tragedy, that she should be squeezed into such a narrow life. She is meant for bigger things, for the quest to solve a scientific mystery or discover a way to prevent illness. It is a waste that she cannot explore that part of herself, and it is a loss for the world. You are a man and cannot help your narrow-mindedness, but I am desperately disappointed in you.

I have cut my hair. Perhaps at least partly because I am angry with you.

Elsie

January 30, 1914
London

Dear Gudiya,
A drawing I have done for you, to always remember how mighty you are. You <u>are</u> mighty, my friend, and wise. Continue with your studies as you are able, and remember, I am always here, your friend forever. I am here, in England, and I would so love to have you visit one day.

Your friend,
Elsie
[Enclosed drawing of Gurdaya on top of a hill]

February 1914
Talwarpur Palace
[In Urdu]

Dear Elsie,
Cut your hair! I do not even know how to address this calamity. I cannot imagine you without your yards and yards of night-dark hair. Why would you do such a thing?

Gurdaya is now married. She wept the entire night before we traveled to her husband's palace. I took your words to heart, for you are right. She should have had more autonomy in determining her life, but while the rights and freedoms of women are emerging in Europe and America, here it is still a distant dream. I do not know how to address it myself—these structures of what men and women can do are deeply rooted and how can they be changed?

The Guru said we are all equal, men and women, king and untouchable, but that is hard to follow in the actual living world. My sister's unhappiness reminds me to consider this in the light of other independence. If we struggle to free India, and yet women are not given the same rights to order their lives that men are, then are we truly free?

I shall think on this more.

Rather than being angry with me and taking me to task, you might remember that I, too, am a part of my society, and I have been trained to think and believe certain things about our roles. Your fierce ideas and my sister's beautiful mind and her great despair are excellent teachers, but I am still a man of my world. I am still learning.

Perhaps in a way this is much like your inability to see where your work might give tribute to colonial ideals, and where it is authentic. No matter how you wish it not to be true, you are a member of the colonial class. You are as tainted by that as I am by my world of men.

Perhaps in this, as in so many ways, we teach each other.

My father has suggested he might bring me with him when he next visits London. If you were not there, I would have no interest, but he insists I must know what the mind of the Englishman holds if we are to navigate the coming decades. In private, he fiercely supports independence, but in public, he flatters and cajoles and makes bargains. I thought once that he was disingenuous, but I have begun to admire his tactics, at least in this mode. He tells me I am too earnest, that too much shows in my expression, and while I know this must be true, I do not know exactly how to hide those things. My brother is far better at these games, though

I must say he has not my father's character. He likes a fast life, with too many women and too much drink. Just now, he's touring Belgium while his young wife languishes here in the palace, lonely and far from home.

Let us make peace, my friend. To that end, here is my small beauty:

We have acquired two more tigers as company for Chhoti Billi. Both cubs, again orphaned, these too young to be left on their own. I have been bottle feeding them for several weeks, and truly, that is a joyful thing, to hold a cub and give it the meal it needs, knowing it is alive because we have chosen to give ourselves to its nurturance. I think of you that first day with Chhoti Billi, holding her in your lap and weeping with happiness.

Which makes me wonder if you have acquired a cat of your own yet. Or perhaps not, living in a dormitory as you do.

Sending branches of peace, my friend.

Tanveer

[Enclosed sketch of a pair of tiger cubs]

From Gurdaya
February 27, 1914
[In Urdu]

Dear Elsie,

Thank you for your letter. At first I did not think I would answer, because I am so angry, and that made me angry with you. You say that so easily—just continue with your studies! As if I would be granted all the books and materials I should wish. That will not be my life, chiriya. It makes me furious that you are free, going to art school while I am married to a man so old his balls swing like an old woman's earrings. He smells of camphor, and I feel I shall scream every time he mounts me. How is this the life I am meant to live? Why wasn't I born a man? Or a woman in a place where she is free?

It is not fair. Which is a child's cry, and yet it is mine nonetheless.

There are free women here. Only look at Mrs. Ganguly, but it seems a woman must be a widow to gain power, and for all that he's ancient, I do not see my husband expiring in any near future. By that time, I shall be old as dirt and unable to do any of the things I so dreamed of.

I am so angry!

And I am sorrowful, too, the weight of a river of tears running through my blood, making me plod along like an ancient elephant.

This is not what you want to hear. I do not know what else to say. It is terrible, and I am grieving, and I do not know how to move forward.

Thank you. I miss you. Be well. Be free. Dance for both of us.

Gurdaya

March 17, 1914
London
[In Urdu]

Dear Gurdaya,

You are a poet and a writer and a scholar. Surely there is a corner where you might place a table, an inkpot and paper to write, a shelf for books to read and study.

I am sending you a collection of essays I believe you shall enjoy. I would love to read anything you write.

Tanveer and I are studying books together so I do not lose my (thin) facility with Urdu. Perhaps you and I could practice this, as well?

Be well, Pyari Sahelī.

Elsie

[Enclosed *Essays and Leaves from a Notebook*, George Eliot]

March 20, 1914
London
[In Urdu]

Dear Tanveer,
I cannot ever be angry with you for long. Your heart is truly one of the kindest I've ever known, and whatever flawed thinking you exhibit over the lives of women, I do know you have been taught this way and can be untaught.

And I must admit I was chagrined to have you turn the tables with my paintings. Could they be tainted by my own colonialism?

Am I so blind? I feel I have painted out of deepest love, for the landscape I grew up in, for the things that fueled my artist's soul, for the faces and people who inspire me. Is that colonial? Or is it love? I don't know how to tell the difference!

It is very complicated and makes me feel weepy and foolish. I do not know how to see what I cannot see. In this way, perhaps it was wrong of me to expect you to see things in light of women's desires.

I do wish we could thrash these ideas out together in person. You *must* come with your father to England! It would be so wonderful to see your earnest, honest face again. The vision of you giving baby tigers a bottle gave me such joy, and made me miss you all the more. Because I do miss you, still, all the time. I have yet to meet anyone in my world who supplies what you give—your good nature and your good mind, but also the ease I feel in your company, the acceptance (and challenge!) you offer me, and that I hope you feel in return.

My heart is suddenly seized with a fear that our connection will be faded in person, that we shall be so changed by time that we barely recognize each other. What if we have nothing to say?

No, I cannot imagine that. Oh, do please come, Tanveer!

As to my hair—I cut it for purely practical reasons. It is very heavy and thick and takes a long time to dry and care for. Many of the women students at Slade have adopted a shorter cut, and it's liberating. A few have also adopted a costume of trousers, and I've followed suit while in the studio, where they give greater freedom of movement, though it is also true that I am awfully fond of my frocks, and do not miss a single chance to wear them.

I considered your gentle prod about whether India will fade for me over time. Perhaps it will, and I do find now that I love portraits of all manner of people, so I can focus on who is around me, though I suspect the faces I find fascinating are still not the illuminated beauties my professors seem to want. Ever I am drawn to people who are not like myself, not only the Indian world of my memory, but the fishwives hawking their wares with their missing teeth, and the African girl in service at Nina's townhome, in the ancient drunks begging near the docks, and in the fine Muslim shopkeeper with his sharply pressed kurta. Painting is sometimes an exploration, a way to really look at anything, and when I look at each of those beings, I see another petal of the flower of humanity.

I have made portraits of my fellows, and more than once one of these bohemian artists have offered up their own bodies for us all to draw. Rocky has modeled for the ladies' life drawing, safely draped. I have not yet got my nerve up to model for others, but I have modeled often enough for myself.

And perhaps I am being indiscreet, so I will halt now. Be well, my dearest Tanveer. I miss you more than I could possibly say.

Please come to London.

Elsie

PS: I do not have a cat in the dorms. Mother has adopted a slew of kittens for mousing in the house at Herewich, and I enjoy them when I visit. She, too, will want to see you. My father has been poorly the past few months. Oddly, he seems to have adapted far less well to returning to his home country than my mother, who never lived here at all.

THE CHILDREN WE DID NOT HAVE

October 1940
London

—29—

Nina rang to invite me to lunch, and I gladly escaped to meet her at Selfridges. It was a gloomy, misty morning, which leant a sense of safety to the journey, for the bombers rarely flew in such weather. My fellow Tube passengers were a silent lot, each of us cloaked in the armor of stoicism. If one didn't think too hard about it all, it was just possible to make one's way through the day.

The tearoom was an oasis of calm, familiar, and my nerves unwound the minute I entered the room. I found Nina already seated, beautifully dressed as ever, with a tilted hat on her smooth hair. I kissed her. "Hello, darling. How are you?"

"I didn't sleep a wink last night," she said. "Did you?"

"No." It had been a wretched night, with endless bombings. "Even mother with her morphine was restless."

"Did you hear about Balham Station? Jonathan stopped in to shave and shower this morning, and I gather it was dreadful."

"What happened?" The waiter soundlessly laid down my teapot and cup.

"I didn't quite gather all the details, but between an enormous bomb and a bus crashing, some waterlines were broken and flooded the station. Hundreds of people were sheltering there."

"Dear God." An exhausted place between my shoulder blades pinched hard. I rolled my neck a little, trying to loosen it. "Nothing is safe, really."

"I suppose not." She picked up the menu and scanned it desultorily. "Oh, I do long for a sole Véronique. And a decadent plate of oysters."

"Mmm. Cheese tartlets and a lobster salad."

"And ice cream."

"And those little petit fours."

Nina sighed. "I suppose I'll indulge myself with Woolton vegetable pie."

"Same for me." I set the menu aside. "It's lovely to see you, dear, but I felt a sense of urgency in your telephone call. Is everything all right?"

"No," she said, and her eyes shone, almost as if she would weep. "Helen is terrified, and she wants to return to her home outside Bath. She feels she will be safer."

Helen was her longtime lover, a woman she'd been involved with off and on since the late twenties. I'd often felt the union was tilted more toward Helen's benefit; she was a lush beauty, some years younger, and Nina was impossibly in love with her. "I'm sorry," I said, as a good friend should do. "I know you'll miss her terribly."

"Whatever shall I do with myself during the raids? Jonathan is always gone, and the servants are there, but I'm essentially alone in the fortress."

"Come to us, if you like."

She shook her head. "Jonathan would not approve at all. The place truly has been fortified as well as anything could be. Perhaps you and your mother should come to me, instead."

"I should dearly love that, but my mother cannot make the trip."

At this, she looked genuinely aggrieved. I reached for her hand. "You will only be alone, not abandoned. Perhaps you should set up a course of study to distract yourself. Or take up knitting," I added slyly.

She laughed. "Don't be beastly. I shan't knit unless I've not even a scrap of fabric to cover myself."

"Mother knits when she feels well enough, but mostly she's been sleeping."

"It must be dreadfully hard on her, all the commotion."

"She is in decline," I said honestly. "The doctor comes when he can, but there's little for him to do. Her liver is failing."

"Oh, darling Elsie, I am so terribly sorry. She is the central light in your life."

It startled me. I would have chosen another for that pillar. "One of them, certainly."

"Your prince is a fantasy, my dear. It's easy to love someone at a distance."

I frowned, slightly embarrassed at the acuity of her comment. I didn't think I spoke of him very often. "We've been friends for decades," I said. "No more."

"Peter mentioned his letters recently, that they arrive in clutches of three or four, every week."

"Peter mentioned the letters?"

"Tanveer has ever been a pebble in his shoe."

Because I had once left him and gone to India when we were in Cairo. I had intended never to return.

Until my hand was forced, once again. A hollow memory of my return to England rustled, and I could not bear it, not just now. "Tanveer worries about us, Mother and I. He asked if I would write every day, so I have been doing so."

"As one would, with a dear friend." She sipped her wine with a droll lift of an eyebrow.

"I wrote many, many letters to you when I was in Cairo and India," I said.

She gave me a piercing gaze, holding her manicured fingers on the condensation of her glass. "We have shared everything, Elsie. Why are you so cagey about him? Do you think I'll judge you?"

A fair question. I had an image of a carved box, inlaid with ivory, that held this secret thing, the thing we barely acknowledged even to each other anymore. "It is the only thing that really belongs to me."

"Not your paintings?"

"Yes, of course the paintings." I grappled with what I meant, what I could say without giving away that sense of private connection, a thing that both lived in the world and not. "But paintings are meant to be public. Even if they're vulnerable or revealing, the entire purpose of them is to communicate with someone else."

She inclined her head. "I am quite sure I have never loved anyone as you love your work." That arched brow. "Or your prince."

Both were a blessing and a kind of curse. "Maybe you will one day," I said. "But perhaps it's easier not to."

"I don't think you believe that for a single moment."

I thought of leaving him in India the last time, and the sound of his voice on the phone the morning after the first horrible raid. "It does seem foolish sometimes."

She reached across the table and covered my hand. Fiercely, she said, "Never."

~

We picked through our lunch. Outside afterward, we paused. The weather was misty but not pouring. "I would like to walk back," Nina said. "Do you mind?"

"Not at all. That sounds wonderful. I've hardly had enough walking the past month." We put up our umbrellas and window shopped as we always had. Some windows had been patched where they cracked, others were taped as a protective measure, but it was still possible to look at the goods within. Such as they were.

I stopped in a stationery shop and bought airmail paper. The clerk said, "Good luck to him," as if all airmail letters went to troops. I merely said thank you.

The streets held a somber tone, vaguely deserted, people hurrying along with their heads down. We passed a section of a block that was a pile of rubble, shops standing fine on either side, a hole in a park where a small bomb had made a crater. Everywhere a mucky grime lay over the windowsills. "I wonder how long it will take them to destroy the entire city?" I said aloud.

"Churchill will stop them long before that happens," Nina protested. "Already the tide is turning."

"Is it?" I said lightly.

As if to underscore the thought, the sirens went off. We were miles from home, and I did not know the neighborhood well. "What shall we do?"

"Let's find a Tube station. What's near?"

"I have no idea. Eventually we'll come to something."

But it was hard to stay calm when we heard the drone of the planes, on their way, and then directly overhead, and I saw one drop a bomb at some distance. I shoved Nina into a doorway and barreled in behind her. We watched it fall, and another behind it. Nina clutched my arm so tightly I knew there would be bruises. When it landed, the explosion shook the walls surrounding us, and we both ducked, trying to contract our bodies. Nina screeched, her hands over her ears.

The second one fell, a touch closer, and dust shook down on our heads. My heart beat too hard through my neck, and I looked left and right to see if I could find a route of escape. Smoke rose over the roofs of the buildings across the street, and the bells of a fire engine rang out. The planes droned away, followed by the rattling of guns, and I grabbed Nina's wrist. "Let's go."

A man in a heavy blue raincoat ran by. "Shelter this way."

We ran after him. The planes droned closer again, circling back, and another bomb landed with an enormous clapping explosion. "In here!" the man cried, and we ran with relief into the Tube station, clattering down the stairs in the din.

Nina held on to my hand with a painful grip. "What about the waterlines? Will we drown like those poor people at Balham Station?"

"I don't know," I said. "But at least we might have a chance down here."

—30—

When the all clear sounded, Nina and I staggered aboveground, brushing ourselves off, and miraculously found a cab. We were shaken, but all in one piece.

When I arrived home, Mother waited in the sitting room, looking wan but otherwise well, her knitting in hand. A pair of kittens frolicked on the rug, chasing each other.

Her condition was bewilderingly variable from day to day. I felt in over my head trying to predict how to care for her.

"Where's Betty?" I asked.

"She went out late morning for rations, and I have not seen her since."

I frowned. "Do you know where she was going?"

"No. She said only rations. She had the coupons with her."

"Have you eaten?"

"Hours ago. She made chicken salad if you're hungry. No apples, but the celery gave it an agreeable crunch."

"I had a good lunch with Nina, so perhaps we'll save that for dinner." I peered out the window, hoping to spot Betty in her chintz turban.

"I wouldn't mind a spot of tea," Mother said.

"Of course." I shed my coat, and as I hung it up, I felt the small hard vial of cyanide. I took it out, so evil and so innocuous at once, and wondered what trauma would force me to use it. When the Nazis invaded? When Mother died and there was no more food? The noise of the bombs this afternoon, exploding and knocking down buildings, came back to me, and I wondered if I ought to keep it on me at all times, in case I was buried alive. How long could a person bear that?

No. I would not give in to such fatalism. Not yet. I tucked it back into the inner pocket, and headed for the kitchen to put the kettle on, lifting lids and opening cupboards to see what might be left from last week's rations. As I was taking out the mugs, I worried where Betty might have gone. I hoped she'd not been injured.

I checked the drawer to see which coupons she'd taken with her. All of them. A concern, but not yet dire. Perhaps I could nip out and see if the fish monger or the baker had seen her.

Just now, I felt a deep need to paint, to express the tangled emotions stirred up by the raid. I took Mother her tea and headed upstairs to the studio, but even as I ascended the stairs, I fretted about those enormous bombs today, all over the city. Surely Betty had not gone far?

—31—

Days passed, and we had no word of Betty. I didn't feel I should leave Mother alone to check the lists at hospitals or care centers, and Peter was swamped at work. We saw him briefly for changes of clothes and a quick shower, and then he was back out again.

In the meantime, I had been working for several days to get the paintings ready to be transported to Nina's. The original plan—to transport them to the country—had been sidelined by a bomb that took out most of the west wing there. Nina had volunteered to put them in her wine cellar, which might not be ideal, but would preserve them better than if a fire devoured them.

My studio was filled with paintings leaning on the walls, piled on tables. Most of them were out of their usual storage places, none hidden as I usually took care to do. I had specially built space in a closet for the ones that would cause . . . outrage, grief, offer too great a view into my private world—mostly to keep them out of Peter's view.

Mother had rallied again, and sat in the parlor. The rain poured down relentlessly outside the windows. A kitten played with a ball of yarn on the carpet. "I want to see your paintings, Elsie," she said without preamble.

Her eyes were clear and straightforward, and although I'd been caring for her for a long time, when she spoke so firmly, I was again a girl.

"Are there any you particularly wish to see? I can bring them down to you."

"The entire body of work, Elsie," she said in a churlish tone that had been cropping up every now and then. "I do not know how to make it more plain."

"What do you hope to find, Mother? Perhaps you can just tell me."

She looked out the window. "I would know what you carried in your heart, Elsie. I would reconcile the choices you have made for my sake." The rest was unspoken *before I die.*

I picked up a kitten and held it to my neck, allowing the rattling purr to pour into my ear, soothing the sudden emotion that rolled through me. Could I reveal myself so fully to her?

Slowly, I nodded.

"I would do it now," she said. "When I feel well."

I rose, settling the kitten on the chair. "Then we shall do it now."

~

I helped her up the stairs. So many we had to pause four times. "Are you sure it wouldn't be better for me to bring them down to you?"

"No," she said with some irritability.

"All right." We finished the trek, and I settled her on the overstuffed wing chair I kept in the corner. She was sweating and out of breath, her lips faintly blue. I flung back the blackout curtains, and I opened the windows slightly to allow some airflow. "Are you too cool?"

She shook her head, but I could see she was exhausted by the trek. "Mother, I can easily bring the paintings down so you needn't—"

"I'm here," she said, again with an edge of peevishness. So unlike her. Was it merely illness? The effort of trying to keep up a good show?

"All right, then. Where would you like to begin?"

"I haven't seen many of the paintings you did in India when you went back."

A stirring disturbance. "Mostly I left them there, of course."

Her clear eyes rested on my face. "Sketchbooks, then."

"Sketchbooks are quite personal," I said, remembering things those books might hold, intimate and revealing things. "I would prefer to leave those on their shelves."

"Oh, come now, Elsie." The thing about my mother people had always discounted was the fact that she had a will of iron. What she set her sights upon, she achieved.

In this, however, I would not allow it. "Let me see if there are any paintings left in the closet."

"While you're looking, choose a sketchbook at random and let me leaf through it."

I'd had several out, remembering the days at Slade, and the juicy summer of 1914, before war was declared and tore it all down. I grabbed one, gave it a cursory glance to be sure there was nothing too shocking in it, and dived into the closet.

It was a large space, fitted with vertical dividers that held paintings of many sizes. I liked a big canvas, so there were a lot of those. I knew I didn't have many from India, for I really had left them all there, but I remembered a handful of studies I'd made in preparation for the portraits of Tanveer and Channan, and when he was born, Kirandeep in her arms. I searched for them, flipping and tugging out many in the same size I remembered doing.

Instead, I found a group of student paintings, experiments I'd engaged in when I was trying so hard to understand what was mine and what belonged to things outside of me.

Smiling, I took a stack of them out to show my mother, remembering the spring of studying artists in all the museums of London, Rocky at my side.

A TRIP TO THE MUSEUM

Spring 1914
London

—32—

Tanveer's letter about Orientalism in my work weighed on me. In the cold of a February afternoon, I went to the studio where I had been assigned a small but agreeable area beneath a north-facing window. My easel was set up with a painting in progress, a rather desultory portrait of a female model, which I hadn't liked from the beginning and liked less each day. I glared at it, hands beneath my armpits.

The studio was a shared space, but few other artists were about today, discouraged perhaps by the wet weather or a head cold that had been making its way through our ranks. A woman I knew very little painted a still life of flowers across the room, and even from this distance, I could see that she had developed her own language of art. In her brushstrokes, her shapes, the palette she employed, a soft garden-like tone on tone of purples and blues, lilacs in a blue vase. Sunlight streamed through a window, a single plum dropped by the vase, and a pair of gardening gloves suggested a person just out of scene.

I crossed the room. "Well done."

In surprise, she looked up. "Thank you." She was a slight, pale girl with nondescript brown hair. Unremarkable in every way but the way she put light on the canvas.

"I'm struggling," I confessed. "I've wanted to attend art school since I was a small child. Not that I'm doing particularly well."

She glanced over to my easel, dabbed a whisper of white over the table. "You haven't found your voice yet. You will."

It stung, like Tanveer's words, like the professor telling me the things I painted were no longer in vogue. I watched her for a while, layering light into the scene in the tiniest drops. "I see that you've found your voice. I can tell a painting is yours before I see your name."

"Thank you," she said with sincerity. "I can recognize yours, as well, but it is because of subject matter. No one else is painting so many Indian characters."

I sighed. "I know. But that is what I loved painting as a child. That was what was around me! I still think they're beautiful."

"Objectively," she said, leaning in to use a fingernail to remove a millimeter of white from the edge of the vase, "they are beautiful. They're not yet very authentic is the thing."

Authentic. A word Tanveer had also used. I sank down on the stool nearby her easel. "What does that even mean? How can I paint what is *not* authentically mine? How did you find out what was yours to say?"

She paused, wiping her brush clean, obviously considering. "I've painted and drawn flowers for as long as I can remember. My grandmother raised me, and her greatest joy was in the garden." She dropped her brush into a waiting jar. "When she died, I was a bit lost. I started painting her things. The gloves." She pointed at a sketch pinned to the wall, showing a hat on a chair. "Her hat. I think I like that feeling of thinking someone is about to be right back."

A little sting burned the corners of my eyes. "I see that in your work." I thought of some of her other paintings, the light, the colors in subdued hues, all very influenced by an English cottage garden. "Huh."

"You are very talented. No one is hard on you because they want to make it hard. They want you to prove you mean it."

I ducked my head. "Thank you." I stood. "You had no reason to be kind to me, but I appreciate it."

She only nodded.

I headed back to the easel and saw that I still loathed the painting it held. But what *did* I love? What did I love to paint? How would my voice assert itself on the canvas?

Our paintings were stored in vertical racks against the wall. I marched over to my section. Most were not particularly large, and I propped them up on a waist-high counter, then stood back to look at them side by side.

The first thing I could see was color. Bright, clear, saturated colors, sometimes even straining credulity. Red and gold, bright cerulean blue, hard desert browns, bright mountain greens. Saris and fruit and jewels. My preference for vivid colors had come under fire, but other painters used them, or had, and I liked them very much—the Matisse paintings I'd admired at the Post-Impressionist exhibit I'd attended with Florence Mallard; Gauguin and the domestic interiors of Bonnard.

What else? With the voice of Tanveer ringing in my ear, I could see the subject matter was a bit stylized, a *bit* fairy tale, even if there was truth in them, the truth of things I really had seen with my own eyes—the tea wallah and the women selling aubergines.

Two paintings were slightly different. Drawn from the same memories, but not the same subjects. The first was the night sky over the palace in the desert, the night we had discussed whether other planets might have many suns. In the foreground was the party, spilling in light and color into the corner of the painting, while most of the canvas was covered with the sky and stars. So many, many stars. Two figures stood with heads uptilted, their bodies in silhouette against the night. It felt true.

The other was of Gurdaya as a child, hair down, cross-legged against the backdrop of the pond where we'd learned to swim. She held a book in her hand and gazed out over the water with a speculative frown. I'd painted it when I found out she'd had to marry against her will. Of course I could not send it to her, but it had transmuted my fury to something more peaceful.

As I stood there, looking and looking, Rocky came into the room. We often ate dinner together and talked over the struggles of the day. "What have we here?" he asked, wiping his hands with the cloth that ever hung from his belt.

"I am grappling with what I should be painting. What's mine and what's some awful legacy."

"Ah, the Orientalism." He nodded, pushing heavy honey-colored hair off his beautiful face. His fingers left streaks of dust on his forehead. "And what do you see?"

I sighed. "I'm afraid there *is* a bit of imitation going on here, in the marketplace, the portraits. I thought it was real, but maybe it isn't."

"Hmm. What else?"

"The colors are bright and saturated, which I know is not the fashion, but it speaks to me in ways all these muted tones do not." I shook my head. "I don't even know why that appeals to anyone."

"Your palette developed in a sunnier, more colorful place."

"So is that authentic or colonialist?"

"I don't know. What do you think?"

Pressure built on my chest. "I don't know!"

"And I, sadly, am not the fellow to help you work this out, as I am fully colonial and have no education in anything else."

"How am I going to figure this out?"

"I don't know, dearest, but I have faith in you." He gestured to the painting of Gurdaya. "I haven't seen that one."

"My friend growing up." I suddenly remembered that she'd been very upset that day before she relaxed into the moment. "Her brother taught us how to swim in that pond. And I just remembered that she was very afraid of what would happen if anyone found out. I dismissed her worry because I wouldn't have been in very much trouble."

He looked at me, his irises catching the light as he listened. "And she would have."

"Yes."

"It is a better painting than the others. Perhaps it's worth doing more to see why."

"But what did I do differently?"

"She's a person you love, not a pretty scene."

I thought about how I felt, painting her eyes, and it was true—what I'd been painting there was love. Would that help me?

"Come," he said, flinging an arm around my shoulders. "I'm famished. Let's find your cousin and a good roast."

~

A week later, he appeared again. "Come, sweet, I have an excursion planned."

I had my sketchbook in my lap, a half-finished drawing lying dead on the page. "I must finish an assignment."

He tilted his head to look at the work. "No." He plucked the charcoal from my fingers, and pulled the sketchbook off my lap. "You've frozen yourself, and we're going to fill you up with inspiration."

"What sort of inspiration?"

"You'll see. Wash your hands and prepare for sketching. We'll make a day of it."

I packed my artist bag with sketchbook, watercolors, a pair of brushes and various drawing utensils. My gray skirt had deep pockets I'd asked mother to sew into it for me, and to avoid unsightly smears and stains, I chose a navy blouse.

"You're going to get lost in the mire of judgment if you don't let yourself breathe, Elsie," he said as we set out. "Today, we're going to stare at the masters in museums. Your assignment is to simply allow yourself to notice what makes you feel something. When it does, sketch it or make a note."

I stopped on the pavement. "I fear it will make this even worse, when I see how far I have to go."

Undaunted, he tucked his hand into my arm. "For today, forget what your work is or what you might eventually accomplish, and let's just enjoy the work of other artists. We love art!"

"We do."

"We're lucky young artists, as well. We *know* we love the work, and we want to pursue it."

"Even when it is difficult," I admitted.

"Yes." He smiled.

That was exactly what we did. We wandered the great galleries and museums of London for the entire day. Starting at the Tate, we looked at the masters of portraiture, Sargent and Gainsborough and Hoppner. I found myself responding to Titian and sketched a pattern of fabric in a Rembrandt, taken by the astonishment of texture. In the Turner room, Rocky teased me. "Your namesake." He paused before an enormous seascape with a sky. "He conveys so much emotion."

I evaluated the painting for the why of the emotion, the interplay of color, the smears of light. Something tight in my heart unfolded. The work was emotional, employing both extravagant and subdued use of color.

At midday we stopped for sausage rolls, then kept exploring. I particularly sought out anything remotely Orientalist. John Frederick Lewis was highly regarded, and I studied one of his works for a long time, a scene of a Cairo courtyard, women in what I would have called salwar kameez, the screened windows of purdah overhead, desert men in turbans and robes. "If I love this, am I still not seeing what I need to see about Orientalism?"

"A good question. I do not know how to answer, but let's study it together." He crossed his arms over his chest, kicking one foot out in front of him. "What do you see?"

"His use of light is masterful." I pointed at the sleeve of a woman in front, the glazing of leaves. "And I love the colors, all that primary red and yellow, the patterns in the fabrics." I continued to study it. "The pigeons give it such a sense of life and movement."

Rocky nodded. "It's a masterful work. The details of the bird wings, and the blankets over the camel, and the woman's scarf." He pointed out the open window. "I love the woman peering out."

I kept looking. "The people are all very attractive."

"Hmm. Yes."

"And it's very tidy and clean, which with all those animals and birds, would it be?"

"I want to look at more Orientalists to compare."

We looked at so many paintings, my mind started to overflow, and as we moved through hallway after gallery after exhibit, I felt the tension in my chest mounting. I could pinpoint things I loved in all the works we viewed, some more than others, some more in line with my view of the world, some not. By the time we both declared an end to our capacities, I was awash in a pulsing sense of near despair. As we strode out into the late afternoon, I stood beneath a tree, overcome.

"Elsie, what is it?"

A man with a truncheon fitted with a bayonet at one end guarded the entrance. His mustache made him look as if he were frowning—a suffragette had slashed a painting in protest not long ago, and they were all on guard. I touched my chest, as if I could calm the boiling, and paced away, returned. Rocky waited, as if he understood my need to collect myself.

Finally I halted and let it all spill out, a tumble of thoughts I couldn't quite pull together. "I still don't see where the line is in my paintings or the Orientalists. I can see a little, but not all of it? I love how much color there is. I *love* those colors. Does that make me a colonialist? Or am I getting it wrong? And where is the difference in my painting what I loved and experienced, and what's the—" I pushed my hat off my head, paced, and came back. "I feel like my heart will explode. I feel that I am a complete failure in my work, that I should never have taken this path at all, but if I don't paint, am I to just become some obedient little wife, shopping for frocks and throwing parties and—"

He captured my hand and drew me to sit down on a bench in the shade. He kissed my fingers, drew me close to lean on him, and at the contact with his shoulder, I found I could at least breathe.

After a moment, he said, "Firstly, you are an artist, Elsie. You shall always be an artist. That you ask such stark questions is as much an indication of that as anything you paint. You're questioning the world and yourself in an attempt to find what truth looks like. Art is all deconstruction."

"But how will I know when I find the actual truth, the heart of truth?"

"Perhaps you will not. Perhaps the questions are the point. The *quest* is the point."

At that, I let myself weep a little. Not dramatically, just enough to allow some of the pressure to leak out.

"Let's get you some tea, shall we?"

Tea always solved everything, I thought, an echo from my father. Tea, which was a crop the British used India to grow. Was it wrong, then, to drink tea? It made my head ache to think of it. Just now, I needed the substance more than the history of it. "Please."

As we ate cakes and sandwiches in a clever little tearoom, I said, "What do I do next? I'm floundering."

"That is why we came out today." He wiped his fingers delicately.

I dropped sugar in my cup, watched it dissolve. Sugar, too, came from the colonies. I sighed. Nearby two men muttered about impending war and the idiocy of the government.

Suddenly, I asked, "Where were the women, Rocky? Do we even think of them?"

"What women?"

"In the museum. On the walls. Where are the women? Did no woman look on those landscapes that Turner painted and long to bring them to life in her way? Were there no women who wanted to capture light like Vermeer?"

"There are some women."

"One or two perhaps. Out of all the centuries of all the painting in all the world?"

He looked abashed. "I did not even notice."

"Nor did I! Which is worse, because I am a woman, and a painter!"

He reached across the table and took my hand. His pale irises caught the light from the window. "Elsie, where were the Arab painters? The Indian painters? Did they not look on those same scenes? Did they not wish to paint them?"

I lifted my eyebrows, and sighed. "I did not even notice."

He gave me a rueful smile.

~

So many years later, I carried from the closet the paintings I'd begun to work on after that intensely illuminating day. "I struggled quite a lot my first year at Slade," I said to my mother, setting them up on the worktable against the wall. "Rocky challenged me to paint in as many different styles as I could bear for one year. These are some of the experiments."

I'd tried landscape Pointillism and sky-centric Impressionism and interior Fauvism; flattened the colors and shapes entirely into boxy little brown worlds. I experimented with the Post-Impressionist styles of Cézanne and Matisse. The paintings were wildly different with different palettes. There was not a single rendering of India or Indian subjects, not even Tanveer, but they all had in common the viewpoint of a female painter, seeing things.

"I see you in this work, Elsie."

"So do I, actually. I started to let go of what I thought I was or should be, and just started learning what I liked."

"I would like to take the one of the table down—"

Outside, the sirens began to bleat. "Let's get you down to the sitting room."

"Get the painting first," she insisted, pointing.

It was an Impressionist interior of the desk in the room I lived in whilst at Slade. An open letter lay on the table in a pool of lamplight, with a half-finished sheet of paper with a pen on top of it. Neither letter was legible, but I remembered them clearly. I'd been writing to Tanveer, or he'd been writing to me.

And then he had come to London with his father.

THE MAHARAJA COMES TO LONDON

1914
London

TELEGRAM

TO: ELSIE TURNER, THE SLADE SCHOOL OF FINE ART

FROM: TANVEER SINGH

WE ARRIVE MAY 19 STOP STAYING SIX WEEKS STOP TANVEER

—33—

I'd had the telegram for weeks by the time Tanveer and his father finally arrived. A ball was to be held in the maharaja's honor, and Tanveer would be there with him.

The day finally came. Nina offered me a bedroom in her townhome in which to get ready, aware only that the maharaja's son was my old friend and I looked forward to seeing him. No one knew of our deep connection, the letters we wrote monthly or more.

I was shaky with anticipation, unable to eat, and had to be helped into the gown I'd had sent up from Herewich for the occasion, one of the frocks made for the parties last summer. It was my favorite, a simple deep-gold sheath with layers of embroidered green gauze over the shoulders and skirt. The square neckline showed off my collarbones and the peacock necklace my mother had given me for my sixteenth birthday, a delicate piece inlaid with small emeralds, shell, and blue topazes, woven of thin cords of silver. She'd had it made before we left India. It was quite my favorite thing in the world.

Rocky and Nina accompanied me to the ball, both invited on their own merits, or rather family standing, and I was relieved to have escorts who knew me. Nina held my arm as we swept up the grand entrance, flanked by footmen. "Why, Elsie, you're shaking! Are you well?"

"I'm afraid I've forgotten to eat all day," I confessed.

She gave me a sidelong look. I pretended not to see.

The ball was held at a London mansion, hosted by the Countess of Asheworth, who liked to be the vanguard of everything. The maharaja was quite popular with such women. My mother had sent her condolences, for all her attentions were focused on nursing my father. He'd fallen ill with cancer over the winter, and Mother didn't want to leave him. *You must bring Tanveer to visit,* she wrote. *I long to hear news of his mother.*

I promised I would make the trip to Herewich, but in truth I did not know if he would be free to make a social call of that ilk. Or if I would even spend much time with him myself. Or how it would feel between us after so long. Letters, after all, were not the same as being face to face, and we were maturing in very different landscapes.

In truth, I was quite sure the opposite was true. And what then?

As Nina, Rocky, and I entered the grand ballroom, the room swirled with scores of people dressed in jewels and silks and feathers. A quartet played upbeat music, and the air sparkled with conversation and tinkling laughter, all muted by the pounding of my heart.

I halted abruptly, annoyed with my foolishness. It was unlike me to be so rattled!

Rocky and Nina paused with me. "Are you all right?"

I took a breath, settled myself into my body. "Yes," I said definitely. We walked the long side of the room. I looked for Tanveer anxiously, but did not see him, even as we traversed the lower end of the glittering space. What if he had decided not to come? What if, like the time he'd written that letter trying to end our communication, he was choosing to keep our friendship at arm's length?

I spied Helen Bonhome from Slade, Diana from Nina's party, and—I scowled—my brother. "What is *he* doing here?"

"Who?"

I pointed with my fan. "My brother."

"No doubt looking for a suitable husband for you," Nina said with some amusement. "Shall I distract him?"

My brother fawned over Nina, both for her beauty and social standing. "Please," I said.

But Rocky halted. "Is that your maharaja?"

I whirled. "Where?"

"Nearby the punch bowl."

I scanned the crowd and located him. My heart plummeted, for it was only the maharaja himself, wearing a spectacular turban hung with strings of pearls and fastened with a great ruby. His mustaches were as showy as ever, wings across his lower face, and he wore a brocaded suit. A tiny woman held out her hand to be kissed, and he made a grand show of bending over it. As a child, I'd always thought him rather fat and jolly, but I now saw a virility that would have escaped me as a girl.

"That is indeed the maharaja. My friend is his son, the prince."

Then, as if Moses parted the waters, a path broke in the crowd, and I saw Tanveer. He was far more simply dressed than his father, in a Western-style dinner jacket cut impeccably, his hair hidden beneath a simple dark-blue turban. For a long moment, the world halted, and all my attention fell on him.

In that exact instant, he spied me, too, and a smile broke across his face. He started toward me, and it shook me from my daze. I hurried toward him as if he were a torch high in the night sky.

We met with outstretched hands.

With greed, I drank in his face, dark brows, and graceful cheekbones and the nose it had taken so many years to grow into, and his eyes, wide and deep and full of a light that I knew must be reflected in my own.

At last I managed a single word, his name. "Tanveer!" Afraid I might weep, I gripped his hands fiercely.

"Elsie!" The word held a dozen layers. His voice was his voice, but it had deepened over two years, and he was taller, even, than when I had left him. "You are so entirely yourself. I am so glad to see you!"

I only managed a nod, feeling my friends join us, their curiosity a living creature winding around us.

Tanveer and I held on to each other's hands, tightly. He abruptly lifted one of mine to his lips, a gesture courtly to outsiders. I found myself focused on his eyelashes, sweeping down. At the brush of his mouth, even over my gloves, a wild joy swelled in my chest.

"I cannot believe you are truly here," I breathed, blinking.

He said simply, "Nor I."

I felt quite faint with the reality of his physical presence. Ridiculous. Steeling myself, I introduced my friends. "Prince, may I introduce my cousin Lady Nina Pendry and my friend Lord Richard Draycott, Rocky."

"Very nice to meet you," he said with a nod. "Lady Turner has written about you both."

"Has she indeed," Rocky said, raising his brows at me.

"You are the sculptor, I believe?" Tanveer said, and again I was startled by the layered sound of his voice.

"I am. Wonderful to meet you, Your Highness."

Tanveer said to Nina, "And you have been very kind, yes?"

Nina nodded, swished her skirt in a little half curtsy, half flirtation, giving me a quick sideways glance. "Delighted to make your acquaintance. We must have you out to the country. The weather is perfect this time of year."

"I should enjoy that," he said, still using his courtly voice.

"Wonderful." She gestured toward my brother. "I'm away. Perhaps we'll speak later."

He nodded.

Rocky simply said, "Excuse me."

And then we were alone, face to face. We only looked at each other, lost, in this moment, now. "I am so glad you're here," I whispered in English, and then in Hindustani: "I wish I could hug you."

His smile blazed once more. "You remembered!"

"I practiced," I admitted.

"Shukriya." He kissed my hand again, and stood for a long moment, only looking. "You are so beautiful, Elsie. I had forgotten."

I laughed. "Forgotten!"

"When I read our letters, I do not think of your face, exactly. Do you know what I mean?"

"Yes. I think of the . . . essence of you, in layers, all of them a little ghostly."

"Well said, as ever." He inclined his head. "You do look different."

"How?"

He lifted a hand as if to touch me, dropped it, tucked his hands behind his back. "Your hair, of course. I thought I would hate it, but I do not."

I curtsied ironically.

"You've learned to dress up, haven't you?"

I smiled. "I couldn't be a tomboy forever, could I?" I drank in the breadth of his shoulders, the shape of his mouth. "You *sound* different."

"Do I?"

"Your voice is deeper." The fluttering sense of faintness returned, and I peered upward, trying to press every detail of his face into memory. The angle of his large eyes, the sooty brows, the warm brown of his skin. "And you have a little bit of beard."

"And you have become a grand lady."

"I can't tell if that's a compliment or a criticism."

"Only an observation," he said, and glanced over his shoulder. "Shall we walk, Elsie?"

"Please."

He held out his arm, and I grasped it lightly, entirely too aware of his size and shape beside me, the flesh of the person behind the words I so treasured. His other hand fell over my fingers. As we promenaded, I could think of not one word to say. Nor did he speak. We simply walked the perimeter of the room, constrained by—what? Eyes? Custom?

"How is Gurdaya?"

"Not well, I'm afraid. She rails against her situation. She fights with her husband." His fingers over my hand moved restlessly, charged and electric, each tiny brush transmitting the power of the entire ballroom. In Hindustani, he said, "She's like a caged tiger."

I paused for a moment to see if I could call up the words for what I wanted to say in Urdu, and tried, "I wish I could rescue her."

He gave me a sidelong look. "You want to digest her?"

I laughed. "Tell me the right word."

"Main usay bachana chahti hoon," he said.

"Ah. I said pachana, did I?"

"Good. I'm impressed."

I said correctly in Urdu, "Main usay bachana chahti hoon." *I wish I could rescue her.*

"As do I, but it is not ours to do."

"Who, then? There must be something that could be done. Why can't she run away to England and live with me here?"

He shook his head. "Her husband is very powerful and wealthy, and while he may not love her, our families have made agreements. It would be an act of war to free her."

"War?" I stopped. "War with whom? Doesn't she have the right to make her own life?"

He tucked his hands behind him, and met my gaze squarely. "No."

Rage edged my vision. "It is so unfair!" I spat.

"Yes." He glanced around us pointedly. "Shall we take the air, Lady Turner?"

So many eyes watched our exchange curiously, and too much of myself spilled publicly. "Yes, please."

He offered his arm once more. "Some things do not change," he said mildly.

A small, pained laugh broke through my fury. "I suppose not."

"I am glad, Elsie. Your fire is powerful."

All at once, I was overcome. Overcome by the sheer fact that he was here, in England, after so long a time; overcome by his physical presence, by the particular scent of him, sandalwood and the hibiscus in his hair and some note I would have recognized anywhere as purely Tanveer.

My throat tightened, and I squeezed his arm, tears welling up like a waterfall from some hidden spring in my soul. I kept my head down until we cleared the portal of the doors to the wide terrace beyond. A pair of men chatted in low voices at one end, but we had our portion to ourselves, and walked to the balustrade without speaking. I struggled to control my absurd emotions, but they spilled wantonly.

Tanveer gave me his handkerchief.

"I apologize," I whispered. "I did not expect to be so overcome by your presence."

"Look at me, Elsie," he said.

When I did, feeling embarrassed, still wiping my tears away, he said, "You are not alone, Mehram. The world is watching, and I am attempting to be discreet. But"—he shook his head—"there is an earthquake inside me."

"I thought—" I cast about for the right words. "Time and distance would have cured me of . . . all this."

"Did you think so?"

"Didn't you?"

"No." In the low light of the gloaming, I spied the shine of emotion in his eyes. "I tried."

The scent of roses and freshly mown grass filled the air, and a low sun hung gold above the horizon. Music drifted through the open doors, laced through the sound of conversation and laughter. Somewhere in a tree nearby, some birds sang in whistling conversation.

In Urdu, I said, "One small beauty is standing here in the twilight, looking up at you."

He replied in the same tongue. "Your eyes shine like stars." His fingers tightened. "Hai, Rabba, I have missed you so much."

"I was so afraid we would feel awkward."

His eyes crinkled. "Somehow I did not fear that."

"Why?"

He glanced toward the open French doors, to the men still engrossed in their fierce conversation, and said, "Shall we explore the garden?"

"Yes." I gripped his arm, and we swept across the lawns, to the rose gardens, and then past a hedge. I turned, intending to ask—

But he turned toward me at the same instant, and before I could speak, he wrapped me in a full embrace. My face pressed into his shoulder, his hands around my back, and I breathed in the shocking pleasure of his scent, something I could not have labeled, but knew instantly.

"I missed you," he whispered in Hindustani, bending to press a kiss to the side of my neck. Dizzy, I held him close, returning the words in the same language, then English.

He whispered against my skin, "The world has color again."

I closed my eyes, gripping his arms, alight. We pressed closer and closer, as if we could somehow mend the torn place inside each of us where we'd missed the other.

So much feeling rose in me, buzzing through my temples, my throat, that at last I broke away and pressed a hand to my chest. "It feels the same."

"More," he said.

"And yet," I said with a small twist of my lips, "nothing at all has changed."

He shook his head, very slightly. "No."

A howl rose in me. "Then what is the point to—*this*?" I pushed against his chest, not truly pushing him away, but feeling tangled nonetheless.

"Will we go so quickly to arguing?" He glanced toward the house, music still audible. "Can we not just take these stolen moments together?"

I closed my eyes. I couldn't breathe.

With a slight sound, he cupped his hands around my face and kissed me. I gripped his coat and opened to his hungry mouth, and then we were lost on waves of connection, weaving back what had been torn by time and distance.

He lifted his head, and we pressed our foreheads together. "All I have thought of is kissing you," he said with some despair. "All the way across the ocean, every day and every night, kissing you. I want to kiss you ten thousand times before we are parted again."

"It's madness," I breathed, but I could only look at his mouth. I felt his thumbs on my face.

"It has ever been madness." He kissed me again, and we fell into that wilderness and might never have returned if not for a pair of lovers crying out on the other side of the hedge.

We halted, suddenly aware of the world around us. "We must return before we're missed," I said. "My brother is here."

"And my father." He gripped my hands. "How may I see you?"

"I will meet you at Hyde Park tomorrow at noon, by the bridge. Can you get there?"

His laugh, soft and warm, spilled through me. "I cannot wait. Will you show me your new paintings, Elsie?"

My heart soared. "Of course."

He squeezed my hand and let go. "I will think of nothing else."

~

Nina spied me as I came in separately. "Your brother is looking for you. Shall we find some punch?"

My body weighed less than feathers, less than sunlight. Only my hand on Nina's arm anchored me to the world.

"You did not tell me," she said, pressing punch into my hand. "Drink. And you must eat."

I did as I was bid, gulping down the sweet juice, surprised I was so parched. I could not help looking over my shoulder for Tanveer, who had been swept up by a balding gentleman asking a serious question. It reminded me all too accurately that Tanveer had not come here for me, but to learn who the players were in this cat-and-mouse game of Indian independence. I must not distract him.

But even as I thought it, he caught my gaze across the room, and I felt his lips on mine in the garden, the heat of our bodies pressed together, and knew that he'd come here as much for this as for politics.

"Why didn't you tell me?" Nina asked.

"I did."

"No, you did not tell me he is your lover. You must be more cautious," she said, turning my body from the room, moving me toward the doors. "When you look at each other, nothing is hidden. Your brother will marry you to the highest bidder before you can whisper another word."

"Did he see?"

"Of course he did. The whole party saw. Flames were shooting from the top of your heads."

I closed my eyes, swooning in the memory of kissing him, and in fear of what we might have revealed. "We have been friends since we were children."

"Mmm." She turned toward the gathering. "Take some time to calm yourself."

As I did so, smoothing my skirt, touching my hair, she said, "I shall have a little gathering, shall I? Intimate, only the closest of our friends, to welcome the prince."

I looked at her. "Would you?"

"Of course. It shall be private, and no one will know. Otherwise you'll wreck everything for yourself. And for the good prince."

—34—

I could barely sleep after the ball, and the morning dragged by as if each minute weighed a thousand pounds. I should have told him to meet me at nine.

At last it was time to escape to Hyde Park. I wore a rose-colored frock, modern and lean in silhouette, a tidy straw bowler over my hair, and walked briskly to the Underground, which I rode to Lancaster Gate. I walked the rest of the way in my little boots, my heart skittering and sliding in my chest as if it had no mooring.

Our connection had not slipped in the slightest, but nothing else had changed, either. I could not make myself care, to weigh it out like a modest female and make considered choices. I only wanted him, Tanveer, his laughing eyes and his hands on my body and his mouth devouring me and long conversations for as many hours as we could squeeze out. I feared anyone looking at me would see an overripe peony, desire leaking out of my skin and eyes, staining the air around me a vivid pink.

The day was fine and bright, not yet hot. Late-spring blooms filled the beds with color, a delicacy of shade that was entirely different from the bolder palette of India. I sat on a bench to wait, pulling out my sketchbook to capture the blushing tumble of roses on a trellis, the fluttering society ladies of irises, and lush, disheveled poppies. I hadn't brought my watercolors out of deference to the fabric of my dress, but I so loved these delicate shades. One iris bloomed white below and peach above, the beard an extraordinary pale orange. It calmed me to sketch.

I spied him walking from the same direction from which I'd come, tall and straight, unhurried and curious. In one hand, he carried a book. Again he wore western dress, which was strange for me, but I supposed he wore it for political reasons, as his father did. He wore a dastaar over his hair, a declaration of his identity, making him stand out in the English crowd. Women admired him from the corners of their eyes.

I quickly sketched him as he paused to examine a shrub, and as I looked back up, he turned and saw me at the same moment. His face lit up so brightly that I thought of Nina's warning, that flames were shooting from our heads, and I tried to school my own face, but it didn't matter so terribly here, where my brother wouldn't see.

I stood, shimmering, and waited for him to join me. He took his time, strolling my way, a very slight smile on his lips. It was highly pleasurable to stand in his regard, to offer my regard in return. In my entire life, I had never seen a man so self-possessed. I thought of him when he was a child, with his too-big nose and knobby joints, and it gave me a rush of happiness that I had known him then, too.

He paused a foot away, tucked the book under his arm, and offered me the greeting of hands pressed together in front of him. In Hindustani, he said, "Your appeal is like that of a bird who takes his blue shimmering color through the sky, shaming the clouds, just like the royal kingfisher."

Even in that language, it was an extravagant compliment, and I laughed. I thought for a moment, then said, "Your eyes are as wild and deep as the ocean."

"As a monkey?" he said in English, eyes glittering.

I thought about my word choices and laughed. "Did I say *monkey*? I meant *ocean*."

"*Bandar* is *monkey*, *samandar* is *ocean*."

"Samandar," I said, and raised a hand to my throat dramatically. "Aap ki ankhen samandar ki gerhraiyon si choon jati hai."

He lifted my hand to his lips. "Good."

"I miss speaking Hindustani with you," I said. "One can think different things in different languages."

"Indeed. If we practice, it will come back quickly." He gave me the book he carried. "I thought we might read together, if you like. I think you will like it very much. *Umrao Jan Ada.* It's a woman's story."

"Thank you. I would like that." I gestured toward the path. "Shall we walk?"

Lacy sunlight fell through the trees, delicate as a whisper. "How are you finding your visit?"

"Frustrating, which was to be expected. My father wants something of me that I find I cannot deliver, and we are at odds over it."

"What does he want?"

He took a breath. "Cooperation with the British. He feels that is the only way we can move forward."

"You disagree," I said, not a question.

"As ever." He smiled down at me. "But let's not waste our precious words on nationhood and politics."

"But politics are part of you. I would hear whatever is on your heart."

"I shall look forward to discussing such matters with you, because I am learning things here I had not expected, but I'd rather not think of them today. Is that all right?"

"Of course." The warm scent of him wafted toward me on a breeze, speaking to some invisible field around my body, teasing and alive. "In truth, I am so happy to be with you that we could say peas and carrots all day and it would be enough."

"Peas and carrots?"

"Never mind." I gestured around us. "What do you think of England?"

"It is beautiful. Everything is softer here. The flowers, the clouds, the air."

We came to a thicket of trees, some as wide as a cart. "What are these trees?" he asked.

"Rowan. They were sacred to the Druids and maybe to witches. Powerful, aren't they?"

He pressed a palm to one, looking up, and I liked that he was a person who would think to do such a thing, befriend a tree another might simply walk by. He looked back at me, and then over his shoulder to the deserted path behind us. He held out his hand.

We dashed into the shadows, hidden by the great tree, and he backed me against it to kiss me. "I could not wait another moment," he said, and then just as quickly pulled me back to the public side.

I clutched his hand tightly. "How have you been so far away all this time? I feel like the world has suddenly straightened itself."

"It feels no time has passed, and too much." He tucked our hands into my skirts as we walked the public path. "I do admire your park, Elsie, but I am quite keen to see your paintings. You speak of it so often in your letters that I long to see the work. Is that possible?"

A swell of happiness strained the confines of my skin. "Yes. Of course. Do you mind taking the Underground?"

"Not at all. It should be an adventure."

~

We made the journey back to Slade, Tanveer admiring the carriage and the stations of the Tube. It somehow calmed my nerves to engage in a simple, ordinary task. "A very helpful invention in a city of such size," he said. "It must be safe if women ride alone."

"Yes. As safe as anything is for a woman on her own."

"And yet you want to move about freely."

"I wish for men to treat women with the respect they offer each other, so women needn't worry."

He raised a brow. "Will that ever be a truth?"

"It will be if we insist upon it."

"Perhaps here. I do not know if that can be true in India."

"Why not?"

He took a breath. "The Guru said we are all equals, men and women, and people of all castes. But many structures will need to be changed and dismantled for that to be true in practice." He glanced over his shoulder at a man pretending not to listen and switched to Hindustani. "We have other pressing struggles just now."

"Why not restructure it all at once? Free women from their chains, abolish caste?"

He gave me a droll glance. "That should be simple enough."

I laughed. Our stop arrived, and we disembarked, Tanveer offering a courtly hand as I stepped out. For a single moment, again I felt swamped at his presence. I shook my head to clear it.

Truly, would I spend all these days in a swoon? Ridiculous.

Briskly, then, I led the way to the school, which would likely be fairly empty on a late-spring Saturday as lovely as this one. As we crossed the courtyard, he looked around but said nothing, simply absorbing. I had forgotten this, too, his willingness to simply be quiet. Rocky and Nina chattered continually, and although I was not so much a talker as they, I had been drawn somewhat into the habit. It was cheering to remember there was more to me.

As we entered the building, cool shadows enveloped us. "This way." I led the way up the stairs to the studios, and he walked behind me, then beside me in the hallway, taking my hand in the folds of my skirt. I gripped him back, feeling nerves return. What if when I saw my work through his eyes, I hated it? What if I could sense he was only being polite?

Outside the room, I halted, my hand on his chest. "I will only show you if you are completely honest in your opinions."

He covered my hand. "Of course. Why would you expect anything else?"

"Very well." I hauled open the door and led the way into the studio. It was, unsurprisingly, empty. "My place is over here."

In the few months since that searing day I had lined up my paintings to see what I could learn about my voice, I'd been painting in a fury. "Sit here," I said, pulling over a stool. "Beware of paint. It's everywhere."

"I shall be aware." He folded his hands comfortably, at ease here as everywhere. I mentally captured the memory for future reference, quickly gathering details, the angle of thigh, the ease in his torso, light falling across his face. Perfect portrait light. I itched for him to sit there long enough to capture it. Perhaps a sketch in a moment.

Instead, I flung off my hat, took an apron from a hook to pull over my head, and started lining up the paintings. First the ones I'd decided to discard or paint over, what was left of them, the Nainital market and the people in India. Then came the first one I wanted to keep, of Gurdaya, and then the night sky in the desert when we'd been at his father's palace. Then more—a vivid, even exaggerated palette expressed in a garden of tulips beneath a spring sky, my mother bent kneeling in her garden; one of Nina, insouciantly draped over a chair, her dress the pink of bougainvillea flowers, and one of Rocky swimming in a lake.

"I haven't worked everything out yet," I said when they were lined up, side by side. "After you challenged me to consider my own colonialism, I admit I had a bit of a crisis."

"And?" His dark eyes held no judgment, only curiosity.

"I discovered that you were right, of course."

"Not 'of course.' I was not offering judgment, only prodding you to find your truth."

Looking back at the paintings, I pointed to the first ones and explained how I'd felt when I realized that they were painted in order to make an appeal to the "exotic," rather than exploring deeply. "But I believe my sense of color is honest. And I do love portraits. I think I am able to see people in a deep way."

"Yes," he said. "I am moved by the painting of Gurdaya. She is so mighty there. Is it the first day we swam?"

I nodded. "I painted it when you wrote that she'd married."

He held out a hand, and I went to him. He looped an arm around my waist comfortably, and I had the deepest sense of home, of rightness. "I love this work, Elsie. Even the vegetable wallah, truly. But Gurdaya and your mother are both filled with such love. I feel peaceful looking at them."

"Oh, dear. That sounds so bucolic. Shouldn't I strive for challenge, or something utterly new?"

"I don't know. Should you?"

I leaned into him, my hip against his side. "The art world would say yes. That this is safe work."

"You're learning, Elsie. Perhaps you don't have to know everything immediately."

I laughed. "What? I'm allowed to be a student for now? What a relief."

He smiled up at me, and he was right there, so close, so I bent to kiss him. Gently, once, twice, and then pulled away, my palms against the line of his beard. "Would you allow me to sketch a portrait of you?"

"I might be persuaded," he said, a twinkle in his eyes, "if you will kiss me again."

I did, lingering this time, falling into the world that belonged only to us, this meeting point of our lips, his hand on the small of my back.

"One more," he said when I raised my head. And then again: "Once more."

"The light will fade!"

"Very well." He released me. "Paint away."

I smiled gently. "It will give me a chance to simply look at you."

"And I will look at you in return. If looking is what you wish."

I feigned innocence. "What else could there be?"

~

So I painted him looking at me, his hand on his thigh, and I knew even as I sketched it quickly that the resulting painting would always be important to me. When the light grew long, he sighed. "I am expected at a function this evening."

I wiped my brushes clean and washed my hands. "I would rather you could spend every moment of your visit with me."

"As would I. But I think my father would object."

We walked down the stairs, holding hands. "Nina has sent out the invitations for her house party," I said. "Did you receive one?"

"Yes." His fingers tightened. "Will this be a bohemian orgy?"

"What?" I laughed. "No, no orgy, or at least not that I know of." I looked up as we emerged into the courtyard. "It will likely be very eccentric." Memories of recent gatherings tumbled through my memory. "And, yes, perhaps a bit more liberal than you are accustomed to. Shocking, even." I winced. "Will you hate it?"

"Hmm. Will there be nudity involved?"

"No." I reconsidered, thinking of the edict to dress as fairies for dinner on Saturday. "Er, well, there might be some very thin coverings."

He looked around the courtyard, then pulled me close. "Will I have time alone with you?"

"Yes," I whispered. "That is certain."

"Then I do not care what else occurs." He pressed his forehead to mine, paused. Then, quietly: "Is it too much to hope that we might lie together again?"

A flash of our limbs entwined, our skin bare and sliding, sent heat through me. To counter it, I said lightly, "As I am already ruined, I suppose it would be all right."

He lifted his head, stricken. "Ruined! By me?"

"No!" I cupped his face, touched his ears. "By me, and willingly."

"That is not ruination," he said softly, brushing his nose against my cheek. "That was our souls weaving together."

The words gave me a vision of a loom, silver and gold threads looped and tightened into a cloth of great strength. "Then we shall weave again." The heat of anticipation rose beneath my skin, enlivening every inch. Then I gripped his shoulders tightly and looked him in the eye. "But we must take precautions."

"Of course." He brushed my hair off my cheek. "It feels a hundred years until the weekend."

"A thousand."

He kissed me, slowly, a promise.

THE CARRIAGE OF TIME

Autumn 1940
London

—35—

October 19, 1940
London

Dear Tanveer,

[In English]: I am removing my paintings to Nina's estate, which involves taking all the canvases from their frames so they can be rolled up and stored. I have moved the most valuable pieces already, those that will be, in some future time, the legacy I have given my old lady self, a source of income if the war ever ends, if the value of my work holds (and I am quite aware that it might very well not—art lovers are fickle, and I have not yet captured the eye of museum curators, which is where the legacy might live).

Just now, I discovered the painting I made of you in the studio at Slade. Do you remember that day?

How young you were! How young I was! How delicately innocent the world was, just at that turning. It is one of my favorites that I've painted of you, although I have many and even more sketches. I feel quite tender looking at young, idealistic Tanveer, and

I want to weep, too, in my desire to protect you from what was to come. Protect myself, too.

But, of course, that is not possible. We are participants in the century that created us, and there is no escape. This war, crashing around us now, is yet another carriage on the train of this time. Will they write about us someday?

We are safe here. Just now, we've had a few days without bombs, so perhaps the Nazis are moving on to some other target and we can breathe again.

[In Urdu]: Mother and I are reading *A Passage to India*, and it reminded me to see if I could find *Umrao Jan Ada*, which was tucked among my books. I read it aloud to myself even if my accent must have degraded over time, just to keep myself in practice. If I lose Urdu, I will have lost a piece of myself.

I've torn a page from my sketchbook to share a moment of those halcyon days that last summer.

Tumhārī Rafīq-e-Jān, your soul companion,

Elsie

[Enclosed drawing of Rocky, Nina, Tanveer, and the lake on Nina's estate.]

—36—

I very nearly did not go to a planned dinner at Nina's. A huge battle took place overhead in the afternoon, rattling all of us, and the blitzkrieg followed all night. Mother slept through the night somehow, bless her, and I'd grown rather adept myself at catching a little sleep even with gunfire and incendiaries falling for hours.

But when everyone had gone to their daily tasks, Mother to her embroidery, Peter to the ministry, I found myself unsettled again. Restless. I returned to my studio, and rather than paint, I found myself organizing my brushes by size, sorting the various pencils and charcoals into tidy piles, tossing scraps of paper and old sketches into the trash. Beyond the windows, rain fell against the glass relentlessly. I had the sense that I'd forgotten something.

Mother had suggested, "Drink some chamomile to settle your nerves, darling. Who wouldn't be rattled in such a din?"

She wasn't, I noticed, but I knew that was her illness coupled with a hefty dosing of morphine. She'd rallied with the infusion of apple pie and a beef stew made with the rump roast Peter had come by somehow. She had not eaten a lot, but it was cheering, and I feasted myself, hungry in a way I hadn't been for years.

Perhaps it was the good food that eventually lifted my spirits. On Friday afternoon, I took a bath and washed my hair, which I'd had trimmed only a couple of weeks before, so it sprang into good order with only a little coaxing, and I took the time to put on a full round of makeup, powder, lipstick, rouge. It was remarkable how much strain it obscured.

Peter was in good spirits, picking me up after work so we could walk together the scant mile to Nina's townhome, a safer choice than driving, even if bombs were falling later.

The rain had stopped, leaving the air cleansed and fresh, all the more noticeable after days of smoky aftertaste. Twilight lingered, turning the sky a soft purple that felt somehow hopeful, and I dared to wish no planes would come tonight. "A night without bombs would be such a luxury," I said. I had not worn high heels in quite some time, and felt myself teetering, clinging to his elbow.

"Indeed." He eyed the sky. "One can always hope."

Peter spoke mildly, about the weather, a friend he'd seen at Paddington Station, and a new secretary in the pool at the foreign office. "She's quite good. Her husband has shipped out to Africa."

I glanced at him, alerted by something in his tone, but his face showed nothing. "She must welcome the work to distract her."

"I would imagine." He patted the pocket of his overcoat for a lighter, and instead pulled out a tiny vial and showed it to me. The cyanide. I'd forgotten about it again. I touched the inner pocket of my own coat and felt the rigid shape. Oddly comforting.

He lit his cigarette. "We've been coordinating troops from any number of directions. Australians." A pause. "Quite a lot of Indians, actually."

"I don't know why they would bother. This is hardly their war." Any more than the last one had been.

"Patriotism prevails."

Patriotism for what land? I wanted to ask, but it would only start an argument, and nothing I said would shift his opinion. "Mmm," I said.

"It's a chance for young men of no means to discover a better life."

Or die, I thought. "Let's not, Peter." We turned the corner, and suddenly, there was a half block in ruins. Both of us halted. I couldn't quite make sense of the rubble, tumbles of gray stone and beams sticking up like broken bones. On an upper floor, a wall had fallen away to reveal a bedroom, the bed still made, a curtain floating in an unseen breeze.

"Good God," Peter said. "Isn't this the building where George and Catherine lived?"

They were acquaintances, a woman my mother had played whist with on Monday afternoons. "It is. I wonder where they are. Will you look into it tomorrow?"

"Of course." He took my elbow. "Are you all right?"

I sighed. "I am, honestly. What does that say about me?"

"That these are trying days for all of us." He looked upward, shook his head. "Good God," he repeated.

At Nina's, she took my coat, kissed my cheek, and gave me a look I couldn't quite interpret. "What?"

She shook her head, drawing us into the room. The usual suspects mingled in the salon, cocktails in hand—a handful of couples who worked with the government and war offices. We'd known them for decades.

Added to the mix were three young women. "We've taken in some refugees," Nina announced. "Everyone, this is Adelaide, Mary, and Gertrude."

"Trudy," she said. "If you don't mind."

Adelaide was a sturdy girl, about twenty, with freckles from head to toe. She'd been bombed out of Kensington, and worked in the canteen. Mary was a plain girl, brown hair, who worked in the library.

Gertrude—Trudy—was remarkably small and delicate, built like a bird, with big eyes and red hair, proved to be Peter's new secretary. A redheaded woman had made a great deal of trouble in my life, once upon a time in Cairo, and I suddenly realized why Peter seemed so much more chipper recently.

A sudden flash of him back then, wild with drink and fury and the unpredictable violence that overtook him, gave me a sense of remembered dread. I fingered a scar I bore across the side of one arm.

But he couldn't touch me now. We had not been intimate since those days in Cairo and never would be again.

Nina said, "Welcome to all! We're so glad to have you."

Despite the reality of rationing, the meal was quite delicious. Jonathan must have been the source of the black-market beef, or perhaps Nina had found a contact through her father in the country. Either way, we feasted on a rich, deep stew, fragrant with herbs, shiny with fat. No butter for the bread, but the rolls were light and fluffy, a masterpiece of clever baking, and for dessert, an actual pie, just like the one Peter had brought home.

"Where in the world did you get this?" Trudy asked.

"One doesn't ask such questions in the modern world, darling," Nina drawled, sipping a sidecar.

"Oh! I'm so sorry!" Her pale face showed her embarrassment, and also her extreme youth. She couldn't have been much more than twenty.

"You've been out of the country," Peter said. "I'm sure you didn't realize."

Nina was in fine form, recounting her best stories to make us laugh. The phonograph played a symphony by Sibelius. I no longer partook of spirits and hadn't for more than a decade, but my mood was lifted by the good company. Peter was his charming best, eyes flashing.

The sirens went off just as we were finishing the first course. Nina stood up with her cocktail. "Right, everyone, under the table."

Titters met her suggestion. Jonathan said, "She is quite serious. Everyone under the table. Take the pillows from your chairs."

I glanced around, startled and amused, and then the guns started rat-a-tat-tatting overhead, and I dived with everyone else into the space beneath the ancient, broad table. Snatching the pillow from my chair, I sat, but couldn't quite get settled until I tugged the dress up over my knees. "Sorry for my lack of modesty, but the skirt is tight."

A boom made the silver on the table clatter, and someone made a little shriek.

"I tell myself it's a thunderstorm," I said.

Nina sipped her cocktail. "Remember the weekend the maharaja came to my humble country house? That was one of the most dramatic storms I ever remember."

"He wasn't maharaja then," I said. "Only prince."

"Right." She gestured toward invisible guests. "Rocky was quite smitten, as I recall."

"Goodness, I miss him," Jonathan exclaimed. "Was there ever a man as exuberant as he? Such a zest for life."

Rocky's face rose in memory, the thick curls, his dancing blue eyes. "Everyone fell in love with him."

"Not the prince," Peter said from the other end of the space. "As I recall *he* only had eyes for Elsie."

That had been the entire reason for the gathering—for us, Tanveer, and me. Peter had been there, too, and Rocky and Grayson.

A whistling bomb sounded nearby, and we all winced, bending over ourselves as it fell, bracing for impact. A trio of small snapping sounds came one, two, three.

"Incendiaries," one of the men said at the other end of the table. "Sounded close. I'll go check."

"I sometimes wish the one that was going to get me would just get it over with," said Mary. "It's so exhausting, never sleeping, never knowing. I'm so tired, it would be easier to just die."

"Bite your tongue," said Trudy in a whispery, baby voice. "Think of all the poor lads out there fighting, taking bullets." She made a sharp noise, and bit her finger, like a movie heroine. I tried not to show that I was rolling my eyes.

"All hands on deck," Gregory cried from the doorway. "Fire in the garden."

"What do we do?" squeaked the sturdy girl.

I pushed a chair out of my way. "Stay here. Not all of us need to fight the fire."

"Peter," Jonathan said, "stay with the women."

A knot of us hurried behind him, and quickly formed a bucket brigade to contain the fire in the garden. It was the first time I'd done it in real time, although we all had been instructed. I was the body just beyond the doorway, and it was the first time I'd been outside during a nighttime raid. I had little time to think about it, passing buckets back and forth, but there was something liberating about not hiding, about standing in the garden beneath the night sky, daring the Nazis to kill us.

We didn't die. The fire was halted, and we trooped back inside. "I say that calls for a drink," Jonathan said in a jolly voice.

"Under the table?"

"Hell no!" Alexander cried. "Fuck the bloody bastards."

No one corrected his language. The rest of the party crawled out from under the table, Peter reaching a hand back to help Trudy stand. She blinked up at him with grateful eyes.

I glanced at Nina, who remembered the days in Cairo as well as I did. I felt a chill of foreboding.

"Never mind," Nina said at my elbow, inhaling smoke from her cigarette. "You don't, do you? Mind?"

"What he does is none of my business," I said. "It's just the—" Eyeing Peter in thrall to Trudy, I spoke my worry aloud. "Do have Jonathan keep an eye on that."

"He has been. We all say it was the war, but I remember that weekend in the country, when the prince was there, Peter was . . . rather rough . . . with a village girl."

A chill twisted through my gut. I'd always believed his violence had been a result of his shell shock in combination with drink. "And you never thought to mention this?"

She pressed her lips together. "It was only the once. And anyway, you were otherwise engaged." She took my arm. "That was a good party—I took care of you."

It had been a beautiful weekend in many ways, but it had also been laced with sorrow and the coming losses. But to reassure her, I covered her hand. "It was an important time in my life."

THE LAST GOLDEN WEEK BEFORE THE WAR

Summer 1914
Clystmere Hall, Kent

—37—

When I arrived at Nina's country home on Friday afternoon, the sky held a purplish layer that captured my attention emphatically enough that I waved to Nina and ran toward the back garden. A storm gathered over the hills to the west, pregnant with rain, and the light turned the grassy hillsides an almost electric green. The undersides of leaves showed pale and restless in the rising wind.

But the mesmerizing thing was a line of copper threading between two banks of clouds, edged with rose and streaks of gold. I drew it as quickly as I could, trying to press the colors into my mind. My paints were in my bag, and I wished briefly I'd taken the time to pull out my watercolor tin.

"Use mine," said a voice behind me, as if he'd read my mind. "Extraordinary, isn't it?"

I saw a man, perhaps in his mid-twenties, dressed casually in a shirt and loose trousers. He handed me a clutch of colored pencils with soft tips, and I sat down to spill them in my lap, using layers to capture the spirit of that light, if not the exact shades. Yellow on top of brown, green layered over white and yellow, the ribbons of pink represented by light lines of red. And over it all, the eggplant sky, muscular and brooding.

"Thanks," I said, standing up. I gave him back the pencils and brushed off my bum. "I'm Elsie. We haven't met."

"Grayson." He had the look of a film star, dark hair a little rakish, a thin mustache across his lip. "I'm a friend of Rocky's."

"An artist, obviously. What are those pencils? I love the marks they make."

"I had them made in Germany last year."

"But that isn't a German accent, is it?"

"Quelle horreur! No, no, I'm Belgian."

"Nice to meet you. I'd best greet Nina properly. I'm sure we'll speak again."

"Au revoir."

~

I heard voices in various rooms as I ran up the stairs to the chamber I knew by now would be mine. A maid was busily unpacking my things, tucking them into drawers, the gown for Saturday night already hung. "Thanks, Matty. I've got it from here."

"You sure, ma'am? I'm nearly done. There's no rush."

"Go ahead, then. I'll go wash."

Nina captured me in the hallway, taking my hand and leaning into my side. "Your maharaja will be here," she said with an arched brow, pointing to the room next to mine.

Blood rushed to my cheeks. "Stop calling him that."

"Maharaja or yours? I think both are true."

The heat worked its way to my ears, and I pulled out of her grip. "No, neither is true, and his name is Tanveer, and you're making it sound—ugh." I cast about for the word. "Tawdry."

She inclined her head. "My apologies. Tanveer it is."

"I'm sorry, I just—he's not—" I looked down the long hall to a window in the stairway. "It's not like that. Some dalliance."

"Oh, my dear, the apology is mine. I did not mean to belittle you, or him, or any of it." She brushed hair from my face, cupped my cheek. "I only wonder how have you never told me about him before this, my dear Elsie? You are so clearly besotted."

I didn't really have an answer for her. There was only a sense that I wanted to keep it to myself, this shining thing we shared. In the world, it could be so easily damaged. "It is a private connection," I said.

She smiled faintly. "Well, then, I won't announce it, but you'll both have to blaze a little less." She brushed my shoulders. "Even now, the light is tumbling off you in little sparks."

"Stop!" I laughed. "Let me go wash!"

As I was about to pass, she caught my hand, and said quite seriously, "Be careful, pet. Protect your heart a little, will you?"

For a single moment, I remembered standing on the deck of the ocean liner carrying us away from India, letter from Tanveer in my pocket. I brushed it away—I was no longer that raw girl. "All will be well."

~

Supper was to be casual, served in the expansive kitchen rather than the large dining room, and I wandered down early, hoping for a glimpse of Tanveer. I'd watched through my window for new arrivals, but he had not arrived with the latest group from the train.

What if he didn't come?

Thinking of Nina's warning to beware of my heart, I occupied myself with sketches of the strange sky. The copper portal on the horizon had been sealed with more layers of clouds, but they were turgid, holding themselves aloof. I wondered how to play with that strip of extraordinary brightness from earlier, what it might signify in a painting, and sketched some ideas, but in truth, I was only waiting for Tanveer.

I went down early to distract myself with conversation, dressed in a simple skirt I wore daily, and a blouse that was one of my favorites, thin white muslin and lace that revealed and hid my shoulders and breasts in equal measure, though looking at myself in the mirror, I did wish for lush breasts like Helen or Gurdaya.

Foolishness. As I'd seen in life drawing, bodies came in any number of arrangements, big and small, soft or angular. Big breasts, small breasts, large penises, small ones—which you could tell even with the draping in class—fat thighs, skinny ones. Some humans were bony, like Nina. Some were softly lush, like Gurdaya.

All beautiful.

A handful of people were gathered in the salon. The French doors were open to the garden, with drinks and snacks lined up on the sideboard. I poured myself an elderberry cordial and headed toward Rocky and his friend Grayson, only realizing from the intensity of their body language that they were lovers, maybe having a quarrel. I hesitated, looking about for another familiar face, and spotted Peter standing alone looking at a ship in a bottle. Veering his direction, I said, "Hello. Do you remember me? We met last summer."

"Of course." His cheeks were rosy, his hair a tumble of corn silk. He was a tall man, angular, and I guessed he would play tennis fiercely. "I'm glad to see you."

"Are you a bohemian, Peter?"

"Oh, good lord no. Nina was short a man, and I agreed to join."

I glanced over my shoulder to the painters having their low argument, to a pair of girls I did not know, coiffed and slouchy at once, playing at being bohemians, and Diana, the Anglo-Indian I'd met here once before. She wore a glowing peach frock that set off her warm complexion. Seeing me, she wiggled her fingers at me over the shoulder of the frazzled-looking girl in front of her. "Who is with Lady Diana?" I asked.

"That would be Henny, who is on the far side of eccentric, I believe. She's a spiritualist."

I shook my head. "I don't know what that is."

"A medium? A tarot reader?"

"Ah, a fortune teller. I met one in India once, at a birthday party for the maharaja of Talwarpur."

A smile played beneath his tender mustache. "Did she give you a good fortune?"

"No, actually. She gave me a terrible one. It scared me so much I ran to my mother."

"Oh, no! Surely that should be against the rules."

"I heartily agree." Outside, a flash of lightning burned across the entire sky. We all looked through the doors at the brightness, but even expecting it, we all flinched when the thunder followed.

A laugh rang out as two things happened simultaneously—the rain began to fall in a waterfall torrent, and two people came in the room. Rocky said, "Quite the entrance, Your Highness."

I spun around to see Tanveer. At last. When everyone looked at him, he spread his hands and said, "I heard it has been a dry summer."

Everyone laughed and surged forward to meet him, speak to him. Next to him was Nina, who looked at me across the room, titling her head ever so faintly.

Beside me, Peter said, "Was it *that* maharaja's birthday?"

"No. It was his father."

"How are you acquainted?"

"We were children together."

"Ah." He took a sip of his drink. "I've always wondered why these Hindus wear turbans. It must be awfully hot, especially in India, I would think."

"That is a Sikh dastaar, actually." I watched Tanveer greet each person with focused attention, hands behind his back, as he gave a short bow to the ladies, a nod to the men. He looked magnificent in a dark western suit, cut to fit his broad shoulders, his long legs. "There are a great many styles of turbans, and many of them help protect the wearer from heat, rather than making it hotter. Bedouins, for example, use them to protect themselves from sand in the desert. But for Sikhs, it's a symbol of their faith."

"Ah, of course. Interesting." He watched the loose gathering around Tanveer. "I'm not quite clear about Sikhism. Is it related to Islam?"

I shook my head. "They're quite distinct, and different still from Hindu practice. Are you religious. Peter?"

"Not at all. My Aunt Genevieve manages the religion for the family."

I laughed.

He added, "At least it's all Church of England here—oh, but you don't like things to be too homogenous, do you?"

I glanced at him, wondering if there was a cut buried in there, but his eyes were guileless. I remembered that he wanted to study architecture. "Have you traveled in the east to study the architecture there?"

"I have not. I would like to. One of my dearest wishes is to visit the Pyramids."

"Oh, my. Yes. That would be quite a sight."

At last Tanveer extracted himself and moved deliberately toward me. "Good evening, jaanu," he said, giving me the same small bow he'd given the ladies. His eyes glittered with humor as he added in Hindustani, "Your beauty shines like a moonlit pool."

I pressed my hands together in greeting. Also in Hindustani, I said, "And yours shines like a monkey."

I was rewarded with his big laugh, so full of life that I saw two people look around and see what caused it. "Tanveer, this is Lord Peter Arbuthnot, Nina's cousin. Peter, this is the Prince of Talwarpur." I looked back to Tanveer. "Forgive my ignorance, but I do not know the correct address for you. Is it 'Your Royal Highness'?"

"Similar, Rajkumar, as I am a son." He offered his hand for an English greeting. "But perhaps you might call me Tanveer in this casual instance."

Peter was charmed, shaking his hand with a smile. "I shall, then. And now I'll leave you two old friends to catch up."

As he moved away, Tanveer stepped close and took my hand, raising it to his lips. "Your eyes truly are shining. Like beacons."

"Because I wanted you to come over here. I was feeling terribly impatient."

"As was—"

A great crack of thunder rattled the glass in the room and made everyone duck, as if something were falling from the sky. The lights blinked out, all at once.

"Oh, dear. That won't be good," Nina cried. "Peter, will you find Mr. Richards? He'll know what to do."

He saluted her and left the room.

Tanveer rubbed his thumb over the center of my palm, and as if all the electricity now flowed through him, into me, I felt quite wildly aroused. "You must stop that." I drew my hand away, and instantly wanted to offer it back.

"Your cheeks are flushed."

I clapped my hands to my face, and I could feel the heat in them. "I hardly know how to stand here with you." I found my eyes on his mouth, framed so artfully by his beard, and wanted only to sink into them.

He turned to stand beside me, looking toward the room, and our arms pressed close. In Hindustani he said, "I have been useless to my father. All I think of is kissing you." He glanced at me sideways. "Your mouth. Your neck."

I laughed, grabbing his arm. "Stop!" I said, "Nina put you in the room next to mine."

"Well done, Nina," he said in English. He looked at me. "It will be an eon until then."

I blushed. "Are we terribly wicked?"

"Are we?"

"I don't know." I suddenly felt shy and girlish and foolish, as if I were tumbling heedlessly into some mire I could prevent if I would only halt now. "We shall never be friends again, will we?"

"We will always be friends, meri jaan." He captured my hand against his thigh in the shadows. "And we will be lovers, too." He used the Hindustani word, *hum-rooh*, which translated more closely to *soul mates* than *lovers*, and this time, his face was quite serious. "But I am patient. If you are feeling frightened, I am in no hurry." He smiled a little. "Well, I am. But I am more patient than hurried."

I suddenly imagined sleeping alone in my room tonight with him on the other side of the wall, and all the time that would be wasted by that. "No. An hour is too far away."

Rocky arrived in our realm then, and Grayson beside him. To Tanveer, he said, "The artists here all want to paint you, good man."

"I am afraid I am a subject for only one artist."

Rocky laughed. "Wonderful." He looked at me with a glitter in his eye. "Wonderful."

~

We ate dinner by candlelight at a rough wooden table in the kitchen. Nina had separated Tanveer and me, placing him between herself and Lady Diana. Rocky was next to me on one side, the husband of the couple on the other. His name was Jameson, and he turned out to be a writer working on his first novel, and not the bore I'd feared. We feasted on roast trout and new potatoes and fresh green beans, with a strawberry tart and cream for dinner.

The storm and good food created a festive mood, and we laughed at the stories Grayson told. Even Jonathan, Nina's most recent beau, who was a serious sort, laughed at his witty tales. Tanveer listened more than spoke, although he and Lady Diana shared tales of the Punjab, which she'd left as a girl. The spiritualist watched everything with eyes too big for her face. It bothered me that she was here, and I found myself remembering the seer from the maharaja's birthday, predicting dire things for my future.

What madness to worry about such a thing? My life had unfolded quite intriguingly since then.

But of course Henny had to read her cards in the flickering candlelight of the salon after dinner. Nina, always one to underline the drama settled in front of her. "What do you need from us, darling? One at a time? Will you read for the group?"

The girl shuffled her cards, worn soft from use, looking from person to person. "I'll do a general reading for the group, and then one at a time for whoever wishes it."

"Goody." Nina leaned back, candlelight shimmering over her dress, in waves of shape, breasts, hips, knees. Diana stood behind her, smirking as ever, but in one little brush of her hand, I saw her sweep Nina's hair from her shoulder, linger on the bare skin there for a moment.

Ah.

Tanveer, freed of the regulation of dinner, sat next to me on the divan. "What do we think," he said in Urdu. "Is she a fortune teller or an imposter?"

"It's hard to know yet, isn't it? She does have the eyes of a medium."

"Mmm. I do not want her to read for me." He looked at me, eyes quite serious. "Or you."

All at once, I was aware of his size, so much more adult than it had been. His thigh leaned against mine, his shoulders broad above my own. That hint of sandalwood wafted through my body, whispering delights. I found my eyes on his throat and imagined myself kissing there. I said, "'Hum apnī taqdīr khud likhẽgē, yahā̃. Ek bistar, do khwāb, kyā ḳhūb hai, wahā̃?'" *We'll write our own fates, just us, right here—one bed, two dreams—what bliss draws near?*

This time, his cheekbones flushed. He took a moment, then said, "'Zamāne kā kyā gham? Chupke se keh ha, ishq kī rāt hai, roshanī kahā̃?'" *Why fear the world? Just whisper yes—this night is love's; who needs the rest?*

I leaned against him.

Nearby, Diana said in Urdu with a droll tone, "'All lovers recite the same old lore—After tea, that tale behind closed doors.'"

I looked up at her and laughed. "Well done, you."

"Oh, share it with the rest of us," Grayson called out.

"It is only an old game from childhood," Tanveer said smoothly. "Of no interest without the context."

The girl divided her cards and divided them again, and began to lay them out in a cross. We all watched as she carefully placed them, one and another and another. A shadow darkened her face, and she paused for a moment, looking at the cards with concern. She held the other cards in her hands. Her gaze flickered up, caught on mine, then on Nina's. A strange hush filled the room.

"Don't frighten us," Diana said, and laughed.

The girl raised her enormous eyes. "Perhaps I should—"

"Oh, no!" Rocky cried, his face flushed with gin. "We're all caught in your web now. You must go on, girl. You must!"

She looked at her hands, at the cards spread in front of her, and then laid out three more. Her mouth did not change, and I thought for a moment that she might weep.

I almost spoke up to say, "Never mind, darling—" when she began to speak.

She pointed to the first card, which showed a sun. "This is the current moment," she said. "A time of innocence and the illusion of safety. Happiness," she added. She took a breath, as if settling into herself. "But it will not last. There is a time of challenge and great darkness coming, and it is very nearby."

Grayson made a little noise. "You heard us talking about the war, I'm sure. That's convenient."

"I did hear you," she said with great calm. "And that might be what is coming. The card"—she pointed to a card with a tower and fire and a man falling from the turret—"says everything will change. All of you will change."

Glances flew around the little group. Tanveer rested his forearm on his leg, close to mine in my lap, and the warmth gave me a sense of grounding.

Henny continued, "This is coming about from the old systems, greed and moral rot that must be broken." She pointed to another card. "Justice asks to be considered, but it will not come cleanly."

The writer spoke up. "'Yet once more I will shake not only the earth but also the heaven.'"

I suddenly had a sense of a miasma entering the room, like a dark fog flowing along the floor, a presentiment of my own. "Oh, let's not be so dour!"

Rocky said, "No, please, Henny, do go on."

She frowned, looking at the cards with great concern. "I don't think anything is going to be the same. A great deal of death and sorrow is showing here, and—" Suddenly, she swept the cards into a heap, mixing them up emphatically.

"Wait, you didn't read the rest!"

She stood up. "I do not wish to finish. My apologies." Scooping up her cards, she hurried to collect them. One fell on the floor, the same that had been at the end. I reached out and picked it up. "What is this one?"

She bowed her head, taking it from me. "The world. Reversed." She shook her head. "Good night."

In the aftermath of her retreat, a vast silence dropped into the room. "That was grim," Rocky said, and tossed back his drink.

Nina clapped her hands. "Never mind," she cried, standing. "Let's dance!"

"Not I," Tanveer said, standing. "I'll take my leave of you good people."

A rush of sweet anticipation pooled in my belly, and I forgot the strange psychic. Rocky also gave his leave, and I waited until Peter followed, then floated up the stairs.

—38—

My room had been lit with oil lamps, one burning by the bed, one on the dressing table. The drapes had not been pulled, and the storm beyond continued to slap rain against the windows. I went to the window, feeling that sense of warning, and looked out. What was coming?

A quiet knock came at my door, and I forgot everything as I flew across the room to let Tanveer in. He had shed his English clothes for a kurta and pajamas, his turban left in his room, leaving his hair in a knot on his head, pieces of it falling around his face. I swallowed, so consumed with want that I almost could not move.

"May I come in?" he said quietly, his hands behind his back. All of the moments of our times came back to me in a rush, weaving together the boy who had drawn tigers with me, and the one who'd shown me the stars and taught me to swim, and taught me to kiss and to make love coming together into a braid of love that shimmered through me, expanding out of me to enfold him, too. I reached for his hand and drew him into the room, tangling arms and then mouths and tongues and hope and longing. I unbuttoned my blouse and shed my chemise, he discarded his kurta, and I stepped out of my skirt, and then he led me to the bed. We took off the rest and pressed bare skin to bare skin, and hands to curves and angles, and everything else moving together until we were one being, woven back together at last.

~

Much later, curled against him, I said, "Do you believe in people seeing the future, like the spiritualist tonight?"

He brushed hair from my forehead, ran his fingers down my face. "I don't know. I am quite sure she believes."

"She was very frightened."

"Perhaps there is a feeling of things in the air, something she can access. It is true there is much talk of war. And that would certainly change everything."

I thought of her looking at the cards, nearly in tears. "Is there going to be a war?"

"It seems there may be. But let's not think of that tonight, shall we? I just want to be here with you."

"It appears we are together," I said laughing. "Tonight, I thought of all the layers of you, the yous I have known. I should like to paint all of them." I drew my finger along the top of his nose. "Your nose, and your eyebrows, they've stayed the same." I brushed his eyelashes, so thick and dark, and drew a line around his eye socket, the lid, as if to create a spell to remember the depth of his iris. So close, it was not unbroken darkness, but layers of earth and sparks of amber. It made me dizzy, looking so closely.

"I would paint your mouth before the beard arrived, when you were small," I said, tracing the dip in the upper, the curve of the lower, and then the line of the beard that was new to me. "And I would paint your beard now, before it's as full as your father's. One day, it will have white streaks in it."

He listened, watching me as I moved my fingers down his throat, to his chest where sprouts of hair had begun to show. It moved me so that I bent in and kissed the place.

"Elsie," he whispered, and nudged my face up to look at him. "If it were mine to paint, I would draw your face full of light, as it is now." He kissed me softly, his fingers on my chin. "I would draw fire in your pupils, and burning in your heart, and I would show those fires the same as my own."

How can I ever let him go now? I thought, but I didn't say it. I only closed my eyes and let him touch me slowly, looking, and whispering about the wonders of the terrain. And so we began again, and it was holy and it was ours and I vowed I would remember it always.

A RIVER OF GHOSTS

Autumn 1940
London

—39—

After the dinner party at Nina's, Peter and I took our chance to hurry home. He was not drunk, and protectively took my elbow more than once when gunfire rattled overhead. When we entered the foyer, our neighbor Mrs. Cotton, who'd come in to sit with Mother, was waiting. "Your mother is quite unwell, my dear. You need to go right up."

I handed her my bag and coat, dropped my hat on the tree, and hurried upstairs. "Mother, I'm here. Are you all right?" I sat at her side and took her cold hand. The palm was red, and I stroked it lightly.

She did not answer, only shifted restlessly. Her belly beneath the blanket was larger than ever, as if she were growing a new baby instead of her death. The thought made me blink hard. "Mother, would you like me to read to you?"

The doctor had been in two days ago, and would no doubt be in the hospital with newly injured people tonight. Outside, I could hear the raid continuing, distant, then closer, and my heart fluttered. How could I help her?

As if she heard my unspoken plea, she turned and tightened her fingers around mine. "I can't find the letter. I had it just now, and I can't find it."

"What letter, Mother? Perhaps I can look for it."

"From William, of course. He promised to write when he arrived in Africa."

My brother. "I shall look for it." On her desk was a basin of cool water Mrs. Cotton had left. I squeezed out the cloth within and folded it to press on her forehead. Quietly, I began to sing a soft lullaby, and for a moment, it gave her no peace. Her legs moved restlessly, and she scratched at her forearms, which were already marked by her nails. I washed the length of them, hoping to give her some relief, and smoothed lotion over the dry skin.

Finally, she began to settle. Bastet jumped up on the bed and curled up at her side, purring as if it were her duty. "Good girl," I said, stroking her head. A ball of kitten tumbled out of the basket on the floor, yelping loudly, and I picked it up to cuddle. Another waddled over, and I picked it up, too, taking comfort in their motor-like purrs. I held them against the chasm of pain in my heart.

I rested my gaze on my mother's face. I could barely even imagine a world without her.

~

In the morning, I had a phone call from Betty's niece, alerting me at last to her whereabouts. She'd been taken to hospital the day she'd gone missing, but it had taken her sisters many days to discover which one. The number of injuries had been so substantial that day that medics had taken her across the river to St. Mary's Hospital in Paddington, one of the last places her sisters stopped.

Mrs. Cotton from next door was more than happy to come in again and sit with Mother while I made the journey to visit Betty.

The weather was dreadful, pouring down rain from low clouds. My feet were wet within minutes, but I was grateful for the respite from bombers, who wouldn't be able to fly in such weather. As I made my way to the Tube, I pondered the absurdity of that—once the clear, dry weather we prized during autumn was anathema, while the rain and dark were valued.

It took two diversions to make my way to the hospital as trains were looped around the damaged stations. Eventually, I emerged above ground to find a landscape I didn't recognize. The bombs had done their work here, often with every other building in ruins or half ruins. Some shops still offered tea and cakes on signs painted on cardboard taped over the shattered windows. In some places, the pavement had been swept, debris and rocks shoveled to one side to offer a clear walkway; in others, the building had fallen so entirely that a path was impossible.

I wondered where the residents had gone. Did they all go to the country? Pile into rooms with relatives?

A pencil of light caught my eye in the debris, and I bent to pick it up. A silver haircomb with inlaid coral, hardly scratched. I held it for a moment, wondering who it belonged to, and if she missed it, amid missing all the other things lost under the rubble. A particular cup, a jumper, a book carried from another country.

I thought of the paintings I'd done after the last war, the memories of domestic life I'd painted after all the losses. It was the only thing I could bear for a time—painting the remains of breakfast, or a homey vase of flowers on a windowsill, a length of fabric over the back of a chair.

Tucking the comb into my pocket, I kept moving, mulling the idea that we all thought about death and injury and staying safe during war, but equally terrible was this enormous loss of homes. I looked at the gaping windows overhead, the revealed privacy of a bathroom, the tiles still on the wall, the tub shattered. I imagined a young woman washing her hair before a man came to take her to the pictures. A kitchen with stove still neatly pressed against the wall yawned nearby, and I thought of a mother making soup, now disappeared.

How could I paint this feeling?

The hospital was an assault—patients tucked into every nook and cranny, beds in the corridors, four or six crowded into rooms meant for two. Weeping visitors, stalwart nurses, physicians hurrying through the crowds. I managed to track down an information desk, and the harried volunteer looked up Betty's name, and directed me to the basement.

"The basement!"

"Safer," she said curtly.

At last I found her, in a room with two others and a bed recently vacated by the look of it. She was asleep as I approached, her face battered, one eye swollen closed even this many days after the event. A bandage circled her head, which gave me pause. A head injury? Her body was covered with a blanket, but one leg was thick with plaster. Gingerly, I took her hand. It was cold, and I covered it with both of mine. She didn't stir.

"She won't know you," the woman in the next bed said. "She's drugged right to the gills, she is."

"Do you know what her injuries are?"

"Broken this, broken that," she said. "Same as us all."

I nodded acknowledgment. Holding her hand, I said quietly, "I'm here, Betty. Your sister tracked you down, and we all know where you are now, so you are not alone. You just get well now, all right?" I stroked her dry fingers, wishing I'd thought to bring a book to read aloud to her. Looking around the room, I didn't see any, and then, tucked behind a curtain, I saw the spine of one. "I'll be right back."

It was an old book, with faded gold letters on a blue cloth spine. *Oroonoko*, by Aphra Behn. "Does this belong to anyone?"

The other two patients simply shook their heads.

I found a chair and sat between Betty and her roommate, then opened the book and began to read. I could not help but remember reading to the injured soldiers near the end of the last war, H. G. Wells and *Gulliver's Travels*.

For a moment, I was washed with acute despair, the ghosts of those soldiers lying beneath the bodies of these humans, also grievously injured by the cold tools of war.

What was the point to any of it, a war to end wars, and then another war to gulp it down, on and on and on forever?

My despair only lasted a moment, for wasn't I still whole myself, and wouldn't I want to be read to if it were me in the bed, suffering? I picked up the book and continued to read.

October 26, 1940
London
[In Urdu]

Dear Tanveer,
It's 2:00 a.m. Bombs have been falling in rounds all day, here and then farther away, then close enough to rock the house and rattle the windows. One small beauty is this circle of lamplight and my hand on the paper, writing to you. I am buoyed by the knowledge of you reading this, far away, but real. Alive. If I think of your face, reading the words I've written, I can take a breath.

A bomb just shook the walls, and I heard shrapnel rattle against the window. It is nerve-racking. I hate being above ground, and wish to run to a shelter, but Mother cannot even manage the stairs. Here we will stay.

Betty is in the hospital, and I suspect she will not be well enough to return to us, though where she will go is a mystery, as her sisters were displaced the first night of the blitzkrieg. I do not know if I can manage another invalid on my own, either. Perhaps I might find an able-bodied refugee. We have a little space.

But that is a task for another day. Tonight (this morning) I am weary in every bone in my entire body, and I cannot imagine there is a soul in this city who does not feel the same.

Reading helps quite a lot. When I visited Betty, I found a copy of *Oroonoko*, by Aphra Behn. It's an old novel, and there are predictable colonialisms about the "natives" and their innocence, but in ways, it's also critical of those same systems. I believe you would enjoy it, although there is a female narrator. I admit I grew so engrossed in my reading that I brought the novel home with me. When I am able to leave Mother with Peter for a few hours again, I shall take it back and read to her some more.

I'm sorry to hear that Channan still struggles. Please give her a kiss from my heart and tell her that I think of her every day and wish I could send my strength to her. It must be difficult to live in a body so riddled with injury, and she is a woman of great courage to have carried her pain so valiantly. I treasure my paintings of her.

Mother is also in poor health, and growing more so. Recently, she seems to forget where she is, or *when* she is, and mentally wanders through her life, dropping into a timeline that pleases her and stays there for a time. I have been with her girlhood self at a tea where she met my father, and rather too vividly in the arms of her husband in America. I care for her as well as I am able, but I see her fading by the day.

How could it be otherwise in this madness of endless raids? It infuriates me!

In truth, Tanveer, I find it difficult to maintain a sense of optimism of any kind. How can London survive this onslaught? There will be nothing left by the end. The papers speak of the enemy's losses, but I know they don't report the full truth. I see the damage of a bomb nearby or on a notable landmark, and often the papers mention nothing about it. It only feeds my sense of certainty that London will fall, just as the rest of Europe has—and then what future will we face?

Forgive my pouring this darkness out to you. There is no other. I must keep a brave face for Mother, and Nina suffers terrors of her own. I barely see anyone else. Peter weaves in and out, here long enough to bathe and sleep, then back to work.

Tell me a story, if you please. Give me a fable I can cling to. I keep thinking of the last war, of the telegrams that arrived, over and over. Of your suffering. Of my brother's. Remind me there is also good in the world, and that we will know it again.

Your friend,

Elsie

PS: The book made me remember that ridiculous picnic Nina staged on the beach, complete with curry sandwiches. (!) Now I've made myself laugh. It was absolutely terrible, and do you know, I am quite certain she does not realize it to this day.

A PICNIC IN BRIGHTON

June 1914

—40—

Nina loved a picnic. On Saturday, she arranged for all of us to go to the beach at Brighton. The whole house party was transported by car and carriage five miles down the road to the beach. She'd ordered an extravagant tent erected, with flags flying above it, in honor of a royal's tent, and a Moroccan rug covered the sand. Chairs within were arranged with draperies of patterned silk. The whole was policed by a pair of grim servants in vaguely military uniforms and turbans unlike any I'd ever seen before. They kept onlookers moving with beetle-browed shakes of the head.

I rode with Tanveer and Rocky and his beau Grayson, all of us a little drunk on sunshine after the storm. As we climbed out of the car, Tanveer remarked, "Extravagant, isn't it?"

"Well there are no elephants, but I suppose the tent is a little much."

He had the grace to tilt his head with a faint smile. "Touché."

"Do you ride on elephants, Prince?" Grayson asked, tossing his hair from his face.

"I have," he said. "More often I use a motorcar."

"Do you have motorcars in India these days?" He bent his head into the wind to light a cigarette. "I've never been there, mind. But my imagination is filled with the things you hear."

"I'm sure they're all entirely accurate."

"My father was there when he was young, though, of course, he was sent back at six, to avoid the language issues and so forth."

"Language issues?" Tanveer asked calmly. "Like mine? Like Elsie's?"

"Oh, no, man. You speak the King's English. It's remarkable, really." Grayson winked my way. "Elsie, on the other hand . . ."

"Mmm." Tanveer gestured to me. "Shall we see what lies within?"

I realized I'd been holding my breath. "Yes."

We ducked into the cool of the tent. More servants manned the feast laid out on the table—little crabs and iced cakes, cold venison pasty, chicken sandwiches with yellow curry powder, an aspic already speckled with sand. The servants had plumes of peacock feathers in their hats. I glanced at Tanveer and pulled my lips into my mouth to avoid commenting.

Nina swirled over. "There you are! What do you think? Have I got some of it right?"

"It's lovely," Tanveer said. I glanced at him, and could read nothing. "I shall enjoy every morsel."

"I did ask if there were things you mightn't be able to eat, so I hope it's all delicious."

"It will be wonderful. Thank you, Nina. It will be a day to remember."

Rocky joined us. "Grayson's an ignorant bastard, but he means nothing by it."

Tanveer inclined his head, in acceptance or rejection, it was unclear.

I filled a plate with little cakes and fruit and sandwiches, and we carried them to a round table with several chairs. As we sat down, Peter approached. "Do you mind if I join you?"

"Certainly not." I gestured toward an empty place.

~

The weather was stellar, hot and sunny. We all swam and ate tiny crabs and fresh bread with sweet butter. The others drank, but Tanveer never drank alcohol, and so I didn't, either. Late in the afternoon, we lounged on chairs beneath big umbrellas and watched the waves roll in.

"I'm enchanted by the sea," I said, one knee propped up.

"What do you like about it?" Tanveer asked. He let his foot fall sideways into the top of mine. I wiggled my toes to acknowledge him.

"Aside from the obvious beauty, it's reliable, isn't it? Wave after wave, one after the other, for as long as time has existed. It's untamable. It's bigger and wilder than anyone, or anything."

"Like the desert."

I looked at him. "I never thought of it that way, but I suppose so."

Peter and Grayson were on the other side of Tanveer. "I'd like to see the desert," Peter said. "Have you been to the Sahara?"

"Afraid not," Tanveer said. "Though Elsie once imagined she might have been one of the builders of the Pyramids. Perhaps she'll remember that former life for you."

I smiled, unbothered by his teasing, and closed my eyes. "I didn't remember, I just hoped."

"Really, Elsie," Peter said, "are you interested in the Pyramids?"

"Oh, very! Who would not be?"

He sat forward eagerly, facing me over the body of Tanveer. His nose was quite sunburned, and his hair had gone askew with salt. He was in some ways much younger than the rest of us, though I couldn't have said just why. His earnestness. Guilelessness. "They're a remarkable feat of engineering."

"Enough slaves, you can do anything," Grayson said.

"Just ask England," Tanveer said lazily, eyes closed.

"You're not suggesting England enslaved the colonies?" Grayson frowned.

Restless discomfort rose in me, and I sat up, ready for—what?

Tanveer raised a brow. "Am I not?"

"Indians aren't enslaved, and anyway, you have your own servant class, caste and all that."

"It's true there is a caste system in India, but Sikhs do not believe in it, and while Indians are not technically enslaved, they are treated by the British like children who couldn't possibly run their own country."

Grayson opened his cigarette case and tapped one against the hard surface. "Fair enough, man, but for the sake of argument, why haven't they got off their arses and tossed the colonials out?"

Alarmed, I tried to think of what I might say, but felt tongue-tied and nervous. Perhaps this wasn't my battle. Tanveer could stand up for himself.

"I believe they have tried," Tanveer said. "I believe they are still trying."

I expected him to say what he believed about independence, and almost boasted on his behalf, and then realized I had no idea what the stakes were in this conversation. It was above me, outside of me.

"Natives around the world are making these noises," Grayson said impatiently. "It's purely economic. The textile trade would collapse without Indian cotton and jute. We face the same in the Congo, the rubber trade."

"Another trade that's famously just," Tanveer said with savage sarcasm.

Peter said, "At least the British have created some semblance of colonial government. King Leopold simply took the entire country."

Nina suddenly appeared, clapping her hands. "Boys, boys, boys. No more politics. Let's all go for a swim to celebrate the day, shall we?"

Tanveer looked at me, shook his head infinitesimally. A burn of color touched his cheeks and temples, and I realized he was very, very angry. "I'd like to walk," he said.

When the others trooped out to the water, I asked, "Would you like to be alone?"

"For a little while," he said.

I watched him go, sun gilding his form as he walked barefoot away from the party. The others had forgotten it already and danced in the waves, splashing each other. I stayed where I was, betwixt and between, a sense of that dense gray fog rising from the ground one more time.

~

That evening, there was a dinner party, and everyone was meant to dress up like fairies. Tanveer declined, arriving only as himself, in a kurta and pajamas with his sandals. I was dressed in a diaphanous gown and wings, with glitter falling off the fabric at every step. When I saw Tanveer, I felt immediately foolish, like a little girl.

He joined me and said quietly, "You look lovely."

A hot aura came off him, and I wished I could run upstairs and change immediately. As I looked at the room, I felt embarrassed of my friends, frivolous and rather too loud, some of them barely glazed by fabric, the fairyland theme an excuse for discarding the strictures of society. I'd known it would be that way, and yet, seeing it through Tanveer's eyes, it reeked of spoiled children, misbehaving because there was no reason for them to behave.

"Prince," Nina cried, joining us. She wore whispers of red that showed off her taut midriff and a lot of lean leg. "Where's your costume?"

"Oh, but it is a costume. My native dress, you know."

She smiled a little uncertainly. "Ah, well, I hope you'll enjoy our little soirée."

"Are you all right?" I asked quietly. We had not spoken about the scene at the picnic, but had gone to our rooms after returning to the house. I slept for an hour after the soporific sun and salt of the day, and assumed he'd done the same, though honestly, I had expected he might join me.

He caught his hands behind his back, and surveyed the room. "It is not what I expected."

"I did warn you."

"You did," he agreed. "Because we are so close, Elsie, I think we are of one mind. And then I remember again that we are not."

Stung, I frowned. "Of course we're not. How could we be?"

"No, I know. I see that."

An undercurrent of darkness wove through our conversation, and I felt something cold in my chest. A warning. "What are you saying, Tanveer? Speak plainly. That's been our pact, always."

He was silent for a long moment. Then: "Walk with me."

We stepped into the mild evening. The sun had not yet set, and I thought of the lake where I'd seen Rocky swim. "This way."

On the forest path, we walked in silence. Birds called out evening songs, robins and sparrows and the punctuating low notes of mourning doves. "The first time I walked through here," I said, "I realized that forests like this are the settings of the fairy tales my mother told me."

"And what sort of fairy are you tonight?"

I fluttered my fingers through the airy fabric. "I am not sure. A tree fairy, perhaps?"

"Did she ever read you tales from India?"

"No," I said. "My ayah told them to me."

We stepped into the clearing of the lake, and I could not have asked for a more splendid view. An egg-yolk sun had half sunk into the water, creating a spill of deep yellow over the lake. Trees framed it with feathery black, and there was even a swan floating gracefully across the scene.

"Perhaps this is what you should be painting," Tanveer said.

"It is beautiful," I said, "but perhaps not to my taste."

"Oh, perhaps you'd rather paint the tent this afternoon?"

I frowned at him. "Are you angry with me?"

"Not angry, exactly. Just—" He sighed. "Disappointed, perhaps."

"In me? Why? The picnic was absurd. Grayson was an ass. I understand all that, but how was any of it my doing?"

He turned, eyes blazing. "You brought me here. You must have known what it would be."

"How could I know?" I frowned. "It's a new world to me here, too."

He bowed his head. "Yes, I see that, too. I just—"

"What? What have I done to so ruin the harmony between us? What have *I* done, Tanveer? Not my friends, not this world. Me."

At last, he took my hands, and he spoke in Hindustani. "You did nothing, jaan. It was that I saw too clearly what lies between us."

"What, Tanveer?" I spoke in the same language, determined to close the widening gap between us. "Nothing! We have our own world, here between us. No one else is here."

"And if it were only that, always, just this meeting place between us, we could live there and be happy. But it isn't. There is no place for me to thrive here, and there is nothing for you in my world."

"But we have now. Why are you fighting with me tonight? We have so little time." I reached for his cheek, touched his neck. "When you return to India, we'll revert to our letters, and distance will shape this thing between us anyway."

He switched to English. "But don't you see? We cannot exist in this place of distance and yearning and love without some toll on both of us. It's beyond foolish. It will be destructive."

Anger flared. "I did not kiss you in the garden that first night. You kissed me." Tears filled my eyes, and I was furious with my weakness. "I said that we might hurt each other, and nothing had changed."

He nodded. "I did. Perhaps I was wrong."

"How convenient! Now that you've swept me into this . . . world with you again, you change your mind and cast me away when it becomes difficult. Just like you did before I left India."

"I'm not casting you away." He made a noise of frustration and bent his head to mine. "You did not step in today. You were one of them. It made you someone else."

I heard the anguish in his tone, and I felt an answering wail. "I was caught in the middle, and I didn't know what to do. I am so sorry."

"I love you," he said. "Like an arm, like water. But I fear there is no way to cross this gulf."

"Stop!" I cried, pushing at his shoulders. "You're wallowing in your superiority. You're judging me very harshly on something I've only had a little tiny taste of. You send me off in exile before I even have an opportunity to try on a new set of clothing. How can you be so gentle in your letters and so judgmental in person?" I felt my face heating. "Is it not the challenge of two souls to learn to navigate the world *with* each other? Am I supposed to know in this very moment everything I must know forever?"

"No, Elsie—"

"I can't speak for anyone else here, but you do know me." Clutching my skirts, I shook my head. "You're not the only person who has feelings."

I stomped back to the party and left him standing on the shores of the lake. The beautiful, bucolic lake with its perfect little swan. I thought he would come after me, but he did not.

My heart bled all the way up the lawn.

~

I had no taste for the party, and made my way to my bedroom, where I shed the foolish fairy dress. Clad in a dressing gown, I sat by the window with my sketchbook, flipping through the drawings from recent days and weeks. The park the day Tanveer arrived, and his hand on his leg, and a quick profile. In my mind, I went over the events of the picnic, and I could see clearly moments I might have spoken or acted in a more supportive way.

But I'd been afraid to upset anyone—Tanveer or Rocky or Nina or even Grayson. My mother had taught me to be polite, and I fell back on that at moments of consternation.

Because it *had* been a moment of consternation, riding up to the tent, seeing the mishmash. Grayson had been an ass from the start, but it was Tanveer who defended me, not the other way around.

I felt as aggrieved as I had examining my paintings. Like a foolish, embarrassing girl who knew nothing.

And in truth, I didn't. I was learning to know myself more in my painting, but this was an entirely new thing, this place where I had to face the role I might play in upholding the old system.

For my painting, I was learning to study everything about my work, and the world of others, to observe where Orientalism started and ended, and how to circumvent it to find something real. Perhaps the same could be true of the greater world. I could read and study, just as Tanveer had.

I stood and went to the window, looking toward the lake. I did not see Tanveer in the gloaming, and rested my forehead on the windowpane. How could it have gone so quickly wrong between us?

A scratch came to my door, and I flew across the room. Tanveer stood there with wildflowers drooping in his hand. "A peace offering," he said.

I flung myself into his embrace, relieved when he clasped me back fiercely.

"Forgive me, Elsie."

"No, forgive me. I am so sorry. I am so very, very sorry I didn't speak up more, that—"

He pushed me back into my room, and tilted my chin up with his thumbs. "We shall learn together, jaan."

We kissed, and then healed the wounds we'd given each other with hands and lips and flesh to flesh. The rocks of our conflict subsided under the high tide of our passion.

It was only later, our bodies close, the quilt enfolding us that he said, "It is difficult to reconcile feelings about England as a political force that has harmed my country with my feelings for you."

A pang struck my chest. "Is it? Do you dislike things about me because you dislike British things?"

"Not personally, not you."

"But I am English."

He nodded. "And the Guru tells us that all of us are equal, but that does not make it easy to love everyone."

"Is it hard to love me, Tanveer?"

"No. Never." Tenderly, he touched my jaw, stroked, the line of my neck. "Our souls are one. I love you easily and always."

I bent to kiss him, his precious mouth, so giving, so rich. Light filled me, head to toe. "That part I know is true." I closed my eyes and tucked myself into his shoulder. "The rest—I don't know." I rested there, feeling whole as I never did elsewhere. How could such a feeling be erroneous? How could such a union be anything but a good force in the world? "What if," I asked quietly, "the whole point is that we do love each other?"

His hand moved in my hair. "Then we are succeeding, at least in this."

At least in this. I shoved the world aside and nestled closer to him. Somehow, there would be a way forward for us. There had to be.

—41—

The weekend couldn't last forever, of course. On Sunday evening, we took our leave of each other and returned to our various posts and responsibilities. Tanveer continued his tour of the world of the English gentleman, much as he privately despised it. I wanted to return to the studio, but I had promised Mother I would visit her. I traveled to Herewich from Clystmere Hall as I had done so many times since arriving back in England.

This trip, I stared out the windows, adrift in memories of the days Tanveer and I had spent together. His laughter rang in my ears, his touch along my skin. I felt more whole than I had since leaving him in India, and with the optimistic heart of a young woman in love, I was sure there must be some way for us to work out a future together. Perhaps it would not be conventional, but I did not think either of us would mind.

Although he did hope to influence the course of his country through politics, a notoriously unforgiving world. The warning rippled through my glow, but I dismissed it. Love would find a way.

To my surprise, my mother met me at the station. She looked vigorously healthy, but a shadow hung in her eye. "Oh, my dear girl," she said, taking my hand. "You are a sight for sore eyes."

"What is it? Is Father declining?"

She sighed, climbing up next to me in the carriage. "He is, but that is not the trouble."

"Then what? It isn't you, is it? You look as healthy as I've ever seen you."

"I am, truly, very well. England agrees with me. Do you know I haven't had a relapse in over a year? It's remarkable."

I squeezed her gloved hand. "I'm so glad." Then I frowned. "What, then, gives you such gravity?"

"You've been the subject of a great deal of gossip, Elsie."

A wash of something—fear?—moved through my body. I knew what the gossip would be.

"Your brother is furious. He's threatening to marry you off to the Baron of Little Field."

"I don't even know who he is!"

"You would be no less horrified if you did, I assure you. It seems he saw you at some function or another and was quite smitten. He's a widower with three children and needs a wife, and spoke to your brother about it last week."

"He can't just sell me off! I have some say."

"Very little, my dear. The bare facts are that you must marry well or Herewich will likely fall to ruin."

"Why does it fall to me to save the family? And why can't *my brother* be the one to marry a fortune? An American millionairess or the like?"

"That is possible. It does not alter the reality that you've been heedlessly ruining your reputation."

I felt I'd been tossed into a cold lake. "Ruining my reputation? What do I care for a reputation? I'm an artist, not a countess."

Her smooth cheeks burned red. "Do not take that tone with me, daughter. I have always had your best interests at heart, and this—entanglement—you insist upon has ever been a detriment to your progression in life. I thought surely moving back to England would solve the trouble, and yet, here we are, years later, facing it again."

"Entanglement?" I echoed. "That hardly encompasses my relationship—"

"Do not," she said fiercely. "Do not defend this thing between you two. I should never have allowed it. It is impossible, Elsie. For both of you."

My youthful optimism bloomed and spoke. "I shall return to India. It will be less challenging there."

"Will it?" She turned to me, her eyes brilliant bright jewels. "Let me speak plainly, Elsie. You have no money, and will have none unless you marry into it. The Talwarpur estates are as poor as Herewich, if not more so. Do you not remember the crumbling rooms in the palace?" She pressed her finger into my thigh. "He is the second son and will earn his way on his wits, which are considerable, but he also has need of a wealthy marriage. Neither of you has a penny."

The words sounded so harsh in her spitting voice. It was desperately rare for her to speak in such a way to me, and the shock of it made me feel as if I should fall weeping on her lap. But I liked less what she said.

"This is not some old novel, Mother. It's the modern world. Things are changing. What need have we of riches?"

She literally groaned, and pinched the bridge of her nose. "Of all the idiotic—" She pressed her lips together. "You might not need riches," she said with an exhausted tone, "but you shall need something. Money does not rain from the sky, and only a girl who has had everything provided for her all her life could be so blind. How will you buy paint? Canvas? Brushes?"

A stone filled my gut, and I reached for her hand, but she pulled it away. We rode in silence for some distance, the only sound the clopping of the horses hooves on the gravel of the road.

Outside the carriage, the fields were green and gold, and balls of sheep dotted the grassy hills. Her words made me acknowledge the precariousness of my position, the foolishness of my dream of having a life with Tanveer.

"It isn't some fleeting love affair, you know," I whispered, trying to hold back tears. "It is a rare and beautiful connection we've woven. It's real and true, and I don't know how I can be happy without him."

She took my hand then, and I could see she was fighting tears, too. "I know. But that does not change a single fact."

A sensation of breaking ran through my entire being, my heart, yes, but my lungs turned to glass, and my head, and my eyes, and all of them shattered. I collapsed against my mother, trying not to fall to a pile of shards on the carriage floor.

Somehow, I would have to see him before he returned to India. At least we should be able to say our farewells.

—42—

July 28, 1914
London
[In Urdu]

Dear Elsie,

I cannot even think of a good thing, one tiny beauty, one single moment of joy because I will not see you again before my father whisks us back to India. He fears war will break out and prevent our return, so he insists we leave immediately. I have pleaded, but he will not listen.

Write to me, soon. I fear you will misunderstand my sudden silence. I am wretched and shall miss you every moment of every day. You are my dearest, dearest love. I do not know how I shall survive without you at my side.

With all my love,
Tanveer

August 7, 1914
London
[In Urdu]

My dearest love,
War has been officially declared, so it appears your father was correct.

I returned to London the day after your ship sailed, and wept for a day at missing the opportunity to wish you farewell. How could we not even have been afforded that single thing, a chance to say goodbye?

I am wretched, rooh ke saathi.

My brother is threatening to marry me off to a man I don't even know. The only glimmer of hope I see is in the truth that all the young heirs will march off to war to do their duty. I wish no ill on any of them, but perhaps it buys both of us a little time.

We have made no promises, Tanveer. We have not even discussed what a future together might be—and perhaps it is impossible, but I find I cannot entirely give up on the possibility that we might find a way. Am I a fool to dream such?

Peter, Grayson, and Jonathan have already enlisted. Although I have no spiritual practice, I do wish for a way to pray for this all to be over soon, and everything safely righting itself.

Yours, always, forever
Elsie

September 12, 1914
Talwarpur Palace
[In Urdu]

Dear Elsie,

It grieves me deeply to say this, but we cannot marry. I have known this always, but you persist in wishing a different future for us.

Please understand that I would be the happiest man in India if I could make you my bride. Truly. You are birdsong and morning, the comfort of sleep, the challenge of noon. Our minds are as well suited as our bodies and hearts, and I cannot imagine a world where I could ever grow tired of your company. Would that we could grow old sparring over ideas until late in the night, then share breakfast in good humor!

This vision makes me weep with longing. For me, it would be the best of all possible things.

But it would be a terrible future *for you*. You are fortunate to enjoy the very edge of modernity in your life in England. You have the freedom to explore your art and your own mind. You have freedom of movement and even the ability to defy the powers that would shape you. You are part of the new world for women, Elsie, and you must step into that leadership by becoming fully yourself. It would be impossible for you to do that in India, with me. No matter how happy we would begin, you would resent me over time. We would end up as old bitter people, despising one another, and that is a future I truly cannot bear.

If we make peace with what the truth is, this truth, that we love each other deeply and perhaps irrevocably, then we can still be friends. We would be free to remain friends, always. Always.

Never doubt that I love you. I feel you moving in the world even when I am thousands of miles away from you. I dream your dreams.

We promised we would put each other's happiness first. I am keeping my vow.

With sorrow and hope,

Tanveer

—43—

London
September 1914

It was, paradoxically, the most exquisite and most wretched evening of the summer. Lanterns had been set out in the garden of Nina's town house. Roses and jasmine filled the air, and the grass beneath our feet sent up herbal notes. I sulked in a corner, as I'd done for weeks, and Rocky was brooding over a fight with his family. Both of us had drunk rather a lot of gin. On the patio, couples danced to a record on the gramophone.

"Nina's going to marry Jon," he said, gesturing. He was quite undone, his hair tousled, his shirt unbuttoned at the throat.

"But he's—"

"Mmm. And so is she. They'll give each other shelter."

I watched them dance, laughing, spinning. "They do seem quite happy in many ways."

"Sex isn't the only unifier, is it?"

A ripple ran over my arms, my back, bringing a fresh wave of grief. I gripped his hand.

He gripped mine back. "You miss him terribly."

"Don't. I'll fall to pieces."

"He is magnificent, Elsie. Everything about him. I know why you adore him. And he clearly loves you in return."

"It's a foolish infatuation," I said, swallowing my grief as well as I could. This was my second round with his rejection, after all. A woman might learn her lesson. I trusted the truth of his love, and only thought he was misguided. Foolish. Arrogantly paternalistic.

But this time, I would make no bid to change his mind. "We'll grow up and get on with things."

He eyed me steadily. "Perhaps."

I took a breath. "Do you ever wonder why we fall in love with one person and not another? Of all the people in the world for Tanveer and me to love, we are the worst choices. If fate meant me to love him, why give me this passion for my painting, too? What's the point of that? What's the point of a prince loving a commoner who will be a terrible choice politically?"

"The world is changing. Surely there is some way? Perhaps not marriage but some other arrangement?"

"I must marry."

He scowled. "A ridiculous institution in the modern age. My father has put his foot down and insisted I will marry by year's end. Though perhaps war will prevent that." He tossed his hair back, eyes glittering. "War will give me a year or two."

"Oh, please. Not that."

Standing abruptly, he held out his hand. "Dance with me, gloomy Elsie."

He was an excellent dancer, athletic and charismatic. We danced for ages, whirling and posing, playing off each other to make the others clap and cheer. It is my fondest memory of him, his hair falling down his forehead in rakish loveliness, face clean shaven, his teeth even and white. Later, winded and sweating, we settled on a stone bench to revive ourselves.

"Thank you," I said. "I was quite devastated when I arrived this evening."

He took my hand. "If I liked women, you would be the one I'd choose."

I kissed his lips lightly. "I know. But my heart belongs to another."

He lit a cigarette, exhaled heavily. Then: "Elsie, I've had the most wonderful idea."

"Oh?"

"We should marry, like Jon and Nina. A marriage in name to save us from"—he gestured—"all the . . . mess."

I laughed. "You would be a most dashing husband."

"I am quite serious." He squeezed my fingers. "It would save us both. Two artists, sheltered. You would have your lover, and I would have mine, and no one need be the wiser."

A breath of hope whispered through the heaviness I'd been feeling. "My brother would swoon in joy." Rocky was a far better catch than the baron. "But how would your father feel?"

"He would have no say. If I choose you, he cannot herd me into marrying some simpering female who would expect me to make love to her." He leaned in, earnest. "Say yes, Elsie. We can protect each other."

In that moment, I saw a future in which I painted freely, and was supported wholly, and could even keep the friendship with Tanveer as long as he didn't marry. Which he would eventually, but at least it bought more time.

I flung my arms around his neck. "Yes. Yes, yes, yes."

He hugged me back, and stood, holding our hands to the sky. "Friends, I have an announcement. Elsie has agreed to become my bride."

~

In a week, it was official. His father was happy enough, and as I predicted, my brother swooned over the union. Even my mother, whom I'd imagined might sniff out the truth, appeared to be very happy with my choice. "I worried so that you'd run back to India and ruin your life, my love."

I did not reply. I held too much fury at her shortsightedness.

October 15, 1914
London
[In Urdu]

Dear Tanveer,
When I first received your letter, I was devastated. Again, you were protecting me from myself, giving me no say in the matter! If I am to be an autonomous woman, the right to make my own choices, for good or ill, remains mine to make. Even if you wish to protect me out of love, you are acting as a father, not my beloved.

But I began to think of how much time and training you have employed in pursuit of India's freedom, and if I am to be true to my vow to put *your* happiness above my own, then I must be truthful with myself and recognize how poor a choice a daughter of the English gentry would be for a man wishing to release India from the shackles of that country. It is exactly the worst of all choices. To insist we would be happy in the face of that challenge is more foolish than even my love can allow me to be.

I do love you, Tanveer.

In the meantime, I have reason to offer some hope for our dilemma. We may not marry, but perhaps we can find some other arrangement.

I am going to marry Rocky. It is, of course, a marriage in name only, since he has no taste for women and I have no taste for anyone but you, but this will appease our families. He's gone to recruit training, but the banns have been posted. It's official, and truly, it's remarkable how happy my brother is.

This may feel a blow, but I hope you will see what a good solution it is. We can be a modern couple, creating our own sort of union.

I say to you, as you said to me, that you are the axis of the world to me, Tanveer. I invite you to meet me in our dreams, where we are free to love as we wish, where we might spend our lives, living one world in sleep, another in the day. Shall I meet you there?

In deepest love,

Elsie

[Enclosed drawing of their hands, linked]

October 20, 1914
Talwarpur
[In English]

Dear Elsie,

It does feel a blow, though it should not. I am a fool to want both things at once, to protect you and to claim you. Rocky is a good choice, which I understand logically. My heart will need more time.

I have joined the army, which I have been trained to do since boyhood. I feel it is my duty to lead the men of our state, and perhaps it will carry weight later. When I know where I shall be posted, I shall let you know.

Your friend,

Tanveer

November 13, 1914
Clystmere Hall
[In Urdu]

Dear Tanveer,
I am heartsick at the thought of you in the army. In danger, constantly, and for what? Fighting for a country you don't believe in? Why did you do such a thing?

Write to me often, so that I know you are safe.

Elsie

BEWARE A REDHEADED WOMAN

Autumn 1940
London

—44—

A spate of bad weather gave us a respite from raids. Mother rested more than she had been able to do, and it improved her spirits significantly, although she continued to decline physically. Nina visited, which cheered me, and we agreed to meet in a week to transport the paintings to her wine cellar, which Jonathan promised would hold up against anything except a direct hit.

Better than I could expect here.

Peter arrived one afternoon and called out from the base of the stairs. I was in my studio, taking paintings from their stretchers, and looked over my shoulder to see what might be visible to his casual eye. Nothing but a painting of a chair with a length of fabric over it. He would not know what that fabric was.

"Studio!" I called, and continued to pull the fastenings from a large painting I'd done during our time in Cairo.

His step on the stair told me he was in good spirits, and he came into the room with an amiable expression. "Well, you've been quite busy!"

"I want to store them with Nina. In case."

"Wise." He was well dressed, his fair hair brushed back from his forehead. I smelled cologne and wondered where he'd been. Wandering over to the table, he touched the top painting, and moved it slightly.

"I'd rather you didn't," I said.

"Hmm." He ignored me, moving another to look below. "I've been exploring the possibility of moving Betty. It appears there might be a berth for her near Guildford. Out of the way."

I plucked a nail from the wood and placed it on the table. "Thank you. It does not appear she'll be working again."

"I'm sorry, Elsie. Wretched to lose her, I know."

I worked on the next nail. "Worse for her."

He glimpsed the painting I was loosening, and came around to give it a good look. "Cairo," he said of the flat light and suggested shapes, one of the more experimental sets, which I loved very much, angles and harsh light, and bright accents, more abstract than much of my work. "I never loved these back then, but I see now why you painted them."

In surprise, I looked at it with him. "You hated these. The whole series."

"I did." He inclined his head. "It looks like a memory, the way you see something in bits and pieces."

"That's lovely."

"Do you have more of them?"

"Of course. Only a few ever sold."

He headed for the closet with its rows of vertical shelving. "Here?"

"I'll find them." I set the hammer aside and hurried over, but he'd already entered the space, and there was hardly room for two.

"I've never been in here before." He flipped through a few at his eye level. "Are they organized by time period?"

"Peter, really, it would be so much easier to find them myself."

He glanced at me, one eyebrow raised. "Are there paintings you don't want me to see?"

"No." A lie. "I'm sure you've seen them all."

"I don't think so." He tipped one out, Channan by herself. "I do remember this. Poor thing."

There was nothing scandalous in these paintings. Still, I sensed a growing tension in him as he pulled one after another out, as if he were looking for something in particular. "Ah," he said, pulling out a portrait of Tanveer at twenty-one or twenty-two, his beard thick and glossy. "Always more of the prince. How many paintings have you done of him? A hundred? A thousand?"

"Peter. There's nothing to be gained from this."

"How many have you done of me?"

I met his gaze with apology. "Only the one." I'd painted him at the Pyramids, one of the only times he'd been reliably happy for any length of time at all. "Would you like another?"

It seemed to pierce him, and he deflated. "No." He shook his head sadly. "I wanted you to love me."

I bowed my head. "I know." I looked up at him. "I am sorry, you know."

He looked back to the vertical stacks. "Will you find one of the Cairo paintings? I'd like to hang one in my office."

"Of course." I backed out of the closet and gave him space to pass me. Our bodies brushed, and he caught my hand.

"Elsie, is there no world in which you would forgive me?" He leaned into my neck, and I stiffened. "Make love to me?"

I did not move, aware that there could be danger in moments like this, when he allowed himself to reveal the truth of his yearning. I waited, still as a stone, as he moved his hand to my belly, and simply rested it there. "I have never stopped loving you."

Still I did not speak. Another silent moment passed between us, and then he said, "Never mind the painting," and left me.

I stayed where I was for a long moment, my heart beating unnaturally fast. My education on his mercurial moods had been far too thorough during our time in Cairo. He'd been moody, prone to fits of fury, often drinking far too much.

This felt like that.

I should have to be wary, especially in light of the instability the bombings could bring to his shell shock.

—45—

November 3, 1940
Talwarpur Palace
[In Urdu]

Dear Elsie,

Do I remember the day at your art school?

I remember the light pouring from your skin as you stood in the ballroom, looking for me, and the blaze that shot from your eyes when you saw me. I felt I had been born for that very moment, when I knew it was going to be all right, that you still loved me. We kissed in the garden, and I thought I might dissolve entirely.

I remember the siren lure of you looking so closely at me as you painted, the delicious anticipation of that hour and the kisses we shared in the courtyard afterward.

I remember the storm at the party and the rain pouring down as we met that evening, alone, and burning. Have there been two lovers more in love than we were then? I cannot believe there ever have been.

What I also remember from that weekend was the terrible picnic, the colonial hysteria of the tent, the absurdity of the mix of decorations, some of it India, some of it Africa, none of it real, and the man (what was his name? Payton?) drawling his superiority into what could have been such a good day. It spoiled my mood, and I regret that deeply. If only we had known that we had so little time, I would have used it more thoughtfully. But isn't that how it always is? "If only we'd known" must be one of the oft-used phrases in the world.

Never doubt I remember. I remember all.

Stay whole, Elsie. Stay alive. I worry about you every day, every hour, thinking of the blitzkrieg raining down on you and your dear mother and all of beautiful London, destroying it.

Tanveer

PS: One small beauty is the camera I bought Channan. She has taken this photograph I think you will like. Gurdaya says he looks exactly like me at that age, which you would remember, too.

PPS: I remember you reading to me, to all of us in the hospital. It might not have seemed to have made much difference, but it was a great kindness. I remember the flowers, too. You brought them from a garden and set a little vase on each soldier's bedside. I am sure there are men from that ward who still dream of you, jaan. I am among them.

[Enclosed photo of Kirandeep, age 13]

A TELEGRAM FROM INDIA

Spring 1917
Herewich

—46—

Rocky was killed in action in France on the nineteenth of January 1917. He survived the Battle of the Somme only to die at the hands of a sniper in that brutal winter. The news reached me on a dark, rainy February day. I doubled over in pain as Nina told me, holding my hand tightly, a handkerchief in her hand. We wept together, not even able to trade stories of his beauty, his extravagant pleasure in life.

The loss was too much for either of us to anything but cling together in our grief.

His death came on the heels of several others among our set, including Grayson, and Nina's younger brother Oliver. One did not grow accustomed to it, the erasure of one young life after the next after the next. I, who had never had a minute of religion, prayed for the end of the conflict before more were sacrificed.

More, in this case, embodied by Tanveer in my mind. We continued to exchange letters, but they were the letters of friends these days, no more.

Life in London grew more bleak by the day as food grew scarce and rations were imposed. My mother had gone to America with a friend after my father's death in 1915, and my brother was stationed in Africa. Tanveer was in France, and wrote letters sporadically, falsely cheerful. I returned the same, for how could I pour out my sorrows and despair to him, who lived in the muddy trenches?

I was cold and lonely and lost.

In desperation, I closed up the London house and took myself out to Herewich, carrying with me only a carpetbag with a few changes of clothing, a sketchbook, pencils, and a tin of watercolors. I took the train from London, staring out the window, heartsick, my stomach grumbling since I'd only been able to find a single potato to cook for breakfast.

In the village, I found a few supplies—a little tea, a loaf of bread freshly made of some imitation flour that smelled nutty, and a rasher of bacon. The proprietor, Mr. Herrick, offered his son and a wagon for a ride to the estate, and I accepted gratefully.

Despite my despair, it was impossible to avoid noticing that spring was in the air, smelling of fresh grass. Late daffodils and bluebells brightened the fields and forest floor. I took the first long breath I'd had in months, feeling it along my spine.

The house had been closed for nearly two years, since my brother had gone to Africa with the war. Eyeing it dubiously, Michael said, "Are ye certain?"

I glanced over my shoulder at the imposing building, the shuttered windows. In the beds alongside the door, tulips were springing up, the bright pink and yellow cheering against the stone. "Yes, thank you."

I opened a few rooms, airing my bedroom, and dusting the small parlor that looked out to the garden. Unlike many of my friends, I was not hopeless in the kitchen, despite the years with servants—in my school days, I'd learned the basics from a cookery book, and could bake bread and make simple meals, enough to keep myself fed.

In the cellar were mealy apples and potatoes, and a great store of carrots that had been advantageously stored in sand. Some were withered beyond recognition, but many were still quite good. Using half the bacon, I made a stew of all the findings, my tongue craving the sweetness of the apples and carrots.

I still did not paint, and I did not write letters, not at first. I swept floors and dug through the clothing left behind to see what I might use. I discovered that my brother's trousers fit me quite well, as did his shirts. I made do with a pair of brogues by stuffing paper in the toe. In the evenings, I made my way through the library, losing myself in Jane Austen and Thackeray, alternating with essays and a great deal of Dickens. I sent Tanveer *Robinson Crusoe* and *David Copperfield*.

Toward the end of the second week, I wandered out to the kitchen garden. To my surprise, things were sprouting, and while I had no idea how that was possible, I availed myself of the offerings of lettuce, radishes, and spring onions. We'd been exhorted to grow corn and potatoes to help the war effort, and the next morning I walked to the village and asked for seed.

"What sort of seed, Lady Turner? Flowers and the like?"

"Oh, I wouldn't mind flowers, but no. I was thinking of potatoes, peas, carrots. The usual things."

"Well, then, I can help you with that. You'll be wanting some muscle to turn the soil after these fallow seasons. Shall I send Michael out to see you?"

"Yes," I said. "That would be helpful."

At the lending library, I borrowed a book on beginning gardening, much to the approval of the librarian, Mrs. Graves. "We have a garden club, if you like." She passed me the book, which I tucked into my bag. "Meets the second Monday of the month in the church hall. I'm sure you'll have questions."

I'd come to Herewich to isolate and heal, forgetting that the village would be inordinately interested in my doings. There were no men about, or many young people. Michael suffered a club foot and could not fight, but all the rest of the boys and men had been conscripted. It loaned the landscape a ghostly feel. "Perhaps I will," I said. "Thank you."

My last stop was the post office, where I had a thin packet of forwarded letters. One from my mother, one from my brother, one from Nina, and one from Tanveer.

I hurried home.

April 2, 1917
[Location redacted]
[In Urdu]

Dear Elsie,
One small beauty: Living with us in the trenches are a great many cats. We welcome them for company and good cheer, and for their impressive rodent killing. They make life less terrible.

Of the rest, I hardly know what to say. I think too much here, life shaped by the opposing forces of boredom and horror.

For the space of many breaths I've held my pen above the paper, trying to think what to say, what I can possibly write about all this, and I cannot think of a way to express it to you that will not be a great sucking hole of darkness. I fight despair daily. How I will return to life at the end of this is a thought that plagues me. How I long for it! The ordinary pleasures of walking under trees, laughing with friends, reading a book that is not stained by mud. We all long to soak in hot baths, and that is what we do when on leave. We soak and sleep in dry beds.

Instead, I will live in memory here, times of happiness. I was thinking of the fete my father held for his birthday and to announce his marriage to his third wife. I was so angry with him for taking yet another wife, and then my mother told me she was relieved, that it made life so much easier for her.

What I was remembering was not my mother. I think of Chhoti Billi and that quiet shed that smelled of hay, and you, and those golden days of that summer. We were so free, so unencumbered by the pressures that would corral us into our proper lives. I truly never know if I am correct, Elsie, in the choices I have made. That I continue to make. I am only trying to do the right thing, thinking of you, and my own responsibilities.

I should not say what I feel, but it seems less and less likely I should survive this war, and so you should know that as long as I live, you are the flame that burns within my heart, the sunlight on my head, the hand I reach for in my mind, always, always, always. You will ever be my love, my life, and I know you feel it, too, that we met somewhere in the ether, beyond any of this, any reality that man knows, and there our souls live always, and perhaps they have forever.

Tanveer

May 20, 1917
Herewich, England
[In Urdu]

My dearest heart and my dearest love,
You have doubtless regretted your words many times since mailing them, but please do not. I swear I shall not hold you to any of it, for I know what it has cost you to continue to hold the line between us, and I have not always made it easy.

But hear me: you are not to give up. You must fight to live, every minute. I can bear the world if I know you are in it somewhere, but not if you depart so soon. You must live this life you were given, fulfill the tasks that so weigh upon you. You are fighting for an independent India, remember that. Remember that your nation will need your hands and heart and vision—and, yes, your passion. That passion cannot be spent on a mere woman (even one so splendid as myself!) and as much as it has sometimes grieved me, I do understand. I understand because I love you, because you are the sugar in my tea and the moonlight on my head. And yes, I must believe our souls live on that other plane, always entwined.

You must live.

When you despair, turn your love to a cat, and allow it to lift your heart. Imagine it can talk.

I am sending books into which you can escape. I'm living at Herewich for the duration, for London is haunted by the faces no longer there, and food grew scarce, and my nerves could just not bear one more hour.

Here, I am painting again, painting the clouds and the flowers blooming in the garden, and I am planting vegetables to eat and share. Imagine me there if you wish, digging and dirty, wearing my brother's trousers.

You are my truest, most beloved friend, Tanveer.

You must live.

One small beauty: Robins singing in the tree outside my bedroom window every morning. It lifts my spirits to know that their children and grandchildren will be singing long after you and I have departed this earth. They'll sing again someday in those fields where you fight, too.

Be well,

Elsie

—47—

Mary delivered the telegram at 9:00 a.m. on a gloomy Monday. My heart stopped as she stood there, holding it out.

I thought of all the people I loved who might be alive until I read their death notice on that piece of paper. My mother. My brother. Tanveer. I halted, and I thought, quite definitely, that I could not bear another death. Not one more. I just could not.

But of course I would bear it, just as everyone else had been forced to do.

And then I realized that I wasn't wife or mother to any of those people, and therefore would not get a telegram. Who, then?

I reached for it, tore it open before Mary had made her way back to her bicycle.

It was from Gurdaya.

> TANVEER INJURED STOP TAKEN TO HOSPITAL IN BRIGHTON STOP HELP STOP HURRY STOP

Injured! How badly? Without a second thought, I whirled around and ran upstairs to gather a bag, taking only enough time to be certain the fires were doused in the two fireplaces I used, in the sitting room and my bedroom. Then I flew away to the railroad station.

In two hours, I was in Brighton, and a half hour after that, I stood at the doorway of the hospital.

"I'm looking for a patient," I said. "Indian. Injured at the front, probably only brought in the past day or two."

The matron, a thin woman with large kind eyes, nodded. "Most of the Indians have been moved out to Africa, so we haven't had many arrive here for quite some time. Come with me."

As we entered the ward, bed after bed after bed after bed of men, a smell unlike anything I'd known slammed me. Instinctively, I covered my face with a handkerchief, then realized how rude it must be, and lowered it again.

The matron gave me a sad shake of the head. "It's all right. You get used to it, but it takes time."

"Is it injury?"

"Some. Gangrene, trench foot, sepsis." She gestured toward a soldier still in his uniform, passed out and covered with a kind of grime that said he hadn't washed in days or even weeks. "Mostly, it's their uniforms."

The smell was so vile it had texture, carrying the scent of death, of rot, of unspeakable things. I wanted to weep, to cover my face, to run away, but if these poor souls could endure what they'd faced, I could stand up straight and meet their eyes as I passed. Some were bandaged, some had lost limbs. Some—I lifted my chin and met their eyes—had faces burned and twisted, uncovered to heal.

At last I saw Tanveer. His body was covered with a blanket, his arms in clean pajamas, but his turban was grimy and stiff with mud. He was the cleanest person I had ever known, and I could not imagine his despair at the layers of dirt and mud and God knew what else layered into it. "Has he not been bathed?"

"His injuries were stabilized in the field hospital." The matron gave me a small smile. "His men would not allow the turban to be removed. And he does not want to be parted from the cat."

"Cat?"

She pointed. Tucked into the blanket at his right side, cradled against his body, was a small yellow cat. This time, I could not help the tears. "Of course he has a cat. Why wouldn't he?"

"It is most unusual, but two men came along with him to make sure the beast wouldn't be taken away." Her eyes were bright blue behind spectacles. "They said he'd saved nine men, but he wouldn't be evacuated because he wouldn't leave her in the trenches."

I blinked my still-welling tears away. "I'll take care of it." I approached and stroked the cat's head. It meowed softly at me, green eyes tilted up happily. To the matron, I said, "What injuries did he suffer?"

Her face was grave. "Abdominal wound, which was treated in the field to stabilize it, and a badly broken arm."

I heard the reserve in her voice. "And?"

"An earlier infection in his leg that was not well treated and has festered."

I swallowed. "Will he live?"

"He requires more surgery, but he seems strong. It will be helpful to have a friend." She squeezed my arm. "Time will tell."

Time will tell. I stood quietly next to his prone, too-still form. His face had grown thin, his cheekbones too prominent. Bruises darkened his jaw and eye. His hands showed scrapes and cuts and marks of all kinds, the oval nails too long.

And yet, he was alive.

I took his hand. "I'm here, Tanveer. You are safe."

"Do not take him," Tanveer growled, an arm covering the little cat. He did not open his eyes.

"Oh, no, I wouldn't think of it."

He made a noise and turned his head away.

"I will take care of him myself."

Nothing. I stood and touched his cheek with the back of my fingers, and found it burning. "Tanveer. You must let me take the cat so you might be treated. Do you hear me?"

His head swiveled at my touch, and his eyes opened. They were red and bleary, full of delirium. In Hindustani he said, "I know it isn't really you."

I leaned in, pulled his free hand to my face. "It is me."

He stared. His fingers moved a little, as if testing the reality. "How?"

"Your sister sent me a telegram. I came right away."

"I can't . . . you shouldn't be—"

"Shh." I held his hand on my cheek. "I will take your cat and give her some food. What's her name?"

"Him. Topaz."

"All right."

"Promise you won't get rid of him."

"I would never do such a thing."

"You smell like Elsie, but I can't really see you."

"It is me. You had a cat name Shera once," I said. "We wept over a tiger that died. And your sister's name is Gurdaya."

He closed his eyes, and I saw a depth of despair cross his face. "Elsie," he whispered. "I am ruined."

"You are not. You are only exhausted and wounded. You're going to get well. I shall be here to help."

He did not look up, but allowed me to take the cat.

~

I found lodgings nearby, where an old woman with a flowered apron allowed me to bring Topaz. He wasn't more than six months old, curious and funny, very happy to curl up on the bed with its piles of quilts. Daily, we traveled back and forth to the hospital and sat with Tanveer as he first recovered from surgery to repair his gut and belly, then to clear and cauterize the infected wound in his leg. Much of the time, he was incoherent or lost in a haze of morphine, and even so, his face was often gray with pain. Topaz eagerly sat with him and purred softly, which seemed to me a thing that would be more healing than many of the other things used to treat him.

I sent Gurdaya a telegram, promising to write a letter to follow up, and as I sat by his bedside, I fulfilled that promise, glazing over the depth of his condition to give her hope so far away.

The ward was overwhelmed, with a shortage of nurses. When Tanveer slept, I offered a hand bringing meals and running errands. The local lending library had a good selection of adventure novels, so I checked out three or four and alternated reading them to one soldier and another. Most of them were desperately ill, wild-eyed. Some had injuries of both the body and the mind, staring sightlessly into nothing. Many of them suffered nightmares and awakened each other with screams. I read *Gulliver's Travels* and *The Time Machine* and even *Alice Through the Looking-Glass*, which seemed a happy favorite.

At Tanveer's side, I read Lewis Carrol and Tennyson. Mostly, I could not tell if he was listening, but sometimes, it seemed it might be getting through.

Day after day, I brought Topaz back to him, sat by his side, read to him, and then spent time with whatever jobs might help the staff. The routine kept me from despairing, for it did not seem as if Tanveer was improving very quickly, if at all.

Time will tell.

I dared not think of the world without him somewhere in it. No.

~

In the evenings, Topaz and I sat in the garden at Mrs. Bolton's. He chased insects and watched birds in branches above our heads, never seeming inclined to stray far from my side. I finished the edge of a long stretch of pale-green lawn provided by Mrs. Bolton from her attic. It had once been a summer dress, airy and light, and would be perfect for my purpose. My stitches were tidy and small, as one learned to do as a gentlewoman, and for once I was glad of the skill.

One warm day, when I arrived at the hospital, the windows were open to a soft breeze, scented with June roses. On my way, I'd gathered handfuls of wildflowers, daisies and campion, and a few stands of pink foxglove. In the hospital kitchen, I found a variety of small containers to hold them. To each of the tiny metal stands near each bed, I added a flower. By Tanveer's bed, I settled a blue glass bottle of oxeye daisies, a clutch of yarrow, and a single stalk of pink foxglove. It was cheery and very English.

Topaz settled on his chest and licked his beard, mewing softly. Tanveer stirred. "Hello, little one," he said quietly.

But he did not acknowledge me, and I did not know whether to be hurt or irritated. I chose practicality. The beds were on wheels, and I asked the floor nurse if I could push Tanveer out to the screened porch where some of the more ambulatory patients sat on warm days like this. "Might I wheel him out there?"

"Course you can. I'll get you some help."

"No need." Gardening had made me strong. Returning to his bedside, I said, "We are going on a little adventure, my friend."

He only shrugged.

It took some doing, but I maneuvered the bed to the wide-screened area. There was no one else out today—once they were well enough to sit and take the air, they were discharged or sent back to the front, a fact that layered yet another horror on top of many others. But they had to make way for more wounded.

Once Tanveer was in place nearby a view of the garden, I left him and found a deep basin, which I filled with hot water and carried back to the porch. I dragged a small table to the head of his bed, placed the basin there. "I'm going to wash your hair, Tanveer."

He scowled. "I would wait and tend to it myself."

"Your arm is broken." When he made no more protest, I began the unpleasant task of unwinding his turban. It had lain undisturbed for the entirety of the hospital stay, but as I unwrapped each layer, the stench of the battlefield rose out of it.

He protested. "Elsie, please—it is too grim a task."

I ignored him, and freed his hair, which was tied tightly in a bun. I let it down, shaking it to unravel the length, then gathered the black mass of it and dropped it in the water. Using a cup, I poured warm water over his head, over and over, working my fingers over his skull, loosening the grime, rinsing again. I squeezed it out and left to empty the basin and refill it, this time bringing shampoo with me.

He had not moved. His hair hung behind the bed, dripping, and I gathered it up and dropped it in the water, wet it all thoroughly once more, and then added shampoo. "It's not as pleasant as the spicy one you like," I said matter-of-factly, "but it will be nice to have clean hair."

I worked the soap into his scalp, using my fingers to massage it deeply. It gave me no small pleasure to so intimately feel the shape of his skull, the smooth places and the small ordinary rises and indentations. Whole. Emotion rose to my throat, but I forced it back down. He needed my practicality, not my emotion.

And yet, when I chanced to look at his face, tears streamed from his eyes. Not a small number and without sound, he wept.

Which meant I could not hold back my own weeping, but I kept it to myself, and let the tears flow as his did, silently, as I rinsed the soap away. "It needs one more rinse," I said. "I shall be right back."

He did not reply. When I returned with a pile of thin towels and the last basin of water, I rinsed his hair one more time, then squeezed it dry. Using one end of a towel, I wiped his face, and dried it, and he allowed it.

Still in silence, I combed his long, long hair, smoothing out the tangles, and then left it loose. "It needs to dry before it's wrapped again," I said. "I don't know that I can get this fabric clean enough, but I'll see what I can do."

He opened his eyes. "Elsie."

I waited, my hands full with the basin and damp towels thrown over my shoulders. As lightly as possible, I echoed him. "Tanveer?"

He touched his chest, and the darkness filled his eyes. "I don't know how to live with what's in me."

I took a breath, steeling myself. "I know."

The very faintest of smiles played over his lips. "Clean hair will help."

I smiled. "Right. Next up, a cup of tea."

~

That evening, he sat up and, as he could not lift his right arm at all, instructed me in how to pull his hair into a topknot and tie it with a small piece of muslin the matron found, likely meant for bandages. This covered his head and secured the knot. I then produced the length of cotton lawn I'd hemmed. "Will this do for a turban? It was the most similar weight to muslin. There isn't a lot of fabric available."

He touched it. "You made this?"

"Every good Englishwoman can stitch a decent hem," I said. "It's no miracle. I only worried that you wouldn't like the color."

"The color is fine." His tone was gruff. "I shall instruct you."

It might have been an embarrassment—my face was hot a few times when I had to unwind it and start again from some early place—but he was as patient as Tanveer of old, although that Tanveer might have teased me.

I finished and stepped back. "I'm sure it isn't the best. You'll be up to it yourself in no time."

He touched it with the hand he could lift. "Thank you. It feels quite tidy."

"Do you want to look in the mirror?"

"No, thank you." He stroked Topaz's long back, avoiding my eyes, and I wondered if I'd done something wrong.

"Have I offended you?"

"No." The word was fierce, but he kept his eyes lowered, and I realized that he was struggling to contain himself. "It was a great kindness. Thank you."

"I'll take Topaz then, and let you get your rest."

As I reached for the cat, who leapt to my shoulder in a routine we'd established, Tanveer touched my hand with his free hand, and said so quietly I almost could not hear him, "Mujh se yeh sab kyūñ sahā nahīñ ja rahā . . ." *Why can't I bear any of this?*

What answer was there to such pain? "Shall I read to you until you sleep?"

I thought he would refuse. Instead he said, "I would like that very much."

THE ELEPHANT AND THE SPARROW

Autumn 1940
London

—48—

November 10, 1940
Talwarpur Palace
[In Urdu]

Rafīq-e-Jān,
I have just received your letter. Do not think you must cheer me. You must pour out your heart in whatever ways it most serves you, and know that I am here, listening, every day. Thank you for the constant flow of letters and drawings. Know that I hold you in my heart every day.

The war has made its presence felt here, and it underlines the ongoing struggles. Arrests have been made of protestors, and Gandhiji has called for a return to satyagraha. The villagers, used to having men in the fields, struggle to do the farm work they rely upon. I have asked a committee of village elders, Sikh, Muslim, and Hindu, to counsel the women on best farm practices, and I am pleased to report that it seems to be reaping rewards. (A little joke.)

One small beauty today. I can smell rotis on the fire. Soon we will eat them for our midday meal, which I suspect will have carrots. It has been a very good year for carrots.

Here is a little fable. Once there was a sparrow who built her nest upon the ground, and a careless elephant stepped on it. Vowing revenge, the sparrow enlisted the help of her friends, a woodpecker, a frog, and a fly. The woodpecker pecked his eye, the fly buzzed to confuse him, and the frog croaked to lure him into a hole, where he fell and died.

England has survived everything thus far. She will survive this onslaught, too.

You are managing a great deal of trouble with grace. Never doubt it. Take care of your own precious self even as you care for others. Paint as much as you are able. Read for escape. Tend your garden. Let a cat purr you into hope. That body of yours contains the soul I love more deeply than any in the world.

Tanveer

I found myself painting for very long hours, whenever I felt it safe to be so close to the sky, whenever Mother rested. The paintings I'd removed from their frames waited in a pile on the table, while others sat in the closet, and I painted new work.

The images of women were stacked, set aside, not quite jelling, the original drive lost somewhere in the bombing. They leaned against the wall, forgotten, while I mixed a palette of soft pastel shades, a dusty golden yellow, the soft dull green of grasses late in the summer, flashes of orange and bright cerulean blue. I painted my memories of India. Tanveer and Gurdaya and I sitting on the banks of our pond, our clothes drying in the sun, our feet bare. The three of us on the rooftop the night we saw the tiger. I painted a memory of my ayah, smoking in a hidden place with a servant whose name I couldn't remember, the pair of them laughing. Childhood, hazy and beautiful.

And I painted tigers, weaving in and out of trees, like Cheshire cats, peering at the viewer as if at that little girl I'd been, longing for connection with a wild, free creature.

Mother was increasingly unwell. Her belly swelled and her breath took on a sweetish smell. But the worst were the days she did not seem to recognize me, or when she thought we were in another time. One afternoon when she awakened after a long sleep, she appeared to be quite lucid, but she kept telling me about her daughter.

"I am your daughter, Elsie," I said.

"No, Elsie has gone to Cairo. She's having an adventure."

I picked up the cat and settled her on Mother's legs. "Is she now? What sort of adventure?"

"She's exploring the Nile! Can you imagine? Her husband is quite the amateur archaeologist."

"I see." I offered the thin oatmeal I'd made. "Will you have a bite or two?"

"Oh, no. I've already eaten today. We had pork tamales. I do not always love them, but Elena makes them beautifully. Such exquisite masa."

It made no difference what I said when she entered these delusions, and it seemed kinder to let her live in them. I kept my sketchbook on my lap and drew Bastet and a kitten who laboriously climbed the coverlet to find her. "I have never had a tamale. I would like to someday."

"Elsie is not happy," she said, plucking at the sheet.

I stilled. This was a new turn. "Oh?"

"She does not love Peter. He is a good man, and he is supporting her well, but she's never learned that we must make compromises."

"*Is* he a good man?" I asked, adding depth to Bastet's fur with a hard mark.

"Oh, yes. Good family. He adores her, but she pines for that prince. Always the prince. She thinks I don't know."

"You did know," I said, unable to resist. "She wrote you letters during the Great War. She told you she wanted to marry him."

"And I told her it was as impossible then as it ever was."

"You were living a life of great freedom in New Mexico, with a great love. Why were you so sure your daughter could not have the same thing?"

She shook her head. "She romanticized that connection. He would never have married her."

How had I never recognized how she really felt about my connection to Tanveer? It seemed she'd always spoken one thing and believed another. "He loved her."

"Perhaps. But how ever would I have explained her marriage to anyone?"

A flush of anger crept up my neck to my cheeks. I could no longer sit with her. "Good night, Mother."

—49—

The raids let up a bit, and twice in a week, I slept deeply, waking up in my own bed. It improved my mood tremendously. Mother, too, seemed a little less delusional, although her physical condition was deteriorating rapidly. Mrs. Cotton offered to come in and keep her company while I ran errands. Peter kept an eye out for a suitable refugee to help, but in the meantime, Mrs. Cotton was a godsend. I'd given her one of the kittens, and I took a pair of kittens to Nina for companionship, and we made plans to move Mother there. Of course, I would come, too.

One morning, I dug up a handful of potatoes. The night had been a long one, bombs dropping for hours, though nothing much landed close by. Even when the bombs didn't fall, the noise of guns and shrapnel and droning planes created enough noise to keep us awake. Mother had had an episode of coughing up blood overnight, and now slept after a tea she'd instructed me to make from milk thistle and valerian. Her skin was raw from scratching, and later I would bathe her in chamomile and oat straw, but in the meantime, I was very hungry and a sturdy potato soup with new leeks would go a long way toward comfort. In the kitchen, I listened to the radio, humming along with a symphony, and scrubbed the skins clean. When the phone rang in the hallway, I dried my hands and picked up. "Hello?"

"Elsie. There you are."

Tanveer.

Every bit of tension in my body drained out, and I sank to the telephone chair. "And there you are. Oh my, what a sound for sore ears."

A low plane flew overhead, and I winced, seeing the shadow pass over the window, but I would not leave this phone even if the bombs dropped in the front garden. In Hindustani, he said, "Tell me how you are, mere chiriya."

I bent myself into the call, making a circle with my body to create a world for our voices. In the same language, I said, "Your voice is a gift. It cheers me immensely just to hear you."

"What are you doing this morning?"

I answered in English, "Scrubbing potatoes. Very glamorous. You?"

He switched to English, "I have a meeting with some members of the Indian National Congress. I do not think it will go anywhere, but I will show up anyway." His voice was warm, low. "It gave me an opportunity to call you again. Are you all right?"

I reached for the words in Hindustani, which I did not practice enough these days. "As well as can be expected. It was a terrible night, honestly. I'm going to move my mother to Nina's so it will be safer for all of us."

"Why is it safer? Fewer bombs?"

"No, it feels like they circle, and hit every area on rotation. She has a wine cellar, and it is quite deep."

"Of course she does." He chuckled. "This sounds like a very good plan."

Such mundanities! "I wish I could say something profound or meaningful," I said. "Something worthy of the call."

"This is the worth for me, Elsie. To hear your voice and know you are alive and well. Shall I bring poems to read to you?"

"Honestly, you could say peas and carrots over and over and I would be happy. It cheers me more than I can say to hear your voice."

"Peas and carrots. You've said that before. I don't know what it means."

"Never mind. I'll tell you in a letter. How is Channan?"

A pause. "No better, I'm afraid."

It made my chest ache. "Give her my love."

A crackle worked through the line, almost too loud. "—for her."

"I missed that, I'm afraid."

"I can't hear you very well."

A harsh sense of loss pierced my chest. "Do not hang up! Not yet!"

The line went dead. I waited for another call, but it did not come. Buoyed and despondent in equal measure, I returned to the potatoes. In the basket by the stove, two kittens curled up together, and I picked them up, burying my face in their fluffy necks, and allowed myself to weep for the space of a single minute. A minute was all I could spare, and when I deemed it long enough, I settled the babies back in their places, dried my face, and picked up the potatoes.

And in some spare gift of grace, I remembered that much of what was seeing me through these dark days was the experience I'd gained in the last war, when I'd retreated to Herewich and learned how to feed Tanveer and myself on meager rations and the garden.

A REPUBLIC OF SMALL THINGS

Summer 1917
Herewich

—50—

Within a few weeks, Tanveer was stable enough to leave the hospital. I arranged for a car to drive us to Herewich, a distance of some two hours. He didn't speak on the journey, only looking out the window with the cat in his lap.

Some part of me wanted to fuss, to make sure he was comfortable, that his legs weren't too cramped, to offer him water. I resisted. The summer landscape offered poppies and daisies and Queen Anne's lace; sheep grazing in green pastures, trees bending down over brooks. A cow stood nearby a pond, clouds reflecting in the water.

I wondered what passed through his mind, if he would ever begin to talk to me again. Aside from a few directions, and the moments when I washed his hair, he had barely spoken since I'd arrived at the hospital.

At Herewich, I realized the journey into the house would be a challenge. The front entrance was approached by a wide, high rise of steps, and then we would face a long journey to the sitting room. "Pull around to the back," I said to the driver.

The kitchen was level with the back garden. "This will be better. Will you help me, good man?"

He looked uncomfortable, which bewildered me, but I didn't have time to sort out judgments or nonsense. "We must get him into the house. I am not strong enough for him to lean on."

Grimly, Tanveer leaned on him, his arm in a sling useless to hold a cane. I wrapped my arm around his waist. "Use my body to keep the weight off your leg."

Between the three of us, we navigated into the cold house, through the kitchen and into the sitting room. Once we had him situated in a comfortable wingback chair, the man brought in our things. I carried Topaz into the house, where he happily sniffed and explored and peered under stoves. "I can use a good mouser, little one."

Tanveer sat upright, but his face was gray with effort. "Are you in pain?"

"A little."

I reached into my deep pockets. "The matron sent morphine with me."

"No. Thank you."

"I shall make tea, and then decide how to make you a bed."

He leaned gingerly back into the chair, closing his eyes. I pushed an ottoman over and lifted his feet onto it.

"Right. I'll get the fire going. There won't be any fresh milk."

"No matter."

"It won't take long."

I hurried out of the room to hide my collapsing resolve. It had seemed such a good choice to bring him to Herewich, where he could convalesce as long as was required. I had not taken into account stairs and drafty cold rooms and the fact that I had no nursing ability whatsoever and he still had a long road ahead for recovery.

In the kitchen, I took a full minute to lean on the counter and bend my head in faint despair, feeling all my inadequacies and the stilted nature of our communication. It was hard to be with this version of Tanveer. At times, I felt he despised me, or if not me personally, then my world; at others, I glimpsed the extreme sorrow that cloaked him like a shroud. I wanted to ease his suffering, not add more.

After a moment, I straightened, blew out my fear, and started the fire. In truth, I was all he had here in England. What I could offer was comfort, kindness, and a brisk attendance to his physical needs.

So I put the kettle on, scrounged up sugar and tea, and what was left of a tin of biscuits. On a shelf in the pantry were three cans of condensed milk, a favorite of my mother's, and it felt like a minor miracle. The potatoes still looked solid, and surely someone in town had some eggs. I should see about purchasing some chickens of my own.

While the water heated, I moved to the sitting room to build a fire in the hearth, pleased with my ability to get it going properly in a matter of minutes. As it caught, I shook open the drapes to let in the light. Blue sky peeked through puffy clouds, and a bird whistled on the branch of lilac bush. Topaz came running to squeak at it. "Mice, little one. Not birds, do you hear me?"

Hands on my hips, I looked around the room to see how to best create a sickroom, or a wellroom or whatever we would call it. I could drag a mattress down from upstairs easily enough, and create a little nook with the chair so he could read by the window and take advantage of the fire.

"Is it always so cold in here?" he asked.

"Afraid so. Centuries of English damp."

"It's summer."

"Imagine what it's like in the winter."

He lifted his brows.

When I brought the tea and the slightly stale biscuits, I said, "I'm going to ride my bicycle into town and go to the market. I'll bring back a boy to help me move things around so you can be comfortable down here without having to navigate stairs." I took a breath and dived into the next question. "Shall I bring you a bedpan?"

He closed his eyes. "Elsie, I don't—"

"I know. It's all terribly awkward, and I don't how to do any of this, either, but this is better than the places they would have sent you, *and* if I don't care for you properly, Gurdaya will never speak to me again."

He gave a slight nod. I helped him with the badly fitted English coat and shoes and left him alone with the bedpan I found in the closet of my father's bedroom.

We managed.

~

I rode my bicycle into the village, finding pleasure in the vigorous exercise. At the market, I found oatmeal and tea, cheese and baked beans. There was no bread, but Mr. Herrick promised there would be in a day or two. Local farmers supplied quarts of whole milk.

The bounty was in the produce—a gorgeous cabbage, spring onions, and joy of joy—cherries! We were lucky enough not to need sugar—I still had a five-pound sack in a glass jar to keep the pests out, left over from before the house had been shut up, long before we knew everything would be rationed. There had not been a similar boon in flour, unfortunately, but I would make do.

At the post office, I stopped in to send a telegram to Gurdaya. TANVEER HOME WITH ME AT HEREWICH STOP CONDITION FAIR, BUT HEALING STOP SEND SPICES LENTILS STOP SEND LADY ELSIE TURNER, HEREWICH MANOR, FOREST VALE ENGLAND STOP LETTER TO FOLLOW.

Mr. Herrick's son, Michael, drove me back in the wagon, and then stayed to help me create a nest for Tanveer in the sitting room. We dragged a mattress down from the bedroom nearest the stairs, along with sheets and blankets I shook out and aired on the line. I wondered if he still preferred a flat pillow, and found one I thought he would like.

After Michael left, I helped Tanveer change into striped pajamas that must have belonged to a guest of the house, because neither my brother nor my father were tall, and these fit him well.

We ate a simple supper of potato soup, made with milk and margarine and some of the spring onions floating on top. He tasted it gingerly, and in surprise raised his head. "You cooked this?"

"I learned to cook when I was at Slade. I hadn't the funds to eat at cafés and the like."

"It is very nice."

"Thank you."

When we finished, it was plain he was entirely exhausted.

"Shall I read to you?"

"Please."

I picked up the novel I'd borrowed from the library before I left and settled in the chair opposite the pallet nestled against the wall. He leaned against a pile of pillows, stroking Topaz's back. He grew sleepy. "Elsie, will you take off my dastaar? I shall sleep more soundly without it. I cannot do it myself."

My heart rustled. "Of course." As matter-of-factly as possible, I knelt beside him, and untied, and unwrapped, folding the fabric as I went. "Do you generally sleep with it or without?"

"At home, always without."

"It's been a while, then."

"So long."

Down to the thin patka; I removed that, too, and paused. "Hair tied up or let down?"

"Do you have a brush?"

"Of course." I found my wide pig bristle, and gave it to him, watching as he brushed with vigor and obvious pleasure. He sighed audibly, a sound of relief. "Do you mind doing the rest?"

I smoothed out the side of his head he couldn't reach, trying to keep myself aloof, above, apart. But my hands trembled slightly as I tugged out a tangle, smoothed curls into waves. His eyes were downcast as I worked, his lashes making a line so thick and dark against his cheek that I was reminded of the child who'd wept with me over a tiger, the youth who kissed me in a hay-filled barn, the young man who'd attracted every eye in Hyde Park.

Emotion filled me like a tide, overwhelming and intense, but I said carefully, "Done." I stood, as if nothing could be more ordinary.

"I would like it back into a topknot, please."

"Of course." This took a little more doing. I knelt beside him and brushed the mass into a rope, winding it around and around until I could secure it at the crown of his head. "That should hold."

"Thank you." He tested it with his good arm. Then: "Will you sleep down here? Next to me?"

I kept my face natural. "Of course."

He must have sensed my turmoil, for he said, "No, no. I'll be all right."

I knelt, pressed a hand to his shoulder. "I don't mind."

At last he met my eyes. For one long moment, we swam together through all the selves we had been, and I reached for him, trying to bring him back, but he looked away. "Thank you."

~

I had to finish evening tasks and my own ablutions. By the time I came back down, wearing a voluminous and modest nightgown, he was very sleepy. I turned the lamp off and settled beside him but not so close we touched.

To my surprise, he took my arm and looped it across his belly. "Is this all right?"

"Yes," I whispered, and pressed my forehead against his shoulder. His belly was warm beneath my forearm, and the precious movements of his breath pressed upward, let go. In the silence, touching him, I closed my eyes, and the long day pulled me into sleep.

~

A simple domestic routine sprang up over the next few weeks. The vegetable garden I'd planted in the spring needed weeding and tying and picking off slugs from whatever they were feasting on each day. I found some young hens, and Michael helped me patch the chicken coop to protect them from foxes.

There was the cooking. I did a great deal of it myself, but in truth, the skills I had learned to feed myself in art school were hardly equal to the needs of preparing healthy meals every day, and I did want to feed Tanveer well for the sake of healing.

I had resisted a servant in the house, but finally allowed Mrs. Newsom from the library to send her daughter, Polly, to help with kitchen and food tasks twice a week.

Michael helped with the heavy chores in the garden, moving and hauling, while I pulled weeds and tied up beans and harvested peas and lettuces until they gave out, then took pleasure in tomatoes and summer squashes. I lost the cucumbers to a pest, and the corn never thrived, which Michael blamed on the damp spring.

The unexpected delight was my mother's cutting garden. Much of it had been there for generations, and I remembered her making bouquets and filling vases. I followed suit, cutting red hollyhocks to pair with white daisies, or fluttery cosmos with sturdy white daisies, sprays of blue delphinium and orange calendula, whose petals shimmered with light. I painted vase after vase in a sunny window in the kitchen, playing with color, shape, light, in a way that felt freer than anything I'd ever done since childhood. I marveled at the petals, the different shapes and pistils and stems.

Of all my tasks, the ones I minded least were helping Tanveer. Until he could lift his arms and walk easily on his own, he relied on my help to wash each day, to bind his hair in the morning, and take it down to brush it at night, to once a week be helped into a bath where he could soak and heal his sore limbs.

My physical body performed these tasks briskly, preserving his dignity and privacy as much as I was able. It mortified him to be so reliant. I often kept up a soft little patter of words, telling him about the garden or the birds I'd seen on a walk, or the weather, which was mild and ridiculously beautiful. The words provided a screen to protect both of us.

Even as my physical self acted efficiently and more adroitly, a ghostly version of me bent to his head and kissed his crown, stroked his shoulder with comfort, whispered kindness and love in his ear. My spirit self tried to coax his soul out of hiding, so it could be tended as well, but it remained hidden.

No matter his ills or how I wished he would talk more freely, I relished the luxury of time I had in his company. I was grateful that he'd come into my care.

And each day, my love for him grew. How could it not?

~

Slowly, he grew more mobile, graduating from spending most days in the chair in the sitting room to a chair I set out in the garden. In the mornings, we ate eggs and bread, which Polly brought to me from the bakery every third day. Afterward, I turned to my chores and he turned to reading, one book after another from the overflowing shelves in the library, where he'd sit in my father's leather chair, facing the open French doors. He read H. G. Wells and Henry James, and Dickens, but never made much commentary. It was as if he used the books to disappear. I'd done the same when I'd first arrived from London.

We spoke a little, here and there, about the weather and the new harvest I brought in. When the hens began laying, he enjoyed collecting the eggs. Topaz had brought home a little tuxedo cat, who had her kittens in the henhouse, teaching the kittens they might be chickens, and it charmed him entirely.

Every evening, we ate by the fire and read our separate books.

And at bedtime, I stretched out beside him like a sister, and he took my arm or my hand, and I nestled against his side, and we slept. It gave him comfort to have me there.

Of course I felt desire at times, when I awakened at night especially to discover he had enveloped me in his embrace, holding me so close to his body that his breath whispered over my ear, when the scent of him filled me with dizzy hunger.

But what I longed for most was his voice, his thoughts. I had never been so long deprived of them. I feared his silence made his suffering worse, like a boil that infects the soul. He had nightmares in which he cried out in despair, shouting until he awakened himself, and could not settle again for hours after.

One morning, after such a night, I rose long before he was awake. He lay on the pallet asleep, his hair fallen out of its knot to spill over his shoulders. His beard had filled in again after the damage of the battlefield, making it thick and glossy, a man's beard, not a boy's. A shaft of light slanted over him, touching his neck, and his long beautiful hands. Looking at him, sleeping there, I was stricken by such a sense of love that I nearly could not breathe.

Sitting at the little desk, I took out a sheet of paper and began to write.

> *July 27, 1917*
> *Herewich*
> *[In Urdu]*
>
> Dear Tanveer,
> This morning, I watch you sleep after a terribly restless night. You appear to be more yourself each day. I see your flesh return to cover your bones, and the color has returned to your cheeks, but I know you suffer still.
>
> I do not know how to help you, but here is one small beauty: I am so deeply grateful that you are still alive, that the terrible things did not kill you and take you off the earth where I could never hear your voice again.

At the same time, I miss you, the you who spoke to me of everything, stars and books and independence and love and duty and ridiculous jokes. I miss knowing what is in your heart, and I think you must miss expressing what's there.

It must be so terribly lonely.

Despite the strangeness of this situation, I expect nothing of you but friendship, so if it is your fear that I will misinterpret this queer intimacy we are sharing, do not worry. I shall be entirely circumspect in every way and never imagine you mean anything but friendship.

But it would be remiss of me not to say that I love and care for you as a person, as my friend, as a man I hope to help live well and whole in the future. How might I do that, mere ham-nafas?

Elsie

I folded the letter and placed it in an envelope with his name in full, just as I would have done to mail it, and I left it on the table. In the kitchen, I grabbed a hunk of the dry brown bread we'd been eating, and headed out to the garden.

When I returned to the sitting room hours later, he was nowhere to be found, but on the table was a folded sheet of paper with my name on it.

July 27, 1917
[In Urdu]

Dear Elsie,

One small beauty: a vase of red and white flowers you've set in the window, cheerful and alive.

Another: the troop of kittens marching into the field behind their mother, off for a hunting expedition, their tiny tails in the air.

Another: your face flushed with steam when you cook, which makes me think of another time your cheeks flush so red.

Another: the delicate feeling of your wrist against my belly at night.

Another: the quick paintings you make, a cat or a flower or me.

Another: the way you hum to yourself when you arrange flowers.

Elsie, I truly do not mean to be cruel. I simply do not know how to reach through the cage enclosing me. I fear if I let any of it leak out into the world, all of it will, and I will be consumed by rage and darkness and that will only add to the evil in the world.

You are not the sun and stars. You are the very earth, the air that I breathe. Please do not think otherwise.

Tanveer

—51—

I sent for my paints and other supplies. Opening them, smelling the oils, made my heart sing, and I bustled about with purpose, setting up an easel left over from my girlhood in the sunny window, where I could paint as many still lifes as I'd like. On the table, I set out charcoals and paper for Tanveer, but he did not use them.

He had grown well enough to take up long walks, much as I had done when I first arrived here, following the public footpaths for miles and miles. It gave him both physical and mental vigor. The fresh air and sunshine worked their own magic.

Slowly he began to talk to me again. Not about anything of his experiences, but about the walks and what he saw. He saw bluebirds, he said, and sat under a willow tree with fingers trailing in the water. He wanted to know the names of the grasses.

Sometimes, at evening, we ambled the back lanes companionably and came back to drink chamomile tea I made from flowers in the garden. Topaz followed us around, disinclined to wander far. I read aloud, or Tanveer did. Nothing in Urdu, for my books were back in London, and his were lost somewhere in the trenches. We found some enjoyment in Shakespeare's comedies, and he proved to be a good mimic.

We had moved upstairs, to my room, where the bed was more comfortable. He no longer needed my help with his dastaar, morning or night, but sometimes he asked me to brush his hair. I wanted to wrap it around my wrists, my neck. I wanted to lean into that place below his ear, the tender spot on his neck.

I did not.

When we first moved upstairs, he asked if it was too much to ask that we continue to sleep together. The unspoken chasteness was there. "I don't mind," I said. I found peace in the stolen time, however it had happened. Peace in the feeling of him close by, the sound of his breathing, the way he always turned to me in the night and pulled me close to his body and we spooned as if we were lovers.

Well, we had been, and learned it then.

His nightmares lessened. His body was healing.

His mind and soul were still desperately injured, and I didn't know how to help.

~

July 10, 1917
Taos, New Mexico, USA

Dearest Elsie,

It took over a month for your letter to arrive here. Thank the heavens that Tanveer survived such terrible wounds, and how very wise of Gurdaya to alert you. I dearly love the boy and wish for him to thrive. I have enclosed two recipes for teas to help heal bones' internal wounds, and one for a poultice should the wound show signs of festering. Washing it once a day preemptively would be a wise choice. You will find the herbs all in jars in the pantry, clearly labeled, but if you should run low, you can find them in the medicinal garden I planted toward the back of the second avenue. It is in full sun there and surrounded by a wicker fence. I've drawn references for each. They will not be hard to distinguish, and should all be readily available. Even after years of neglect, I suspect they will be growing vigorously.

While I am relieved Tanveer has survived, I cannot help but express concern over your tending him. Is there no other place for him to go? I suppose there is not, but I well remember the state of my daughter's heart at the end of his last visit to England—and before that, when we left India. You are raw with the losses of war and will be vulnerable to your old feelings.

Protect yourself, my darling. He means quite well, as do you, but I fear this episode will only lead to more suffering for both of you.

In other news, I am settled in Taos, New Mexico, which is a landscape that would take your breath away. Towering red rocks and impossibly deep canyons, and a sky so blue and endless I feel I could fly right away. I understand why so many artists are drawn here, and I hope this war will someday end and lead you here to visit me. It would excite your imagination deeply, I know it.

I remain quite smitten myself with Garvey. It is such a delightful adventure to follow him out west, giving me the opportunity to see things I never dreamed I would see at such a late date in my life. To find love after forty, and travel across America, imagine! The wonders of life.

I love you very much, Elsie. Send me a painting or two.

Mother

~

In late July, I made a pudding with the blueberries ripening in the Moores' field, sweetened with honey and covered with cream. The day had been hot, and the rooms inside the house were muggy and still. We carried our bowls outside to the terrace and sat in the still evening. Gold light slanted through the woods to the west, like fingers poking through branches. A pair of sparrows whistled somewhere close by. Crickets whirred in the grass.

"It is so quiet here," Tanveer said.

"Mmm. Peaceful." And then I worried it was the wrong word to use, but pushed forward. "Not like the trenches, I suppose."

"Sometimes it was quiet there."

He finished the berries and set the bowl aside. I found my gaze on his hands, folded calmly, the length and grace of his fingers, the oval nails, and I wished I could reach for them.

Unexpected emotion rose in my throat, fierce and insistent. "I hate that there is this gulf between us, Tanveer," I said. "All of our lives we've been able to talk, and now you've gone somewhere else." I blinked, irritated with the tears welling up at this burbling truth. "I miss you, and you're sitting right here."

He did not reach for me, only looked up to the treetops. After a long moment, he said, "Do you know the story of the Battle of the Saragarhi?"

"No, I don't think so."

"In my father's youth, there was a skirmish at Saragarhi, on the outskirts of the Afghan border. Twenty-one Sikh soldiers squared off with ten thousand Afghan tribesmen, and decided to fight to the death rather than surrender."

I listened.

"Of course they were all martyred, but they fought so bravely that even the British honored their sacrifice, and their bravery was held up as an example of Sikh mightiness, and what a good soldier would do for the empire."

He paused so long that I thought he'd finished. "As a boy, I imagined myself as one of them, taking down a dozen Afghans with my sword before we all fell to the glory of battle." He tapped his chest. "I believed in that bravery, that glory. The fierceness of battle, the lions of the Punjab."

I remembered, suddenly, Tanveer the boy slashing the air with swords made of tree branches, leaping to the top of rocks to fight off his invisible enemies. "I remember your tree swords."

He looked up at me, surprised, as if he'd forgotten I would know such a thing. "Yes." He shook his head. "I went to France because I was proud of my warrior heritage, proud of the grand deeds I have heard about all my life. I believed that if we could turn this tide for the empire, we might truly win independence at last."

A pinch ached in my lungs. Above us, a blackbird called out its sweet song, and another answered deep in the forest.

He continued, "The Sikhs I fought with in France did not die in honor. We did not give our bravery to any great cause. We swam in the mud, mud layered with the dead, for the very people who are going to destroy my people." He looked at me. "Why did we do that? Why did I do it? I knew better."

His eyes burned. I placed my hand on his arm, lightly, and did not look away.

"There was no honor in that slaughter, Elsie. Maybe there never is. Maybe the battle cry is a lie. It serves no purpose but building the fortunes of men in castles far away."

I hardly knew what words to choose to allow this boil to continue to drain. I chose no words, only my hand, steady on his arm.

"I do not know how to move forward from this, from what I saw, the things that haunt me. I cannot bear to tell you, to put those visions in your mind, but I feel the poison of it in me."

"You are a storyteller, jaan. Perhaps you should write it all down."

"And then what?"

"Perhaps nothing. Perhaps you'll burn the pages when you're done, and let the alchemy create something . . . else. Maybe a world that's better."

He looked toward the rooftops again. "I will consider that." His hand turned, palm upward, and I reached over to place mine against his. He closed his fingers over mine, and then surprisingly, lifted my hand to his lips and pressed a fervent kiss there. In Urdu, he said, "I miss you, too, Elsie."

I kissed his hand in return, and then we sat in a quiet evening that was slightly less lonely, side by side.

—52—

We carried the bowls and spoons into the kitchen, and as I washed them, Tanveer called for Topaz, who came running at his name, and twirled around the kitchen hoping for snacks. Tanveer spoke in a lilting singsong, sliding between Punjabi and Hindustani and English in a combination I couldn't follow. I smiled as I dried the bowls.

Tanveer moved behind me, and when I began to shift out of the way, he stopped me with a hand on my shoulder. Softly, he bent to sweep the hair away and planted a kiss on my neck. I did not move, waiting, my heart suddenly pounding, as he kissed me again, this time at the joining of my shoulder and neck. His hands curled around my upper arms, and then slid around my torso, pulling me closer to him. "I miss you," he said quietly. He kissed my neck, my jaw, my temple. "I miss you."

The simmering heat in my veins, held so tightly for months, flared with such ferocity that I feared he might burn his hands on my skin, that his lips would blister as they crossed the terrain of my shoulder. I turned, lifting myself up to capture his face, holding it between my hands, half beard, half skin, as he bent down and we met in a kiss that seared my lips, our tongues both hot and soothing, exploring and diving. Our hands pulled at each other's clothes until I broke away and took his hand. "Upstairs."

In the moonlit bedroom where I had ached for him so many times, we shed our clothes, and moved together, flesh to flesh, familiar and yet so new. We made love with greed, filling the room with all the light in the world. I wept as a lock of his hair fell on my face, and he kissed me as if my mouth were the source of all things. He filled me and I held him.

If something had struck me dead right then, I would have lived enough.

In the darkness, above me, he said, "You are my only one, Elsie. I will always love you. Always." He kissed me. "Hamesha." Kissed me. "Hamesha."

Later, in the dark, as we lay cradled together, he traced the line of my ribs upward to my collarbone, and back down, watching his fingers make the journey. In Hindustani he said, "It is so mysterious, why we love who we love."

I could not always be as articulate as I wished in Hindustani, so I replied in English. "Is it mysterious, Tanveer? I well know why I love you."

He smiled a little, and that smile was itself a triumph. "Do you? Tell me."

I had to pause and consider how to express it, and I wanted to say it in Urdu, our meeting place. "Because you say what you mean, and mean what you say. You're never some pretend version of you." I touched his head. "You have a fine, rich mind, and you like to talk."

"Not so much lately."

"I have faith it will return."

"I do want to talk now, to you. And hear more of my attributes."

I laughed. "You talk and perhaps I will give you more."

He leaned over to rub his nose over my cheekbone. "I love your smell, like roses and cardamom, and something I always feel like I should recognize, but I think is only you. I love the way you laugh when you're surprised by something, this loud shout that seems very large coming from a fairly small person."

"I am hardly small." I wiggled closer, taking delight in the brush of his thigh against mine. "But do go on."

"I love how you see things, everything. Petals and teacups and faces, and then put it on paper." He tucked a lock of hair behind my ear, lingered on my earlobe. "You are mighty. You stand up for what you believe. But mostly, you are just you. No other."

"It is impossible to imagine anyone but you standing in this place in my heart," I said.

"I have never tried to imagine anyone but you."

The looming impossibility of all the things that still stood between us walked in to the room then, but I ignored them and flung my legs over him. "I never have, either. There is no other you, my love." I kissed him. "Hamesha bas tum hi." *Only ever you.*

~

Of course I did not think he would be instantly healed by a sliver of confession and our renewed physical connection. He was not. He still suffered nightmares, and walked for miles to pace out his torturous thoughts.

But the physical overtook us on those hot August days. We tangled and tumbled and spent more time naked than clothed. All I could think about was the taste of him, his hands on me, the slightly drunken glaze of desire over each day. He reveled in it as much as I did, waylaying me with kisses on the stair, or biting my neck playfully as I cooked food, or sliding a wicked hand under my skirts.

I did not think him healed, but it did appear he was healing.

—53—

September 2, 1917

Dear Mother,

I am so delighted to hear about your life in Taos. It suits you, and I can feel the energy in you glowing across the sea. Tanveer is healing, though he cannot walk without instability yet, a good thing because he has declared he will not participate in the war any longer. He does not speak of it in any detail, but the horrors of the trenches have left a mark on his soul.

Of course, he cannot return to India just now, either. We stay in Herewich, living an ordinary domestic sort of life, time out of time. I paint and cook, he walks and collects eggs and is making his way through the entirety of the library, and in the evenings, he writes and writes and writes, working out for himself the history of colonialism, and the British in India, and how to move forward from it. He has been corresponding with some of his fellows in India. They have elegant arguments and debates about the way to shape the future, and trade books on various ways to tackle the subject. I fear I do not have the same power of mind as they display, but I grasp the need for deep change, and the difficulty of creating a new India with so many disparate parts. How to unify them?

And you may surmise we have formed a unit again, as we have in the past. I know you worry, but I am an adult woman now and realize that not all connections have a fairy-tale ending. He will return to India. I will return to London to paint. Perhaps we will meet again, perhaps we will not.

But I refuse to believe this is a wrong choice. To say I love him is entirely inadequate, like comparing the twinkle of a distant star to the force of the noonday sun, and it is the same for him.

At any rate, it was inevitable that it should happen this way. I could not leave him in hospital.

Please don't worry. I would rather have these days and months, knowing they will shatter us (again) than to never experience this depth of love. Not everyone is so fortunate as to love and be loved in such a way.

Now we are going to walk the lanes, but not to town. Harriett Snowden lost her son Jake two weeks ago, and every time she sees Tanveer limping through the streets, she sneers that he could be back at the front.

How long until it ends? Daily the death of another one of my group, or another student from Slade, or a son of the village, comes by letter or grapevine. At least Tanveer has not died. And my brother so far survives as well. I had a letter from him a week ago. It was quite strange, fanciful, and Tanveer said perhaps he has desert madness. It is said to plague men sometimes.

Please write and entertain us with cheerful stories from the American West! I want to know everything.

I miss you.

Love, Elsie

In early October, the rain began. Tanveer was trapped inside the house, and he paced like a tiger, down the passageways to the closed-off rooms, up the stairs, circling the ballroom that was shut up and mildewed, the wallpaper peeling. He discovered a leak in the library and moved dozens and dozens of books from that wall, but they were already destroyed. "Herewich is crumbling just as Talwarpur is," he said.

"I don't know how any of these big estates will survive in the modern world." I washed brushes in the sink, pumping water with my foot. Blue and red and yellow ran in rivulets over my fingernails, across my wrists. "Nor the palaces in India."

He nodded, deep in thought, as he stared out the window. "Perhaps this war will finally change things, create a more equal world."

"Will you mind if your family palace crumbles, if there are no more queens and princes and maharajas?"

He leaned on the sink, arms crossed. "That is a very good question, and I don't know the answer. Of course I would mind losing my home, but I would like to see an end to royalty."

"Will you be the same person if you are no longer a prince?"

"I shall still be myself." He tilted his head. "Will you still love me if I am a common man?"

"It would be easier, if you were."

"Is it so difficult, though, Elsie? Or are those stumbling blocks in our minds?"

A faint hope, like pink smoke, blew through me. "What do you mean?"

He stepped closer and picked up my wet hand. Using a tea towel, he dried my fingers, one by one, and my wrist. "I have been thinking that there must be a way for us to make a life for ourselves. Together."

"And what might that look like?" I asked, weaving my fingers into his.

"I haven't worked it through, but why would the fates conspire to bring us back together, over and over, if it was not meant to be? If our union would not bring some good into the world?"

"Why indeed?" I whispered, and stood on tiptoe to kiss him, wrapping my arms around his neck so he wouldn't see my tears.

But he felt them, wet against his throat, and brushed my hair away from my face. "I do not want to live a life without you in it," he said, and smoothed a thumb over my wet cheek.

"Nor do I."

"Perhaps we live in both our countries, here and there."

"Art here, politics there."

He smiled. "Perhaps." He held my hands. "We shall marry then."

I closed my eyes, thinking of my mother's warning years ago, that neither of us would have a penny if we didn't marry well. "We have no money, Tanveer, either of us."

He chuckled. "The palace and this place are crumbling, love. No one has any money."

"How will we live?"

"How does anyone live? You'll paint, and I'll go into politics, and we'll get by."

I looked up at him. "Will we hate each other in a decade?"

"What do you think?"

"No." To have the opportunity to eat meals with him, to walk in the evenings with him, to perhaps one day bear his children, seemed an absurd blessing. "I shall teach if need be. And you have many talents."

"Yes," he said, and lifted a wicked eyebrow. "I do. Allow me to show you."

~

As the days grew shorter, Tanveer embarked on a course of deep study. In the Herewich library, he found copies of *The Rights of Man* by Thomas Paine, and texts by John Locke and Thomas Hobbes. "Who among your ancestors was so interested in democracy?" he asked.

I knew exactly who it was. "My father."

"Ah. That explains a great deal."

A package from India arrived with books from Indian writers, *Poverty and Un-British Rule in India*, by Naoroji, and speeches by Gopal Krishna Gokhale, but the pamphlets by Gandhi, mentioned in the letter, were removed by censors.

All through the winter, he wrote and read and walked on fine days. Often he read his own writings aloud to me, asking for feedback and argument, so I had to read the texts, too, so I could understand what he grappled with.

I painted and painted, finding some truth in domestic scenes I had never noticed. It had once felt unimportant to paint kitchens or food or cats, but it felt powerful to me now. A battlefield cannot have an easy kitchen scene. A bombed village leaves no space for gardens. A home is a powerful thing, and I was glad to claim that idea for myself. As winter tilted toward spring again, it began to seem as if a new world might be possible.

Once the bloody, brutal war was over.

In a way, I felt protected by it. As long as it raged, nothing in this sacred, special time would end. We could live, Tanveer and I, in the crumbling house in our four little rooms, eating simply, and painting, and reading, and writing, with a pair of cats and buckets of love, and all would be well.

—54—

The telegram arrived by bicycle on a bright April morning. "Sorry, Lady Turner."

I took it with a trembling hand, sick to think it was my mother or brother.

Instead, it was addressed to Tanveer. It was brutal and to the point.

MAHARAJA AND PRINCE DEAD IN AUTOMOBILE CRASH STOP YOU ARE HEIR STOP RETURN HOME AS SOON AS POSSIBLE STOP

He read it once, twice, three times. His fingers trembled. I guided him to a chair. "I'll fetch a cup of tea."

When I brought it back and set it on the table, he had not moved, only held the paper in his hands. "I can barely comprehend this."

I sat on the settee facing him, my hands on my thighs. I thought of the night my father and mother told me we were leaving India, and how the world had tilted. I felt it tilting again.

"Of course I mourn my father and my brother, but I do not want this," he said fiercely. "All the work I've done"—he gestured toward the table, piled high with his books and notebooks and inkpot—"will disappear under this mantle of maharaja."

My heart felt as if an elephant stood on it. Here it was, the disaster that would rip him out of our little cocoon. But he looked pale with reaction, and I squeezed his hand. "Take a moment, Tanveer. It's a shock."

He took a breath, set the telegram aside, picked up his tea. His hand stilled, but he stared into the cup with despair. "I do not want to leave this space of study and quiet."

I nodded, lungs emptying as the truth set in. Inheriting the title and everything that went with it also meant the end of the future we'd imagined for ourselves, living between England and India. I waited for him to know it, too.

"How quickly can you be ready to close the house?" he asked. "We'll go to London to find transport."

I only gazed at him.

His face sobered. "You will not come with me."

"Think, Tanveer. How can I? You shall need to find a proper wife, an Indian wife, someone to help you forge the alliances you need."

He shook his head. "No. You are well versed in these things. You have studied beside me. We shall create a new kind of world."

Tears welled in my throat as I saw the vision he spun, but my heart still felt the weight of truth. "I so wish that could be true, mere rooh ke saathi."

"Will you so quickly give up?" he cried. "You will still do your art, and I will still help create a true democracy for India. We can travel between England and India, just as we said."

"We could have done that if you were a second son, a prince. We cannot if you are the maharaja. There is no money in your father's estate. Now it is your responsibility. You will need a wealthy wife."

"No." He narrowed his eyes, hands in fists on his thighs. "I shall not marry. It would be cruel to that wife, and cruel to you, and I shall not do it."

I looked at my bare fingers. "It is not only that. You said it yourself, years ago. How can a man who wants to create freedom for his country marry the daughter of the colonizers?"

I saw the knowledge land. He stood and strode from the room.

~

For three days, we debated the situation. Three days of debate and arguments and presentations, of making love and declarations, of fiercely trying to find solutions.

In the end, I held the line when he could not. He insisted we could marry and find ways to build a life in India. I knew my mother had been right all those years before. He would need a wife who could bring money into the principality. I was not that woman, and however that grieved me, my first vow to him had been to support his happiness over my own. I would uphold that vow, no matter how it shredded me.

He was angry with me as he gathered his papers and books and packed his meager wardrobe. I watched with the blood running out of my body, leaving me cold and lost. How would I bear it? How could I possibly let him go?

But in the end, he knew the truth of my stance, and met me in the bedroom we had shared for many months, dreaming of better things. We held each other and mourned. "Why give us a glimpse of this thing we cannot have?" he whispered. "Why shred our hearts over and over?"

I pressed my face into his chest, my body into his side, memorizing the feel of him, so precious and now so fleeting. My grief was too deep for tears, and in truth, I didn't know how I would live after his departure. "I will miss you always."

"We should not write letters for a year," he said.

"A year!"

"That will give us time to adjust to the loss."

I would not adjust, but in time, this would be the choice that would lead to his happiness.

"One year," I agreed.

A SINGLE SPOONFUL OF JAM

Autumn 1940
London

—55—

We had a few days' lull in the bombing, giving me a chance to rest deeply. After the third day of actually sleeping through the night, I realized how foggy I'd become without it. My mood was better, and I even found myself humming under my breath as I made toast for breakfast, drizzling the tiniest bit of honey over the finished product.

When I checked on Mother, she was still sleeping. A blessing, both for her and for me, for her sense of time had slipped so much that I did not think she was aware of time and place more than a few minutes at a time.

And who could blame her? Between her failing body and the endless bombings, the current world was hardly worth occupying. I smoothed her blankets. Cold November light came in through the window, illuminating the fading sight of her. Each day a little less, her skin more translucent, the underlying muscle and fat all but disappeared, so she was simply a skeleton draped with flesh. Her hair remained beautiful. I glanced at the painting above her bed, of the house in Nainital and the three children on the steps. I wondered if she would mind if I moved it to Nina's. It was one I would desperately hate to lose.

She will never even notice, a voice said in my mind. And while I knew it was true, I couldn't bring myself to take it down.

I applied myself instead to getting the rest of them ready to move. I'd asked Nina if I might bring a group of them over, and arranged for

Mrs. Cotton to come sit with Mother. I hadn't seen Peter for a few days, which had been a surprise since the raids had been less problematic.

But who knew what intelligence swirled at headquarters? The raids were visible to ordinary people, but they were only the tip of the war machine.

I felt an odd urgency as I gathered the paintings I'd already removed from their stretchers and began layering them, paint side up, with sheets I'd cut for the purpose between each layer. I had already moved the most financially valuable paintings to Helen's, and these were in a different tier—works I loved that had not necessarily appealed to collectors, some of the experimental landscapes I'd painted in Cairo and then India; more interiors, quiet moments within a woman's world. Finally, I brought out the Tanveer portraits, from youth to full manhood, Tanveer bent over books by the fire at Herewich, as a maharaja in his black coat, Channan at his side. The formal portraits I'd left with them, but I'd brought one back for myself, too.

When I was finished, I rolled the lot into bundles and tied them with string. They were heavy and unwieldy, but not unmanageable. I loaded them in the Austin, then went back up to the attic.

I'd dithered about my sketchbooks. They were not in the least valuable to anyone but me. But it would grieve me to lose them nonetheless. Resisting the urge to flip through them, I loaded stacks of them into cardboard boxes I'd collected from the grocer, focusing on periods of great productivity or growth—living at Herewich in the last year of the war, the vivid painting experiments in Cairo, living in Talwarpur Palace in India, and earlier, at Slade, when I'd been so desperately trying to find my voice. I had five boxes, and when they were filled, I left the years that would not fit on the table, neatly, each with a note on the spine, *Greylake* or *Interiors, 1932*. I would have to stop and ask for more boxes on my way back home.

Going up and down the stairs several times, I loaded the sketchbooks in the boot, and was on the way back up for the last one when I had to sit down in dizziness halfway between the first floor and the second, where my mother slept. It was dark because I hadn't opened the blackout curtains, a task Betty had ordinarily performed. Even in the dimness, I could see dust on the balusters, thick enough they'd collected long bits of hair. How long since anyone had dusted? I didn't know. The thought of another task winded me.

As if he sat right beside me, I heard Tanveer's voice. *You must take care of yourself. You must endure.*

Right. I touched my empty belly, tried to remember what I'd eaten the night before. I'd had little energy left over to be creative with our rations, and had been eating mainly potatoes I dug from the garden, bread with whatever bacon or other meat we had week to week, a little cheese. And eggs. Always eggs. A blessing, even if I'd never much cared for them. Most of the food I tried to fashion into things mother would eat—broths and easy, soft foods that did little to entice my appetite.

Foolish. If I meant to survive this war, I had to care for the body that carried me. When the dizziness passed, I headed to the kitchen and made a cup of tea with a full teaspoon of sugar and plenty of milk, then made a porridge of oatmeal and milk, and topped it with a small spoonful of jam.

I intended to survive. I ate the meal. I drank the tea.

~

Nina's yardman, Hugh, a spindly old man with arms that belied his age, helped me bring the paintings and boxes into the house, and then down into the cellar. Once they were settled, Nina and I drank tea and ate some little cakes that hardly seemed as if they'd been made with fakery. "Sassy is a genius with substitutions," I said. "She should submit this recipe to *The Kitchen Front* on the radio."

"She should, indeed. Have you found a new housekeeper?"

"Peter was meant to be looking among the refugees, but I haven't heard anything from him."

"Mmm."

I looked up. "What is it? Has he done something again?"

"I don't honestly know, Elsie. Jonathan has been awfully out of sorts with him, but, of course, all the secrecy means he can hardly say a word."

"Drinking, is it?"

"Perhaps." She shrugged, shaking her head. "He had seemed better, hadn't he?"

"Yes. Much better, almost as solid as after he returned from Kabul."

"But?"

"I haven't seen him in a couple of days. I noticed this morning only because the raids have been somewhat quiet, and I supposed he might come home to sleep and shower instead of staying at headquarters."

Again, a little information flitted over her mouth.

"You would be a terrible spy," I said. "Out with it. You know I have no attachment. Is it that girl, Trudy?"

She nodded. "From all accounts, it's quite torrid."

I'd been certain of this outcome from the moment I'd seen her. "Exactly his type," I said.

"I think his type is beautiful," Nina said with a roll of her eyes. "He's always loved to worship from afar, like women are all the lost fairy queen he can't quite attain."

"Lost, yes," I added. That had been the piece I hadn't quite seen in Cairo. Margo had been a widow mourning her husband when she and Peter met.

"His womanizing is a surprise," she said. "As a youth, he was so . . . earnest. Do you remember?"

"Of course."

"He fell for you that very first day, and never gave up, did he?"

"No," I said with some weariness. "But it was never *me* he wanted. Any more than he wants Trudy, the actual woman, or wanted Margo in Cairo. He falls passionately in love with . . . an ideal, some imaginary vision of what she will be."

"Isn't that what all men want?"

"No. Not at all." I scowled. "Peter is driven to possess beauty, as if it's something he can buy." I paused. "A lot of men are that way, of course. And we're taught to pander to it, offer beauty in whatever way we can to capture their attention. But not all men."

"Not your prince."

"Why do you always say it that way? So droll, as if it's something foolish."

"What did I say?"

"'Your prince,'" I echoed in her lightly mocking tone. "That is a title he inherited. It is not the summation of him. And yes, I am thinking of him when I say all men are not like that. He has values and lives them. He looks beyond beauty."

"But how would you know? You're beautiful yourself. Perhaps he, like Peter, was only smitten by your face and body."

"No." It would be easy to trot out Channan as the exhibit of the day, but I would not use her that way. "Integrity truly exists. The ability to see women for more than their beauty or usefulness to men also exists." I shook my head. "Jonathan, for one."

She rolled her eyes. "Queer men don't count."

"I disagree, but let us change direction now. I don't want to fight with you, my dear friend."

"Oh, do ignore me! I am wretched in Helen's absence, and Jonathan is so busy. Please come stay with me here, Elsie. We'll transport your mother, and then you and I can while away the war playing rummy and whist."

The image gave me such a sense of relief that I nodded. "Yes, let's do that. I need to bring the other two kittens and their mother. Is that all right?"

"Of course. They're being little darlings."

"All right. I shall see what needs to be transported."

"Truly?"

"Truly."

As I prepared to leave, Nina laid a thin hand over my forearm. "Are you safe with Peter, Elsie? You've always been quite vague about what happened in Cairo."

"You needn't worry," I said. A ripple of memory warned me that was not at all true.

LETTERS AFTER THE WAR

1919
England

—56—

February 19, 1919
Greylake, England

Dear Mother,
It grieves me to write this letter, but I have had a telegram about William, who survived the war only to succumb to influenza on his way home to England. A friend of his wrote to me (I am enclosing the letter) to say he went very quickly and did not suffer, but I do not think that will alleviate your sorrow very much. I made arrangements for his body to be interred at Herewich with his ancestors.

I weep as I write this, knowing how hard it will be for you to hear. It is terribly cruel that he managed to get though the war and then fell to illness so close to the end. I am sorry that he did not have a chance to marry, or test all his grand theories on how to build Herewich into the thriving estate it once was, and I am desperately sorry that I cannot ever embrace him again.

Of course, the estate now passes to cousin Harold, a feat that once would have seemed impossible, but the war has killed so many more than our William that a distant cousin is the only male of our line left to inherit. I am furious that we shall both be left without a dime, when I am alive and breathing and as much my father's child as my brother was.

But what is there to be done?

For now, I've gone to Nina, and you must stay where you are, living cheaply with your husband. There's nothing left in England for us.

I love you, and I wish I could be there to share your grief.

Elsie

[Enclosed letter and a sketch of William's grave site]

March 29, 1919
Palace of the Raj
Lahore

Dear Elsie,

I am enclosing two things for you today, perhaps to cheer you up. One is a newspaper article about Tanveer and the Indian National Congress. He gave a fine speech last week and is highly respected as a member of the party. His time in England made him a fiery warrior. It's quite thrilling to watch.

The other is a bit of a surprise. Please check page 16 in the enclosed magazine.

Your friend,

Gurdaya

[Enclosed newspaper article about Maharaja of Talwarpur and his speech]

[Enclosed copy of *The Bombay Storybook Magazine*, with an older woman in spectacles and a dupatta peeking through a curtain with a spyglass in her hand. *Aunty-Ji, Investigator*, by Guriya Kaur.]

June 1, 1919
Greylake, Kent

Dearest Gurdaya! I could not be more proud of you! I cried with happiness. More, more, more!

Another letter soon.

Your friend,

Elsie

April 7, 1919
Talwarpur Palace
[In English]

Dear Elsie,

I am startled to hear from Gurdaya that your brother died. You could have written to tell me such tragic news, surely!

It has been one year to the day since I left England. I have picked up my pen a hundred times since then, but I wanted to give you space to consider your foolish stand. Perhaps I should proceed in the way we are meant to go on, as dear friends.

But I sit at my desk and do not know how to do that. How to pretend you are only my friend, when that is not true, has never been true, will never be true. I miss you most desperately.

I heard that you had to vacate Herewich. Please come to India where I can give you a home. It might crumble to nothing around us, but it will be ours.

Please forget this ridiculous prideful plan of yours and come home.

Ever your love,

Tanveer

April 29, 1919
Greylake, Kent
[In Urdu]

Dear Tanveer,

I am so relieved our year of abstention has passed. I thought of writing you a thousand times.

Yes, my brother died. I have landed with Nina and Jon in the country for now. They've purchased a small estate not far from London so that Jon might commute easily. Nina has given me studio space in a shed overlooking the river, where a towering willow tree bends over to trail her fingers in the water. It makes me think of you, how delighted you were with the brook near Herewich and the bluebirds who drank there.

England feels like a hollow landscape. All I can do is paint and paint and paint.

I paint portraits of you because I miss you and it helps. I paint scenes of Herewich, lost to me forever through some foolish ancient law that punishes women, and it makes me furious. When I paint, I can own it again, my garden, my bedroom, the cozy, warm kitchen where we cooked and ate, the hearth where we took our cushions and read to each other. I paint the great old claw-foot tub where we bathed.

I knew a woman at Slade who painted rooms where it seemed someone had just left, a glove on a table, a hat on a chair. She had lost her grandmother, and it helped to think she might return momentarily, and thus I paint the possibility that we might be returning to those rooms any moment. The coverlet and sheets still rumpled from our lovemaking, Topaz asleep in a little ball at the thickest part, the fabric of your dastaar draped over the chair. I paint the table with our dishes still upon it, and a pot steaming on the stove. I paint the garden with our shoes discarded at the edge, side by side.

You ask me to come home, and home truly would be you, wherever you are, but I also know that this time, it is I who must protect you from the quixotic gesture of marriage to me. I hear the news out of India, and I know that the struggle for independence will continue to be central to your life in the next decades. I know this because I know you and I love you more than mere words can possibly express.

I cannot be the wife you need at such a time, and I will not distract you from those tasks you were born to complete. It gives me joy to know you are unencumbered to do the work.

But I do question what forces made me love you with this unshakable depth if we must spend our lives apart. What is the purpose of that? For either of us. Does my longing imbue my work with some beauty it would otherwise not hold? Does your love for me allow you to give more intently to the women of your world? I cannot pretend to answer.

I must admit that my resources are very close to nothing. I should have married at my brother's urging when I still had some connection to the earldom. Now my worth is only that of a commoner, and I am hardly a spring chicken.

Please remember that I made a vow to young Tanveer, a vow to always put his happiness above my own. I am doing that, even if it does not seem that way to you. I hope we can continue our friendship as time eases our pain.

In the meantime, I remain yours,

Elsie

June 1919
Talwarpur Palace
[In English]

Elsie,

I write to you over a horrific event, that you will not have heard of and has shattered any faith I might have held in the possibility of a peaceful transfer of power.

There has been a massacre at Jallianwala Bagh. These are the barest facts—during a festival in Amritsar, the army surrounded the enclosure of Jallianwala Bagh and blocked the exit, then fired upon the trapped crowd until their munitions ran low. Thousands were killed and injured. It was said to be a warning against the protests that are breaking out over arrests of Indian leaders, but, Elsie, many of those people were there to celebrate a holiday. They were there with their families, their children—

My ribs break with the pressure of my rage. I despair of the darkness in mankind that will allow us to rain such violence upon each other. It has awakened my dreams of the trenches, and I do not sleep.

This must end. It must end.

And what I have seen, at long last, is the truth of your stand against our marriage. I cannot do this work if I am married to you. I fear my anger would poison me against you in some twisted way, even if it was unfair.

I shall mourn what might have been forevermore, but thank you for your devotion to the vows we made to each other so long ago at the pond, to assign ourselves to the happiness of the other above our own. I will offer my own devotion to them in this: You must marry and try to find some happiness in family life. I shall do the same.

Know this—my love will never alter. As long as I live, you will hold my heart. Hum aik jan hain. We are one soul.

When I feel I can write with sanity to Elsie my friend and not my lover, I will inquire toward your feelings, and perhaps we can continue our friendship, and share again our love of books and life and art and freedom. Until then, be well.

Always,

Tanveer

WEDDINGS AND PYRAMIDS

1920–24
England and Cairo

—57—

For several years after the war, parts of me were so crushed that I could not find my painterly voice. In the shed at Nina's, I painted my memories but more as sketches of all that was lost than works of finished art. I piled them up, canvas after canvas of small domestic things I was unwilling to show the world. My confidence disappeared. I was adrift and unhappy and drinking in the evenings with our small band of survivors. We all drank too much. Our souls had been twisted and tortured, and we took refuge in gin while we desultorily played backgammon and rummy and bezique.

It was during those long winter evenings in '20 and '21 that Peter and I became friends. He, too, had suffered badly in the war, as a prisoner of war in the desert, but he'd found a place in the diplomatic corps with Jonathan, and often accompanied him down from London at the weekend, sometimes with one or two others from the office. Rations had ceased, so we poured too much sugar into our tea and feasted on decadent cakes.

Or more truthfully, we pretended to feast, just as we pretended to return to ordinary days.

August 8, 1922
Talwarpur Palace
[In Urdu]

Dear Elsie,
I have important news to share. My pen hovers over the page, as I know how hard this will land with you, but there is no other way to say it:

I am to be married. My bride shall bring a dowry to replenish the starved coffers of Talwarpur, and, of course, that is much required. She is the daughter of a local raja with far more land than we enjoy, and the savvy to manage it. We share a view of the future, and our unity will be politically smart. At another time, she would have been a brilliant catch, and I could not have hoped to negotiate a marriage to her, for she was much in demand.

Two years ago, she was attacked by robbers on the way to Lahore. Her servants were killed, and she was brutally beaten, then left by the side of the road. Her health understandably has suffered, and her injuries left her unmarriageable. She is quite intelligent and well educated, and has a clever sense of humor.

I do not marry her out of pity, but out of a need to make an alliance with someone I can trust to be honest, and with whom I can be entirely myself. I have been as honest with her as I am able, Elsie, about our long friendship. I have not told her everything, of course, for that is our private treasure, and I shall keep it for my own.

It was always going to come to this. I am grateful for your wisdom in this matter, but I also pray that

> you do not desert this good friendship between us, for I do not know how I would live without it.
>
> Your friend eternally,
>
> Tanveer

Although I had known it was coming, I was utterly crushed by the news of Tanveer's marriage. In some bizarre twist of alliances, the only person I wished to share my grief with was Tanveer himself, which, of course, was impossible.

Instead, I walked endlessly, for miles and miles on the public footpaths that looped across the entire countryside. I wept and walked and walked and cursed. I was raw and exhausted, completely dependent upon Nina for a roof over my head. Peter and I gave each other comfort at times, sex halting for an hour the darkness of both our memories. He was a surprisingly skilled and imaginative lover, and the pleasure gave me a kind of hope I hadn't anticipated.

Peter first phrased his proposals with that in mind, mutual solace and pleasure, as well as a path out of my dilemma. I refused, for months. What could he possibly gain from such a match?

After a time, he changed his suit, saying he would happily gain a beautiful wife for the enjoyment of seeing me paint and find myself again.

I was by then nearly twenty-seven. The only man I'd wanted was married to another woman. In another era, I would have been declared a spinster, but there were so few men and so many women my age that the usual shame associated with that status had been nullified.

It was a desire for children that swayed me in the end, and a desire to see to the support of my mother, who'd also been left penniless with my brother's death. I wanted shelter, craved hope, for both of us.

And yet, I feared he would mistake my motives. "You know I don't love you."

"I know. I like to think you might over time."

"What if I don't?"

He laughed. "Well, then, we'll just be another British couple, making do."

In the end, he was given a posting to Cairo. He made one last bid for marriage, offering me studio space wherever we lived, and full support of my mother.

I agreed. We were married in a small ceremony just before we sailed. I began to look toward the future for the first time in at least two years.

Cairo blew a bright, strong wind through the darkness of my soul. I awakened to the hot white light of the desert and the hard blue skies, the thronging humanity in the markets and backstreets, which I wandered regularly, sketchbook in hand, dupatta over my head. Peter insisted I be accompanied by a servant at all times, which I adjusted to quickly enough, and she proved to be a great companion. Once she saw that I wanted to paint everything, she led me to mosques and churches and bazaars off the main colonial routes.

Egyptians were weary of colonial occupation, too, but I discovered that if one was respectful, if I wore a scarf over my hair and spoke a few words of Arabic, it went a long way toward facilitating friendships. Not that I made the mistake I had as a child in India. I knew I did not belong, even if I loved it.

We traveled keenly, on the Nile, and to explore sites of antiquities, and somehow the ancientness of history eased me, too. People had survived dark times before, and we would again.

A new voice emerged in my painting. I copied classic styles to paint ordinary women in ordinary pursuits—sisters laughing as they walked to market in the luminous alleyways, a grandmother with only her laughing eyes and sliver of mouth showing over her scarf. I painted English women sweating and red faced in the heat of a hotel garden, and a mother plaiting her daughter's hair, both of them freckled and a bit gap toothed. I showed a group of the paintings at a local English gallery, and all but one sold the first day.

Perhaps I'd finally found something authentic to myself. Encouraged, I sketched women at household tasks around the city, and sketched the settings of their lives. The stove on the floor, the pot on the stove, a pile of carrots and the knife that cut them. I painted my own domestic life, as well—kitchens, tables, gardens with forgotten tools. And then more intimate—a towel on a rack, with a pair of slippers and a discarded skirt on the floor. An unmade bed with only one side slept on.

One of the women I'd become friends with commented, "Every painting is so lonely, Elsie. Why don't you paint happier things?"

Others must have shared my loneliness, however, for they sold as fast as I could paint them. I developed a language of intimacy that sometimes was too deep for the conservative Cairo market, and I began to set those aside for a London show. A window with an opened letter on a table below it. A road leading into the distance. A book in Urdu on an armchair, an empty cup of tea beside it.

We had been there for two years before Peter had his first episode. He had continued to drink a great deal, but so did most of the diplomatic corps. Gin was the language of the foreign office, and he partook as heavily as everyone else. When he grew sloppy in public, I got him home and into bed without much incident. He often tried to have sex with me at such times, which felt vaguely dangerous, but it was easy enough to slip away.

I always understood, from the very first time he proposed, that there was a risk he might end up being very unhappy in a marriage with me. I'd talked it over at length with my mother and Nina, dissecting the reality that while I enjoyed his company and had found him an agreeable lover during those lost days after the war when we were all trying simply to recover, I would never likely love him.

My mother said that I would get over my attachment to Tanveer over time. It was young love, first love, and would fade. Nina simply said no one is ever happy in marriage—one did one's best.

The first couple of years in Cairo, all was well. I painted with new vigor, and Peter liked his position and his superiors, and we made expeditions to the ancient sites he so loved.

Two years in, he was mugged in the street on the way home by a band of thieves who beat him and stole his father's watch. He staggered home with blood on his shirt and an eye that was swollen shut, but it seemed minor. Such things happened.

Except that shortly afterward, he began to have nightmares of such vividness I found it difficult to sleep next to him for the thrashing. He never wished to discuss what he dreamed. I, remembering Tanveer's torturous memories, did not push. I did ask the physician for a sleeping draught, but that seemed to make things worse, for he would not leave drink alone, and the combination would knock him sideways. He'd wake up not entirely himself, flailing about in a fog of insensibility.

The first time he attacked me was in the early morning hours after such a night, when he had begun fighting invisible monsters, yelling and throwing things. I tried to soothe him, and he turned on me, flinging me down on the bed and holding me down. I thought he might strangle me, but I managed to roll away and get out of the room.

When morning came, he was abjectly sorry but remembered very little of it. I refused to sleep in the same room with him after that. Mostly, in the daytime, he was himself, if a bit more hungover than he had been. His supervisor, seeing Peter's ragged health, sent him to England for a few weeks to recover, and I went with him, taking paintings to London to see if I might find a gallery.

Which I did, quite happily. It was a prestigious place, on St. James Street, and I promised to deliver a show by the end of the following spring.

The time in England calmed Peter, and we found an even footing once again. We returned to Cairo, me to my paintings, he to his work and archaeological digs.

He was not, however, the Peter I'd come to know. He brooded more, drank more. When he was in his cups, sex was sometimes so rough I was wary of it at all, so intimacy between us dropped. He complained about it but would not moderate his drinking.

There was an incident at a brothel that was swept under the rug, but I gathered he'd had an episode after falling asleep with a girl, and she'd barely escaped injury.

And yet, I was happy in Cairo. I painted the best I had in years. I read deeply on many subjects and made friends among both the expats and continentals and Egyptian artists. After a hiatus of more than a year after our marriages, Tanveer and I had recommenced our friendly, intellectual letters. If my marriage was less than ideal, it was not appreciably worse than many others. Peter's troubles were an illness. I tried many ways to help him bleed the boil, as Tanveer had done in Herewich with his writing and walking, but Peter was inclined toward neither. His condition continued to worsen.

After a terrible night of his nightmares and the omnipresent fear of his delusions, I finally asked for help from the one person who might have insight into the problem.

—58—

December 3, 1925
Cairo

Dear Tanveer,

[In Urdu]: I hope this letter finds you well. I continue to enjoy Cairo, with all its many discoveries and layers and colors. It is so inspiring to me as an artist, and my work is improving daily.

I've read both of the books you mailed, Müller and poetry of the Afghans. I'm particularly interested in the poetry of the Afghans as Kabul is a possible next posting for Peter.

I'm delighted to understand how closely connected Arabic and Urdu and Hindi are, all languages in a single family, as Latin, French, Spanish, and Italian are. Not that I have learned to speak any of those with any skill, but I did know they were a family of languages, where I did not know about the Indo-Persian family. That seems an oversight of my education, which has been so terribly Western centered, all of it, even in India. I remember your complaints as a student about such things. How, I wonder, were you so clear about things, even as a youth?

I write today with a matter of some delicacy, and I would ask your discretion and honor. I am concerned about Peter. He suffers greatly from a malaise related to his war experiences, including terrible nightmares from which he acts out and is not himself. He drinks to subdue them, and that seems to make the trouble worse. I have also noticed that at times he is fully awake, but a loud noise or a particular scent will send him into a sort of fugue state in which he is no longer living as himself, but again, acting out some kind of memory. He can be violent at such times.

I believe it is connected to his memories, which he will not share. I understand, for you, too, struggled with sharing your war experiences. It seems a common theme among soldiers of this age.

I wonder if you might have suggestions for another man suffering that particular hell. He will not write about his experiences, as I have suggested that. He only drinks.

I do apologize for digging into what are terrible memories for you. Forgive me. If you do not wish to discuss it, I will never mention it again.

[In English]: Give Gurdaya and Channan my love. It is such a joy to read Gurdaya's stories and see her so happy!

Tell me how you are, what you are pursuing, what insights you've uncovered. I'm sending along a book I enjoyed most earnestly by William James, on the ways we experience religion. I would love to discuss if you read it.

Again, please forgive me if I overreach.

Best,

Elsie

January 2, 1926
Talwarpur Palace
[In Urdu]

Dear Elsie,

Happy new year, my dear friend!

You do not overstep. I am honored you would bring this concern to me, and I thank you for trusting me with such a delicate matter.

I do not have any insight into your husband's particular troubles, but what you describe is not uncommon among survivors of the war. Despite the disdain with which many in society hold the sufferers, I do not think there has been war of this nature before now, where mechanistic horror made the always burdensome experience of battle a particularly torturous one. We have seen the lingering effects in India, too. Men who cannot hold a job, who fall into rages or alcoholic stupors. Men who simply do not function well.

As for how to help drain that boil, I do not hold hope for a man who will not quit drinking. I am sorry to be so frank, but alcohol seems to aggravate and increase the symptoms. Perhaps you might start there.

I ask you to protect yourself as you must. I shall worry if you do not reassure me, and I ask you to forgive my directness in that.

I will write again when I have read the William James. Please say more about your experience reading Müller, and the poets. Were there any poems you particularly enjoyed or did not enjoy? I've tried to engage my sister in this discussion, but she is only interested in fiction. Poetry, she says, is for lovers and mystics, and she is neither.

Be well,

Tanveer

—59—

In March, the winds came into Cairo, picking up sand and dust from every corner of the desert and flinging them across streets and through any open window, and through the cracks of the closed doors. My teeth constantly had grit between them, and it was impossible to keep the floors swept.

The wind brought a kind of insanity to the expats. Peter had been remarkably stable since an invitation to visit Luxor, but the winds ruffled his nerves once again. I steered clear of his moods and painted trees bent in one direction and sand piled over a pair of shoes, only the toes still showing.

I'd rented a studio away from our little house, a set of rooms at the top of a colonial building, the windows enormous. Here, too, I had to sweep constantly, never left a painting uncovered overnight, and hired a girl to come in every morning and keep it clean. I kept a hot plate for tea, and a small number of groceries.

Peter disliked the studio, and he especially hated when I slept there. I gave him keys to the place so he wouldn't suspect infidelity, and he often popped in on his way to and fro—to work in the morning, to zinc bars in the evening. He, too, spent nights away from home, but I did not question him.

Most nights, I did go home to sleep, and sometimes I cooked for him, for I was learning to cook Egyptian dishes. He enjoyed exploring the flavors, but I suspected that he most liked being tended by his wife.

One night I had proudly made mulukhiyah, a green stew made with jute leaves and spiced with cardamom, cloves, and bay leaves. The scent of it filled the room, and I danced a little to the radio, an Egyptian woman named Umm Kulthum singing a mournful song I couldn't understand and loved anyway.

Peter blew in, his hair askew with the wind, a restlessness in his pacing. He poured a gin, and drank it quickly, then made another. As if the wind fueled his speech, he tumbled out a series of anecdotes and stories from his day, bouncing from topic to topic in a way that warned me he was on the verge of an episode. "Peter," I said, "will you dance with me?"

The radio had switched to "After You've Gone," and he lifted his head with a smile. "We danced to this a lot at Nina's, didn't we?"

"We did." I took off my apron and offered my arms.

His entire being softened. Unbuttoning his shirt a little, rolling up the sleeves, he stepped forward with a half smile that made me remember his young self, the earnest boy before the war. He had always been a nimble dancer, and that had not faded. It was a relief to sway, to spin, to laugh at some fancy dip.

The music changed, and we danced to that, too. His mood eased, and he kept up a happy patter of conversation about mostly nothing at all.

And then the wind knocked something down outside. With a crash, a projectile came through the window, struck me sideways and hit Peter in the ribs. He cried out in terror. I stumbled sideways, trying to see what had come through—

He slammed me to the floor, knocking the wind out of me. "Don't move!"

"I can't breathe! Get off me."

"Shut up. You'll get us killed."

Struggling to regain my breath, I was seized with panic, struggling sideways back and forth, gasping and hurting from the weight of his body plastering me to the floor and the impact of landing on the tiles and whatever it was that had struck me. "It was the wind—"

He plastered a hand over my mouth, bending very close. "Not a sound."

I began to weep, fearing for my life, and shoved at him with my hands against his shoulders, my knees against his legs. He pinned me harder, grabbing one arm above my head, pinning it to the floor, wrenching my shoulder.

I moved my head hard, dislodging his hand over my mouth. "Peter!" I cried. "Stop! You're hurting me!"

"Stop resisting!" Spittle flew from his lips as he scanned the world around us. Leaning into my ear, he whispered, "They'll hear us."

Tears leaked from my eyes. His elbow bruised my forearm, and my lip was bleeding from his grip over my mouth. I stopped struggling, hoping he would regain his senses.

The radio played and the wind blew, and Peter kept me pinned to the floor for long, long minutes. It was the shift of the music that seemed to bring him to his senses. All at once he said, "Oh, God, Elsie. Jesus." He scrambled backward, freeing me, and I rolled away, gasping to fill my lungs.

He bent to help me, and I waved him away, tasting the coppery blood in my mouth. "Get away from me."

"Let me help you."

"No." I struggled to my feet. My hair fell in my face and my dress was twisted.

He stared at me in horror. "Jesus," he said again. "I am so terribly sorry. Do you need a doctor?"

I waved him back with a hand and retreated to the bathroom, where I took inventory of my injuries—bloodied lip, the suggestion of bruises on my cheek, my hair askew. A bump grew on the back of my head, and I could feel the bruises on my shoulder and arm, as well.

Running a face cloth under cold water, I stared at myself in the mirror. He might have killed me. He *could* have killed me. Wiping away the blood, gently, I let the cold reality sink in.

Peter's war experience had twisted him, and as long as he suffered these episodes, he was a danger—to me, to others, to himself. What could I do?

He'd been moody in England at times, but never dangerous. That had only started here. Perhaps something about Cairo triggered his memories. Perhaps—

My mother's face floated over my reflection, as she'd tended a woman severely beaten by her husband, long ago in India. "A brutal man will never change, Elsie. Remember that."

But Peter was not brutal. He was tortured. Was there no help for that at all?

I opened the door and found him in the living room, drink in hand, his expression bereft. As I approached, his eyes filled with tears. "Elsie, I can't even—"

I shook my head. "No. I know you were not yourself." I narrowed my eyes. "But I will not stay in the company of a wounded tiger."

"Don't leave me, Elsie. Please. I'll find some help somewhere. Somehow."

"I will not leave you." I took a breath. "I owe you for rescuing me, and in light of that, I will remain your wife." I paused to give my words weight. "But henceforth, I will be spending the night at my studio, and you will quit drinking."

"Yes, of course. I felt so much better in the desert. Perhaps I should go back there, dry out, get my head together."

"That is not a terrible idea." I touched his arm. "I do think, Peter, this is not the best city for you. It seems to unnerve you."

He looked away, suddenly looking a husk of himself.

"Do you want to talk about it?"

"I don't know how."

I sat, took his hand, drawing him down beside me. "Perhaps you could write me letters, as if the experiences were happening now."

He closed his eyes tight. "No."

"Perhaps not to me, then. Someone else. Someone who will listen and not judge."

He growled, yanking his hand away. "There is no one who will not judge. You think you know, but you do not."

"I don't think—"

"I'm not your precious prince, to be patched up and sent on my way." He reeled way, pushing his hands though his wild hair. "It's this wind. It's this place."

"Perhaps you could ask to return to England? We were all right there, weren't we?"

He swung back. "We were. It's early, but considering all, perhaps they'll send me back."

"It's worth asking."

With sudden drama, he fell to his knees and buried his head in my lap. "Elsie, you are the dearest thing in my world. I can't bear hurting you."

I hesitated for a moment, blood still on my lip. But I had married him, and he deserved the ministrations of a wife. In truth, I was fond of him, even if it wasn't quite what he hoped. "Dear Peter. I'm sorry for your suffering. I truly am. But we must take action."

He lifted his head. "I shall go to the desert this week, and speak to headquarters about a transfer before I go." He kissed my fingers. "It will be all right. You'll see."

—60—

Fate conspired to bring Gurdaya to Cairo not five days later. She was accompanying her husband, who had some business to attend, and she intended to shop. I'd been looking forward to seeing her for months, but on the morning we were to meet for lunch, I very nearly canceled. My lip was no longer swollen, but the cut still marked it, and a quadrant of finger bruises showed on my jaw. I covered them with powder and foundation, and wore long sleeves to cover the bruises on my arms. I couldn't bear not to see her.

We were to meet at her lodgings, Shepheard's Hotel, a glamorous place known for its international visitors, and a terrace overlooking the Ezbekieh Gardens. It was bustling in the bright late morning, waiters in uniform discreetly serving and whisking away dishes and pouring coffee from silver carafes. I paused at the doorway to see if I could spot her, but there was no one who matched the girl who was in my mind.

A woman stood and raised a hand. She was clad in a western dress of yellow silk, and her thick, black hair was swirled into a fashionable twist, showing off the face that had matured even more beautifully than I remembered.

My mouth opened, and I hurried over, taking her hands. Her childhood nickname slipped out: "Guriya!" She was taller than I, and regal in her bearing, which I supposed fitted the wife and daughter of a raja. Ropes of pearls circled her neck and fell in cascades over her chest, and her wrists were adorned with bracelets.

"Elsie!" she cried, kissing my cheeks in continental fashion. "You are stunning!"

"And you!" I laughed. "I did not expect you to be the last word in modern girls!"

We sat, and the waiter poured coffee and brought cream, and then bread and olives and tomatoes for us to graze. "I hardly know where to begin," I said, a little breathless. Of course I could see Tanveer in her face, in the same high-bridged nose, the full lips. "Or, I suppose I do—I am so delighted by your writing career!"

"It is so wonderfully surprising, and so very enjoyable. I love the writing, and the publishing. I am a tiny bit famous in Bombay." She mimed a movie-star pose with hands below her face. "Not as famous as you! I saw your paintings in the gallery."

"You did?"

"Of course. I made a particular trip. Baldev also found them striking. He said you must come to India and paint our world."

I laughed. "How kind! But I spent my first years in school unlearning all my India styles."

"That's terrible! Why?"

"Not at all. I had to find my own voice."

"India must be part of that, surely."

A wash of late summer evenings moved through me, the sound of cicadas loud in the trees. "It seems far away now. Long ago."

"We were fortunate children. What a gift it was when my mother moved in next door to yours!"

I couldn't even imagine my life without Tanveer in it, but I did not know her feelings about our connection, or how much she really knew. Of course she knew I'd gone to him in the hospital in Brighton and brought him back to Herewich to heal, but how much more than that, I did not know. As lightly as possible, I asked, "How is your brother?"

"Has he not written of late?"

"No, he has." I dropped sugar cubes into my coffee to hide my expression. "I assume you must see him now and again."

"I do. And Channan, frail as she is. Poor dear. It's always been an amazement to me that he married her. Baldev and I think him a bit of a saint."

"A saint!"

Gurdaya inclined her head. "Do you not know her story?"

"A little. She was disfigured in a robbery."

She lifted her chin, and waved toward the waiter. "*Disfigured* is a mild word. She was beaten and burned. It was a miracle she did not die—and it might have been kinder if she had."

I found myself suddenly protective. "Oh, surely not. Tanveer praises her good mind. Beauty is not the only measure of worth."

"Oh, no, of course not." She touched my hand. "How kind that you defend her." The waiter brought grapefruits and toast. "I only meant that without Tanveer's protection, she would have suffered."

I hadn't realized her condition was so severe, and it gave me a twist of new love for him. "That is in character, isn't it?"

"It is," she said. "He has ever sought to protect the defenseless. And you, Elsie? How do you fare?"

"I'm well!" I said brightly. "Cairo has given me so much to paint."

"And your husband?"

"A junior ambassador, but likely to move up, I'm sure. He's an amateur archaeologist, so, of course, he loves Egypt."

"Is it he who gives you those bruises?"

The inquiry was so direct it disarmed me entirely. I looked at her without speaking. She waited, and then cocked one elegantly arched brow. I nodded. "He suffers war troubles, and the winds have set him off. He did not mean to hurt me."

She blinked. "Are you in danger?"

Again, the directness took me aback. "No," I said, even though I was not sure. But I would not burden Gurdaya with it, nor Tanveer if it got back to him. "Not at all."

"Would you tell me the truth, my old friend?"

I met her gaze and lied. "Yes. Now, tell me about your husband and your children."

She allowed the redirection, but as she spoke of Baldev, her eyes glittered. I could see that she loved him, and her four children.

"It's wonderful that it has turned out so well. I remember how distraught you were when you married."

"I was. And it was you who challenged me to write, and when I did, when I discovered some outlet for myself, I found I did not have to hate him, and in fact, I found some joy." She raised a brow. "He is quite handsome."

"But older, yes?"

"A decade, which seemed much more when I was fifteen than when I am thirty." She laughed. "Come, I must find a dress for a dinner tonight. I'd like your feedback."

"Would it be too plebeian to ask you to bring your husband to dinner? I shall cook."

"I would so love to, but we are only here for a whirlwind." She reached for my arm. "Won't you come to India? Come and paint."

The idea had dangerous appeal, but, of course, I could not. "My life is here."

She gave a little shrug. "One can travel, you know. Think about it. We should so love to have you."

AN INVITATION FROM CHANNAN

1926
Cairo

—61—

Peter stabilized again over the following months. He began speaking with enthusiasm about a woman archaeologist, Margo Lang, who turned out to be a stunningly beautiful redhead, and so far out of Peter's league that I couldn't believe he even had a crush on her. An American doing research at the Valley of Kings, she was in town for a few months. She circled the edges of our set, and I met her a few times at dinner parties, but we had little in common. In truth, she rubbed me the wrong way a bit—too bold and bright, with a wide red mouth and large breasts and a way of moving that seemed just this side of tarty.

And yet, one night, as everyone danced and I sat on the sidelines, watching, I found myself pondering my reaction to her. Why did I judge her? From my deep bag, I withdrew my sketchbook and began to draw the flying hands, the mouth laughing, wide open, the vigor of movements. Surprising that she'd chosen archaeology with its careful, studied movements, the silence of the desert. Perhaps I would ask her why.

She was known for her prodigious ability to hold her whiskey. Maybe that was what she shared with Peter, who didn't seem to be the kind of man such a woman would choose. He was utterly smitten. For quite some time, I wasn't sure if he was actually having an affair or just worshipping her from afar. Honestly, I didn't care. Our physical relationship had halted the night he held me down on the floor.

He knew I would not sue for divorce. Apart from the scandal and the likelihood that my suit would be denied, I had no income of my own, other than dribs and drabs that came in from painting. I depended upon his goodwill.

Better to keep the arrangement we had.

I kept my focus on my work. My reputation was growing, both in England and Cairo, and now with a push from Gurdaya, I'd been approached by a Bombay gallery. It made me a little giddy, and I spent most of my time in the studio, which I'd furnished for my comfort. Peter and I still kept up the appearance of a marriage—I attended events on his arm, and we entertained as required by his position, but I limited the amount of time we spent alone.

One night, after a successful dinner party with three couples from the embassy, he brought me a coffee as I collected my things in the bedroom. "You don't have to go, Elsie. I'll sleep on the sofa."

"That's not necessary. We both might as well be comfortable."

He tucked his hands in his pockets. "I rather miss your company."

I paused. He was quite thoroughly sober, having limited his intake during the dinner. From past experience, I knew he'd likely settle in and drink a fair bit of whiskey before bed, but for now, he was the Peter I knew. "I'm sorry." I sat on the edge of the bed. "I supposed I thought you were happy with this arrangement."

"I know it makes you feel safer, and for that reason, I am willing to go along. I deserved this judgment."

Something about the way he ducked his head brought the youth he'd been into clear focus. I patted the place beside me. When he'd joined me, I said, "It just seemed wise to give you wide berth until you find a way to avoid violence when the demons plague you."

He bent his head into my shoulder. "Don't leave me, Elsie. Please."

I laughed softly. "I have no intention of leaving you."

He raised his head. "Truly?"

"Why would I leave you?" I made my voice light. "Truth be told, I'm married to my painting, and you do not seem to mind that."

He allowed a smile. "I do not. I am quite proud of you."

"You are?"

"I boast to everyone what a gifted artist my wife is." He touched the place on my chest above my buttons. "Beautiful and talented both." He raised his eyes, and I saw that whatever transpired between Margo and him, he still loved me as much as he ever had.

Perhaps out of guilt or pity, I leaned in and kissed him, and allowed him to take off my dress and make love to me, gently, deeply. We slept in the bed together, and he did not go back out to the living room for more whiskey.

Perhaps he could heal.

~

Not more than two months after my day with Gurdaya, a letter arrived from Talwarpur Palace. But not from Tanveer.

> *March 30, 1926*
> *Talwarpur Palace*
> *[In Urdu]*
>
> Dear Elsie,
> Please forgive my forwardness in writing to you directly. I found your address on my husband's desk. I wonder if you would consider visiting us in September, in time for Tanveer's birthday. It is a lovely time in the Punjab, as you may remember.
>
> My main wish is that you might paint our portrait. I saw the painting Gurdaya brought home from Cairo, and I was quite deeply moved. Your work has a depth of compassion and true seeing that is most unusual. I have longed for someone who might be able to see through the damage of my face and paint me in a way that shows who I am. (I assume you know that

I was badly burned as a young woman, but perhaps you do not.)

And to be frank, Tanveer is not well. It is not a disease of the body, but one of the soul, for there is much division among the people of the Punjab, and the British ever try to widen the gaps. I am not a political or philosophical being, and I know he takes courage from your exchanges.

He speaks of you often, sharing your insights and travelogues, and I know that he holds you in very high regard.

Will you consider it? Cairo is not so terribly far, and you must have sometimes wished to visit your childhood home. You would be free to stay for as long as you like, and I have just the space in mind for a studio.

I hope you will say yes.

Your friend by association,

Channan Kaur

I would not go, of course. I suspected Gurdaya's hand in the matter.

April 7, 1926
Talwarpur Palace
[In Urdu]

Dear Elsie,

Channan told me that she wrote to invite you to come here and paint our portrait. It would honor her so deeply for you to do such work, and I thank you for even giving it a single moment of consideration.

I suspect you will hesitate. I have vowed to be as truthful as possible with you and I will not stint

> here. Gurdaya was quite concerned about you after her visit, and I felt similar misgivings over your letter about Peter. Perhaps taking a time for a leisurely visit to the world of your childhood would not go amiss? Channan has already put servants to work making over a room with good, clear light for a studio, and you would be able to visit the tigers and see the work we have done there. We should be free to debate religion and thought and politics until we're both completely weary of it. It would cheer me to no end.
>
> As for the other, surely after so many years, our youthful attachment will have resolved into a mature and respectful friendship?
>
> Please come.
>
> Your friend,
>
> Tanveer

Tanveer's letter haunted me for weeks. *Had* we matured to such a place? Perhaps we had. We were nearly thirty, settled into our own lives, both of us married.

But still I resisted. Even when Gurdaya sent a letter about the Bombay gallery, I resisted. I had made a kind of peace with the way of my life, and going to India seemed a fool's errand, a way to torture myself. What things might be awakened there?

My rational side argued he was a man who kept his word, and he would keep his word to his wife. There would be no danger of dalliance.

In truth, I longed to go. To walk those landscapes, to debate ideas with Tanveer, even to have a chance to meet Gurdaya's children, and see the tigers. Every time I considered it, a fresh wind of possibility blew through my soul.

But had I truly let him go? Would my old sorrow be reawakened in his presence?

In my studio, the bickering voices battled for days, until I realized that if I actually did travel to India, I would spend the entire time there in this state of anxious longing. Absurd for a woman of my age and status.

I would not go.

~

The love affair between Margo and Peter began to be a subject of gossip. I only heard the edges of it, of course, as everyone imagined I wanted protecting. They traveled to a dig, and he came home in a sour state. She returned to Cairo a month later, and they took it up again, famously fighting at a club known for hard-drinking expats. They drank and fought and presumably this fueled less visible sex. He was both more alive and more prone to his instability, and I pushed again for a move back to England or to a different posting. Perhaps Kabul, which was a nondrinking society. He was not interested.

It came to a head when Peter arrived at my studio rather late one night. He was quite drunk, had a scratch across his face. I could see by his bleary eyes that he was in an evil mood. "I need a cup of tea," he said.

"You cannot come in," I said, holding the door. "Not in this state."

"Just give me a cup of tea, Elsie. For God's sake, you're my wife."

I did not move. I'd already changed for bed and felt vulnerable in my nightdress and robe, my feet bare. "I am your wife, but I cannot help you when you are drunk."

"I'm not that drunk." He pushed at the door. My nerves jolted. "I just want a cup of tea."

"It would be better if you find it elsewhere." A little ribbon of warning ran down my spine, making me alert to every small movement he made, his feet, his eyes, his hand flat on the door. "I was already in bed."

"Well, let me sleep next to you then?"

"No, Peter." I braced my hip against the door. "Is there something wrong?"

He scowled. "I'm tired of women who think they run the world. Where would you be if it weren't for me? Hmm? Living in some bedsit, without a penny. What makes you think you can tell me how to live?" With a sudden movement, he pushed the door, and I lost my hold. "You are my wife. I am the master of this family."

I cried out as he barreled into the room, holding up a hand as if he would hit me, and that infuriated him even more. "You act like I'll beat you! Have I ever lifted a hand to you?"

"No." Not exactly, although he'd become more and more unstable when he drank.

But my body reacted to the memory of him knocking me to the ground the night of the winds. My lungs felt compressed, and the hairs on arms lifted, and I could not help but use my peripheral vision to see what I might use to defend myself if need be.

"Of course not!" He stalked around the room, restless as a tiger, taking an apple from the dish on the table, taking a bite, rounding the room toward my easel, where I was working on a new painting of Gurdaya, in her new guise as a mighty woman. "Who's this?"

"A friend from my childhood who came to see me."

His gaze sharpened over his shoulder. "A friend? Have you seen the prince, too?"

"No. Peter, you need to go. You're in a terrible mood."

He continued his pacing and started a nonsensical rant about women and how they were ruining the world for men like him. Suffragettes and women in the workplace, artists and archaeologists.

"Is this about Margo? Have you had a fight?"

"What do you know about Margo?" He tossed the apple core into the sink.

"Everyone knows about her," I said, wearily. "You two have been spotted drinking and scrapping across all of Egypt."

He went still. "That's a lie."

"It is not a lie." I was exhausted by him suddenly, by all of it. "The two of you have not exactly been discreet."

"How dare you!" He slapped me.

It was so sudden and violent that I staggered backward, tripping on the edge of a rug and nearly falling down before I righted myself. Fear ran cold through my veins, and as I straightened, I took the offensive. "Get out!" I cried, shoving him. "Go home and sleep it off."

But he shoved me back. "You're my wife. I pay for this space." He pushed me against the wall and held me there, his face inches from mine. I struggled, pushing back against him, but his grip was harsh, his size an advantage. True fear made my limbs shake. "You always think you're so much better than me, doing me such a favor." He pressed a forearm against my chest, and with his other hand, tore at my robe.

"Peter, stop!" I cried, trying to grab the fabric back around me, push his hand away. "You will hate yourself."

"Will I?" A little smile turned up his lips, and he unbuckled his belt.

I shoved again, unbalancing him, and ran for the door. He got there first, and yanked me around, pushing me to the bed, holding me with one knee and one arm while he dropped his pants. "I don't know what you're fighting about. It's not like we haven't done this before."

Gathering all my reserves and my anger, I screamed as loudly as I could. It took him aback, and when he was off guard from the noise, I managed to roll off the bed. I fell on the floor and scrambled away. I heard him behind me, and grabbed the closest thing I could see—a shoe with a substantial heel. With a feral sound, I slammed the heel into his temple, once, and then again. He staggered away, hand to his head, blood trickling from a cut.

"Get out," I cried. "Out!"

He stared at me for a long moment. I could not tell if he was himself or the monster. I screamed, as loudly as I could manage in my raw throat, "Out!"

He left.

I dropped the shoe, and ran to lock the door, then fell into a chair, trembling, panting.

Enough.

—62—

TELEGRAM

Handed in at: SS RAJPUTANA (MARCONI ROOM)
25 JUNE 1926
Received at: PLYMOUTH WIRELESS STATION
26 JUNE 1926
Forwarded via: POST OFFICE TELEGRAPHS

TO: MAHARAJA TANVEER SINGH
TALWARPUR PALACE
EN ROUTE TO BOMBAY STOP
ARRIVING JULY 5 STOP
PLEASE ADVISE STOP
ELSIE

TO: ELSIE TURNER
SS RAJPUTANA
HAPPY NEWS STOP
WILL MEET YOU AT TERMINAL STOP
ALL IS WELL STOP
TANVEER

All I took to India were my paints and clothing. I withdrew every penny I had from the art account I had established, and it was enough to cover my fare with a small amount to live on for a few weeks. Once I arrived in Talwarpur, I could make arrangements for the rest of my English accounts to be wired. It was not a tremendous sum, but I'd saved it for just such emergencies.

On the trip, I found myself sleeping, unable to think about the past or the future, or even sketch. I read on the deck, letting the salt air sink into my pores. It wasn't until we approached Bombay that the freeze began to crack.

India.

I stood on deck and watched the skyline of Bombay approach, feeling enormous waves of emotion I could barely even name. I felt my mother beside me, that long ago day, felt that girl I had been coming alive, rejoicing that I had, at last, brought her back.

In the terminal, noise of passengers and the general assault of humanity roared through the air. Shouts in a dozen languages, and flashes of color—the orange of a turban, a vivid turquoise sari, the embroidered collar around a goat. Small bells rang from ankles and collars. It smelled of dung and heat, coriander and smoke, urine and dog and sandalwood, a mix so heady it made me feel faint. Overcome, I halted, allowing some deep part of me soak it in, fill me up.

I looked for Tanveer eagerly and thought I spied him a dozen times, a tall man, a man in a suit, in a kurta, three times in turbans and beards.

And when it was finally him, he was so much older than he had been, wearing a dark-blue dastaar and a maharaja coat over his kurta and pajamas. His beard was thick and full. I halted, suddenly shy after so long a time. Breathing in, I willed my emotions to settle, but even as I fought for calm, it was the same as it had been years before at the ball. The more I tried to exert control, the more tears poured from my eyes.

I couldn't move, and instead, he crossed the space between us. So close, I saw that he, too, was emotional. He took my hands, and said in Hindustani, "You're here." His tone was gruff.

I closed my eyes, feeling the pouring heat of my tears, and opened them again. He was still there. His fingers gripped mine tightly.

"I am so sorry," I breathed. "It is just so good to see you."

And then Gurdaya was there, arms flung around me, her enthusiasm much less controlled than ours. "Behen!" I was swept into her embrace, and hugged her back, feeling suddenly tethered to the world again. "I am so happy you have come!" She took my hand, lacing her fingers in mine. Her hair was tucked beneath an elegant dupatta, pale rose and embroidered with gold, and her silk salwar kameez was deeper tones of rose and yellow. She looked every inch a rani.

I looked from one to the other. "I can't believe we're together."

"Shall we go swimming?" Gurdaya asked.

We all laughed. "I still love swimming," I said.

"So do I! We have a pool. I made my husband build it for me."

I was terribly aware of Tanveer on the other side of me, quiet and contained. I could not look at him, but saw him in flashes, the sleeve of his black coat, embroidered with silver, the lift of a knee. In front of us, a servant waved the crowds away so the pair of them could pass, and I felt curious eyes on me, too. When we were children, they were children like me. Now that we were adults, they each carried the glow and power of royalty. It made me feel dizzy that I did not realize, that I had been so foolish to think we had all maintained our status. I had not felt this in Cairo with Gurdaya, but I did now.

A car met us and whisked us to the Victoria Terminus. In the car, Gurdaya poured water and I drank deeply. "We shall eat on the train. It leaves at five. Will you be all right until then?"

"Yes. Thank you."

"Are you all right, Elsie?" Tanveer asked.

I looked at him, and the truth tumbled out. "I am a little overwhelmed, I think."

"Most understandable."

At my side, Gurdaya swept hair from my face. "You are tired from the journey. We shall have plenty of time to rest on the train."

I nodded. The soul of me seemed somewhere else, far away, as if she were watching. Watching me look through the window to the streets milling with people, and animals. Watching Gurdaya and Tanveer exchange a glance. I remembered when I brought Tanveer to Herewich from the hospital, and how little he'd spoken. My pain was small in comparison, but I understood now how hard it could be to speak shame aloud.

"Gudiya," I said at last, rousing myself, "tell me about your children."

She was happy to oblige. Her love for them carried us straight through to the train, where we were settled in a luxurious suite of rooms. The same servants who had waved a pathway through the crowd at the terminus now served tea from silver pots and offered cakes and samosas. "There is no coconut," Tanveer said, a slight glitter in his eye.

"You remembered."

"Of course."

I ate hungrily, aware suddenly that it had been hours since I'd picked at my breakfast, too nervous to really eat. The samosas were filled with potatoes and peas, and I ate two small cakes layered with jam before I leaned back into the velvet comfort of the seats. The train began to move, and I looked out sleepily. Across from me, Tanveer stretched his long legs under the table and crossed his arms.

"Now then," Gurdaya said. "I've brought cards and games. Which would you prefer? Rummy? Parcheesi?"

Tanveer spoke to his sister in Punjabi, and the words spilled over me, a happy memory, the way they'd moved between their languages, English to Punjabi to Hindustani, a river of languages flowing together. To me he said kindly, "I told her to let you sleep."

I protested, sitting up straight and blinking. "I don't mind."

"Dear girl," Tanveer said. "You will fall over any moment."

Gurdaya spoke to the servant in Punjabi, and he disappeared and came back with a soft blanket and softer pillow. I curled up in the corner, safe after the long journey, and allowed myself to sleep.

~

The train took three days, time we spent playing card games and reading aloud to one another from a book I'd had with me on the ship, Agatha Christie's *The Man in the Brown Suit*. At night, we were tucked into our beds, and I looked up at the stars flowing by while I listened to the others breathe. Sometimes I slept, but I sometimes jolted awake in terror, crying out and shaking off my blanket. One or the other of them woke up and sat with me, bringing me water, covering me again as if I were an invalid. In the soft dark, it was easier to be comfortable with this new Tanveer, the husband who was also my friend. He sat with me quietly, holding my hand, but it was only kindness, and I did not make it anything more.

After lunch on the third day, Gurdaya fell asleep so deeply that she snored. I fondly covered her with a blanket and lifted her head to another pillow. She barely moved, her body a deadweight.

I found Tanveer looking at me when I sat back down. It was the first time she had not been there to distract me, which I thought might be the point. I allowed myself to take him in. He seemed to be making the same catalog of me. He said, "What made you change your mind?"

I looked out the window, thinking of the near rape, the mindless, unfocused rage Peter had displayed. Shook my head. "I don't know."

"Gurdaya has been worried about you since she visited in Cairo."

What could I say to that? I only nodded. A sting of grief, or perhaps fury, ran through my midsection, but I could not bear to listen. "Channan can be very persuasive."

"That is quite true"—he leaned forward—"but not the reason you are here."

I took a breath, and in that air he occupied with me was the scent of his skin, so intimate and deep I could feel an echo in my own body, in my elbows and knees. He was the same to me, would always be the same, but I also felt in me the strength of adulthood, the ability to stand firm in reason rather than passion.

But I could not bear to tell the truth, either. I only shook my head in answer, pushing all the rising emotions back into their box.

For a moment, he measured me, then picked up the book we'd all been reading. "Shall I read?"

"Yes," I said, relieved. "We can take turns."

But as we settled, our legs brushed, calf to calf, and I knew I could not stay long. Long enough to do the portrait, and then I would have to go to America and my mother.

A DEMENTED DEMETER

1940
London

—63—

After the lull, the raids started up again midweek. Mother was too ill to move, which meant I had to sit with her on the second floor, where I listened to every falling bomb with a fear that we would be buried any moment. Bastet sat with me, as if she knew I was terrified. An incendiary fell in the garden across the back, and I came out the next morning to see the fence charred.

When the all clear sounded, I washed Mother's face and hands. She rambled, unaware of where she was, sometimes in India as a child, sometimes in America, sometimes with me as a little girl. This night, she asked for the letters from her husband.

"What letters, Mother?"

"The ones he wrote to me."

"Do you mean your husband Leland, my father? Or your husband Garvey, the artist?"

"Oh, Garvey, of course."

I considered thoughtfully, wondering where they might be. And if I found them, would she remember that she'd asked for them? "Letters when you lived in America?"

"No," she said, as if it were obvious. "When I came back to England."

She often confused events, but Garvey had passed away in California of stomach cancer. Surely she would remember that. Peter, who had returned from Kabul by then, had set her up in this house.

I hesitated, unsure how to answer in a way that wouldn't upset her.

"Mother, I'm sorry, but Garvey died before you came back to England."

"Oh, don't be silly. He didn't die. I left him."

"I don't think so. You loved him."

"I adored him. But when it came to Elsie or Garvey, I was always going to choose my daughter. I had to save her."

My limbs went ice cold. "Whatever do you mean, Mother?"

"From another broken heart. I loved Tanveer, of course, who would not, but he could not make her his wife, and she was living as his mistress. I feared she would not survive another shattered heart." She took my hand, looking right into my Elsie eyes and not seeing me. I wondered faintly who she thought she was addressing.

"Your husband did not die?"

"No." Her eyes, so vividly blue, filled with tears. "For the rest of his life, he begged me to return, but a mother does what she must."

A pulse hammered loudly in my ears. Was this true? Was she imagining some other reality that had never happened, smoothing out the painful loss of her husband to make another tale?

"I shall see if I can find the letters," I said. "Where will they be?"

"In the blue hatbox in my closet."

With a buzzing sensation along the edges of my brain, I opened the wardrobe. On a high shelf was a stack of round hatboxes, a pale-blue one on the bottom. One by one, I took them down, stacking them on the floor by my feet, until I freed the blue one.

With trembling hands, I pulled off the lid. Within were dozens of letters. Some were from me. Some from names I didn't recognize in America, some from friends around England and India.

And there, in a cream-colored envelope, thin, with a light sketch of a desert landscape, was a letter from Garvey Martin, Taos, New Mexico, postmarked March 3, 1930.

Some four years after he supposedly died.

I flipped it over, lifted the flap, and unfolded the paper within. One page in a clean, readable script. *Dearest Violet,* he wrote—

Such fury filled me that I could not even see. Dropping the letter in the box, I left it on the floor and looked for a long moment at my mother, who appeared to have fallen asleep.

How could she have lied to me for so long? And what made her do such a desperate thing?

I wanted to scream at her, fling all the letters over her body, but I also wanted to fall against her hand and wail. What a terrible sacrifice, to leave a man and a world she loved to "protect" me!

And for what? For what?

Whirling, I stomped upstairs to my studio. The nudes I'd abandoned at the start of the bombing reclined against the wall, and I grabbed one, tied on an apron and began to paint, transmuting anger into art, my fear into life.

I am alive, I told myself. With every brushstroke, *I am alive. I am alive, I am alive.* Tears of fury and release ran down my cheeks. I painted a furious goddess, a demented Demeter.

I have seen the world. I am a witness to it, beautiful and terrible.

I am alive.

I am going to stay alive.

November 9, 1940
London
[In Urdu]

Dear Tanveer,

Tonight, I painted for hours and hours. There were bombs early, but they haven't returned, and I left Mother sleeping. I have not been back down to check on her, and I know I should go, but I am incandescently angry with her, and I don't even know if I should be. She is most desperately ill; two days ago her physician said simply that we can only keep her comfortable now. He has left morphine for the pain, which makes her sleep, and when she wakes, she hardly knows who she is or when she is. She rarely knows who I am—one day I am your mother, another my father, another some invisible confessor who knows all her secrets.

Tonight, she matter-of-factly told me that her husband in America did not die. She left him, and she did it to manipulate me to come back to England from India.

I write that and my hands shake all over again. I am so furious with her. I am heartbroken for her and for myself, and for you, for us, for everything that—

Oh, it doesn't matter. You know.

And yet, I also grieve that my mother, my beloved, beloved mother, is fading. I grieve that I may never have an actual conversation with her again. How can I be angry and grieving and love her so deeply and feel so appalled at actions that have caused me—both of us—genuine harm, all at once?

I did not return to England because of her manipulations. I would not have. So why am I so very furious with her? And how do I make peace before she dies?

I feel quite lonely. I miss Betty's competent cheer. I am mostly alone with my mother, who is no longer really here, and she is too ill to move to Nina's as I'd hoped to do.

Enough of my sniveling.

One small beauty is the silver comb I found in the rubble when I went to visit Betty. I've enclosed a drawing. It's quite beautiful, and I polished it to wear, thinking of the woman who lost it. Perhaps one day I'll be in the market and she will see it and say, "That is the comb I lost in a raid. My grandmother gave it to me!" And I will happily, in peacetime, return it to her.

Fanciful, but one never knows.

Love,

Elsie

A MATURE AND RESPECTFUL FRIENDSHIP

1926
Talwarpur, India

—64—

The train station was the same one where we'd arrived for the maharaja's birthday so many years before, and for the first time I felt true joy. "No elephants?" I said as a car was brought around.

"Elephants?" Gurdaya asked.

Tanveer grinned. "The party for Baoji when everyone came. Elephants brought everyone from the station to the palace."

"I had forgotten! What a spectacle!"

"My mother was so thrilled," I said and remembered Rocky's lover Grayson, long ago at the picnic, asking Tanveer about riding elephants. Grayson, who'd been a boor, but now was a dead one. He'd been one of the first to die in our group.

I brushed the memory away. A rising sense of possibility filled me as the desert passed by the windows. The siblings chatted back and forth in their mix of languages, perhaps making plans, perhaps something else. I caught a sentence here and there but mostly let the mingled languages wash over me, bringing with them sunstruck memories of childhood. "Do you ever go to Nainital now?" I asked.

"I haven't been there since we were children," Gurdaya said.

"I have been. We still hold the house there for summer. Channan has not been able to make the trip for some years, but I have been a few times. Would you like to visit? It could be arranged."

A dangerous place in my current state. I lifted a shoulder in pretend disinterest. "Perhaps. I just thought of it."

"The swimming," Gurdaya said, and sighed.

I dared not look at Tanveer, but felt the heat crawl up my neck. He banged my knee with his, and I looked up to slam into a bland expression, a quick, sidelong glance. I banged him back and scowled. "Is your husband's palace far? I should love to swim in your pool."

"It is a journey," she said with a sigh. "And I will not linger long at Talwarpur, only a day or two. My children will want their mother back."

"And their mother wants them back," Tanveer said.

"It was good of you to make the trip."

"It wasn't good of me," she protested. "I couldn't bear to wait until you could come visit me. This way, I will have a little taste of your company, and you might come in a few months to stay with me. They can't have you all to themselves."

A few months! When I'd fled Cairo, I had not considered how long I would be here. I covered her hand. "I shall."

As we approached the village outside the palace, the car slowed. The driver said something I didn't quite catch.

Tanveer muttered under his breath, peering out. "It's a small group. Carry on."

"Protesters again?" Gurdaya asked.

"Yes."

"What are they protesting?"

"The British, the wealthy, the laws." He shook his head. "Legitimate, but dangerous. Last month, they attacked a car outside of Jalandhar, and the family barely got away. They set the car on fire."

As we passed through the crowd, it parted, but a rock hit the car, and then another. Nothing else. We made it to the palace, and the gate closed tight behind us.

The palace was as massive as I remembered, but shabbier. How thrilled I had been that first visit to have a sketchbook in my hand at all times, drawing the various forms of tile work, the arches and the hallways, courtyards with their tinkling fountains and bougainvillea. A blaze of flowers still climbed the walls, and as we stepped out into the blast of heat, I heard a fountain nearby.

And there, waiting for us, was a small woman in a soft blue sari. Tanveer took my hand and drew me to her realm. I towered over her—she could not have been more than five feet tall—and she'd draped her face with her veil. As I came forward, she pulled it away and held out her hands.

I'd been afraid of what I might see—burning and scarring and misshapen features. All of those things did exist. One eye and her mouth pulled toward each other in a web of scarring, and long white scars marred the other side of her face. Even her hairline had been shifted by that injury long ago.

But she held her chin proudly, and there was such a glow of joy and welcome in her expression that all the rest was swept away. "Dear, dear Elsie. I am so glad you've come."

I bowed my head, offering a namaskar. "Maharani Sahiba."

"Please," she said. "We shall not stand on ceremony. You are the sister of my sister. Come inside. I wish to show you the studio I have prepared."

She reached out her hand. It, too, was scarred, the flesh white and brown and pink. I took its smallness in my own. "I cannot wait to paint you," I said, and meant it very much.

Tanveer had hung back, and now he said, "I shall leave you to it."

"We shall have an intimate supper," Channan said. "Gurdaya, come with us to see the suite."

~

The rooms were in a tower. Channan rested every fourth step, and I protested. "I'm sure Gurdaya can show me the room!"

"I have been anticipating this moment."

"As you wish." But I slowed my steps more fully.

We made our way, and entered a suite of rooms through a pair of tall carved wooden doors. It was bright and airy, high up, with open archways in the tower portion. Through the arches, I could see in all four directions. Across the plains, the austere desert with dusty trees, all the way to a line of mountains in the distance. From another angle was a courtyard of the main palace, and from another, the open balcony of another tower. Last, the fourth direction looked on the ruined tower I had painted so often. "Do griffins still nest there?"

"They do," Channan cried. "And you will see pigeons, too."

The bedroom was richly appointed with a wide bed and curtains threaded with silver. An adjoining room was furnished with a wide table and an easel. "Will that do?"

"It's beautiful, Channan. All of it." I turned to her. "I feel like a princess myself."

"An earl's daughter is not such a low form of life," Gurdaya said drily, picking things up and putting them down, rounding the room as if inspecting it.

"The earl died, and so did his heir, I'm afraid, so I am anointed no longer."

"Nonsense. You were born as you were born."

A sense of depletion suddenly flooded my limbs, and I sat down suddenly.

"You must rest," Channan said. "And drink water. I'll send a servant to bring you water for a bath before dinner."

I nodded. I'd brought two gowns suitable for dinner at the palace, which would see me through for a bit. "Thank you."

Channan paused at my side. "I will see you tomorrow in my chambers at nine."

"Of course."

"I'll send my servant to lead the way." Her hand rested on my shoulder. "I am very glad you've come, Elsie. Thank you."

Gurdaya waited until she departed. "Do you need anything? Your luggage is very thin."

I glanced at the small cases. "And most of it is paint," I said with a rueful smile.

"As I thought. I shall see to it."

"Thank you."

"Elsie," she said. "He hurt you, did he not?"

"I am all right now that I'm here."

"I could have him killed, you know."

The offer was so surprising, I burst out laughing. She raised her eyebrows.

"I know," I said, still smiling. "Perhaps that won't be necessary."

She shrugged and left me.

~

I awakened from the deepest sleep, slightly confused about where I was. It was dark, and the bed was deeply soft. A shadow stood over me, and I bolted awake, terrified, scooting backward. "Leave me alone."

"Shh. Elsie, it's me." The voice was familiar but out of place. He leaned in, spoke in Hindustani. "I did not mean to frighten you."

Tanveer. The world coalesced. I was in India, in the tower room Channan had prepared for me. "What are you doing here?"

"There is a meteor shower. I want you to see it."

I blinked, took a breath. "Did I miss dinner?"

He chuckled softly. "Dinner and breakfast and dinner again."

"I've never slept like that in my life!"

"A long journey," he said. "Come, get dressed, and let's see the Perseids. I have food waiting."

That caught my attention. I pressed a hand to my empty belly. "I *am* hungry."

"I shall wait in the corridor."

I nodded, throwing the bedclothes off me, and hesitated. "Is it all right for me to go with you to the roof alone? Seemly?"

He nodded. "It is all right. I promise."

I scrambled to wash my face and don a skirt and blouse I found in the cupboard, and the slippers that had been left in the bathroom. It registered for the first time, a luxurious space with a deep tub and tiled appointments. Very modern. In the mirror, I looked clear eyed.

Two days!

I joined Tanveer in the corridor. He wore a simple kurta and carried a lantern flickering orange, casting shadows on the walls. He held out his hand. "The way is shadowed."

His palm and fingers enfolded mine, as if I were home. And perhaps I was in a way. It had always felt that way with Tanveer, whether we were friends or mental sparring partners or lovers. Now something more and less, friends who had shared a great deal of life. At the thought, a tremendous amount of pressure soughed from my body.

He squeezed my fingers lightly, then held the lantern high so I could climb the stairs. Lizards darted in front of me, making me squeak and hold back. He paused. "They will not hurt you."

"I know. They just startled me."

"Of course." When the way was clear, we kept climbing.

The steps opened to a rooftop. Another lantern sat on a small table, where I could see a pitcher and glasses and a tray of food. My stomach growled and without even knowing it, my body headed straight for it.

"Wait," Tanveer said, touching my arm. "Take a moment to look up."

I hadn't yet noticed the sky. Horizon to horizon, it was dark, moonless, which made every star and galaxy all the brighter. I took in a breath of wonder at the endlessness of it, tipping my head back to take it in. The Milky Way was directly overhead, stretching across the midheaven in a display of endless galaxies, and even as I watched, a streak of red crossed it. I cried out in delight. "I saw one!" And I spun, but felt overbalanced, and reached for his arm.

He offered his elbow. "Steady."

I lowered my head, realizing that all I had to do was stand there to be absorbed into the endless array of stars. "I feel as if I am floating, as if I am a star myself."

"We are stars," he said quietly, looking upward. He pointed. "Another one."

"And another!" This one was smaller, slight and pink.

"I was right to wake you, then."

Startled, I looked at him. "Of course! How could you think anything else?"

"Good. Have something to eat, and we can lie on our backs. I brought cushions."

I was famished, and filled a little plate with pakoras and wedges of paratha, nibbling them at first to test the heat after so long a time, but they were exquisite. I washed them down with salty lassi, refreshing and sour, and guava. Licking my fingers, I said, "I apologize for missing dinner. Did a servant come to wake me?"

"They did, but when they said you were still sleeping, both Gurdaya and Channan insisted you be able to sleep as long as you required."

I gave a little snort of laughter. "Two days is a bit long."

"It can be good to sleep at times of transition."

Transition, I thought, finding a knot of sorrow in my throat. Had I truly left Peter for good? "I suppose that's true."

"I hope you will feel you can talk to me again, Elsie," he said and offered a fresh date from a small bowl. "That we can find a way into . . . whatever form this takes now."

I didn't want to talk to him about what had happened with Peter. Even the thought of it made shame crawl up my neck, heating my ears. I looked away. "If I don't, it has nothing to do with our trying to find a new footing."

"Then what?"

Words welled and then caught in my throat. I shook my head.

We stretched out on cushions covered by patterned blankets, and the night was cool, so we wrapped up with the blankets, lying side by side. "I cannot believe how many stars you can see."

"It is quite arid here, and that makes the view very clear." He pointed. "Meteor."

I watched it streak across. "What other constellations are we seeing now?"

"Garmi kā Musallas is the summer triangle, made of Vega, Deneb, and Altair." He pointed toward each one, brighter than many around them. "Of course, Thurayyā, the Seven Sisters. Famous in poetry."

"Mmm." Some piece of me that had been taut for months, maybe years, began to unwind. "Why are they called the Seven Sisters?"

"Ah, that is a good tale. The sisters were the offspring of Atlas, who was condemned to hold up the sky, and Pleione, a sea nymph. When al-Jabbār, the hunter, saw them, he fell in love and pursued them across the earth."

"He fell in love with all of them?"

"Gods have mighty appetites."

"Ah."

"When their father heard about the pursuit, the sisters were exhausted and weary. Atlas took pity on them and turned them into stars, where even in the sky, they huddle together for safety." I watched him trace the cluster. "Al-Jabbār pursued them into the sky, and now chases them for all eternity."

"Justice for his greed."

"Indeed."

"You rhymed."

"I did." He glanced at me. "On purpose."

Dying stars fell across the sky in red and white and green. Next to me was the solid, breathing presence of Tanveer, whom I'd missed for literally years. I'd missed the sound of his voice, his particular phrasings. Missed his chuckle. Missed this way he had of telling a story at every turn. It did not matter that we were not lovers. I felt the tattered bits of my soul, shredded so badly over the years of struggle, begin to reweave themselves.

"I am very grateful you're here," he said quietly, reading my mind. "The world rights itself when I'm in your company."

"Yes," I said, and looked at him. "Has your world been akilter?"

"It has. A society in upheaval seems to always turn to violence, no matter how we try to structure it more carefully."

"What of Mr. Gandhi's nonviolence?"

"A good movement, but I do not know if it will be enough."

"I'm sorry."

"This, too, shall pass."

I said, "And the stars will keep shining."

"Long after we are no longer here to fight beneath them."

"Or find joy in them."

He looked at me, and feeling it, I turned my head. A faint smile lifted his mouth. "A good reminder. I am here now, under these stars, and you are with me."

For a fleeting moment, I wondered if we were tempting ourselves too much in this exercise, but then he looked back up to the sky.

"Here we are," I said, and let myself fly into the darkness lit by ten thousand stars.

—65—

Channan was deeply unwell for several days after the night of ten thousand stars. She sent word that I should explore as I wished, and eat well, and paint to my heart's content. Tanveer had business in Lucknow and traveled with Gurdaya.

So, indeed, the palace was mine to explore. I wandered without restraint, finding vast empty rooms meant for state functions or balls, and intimate little parlors decorated with lush rugs and draperies. I got lost in courtyards and then could not find them again. I explored rooms where ceilings had fallen down and birds roosted. There were many cats of many colors. Some appeared to be pets, very friendly and companionable. I made particular friends with a hefty black beauty with yellow eyes and extra toes. Others were more like barn cats and not interested in human companionship. They skittered away if I came close. I began to carry small bits of meat in my pockets for them.

One afternoon, I sketched in the sunshine of a courtyard. Something about the sun on my feet made me think of my ayah with a sudden and piercing sense of longing. Was she still alive?

I paused my drawing, remembering. A cat came from a hidden place, pale yellow with long fur, and I sat up. "Topaz! Is that you?"

He turned toward me for a long minute, and we studied each other. Perhaps this was not Topaz himself, but a descendant. But I called him anyway. "Topaz, come here, kitty. *Psh psh psh.*" I held out my hand. "Do you remember me?"

All at once he *mewp*ed with excitement and trotted toward me, meowing all the way. He leapt up into my lap, and when I laughed, putting aside my sketchbook, he butted his head against my chin. "I am so happy to see you!" He purred and meowed an entire conversation. "You've grown into quite a big cat."

I held him close and bent my face into his fur, thinking what a life of adventure he'd lived, from the killing fields of France to England, to the palace.

He followed me back to my room and jumped on the bed as if he belonged there, watching while I sketched a great rolling storm moving in with towers of clouds and lightning shooting across the landscape.

His presence seemed a little miracle. A small wonder, to be sure.

July 16, 1926
Talwarpur, India

Dear Mother,

I hope this finds you well and continuing the pleasure of your life in Taos. I write this from Talwarpur Palace, where I have come to paint a portrait of the maharaja and maharani, at the request of the maharani. It has been deeply enjoyable so far. Channan, for she has insisted I call her that, is a charming and gracious woman, and I am greatly looking forward to painting her.

I find myself coming alive in a way I had forgotten. Cairo is lovely, and I love the desert, but Egypt is not India. I wept when I saw Bombay from the ship. Every minute since has been more of the same joy.

Peter and I have struggled in our marriage, as I think you know. This time will give us an opportunity to—

I paused. What did I mean here? An opportunity to think things over? An opportunity to heal? No. What I felt in my gut was that I would never return. I would find some way to live in India. Gurdaya had contacts in the art world in Bombay, and perhaps I could make a living as an art teacher in finer schools, to supplement whatever I could earn from my paintings. Perhaps, if the commission of the maharani was beautiful enough, I might attract more such portraits.

> —discover a new arrangement for ourselves. His shell shock combined with drink creates a violence that is untenable. I have tried to find solutions, but as long as he continues blunting his wounds with gin, I do not feel safe. While I have little hope I would be granted a divorce, I can choose to live apart from him. I know how fond you are of him, but please understand this is not something I have undertaken lightly.
>
> Always your loving daughter,
>
> Elsie

After three days, I was hungry for companionship and asked an older servant woman, someone who appeared to be in charge of things, if the maharani was too ill for company. She shook her head and gestured for me to follow her. I remembered the last time I visited the palace, there had been armies of servants in corridors and gardens, sweeping parlors and cleaning tiles and carting things from place to place with an air of purpose. Now I spied one girl in the courtyard, sweeping, and could hear the sound of people in the kitchen. A guard at the gate.

Very few.

In my girlhood, the palace had overflowed with people, the wives and all the children of Tanveer's father, who had clearly not followed the usual Sikh practice of only one wife, but took four or maybe even five by the end. I thought of him at the ball in London, virile and charming, a man who'd made his own way, navigating between the Hindi and Muslim majorities in India, and manipulating the British as well, his small principality doing well over time. I knew from Tanveer's letters that drought and plague had diminished the entire Punjab since the war, and when the population revolted, they'd been crushed by the British, more than once. The worst, of course, had been the attack at Jallianwala Bagh, but there had been others.

The emptiness now in the palace seemed lonely. I was quite sure when Gurdaya and her family visited, it could be as noisy and colorful as when Tanveer was a boy, but now it was so quiet I could hear my slippered feet on the swept floors.

The servant opened Channan's door and went in. I waited in the corridor, book in hand. Within, I heard an exchange in Punjabi, and then the woman was back, waving me in. "I will bring tea, memsahib," she said in Hindustani. "Would you like cake?"

"Oh, please!" I answered and then left the shadows for a sunny room that faced south. Tiny Channan sat on a chaise, legs covered with a blanket. Her hair was braided in a long fall over her shoulder, and she wore a simple dressing gown in a soft peach shade, with ribbons in red. Without her veil, I could see the uneven terrain of her hairline. A tiny black cat curled in a ball at her ankles, opening one eye as I came in.

I bowed in deference to her status. "Hello, Maharani Sahiba."

She shook her head slowly. "I have already said we shall dispense with titles, my dear. Please, come sit with me."

I took a comfortable chair nearby the chaise. "I did try to leave you alone," I said, smiling, "but I admit my mother always said that, when I was a little girl, I so required conversation that I made up names for teapots and dishes and had conversations with them."

She laughed lightly. It made her cough, and she pulled a handkerchief from her sleeve and spit into it. "Forgive me," she said, touching her chest. "I have weak lungs."

"I shall endeavor not to make you laugh, then," I replied.

"Oh, please, I'd rather laugh and cough than not laugh at all." She measured me for a moment. "You are much invigorated after your long sleep."

I laughed. I'd almost forgotten that I'd slept for two days upon arrival. "I am so sorry I slept through your welcome dinner and our morning appointment. Will you forgive me?"

"Nothing to forgive. You looked quite wan when you arrived." She inclined her head. "Is it being back in India at last that enlivens you? Or"—a sideways glance—"have you left your husband, then?"

Startled, I gaped at her. "I—er—"

"I have been told I speak my mind too frankly," she said, "but life has taught me that the things we think matter so much are not the right things at all."

I met her straightforward gaze, feeling humbled. "I welcome your frankness. It has sometimes been a flaw of mine, as well."

"You say *flaw* when I believe you mean *virtue*."

I chuckled. "Yes."

"So, have you left him?"

I took a breath. "Yes. He is a decent man when he's not drinking, but he's very cruel when he is."

"Did he hurt you?"

A sting of tears made me look away. "He did," I said at last. "But I would ask that knowledge remain between us."

She nodded, reaching for my hand. I tugged my chair closer so that I could easily hold it. "Your truth is my secret."

"Thank you."

"My husband said you watched the meteor shower together the other night."

"It was so beautiful. I'm sure you've seen it."

"Once or twice. I am not terribly fit for stairs, and there are a great many to the roof."

I nodded, but in fact, my fingers were itching with the need to sketch her. I took my sketchbook from my deep pocket. "Do you mind if I sketch you as we talk?"

"Not at all."

"Do you have family nearby?" I asked, drawing a line from the top of her head to her toes, then back up.

"No, they live quite far away, near Udaipur. I sometimes see my sister in Jaipur, but—" She spread her fingers. "They find it hard to look upon me. Without Gurdaya, I would be quite lost."

I absorbed the shape of her chin, the angle of her neck. "Must Tanveer travel often?"

"Yes, but—oh, it is not the company of a man I long for. I miss my sisters."

"I do not have sisters, aside from the time I spent with Gurdaya." Sketching the line of her shoulder, the shape of fabric over it, I said, "How many do you have?"

"Three, but one died in childbirth. I was still a child, so I do not remember her well. Gurdaya has been a comfort to me, certainly. She is a very lively companion."

"She is, indeed. She has fashioned a life that suits her very well." I sketched the shape of the cat at her ankle. "I am sorry you're deprived of your sisters."

"Oh, no. Do not misunderstand. I do not complain about my lot. I am very fortunate that Tanveer agreed to marry me and bring me here. Else I would have spent my life on the edges of my father's court, pitied and ignored. At least this way we do entertain, and I have some social intercourse. When I am well enough."

I nodded. With a light hand, I suggested the scars on her face, with a heavier hand, made her eyes black as a new moon. "You have beautiful eyes."

"May I see?"

"Of course." I held up the drawing and she stared at it for a long moment.

"You've made me beautiful."

"I have only drawn what I see."

The servant came in with a tray of tea and cakes and settled it on an inlaid table at Channan's elbow. The woman spoke in Punjabi, and Channan dismissed her. "Will you serve, Elsie?"

I set my book aside. "I feel you must have spent a great deal of time with the British."

"Yes. My father wanted us all to know your manners and customs. He believed we should understand our enemy." She smiled, taking a delicate cup.

"Like your husband," I said.

"Exactly. They met through politics, after the Amritsar massacre."

That had been the moment Tanveer had recognized a marriage between the two of us would never be possible if he were to accomplish the goals he'd set for his life. The memory clanged a dull gong in my chest.

"Have I said something wrong?"

"No." I shook off the selfish memory. "I was just remembering how terrible it was."

She leaned back, as if suddenly exhausted. "It was, indeed."

"Shall I read, Channan? I've brought a novel I have found very enjoyable."

"That would be lovely."

So we had tea and I had cakes and I read Agatha Christie. The rains moved in hard late in the day, and I wandered back to my rooms where I sketched whatever crossed my mind—the kittens around the palace; Gurdaya in her rose-colored sari, the look of the train compartment, and Channan, fast asleep.

I had feared I might resent the woman who had married Tanveer, but instead I found in her a friend.

What a surprise she was. What a surprise all of it was.

—66—

August 20, 1926
Taos, New Mexico

Oh, Elsie, what have you done! I received your letter and one from Peter on the very same day, and you present quite different stories. He admits to drinking heavily in Cairo, and regrets his behavior. He did not elaborate, but I can piece things together myself. British men are often known for their wandering eye, and while regrettable, it is not grounds for this kind of drama. Running away!

It is also not safe for an English gentlewoman in India now. The turmoil reaches us even in America—riots and trouble and even people murdered.

I am distraught. Please write and tell me you have ended this mad sojourn and have returned to mend your marriage. Peter offers me a great deal of financial support of which I do not think you are aware. My husband is not a wealthy man, an artist who lives very simply. Those funds from Peter are my lifeline.

Go home to your husband, Elsie. You have never thought clearly about the prince, but you cannot risk everything to live in India no matter how much you wish to do so.

Mother

The letter came with the morning post, an airmail envelope that looked battered and stained. I read it and then sat on my balcony holding it while I let her words sink in. *You present quite different stories.* Why had she believed him instead of me? The scolding tone of the letter made me feel strangely ashamed, even as I knew I was in the right. But if my mother did not support my choice, even when I told her the truth, what hope of anyone else giving me the benefit of the doubt?

In that case, why would I bother to return to that world? Why wouldn't I stay in India, where I felt loved and welcomed?

In the tower across the courtyard, I saw Tanveer emerge, toothbrush in hand, his chest bare, his hair not yet bound. He faced the mountains, and tucked the toothbrush into his mouth, then stretched tall, arms overhead.

I was entirely riveted. His bare arms were a burnished burnt umber, and his hair fell nearly to his waist. When he swung around, I saw the black hair across his chest, something that had been missing when I had last seen that chest unclothed. Virility surrounded him like a sheen, or perhaps it was only my eyes, devouring the surprise, coming alive to a hunger I'd done very well to ignore.

But, oh, he was so beautiful standing there in the morning light! So easy in his skin, so cheerfully looking out at the world. When he caught sight of me, he grinned and waved, then crossed his arms in jest as if to cover himself. I waved back, shaking my head.

He disappeared into his rooms. I stood at the wall with my mother's thin letter in my hand. With sharp gestures, I tore it into ribbons and flung it into the air to be carried away by the breeze. My limbs shimmered with life and a longing I could not satisfy, but it was still better to be alive here in this place, with these challenges, than in the life I had fled.

I would not go back.

~

Life settled into an easy rhythm over the new few weeks. I spent my mornings painting and sketching and reading, sometimes writing letters to Nina and Gurdaya. I did not write my mother or Peter, even though letters did arrive from both of them. I threw them away unread. Tanveer held durbars with various villagers and officials and his munshi. Often, we had a light midday meal together in a small courtyard that was deeply shaded until very late afternoon. I told him about my painting and he shared stories of the durbar—a Hindu farmer complaining about his Muslim neighbor's cow, a road that needed work, complaints about celebrations that had grown too loud. Sometimes there were more serious problems—a conflict over the gurdwara in the village that had been recently reclaimed, the struggles of cells of radicals who wanted more visible action against the British, but this was only spoken of in low voices.

Channan rarely joined us at midday. She reserved her small pools of strength for our afternoon portrait sessions, and for the more festive evening meal. Festive in the fact that we all three were there, and sometimes were joined by visiting officials or politicians, even some locals who were not of high status to show that Tanveer embraced the Guru's edict of equality between classes and between the sexes, a philosophy that had led to the names of Singh for men, and Kaur for women, since Indian surnames revealed the caste of the bearer.

The discussions on such evenings was lofty and illuminating, and quite lively. Often the discussions with the men would continue long into the night, plans and problems and the worries of danger. Channan and I took tea into her chamber where her maid readied her for bed. I read to her and we talked about the readings, or simply sat quietly. She loved needlework, and claimed it kept her fingers flexible. When I returned to my chambers, I could often see the lanterns flickering from the parlor below, men's voices rolling out indistinctly into the night.

In the afternoons each day, when the sun was too high for comfort, we gathered in a courtyard on the north end of the palace, shaded by neem trees and cooled by an ancient system of water pouring through a grid in the walls. It was still quite warm, but Channan suffered more if the air was cool, and she preferred the courtyard to any other room in the palace. Pots of bougainvillea and hibiscus bloomed against the tiled walls, and a fountain burbled cheerfully.

I'd kept the easel she supplied in my room and asked the carpenter of the palace, Ramu, to make me one that was larger and sturdier in preparation for the size of canvas I planned. The palace walls were enormous. The painting needed to be, as well.

Before I officially began, I did watercolor studies in various poses. Channan always sat. Sometimes, Tanveer sat beside her, sometimes stood behind. He was so much larger than she that I felt we had to balance the painting in some way or she would appear a child. And there was the challenge of painting her both as the woman who had been so badly hurt and the woman who had survived, the courageous lion who lived with joy, despite her physical frailty. I tried various saris, discarding them all, until her maid brought out one of layers of green with gold embroidery. It brought her alive.

Tanveer resisted the trappings of a maharaja. He wanted to wear the simple fabrics of the area, as Gandhi asked, but Channan was irritated by this. It would be a royal portrait, after all. He must be in royal dress. "Aside from my desire to break from this absurd tradition," he protested, "it is too hot for such clothing."

"Elsie," Channan said, "do you agree with me?"

I held up my hands, out of the fight. In the end, he wore the black maharaja coat he'd been wearing when he and Gurdaya fetched me from Bombay, and a dastaar made of black silk with a brooch of rubies and pearls I remembered from his father's day.

Each day when we began the sitting, I settled into my painting self, not seeing humans or objects, only light and color and shape, the shadow of an arm, the circle of a jewel, the color and shape of a fingernail. My focus was deep and clear.

But each day, at some point or another, I would fall back into my body, and I would see Tanveer looking back at me with his soft gaze. For a moment, we would rise, suspended in the gold-tinted air, and then I would breathe and return to my selfless self and remember to think of shape. Of light. Of color.

~

Despite the hours we spent on our own, Tanveer and I were models of honor. We quickly fell back into our long-established modes of debate, talking over ideas in the books we shared and sometimes just sitting side by side to read. We walked the perimeter of the palace, along a section where the grasses were kept low to discourage snakes, and talked about everything, speaking in English and Hindustani in the same way our letters had moved back and forth, to talk about books, history, time, place, the skies, ourselves.

One overcast morning, he took me on a high wooden walkway that had been built above the tiger enclosure, and I glimpsed two tigers sleeping in the long grass. "You may come here to draw them whenever you like," he said.

I thought of the tiger we had mourned together, so long ago. "It is quite moving that your love of that first tiger led to this special place."

He leaned on the railing overlooking the vast enclosure, hands clasped. The steel kara on his wrist caught the light, and blue ink stained his thumb. "*Our* love of that tiger," he said.

I nodded, thinking of her enormous paws, the way we wept over her. I thought, too, of the tiger he'd rescued, and how it felt to hold her, and how everything had changed between us that day. "Is Chhoti Billi still alive?"

"She lived to be twelve," he said. "And nurtured the other ones who came in."

I did not spend any time thinking of that hay-filled room, but my body remembered, a whisper of the lost erotic at the back of my throat, a shimmer over my scalp. I shook it away.

Perhaps it was the same for Tanveer, for he straightened and gestured for me to head back the way we came.

~

The one thing we did not do was read or speak of poetry. Beneath our civility ran an unspoken simmering, one that flared to high heat if the bare skin of our hands brushed or an exchange of repartee strayed ever so slightly too far into the risqué, or something reminded us both of a memory that held a heat or story of its own. There were so many markers of that shared time, of our braided life, braided time. Sometimes at night, I could see the lights burning in his chamber, and it pained me to know he was there, alone, and I was here in my own room, alone except for Topaz, who slept next to my pillow.

For his part, Tanveer gave no indication that he felt anything other than friendship for me, which made me feel ashamed for the fleeting desire that speared me in odd moments.

Thus we had achieved that mature friendship we'd sought. For me, I was only grateful to be in his company again. To hear his voice and see him laugh. It felt like dawn had risen in my life again.

One late morning, I helped Channan downstairs for a rare luncheon appearance. She'd been feeling well, and I helped her settle in a wide, soft chair she loved in the parlor. Finishing his durbar of the morning, Tanveer walked into the corridor outside the room, trading jokes in Punjabi with a local man, both of them taking pleasure in the kind of one-upmanship so many men seemed to enjoy. Tanveer abruptly laughed, a sound as large as the sun. Channan and I both looked up. Tanveer slapped the man's back and led him to the gate.

"I have not heard him laugh so much," Channan said. "He is so much happier with you here."

"Oh, I am quite sure that is not true."

She looked at me quite seriously. "I assure you that it is. I have never known this Tanveer."

I sat next to her, smoothing my salwar kameez, for I had taken to wearing the simple outfit. The style was as comfortable as my brother's trousers, if not more so. "How so?"

She gathered her hands to herself. "He has ever been kind and good, of course. But never particularly happy." She shook her head. "And never playful."

I hardly knew how to respond. It seemed an intimate observation of a wife about her husband, and I did not think it my right to comment. I remembered him as a boy, full of energy and light, as a young man, teasing and alive, in England, and then the sorrowful man he'd been after the war. But I could not offer those memories here. "Perhaps it is simply that we are connecting to our childhood selves."

"No." She took my hand, a little smile on her mouth. "You must listen, Elsie."

I opened my face to show I was receptive.

"My father was a forward-thinking man, just as Tanveer's father was, and he saw to it that all his daughters were well educated. I speak six languages, and read four with some proficiency."

"Like Gurdaya," I said, smiling. "Do the two of you trade Latin asides?"

She gave an appreciative chuckle. "She is even more accomplished than I. My Latin is poor." She passed a thumb over my knuckle, back and forth. "No, but I do read Arabic, which you may not know is very close to Urdu script."

"I have only recently learned that, when I was in Cairo."

"I do not think Tanveer quite realizes." She swept a hand over her skirt, brushing away a leaf that had fallen in her lap. "He writes ghazals in Urdu," she said. "Poetry. All of them are about you."

I flushed deeply, and could not think what to say. At last I managed, "Perhaps he did at one time," I said softly. "But it must not have been for many years." And that seemed not quite right, and I added, "I am so sorry if that caused you pain. We met long ago."

"It did not cause me pain," she said in her sensible voice. "From the beginning, our marriage was a clear agreement." She pressed her lips together. "My injuries caused more damage than my face. I was scarred within, as well."

The implication of that simple confession burned through the core of me, but I would not insult her dignity with overt emotion or even a whiff of pity. I covered her hand where it rested on the chair.

"We will not speak of it again. Not even Gurdaya knows, or any of the servants. But I would not let Tanveer marry me until I told him, for not only will I never have children, Elsie, but I cannot participate in the acts that will create a child, either."

I swallowed hard, willing myself to simply be a witness.

"He married me to give me a good life. My dowry was helpful, but it was not enough to make even a splash into this"—she waved her hand toward the ceiling—"crumbling place."

At that, I could not help the tears that spilled from my eyes. It seemed a very quintessential Tanveer act, not a sacrifice but a stand.

"He told me at the time that his heart belonged to another, so we have been very honest with each another," she said. "The ghazals are not old. He is laughing and alive in this new way because he is alight with you here."

My heart beat too hard, too loudly. I did not let go of her hand.

"He loves you. I believe you also love him."

Again the flush rose in my cheeks. "There has been nothing untoward between us, Channan. I would never betray you, nor would Tanveer."

"I do know." She took a breath. "What I am saying is that you will not betray me."

A small low trembling began in my legs. "What do you mean?"

"Allow him to love you. Love him in return. A man should not be so long without a woman in his bed."

My breath disappeared, and for a long, long moment, I had no air in my body. My vision prickled at the edges, and I tried to imagine what this could mean, how it would even be possible when both Tanveer and I loved Channan, and we had found this peaceful, loving existence.

And yet, a song began to hum along my nerves. What if? What if I could kiss him again? Touch him again? Lie with him?

I heard him enter the room, feet shushing over the floor in his slippers. "What is this secret conversation?" he said, dropping to an ottoman.

I looked at him, my ears roaring. So many conflicting emotions swirled through me that I would have leapt to my feet and fled immediately if Channan had not increased her grip on my hand, holding me there. He looked back at me with a tilt of his head, and then to Channan. In the instant before she spoke, he seemed to sense the intensity of the moment. She held out her hand and he took it.

"I have just been telling Elsie that I read Urdu script. And I apologize for reading your ghazals, but they are enchanting."

"You read my private papers?"

"I did," she said without apology. "That is not the matter here." She sandwiched our hands together between her tiny ones, his on top of mine, hers above and below. "The truth is that you share a deep love, and it deserves life."

Tanveer met my eyes, and I had no sense of what he was thinking. My discomfort was so high I would have gladly slipped out of my skin to run away, but the weight of our entwined hands held me there.

And, too, what held me was a longing to slip into his flesh, find again that place where our souls met.

We stared at each other. Possibility rose like lavender smoke, wafting through me, between us, circling his head. He was as surprised as I, and after a moment, he said, "What exactly do you mean?"

She laughed. "You both know what I mean. Shall I say it? You should be lovers."

He closed his eyes, as if steeling himself. For a long moment, he stayed in that posture, and the tension of the moment nearly squeezed the life from me.

And then he abruptly pulled our pile of hands forward and bent to kiss them. His lashes fell over his cheek, and I saw a single bright tear slide free. I looked back to Channan, and there was no conflict in her face at all. Only love.

My ears still roared, and I could not think clearly, and yet, the world felt wider, brighter, more beautiful. Our hands were tightly woven, a promise. I wanted to touch Tanveer's head, to kiss Channan's cheek, to bend as he'd bent, and kiss our laced fingers.

At that moment, the gatekeeper called, "Maharaja Sahib, Colonel Barrington has arrived to see you."

"What?" Tanveer straightened, and our hands all flew apart.

A white man came into the room, calling out, "Hello, hello. I tried to get here for the durbar, but I see I was too late." He gave a jovial chuckle. "I've been in India so long I'm developing Indian habits. Good to see you, Your Highness."

Tanveer stood. "Colonel Barrington. Good to see you." Recovering, he crossed the space to meet him with an outstretched hand. "What brings you to our little world?"

"Oh, this and that, this and that. I heard you had a spot of trouble last week."

"It was nothing. We managed all right."

"Of course, of course."

Channan said smoothly, "We are about to enjoy luncheon, Colonel. Won't you join us? Very simple, I'm afraid, only rotis and dal. Our cook has been making milder dishes for the palate of our English friend, so it may be to your liking."

He gave me a sharp look, perhaps registering my presence for the first time. "I haven't had the pleasure," he said. He had ginger hair shot through with white, and a thin mustache. "Colonel Barrington."

"Elsie Turner," I said. "Old friend of the family. My father was in the ICS when I was a child."

"Is that right? Good to meet you." He held his hat, shifted, thought. "I believe I would love to join you, Maharani. Been a trek out here."

"We would be honored," Tanveer said. He gave me a glance over the man's head. "All of us."

"Of course," I said. "Perhaps I should run upstairs and change."

"Nonsense," Tanveer said. "We stand on no ceremony for a simple lunch. You don't mind, do you, Colonel?"

"No, no. As you are."

We trooped into the courtyard with its deep shade, where a table had been set for three. "Another setting," Channan said, and the girl scurried off.

The Englishman seemed off-kilter as he looked around, eyeing the cat sleeping in the corner and the splendid table setting. Tanveer made no move to make him comfortable, only gestured for him to take a seat. I wondered if it was deliberate that the view was of the crumbling tower, which put him opposite Tanveer, with Channan and me between the men.

The quarters were rather too close, and my knee brushed Tanveer's thigh below the table. I looked up, then away, feeling as I had that long ago day when I'd come to the palace and discovered the new Tanveer stirred all manner of things—I was too much in my body, too deeply aware of his physical person. He nudged me and I looked up. His gaze was serious, direct, and I found myself nodding as if he'd spoken.

The luncheon was interminable. Channan kept up a graceful sort of conversation, and I must have participated, but my eyes dragged on Tanveer's long hands as they folded a roti and dipped it in dal. I was aware of the heat of his calf nearby my shin. My gaze snared on the edge of his ear peeking out beneath his dastaar, the few inches of neck above his collar.

My mind whirled. He might not even wish to accept her offer. He might be angry, even. I could see a scenario where that might be true. My ears burned again, and I had no appetite.

And then I thought of him bending over our clasped hands, and I knew he also wished for the things hanging in the air.

It was painful to want anything so much. I had wanted and lost this lover more than once. He was so close I could smell the oil he used in his beard. His foot grazed mine under the table. My foolish brain remembered the kisses in the tiger enclosure all those years before, that first kiss, right in this very palace.

The servant who minded the table brought out a big bowl of cubed watermelon. "Memsahib," he said to me, for I'd been eating enormous amounts of the fruit. I loved it madly.

"Thank you," I said, and it gave me something better to focus on.

"So, Miss Turner," the colonel said. "It is Miss? Where do you visit from?"

A chill touched my neck. Was he here because Peter had sent him, or sent word? I piled cubes of watermelon on my plate, one at a time, and lied. "South of England. My father was the Earl of Herewich. Are you familiar?"

"No, no. Spent most of my life here in the Punjab in one spot or another." He frowned a little. "Wait, I'm remembering the ICS officer with an extraordinarily beautiful wife, who went home to take up the title, must be what fourteen, fifteen years ago. Is that your family?"

"Could be."

"Well, I'll be. What a small world. I worked with your father in Lucknow for a bit. He was always a bit of a radical. You have the look of your mother, I'd say."

The story cut too close to truth. Of course Peter knew where I was because my mother had told him, but I seriously doubted he'd storm the palace and try to drag me home. Still. I felt dizzy with everything. I stood, feigning a headache. "I'm so sorry, will you all excuse me?"

I fled.

A TERRIBLE NIGHT, PART ONE

Autumn 1940
London

—67—

As I made dinner for myself and Mother, I listened to the radio, keeping half an eye on the weather, which promised to be clear and cold with a bright moon. Good flying weather. My nerves were on alert, and I kept the kitchen curtain open as I cooked.

The radio provided some company. Lately, the news had been a little better, with a big naval victory and Roosevelt's re-election, but I was happy when music came back on. I was trying my hand at mock fish cakes, made with a very small amount of mackerel mixed with mashed potato, and was quite pleased with the way they looked when I fried them. With some mayonnaise mixed from eggs I'd got from Nina, and a half a head of cabbage, dinner would be rather appealing for a change. Mother wouldn't eat much, of course, but I had enough for three, and I could put the extras away for tomorrow.

I fed Bastet and her kitten, whom I'd still refused to name, although he was clearly staying, then I sat down to the table. I saved my letters for dinnertime, and although they didn't arrive every day, I'd had one this afternoon. It was a ritual to sit down and open it, taking my time to read his handwriting. We'd been comparing English and Indian poets at the turn of the century, and I had made some mocking attempts at imitation, which he then expanded. It was lighthearted, and gave me a smile, as it was meant to. After I saw to Mother, I'd write my daily letter in return.

The letters were a lifeline, even if we were out of sync because they took so long to arrive. I'd often receive three or four in a day, some long, some short, some a simple drawing meant to make me laugh or remind me of something I loved. Sometimes, he enclosed dried flowers or rubbed the paper with spices so they would fill the room with the fragrance of the Punjab.

When the letter was over and my dinner was finished, there was only the empty room with its overhead light shining too brightly on my bare table. Beneath the music was silence.

In the silence, with my single place setting, loneliness descended. It walked with me every hour. These were Mother's last days, and I wished I could share the sorrow with someone.

So when I heard Peter's step in the front hall, my spirits lifted. I hoped he was in a good mood.

I could see the minute he came through to the kitchen that he was not. His eyes were rimmed with red, and his hair was askew. "Peter!" I cried. "What is it?"

"I've just heard that one of the office girls was killed in a raid last night. Last night! There were only a handful of bombs because the weather was so terrible."

"Oh, my dear, I am so sorry." I pulled out a chair. "Sit down. Let me get you some dinner. It's not terrible, and I have real mayonnaise."

He dropped in the chair, head in his hands. "I can't believe it."

"Who was killed?" I filled a plate with a fish cake and some of the fried cabbage. "Anyone I would know?"

And the second I settled the plate on the table, I knew.

"You met her, the night at Nina's. Trudy. Just a girl, only twenty years old."

A clutch of warning moved through my middle, but I brushed it away as a memory of another time. I touched his shoulder. "It's awful. I'm so sorry."

From upstairs, I heard a cry. "That's Mother. I have to check on her." At the door, I added, "Will you come up and sit with us? She likely won't know you're there, but you can bring your plate up."

He raised his head. "Of course."

~

Mother was restless, clearly in pain. I tried to give her some water, but she couldn't take it. I wasn't sure she was with us in any way, but Peter held her hand and told her a story about a childhood game he lost. She fell into a deep stupor after a time, and we left her, a lamp at her side.

"Would you like to play cards?" I asked. "I have some Ovaltine."

If he was surprised, he didn't show it. "That sounds lovely, Elsie. Yes, please."

As I boiled the milk, he said, "She hasn't long, has she?"

It gave me a sharp pain through my ribs. "No. I don't think so." I thought about the revelations she'd spilled, and wondered if I should ask him if he'd known, and then chose not to. What difference did it make? None of it mattered now, and as I'd said to Tanveer, I hadn't left India for her sake.

"Will you leave me then?"

"What?" I looked over my shoulder. "I'm going to stay with Nina, which you already knew. It will be safer."

He nodded. "I can see it would be lonely here, by yourself."

"Yes." I sliced the cheese ration for the week into small squares and arranged them on a plate. "I miss Betty terribly. Any news of her?"

"She was moved to Oxford, but I haven't heard anything else."

We sat down with our malty drinks, and I passed the cards across the table.

"Do you suppose we'll ever have a true marriage again, Elsie?"

Again that wash of warning edged around my gut, my elbows. Why this concern when he was clearly grieving the loss of his mistress? It was too much like the nights in Cairo.

Lightly, I said, "It's as true as many others, I reckon."

"Don't you ever want more?" His eyes were red as he looked hard at me. "We could start again, you know."

I thought of my mother upstairs sleeping, of the moon rising, of the winds in Cairo that drove the British mad. "Considering all we've endured, our good friendship is a treasure, wouldn't you think? How many are miserable? We are not."

He sighed. "*You* are not." He calmly placed his cards in the middle of the table. "I believe I need a drink."

"Peter," I began, but he was gone. For a moment, I sat at the table with its two filled cups of Ovaltine, and the stack of cards. My intuition prickled, running up and down the back of my arms in warning. Should I collect my things in case he showed more signs of instability? But I could not leave my mother. A stab of fear and fury twisted in my chest.

And the sirens began to sound.

CHANNAN'S GIFT

1926
Talwarpur, India

—68—

A servant came to my chambers in the late afternoon. The day had cooled considerably, with heavy clouds moving in, promising thunderstorms and monsoon rains before dark. I wrapped a shawl around my shoulders as I did the only thing I could do, which was paint. I could not paint what I wished to paint, which was Tanveer's beautiful hands, or his freshly washed hair and his bare shoulders that morning on the balcony, a memory I had put out of my mind until now.

I could not paint those things for, as it was, I could barely hold the emotion surging through my body, pouring through veins and joints. I could see it, heat and light just below my skin. A door had been flung open in my mind, and from the dark room where I'd stuffed all my feelings came an outpouring of memory and longing and wishes, hope and fear. So much fear, rooted in our history. Leaving him now, even our renewed friendship, would be wrenching.

If we walked through the door Channan had flung open, what then?

When I answered the knock on my door, Sughra, Channan's maid, stood there. In Hindustani, she said, "Maharaja Sahib asks that you dress English for dinner. The sahib will stay overnight because of the rains."

"Will maharani-ji join us as well?"

"No, memsahib. Two meals in one day would be many for her."

"I understand."

"Do you wish help dressing?"

I looked at my hands, spattered with paint, and my apron. "I'll need to wash first. Return in a half hour. The buttons are impossible without help."

She gave a short bow.

If Tanveer wanted me in English dress, I should have to bring my Lady Turner self to table. It had been weeks, but I dutifully bathed, and scrubbed the paint from my fingers, brushed my hair into a short bun, and applied makeup, what little I had—powder and lipstick and the small cake of kohl I'd purchased in Cairo. When I stood in my shift, waiting for Sughra, I stepped back to check my look in the mirror.

And I couldn't believe the difference in myself in just a couple of months. The sharp angles of shoulder and elbow had been enveloped in a layer of soft flesh, and my cheeks no longer looked so haggard. My eyes held a spark I had not seen in a long, long time.

I have never known this Tanveer, Channan said.

I had not seen this me. Not in years and years, not since the day he'd left England with Topaz in a basket. Whatever other thing was in Channan's mind, what mattered to me was being able to stay, to grow and live here in Talwarpur, where I felt loved and accepted.

Where I felt at home.

Sughra knocked and I let her in. The dress I'd chosen was pale green, beaded with tiny silver flutes that shimmered over breast and hip. The back was low and met just above my waist, and fastened with buttons all the way down. I'd had it for years and worn it countless times to various functions and dinners and balls, and tonight, I was glad to own it as it fell down over my body. A thin chain hung with small square emeralds and diamonds draped down my spine.

Sughra exclaimed, "So beautiful!"

I swayed to make the beads dance on the hem. "Thank you. It's long been my favorite."

As she headed toward the door, my painting caught her eye, a tiger with stars overhead. Not quite a real tiger, but the one from my child-hood imagination, the version of a tiger who would have befriended me and ridden off into the night with me and Tanveer on her back. I had not yet painted the children, but they were sketched in thin lines. On the sidelines Gurdaya stood, arms crossed and worried. "You should paint the tigers here," Sughra said.

"Yes. I shall."

~

As I walked toward the small dining room where we would eat, I heard the colonel's voice. "You've got to root them out, man. These cells are going to rot the empire."

I slowed, listening.

"They are harmless," Tanveer said, and I knew he did not believe that. He had warned me several times about straying too far from the palace without escort. British citizens had been killed across the Punjab, including women, some of whom had been targeted directly. "If you spend too much of your enforcement upon them, the problem will only grow worse."

"The crown has noticed your complicity, Singh. It is well known that you have hosted radicals in your own home."

"Those radicals would be my old school chums, Colonel, who come to share stories of their lives, not their politics."

"Look around you, man. This palace is falling down. How will you keep it up if you lose the support of the British?"

Smoothly, I entered the room, as if fresh out of the bath. "Good evening, gentlemen. I hope I'm not interrupting."

The colonel, dressed in black tie, bowed. "Good evening, Lady Turner."

Tanveer greeted me with prayer hands, one raised brow acknowledging my timing. "You look splendid tonight."

I gave a slight curtsy, setting the beads on my hem alive. "As do you, Maharaja-ji." He had donned his high court turban and coat. Emeralds and rubies the size of lozenges shone on his long fingers, and the turban was draped and crusted with more jewels than I'd ever seen him wear—strings of pearls and an enormous diamond brooch and lesser colored stones pinned in the folds.

An impressive display.

"Lady Turner is staying with us to paint a portrait," Tanveer said. "My wife asked for her specifically. She's known for her work around the world."

"Is that right?" The colonel's nose was red with drink. "Anything I would know?"

"Oh no. I've only shown in a few galleries."

"She is too modest," Tanveer said. "She has shown in London and Cairo and will show in Bombay, too, if my sister has her way."

The mention of Cairo made me nervous. Would the tale of my flight from my husband have circulated this far? I doubted it, but still. "You mentioned my mother earlier, Colonel. Did you ever meet her?"

"Only once," he said with some regret. "We danced at New Year in . . . must have been '08 or '09." He raised his glass. "You resemble her."

"As a puddle reflects the sky," I said. We all laughed. So jovial.

~

The rain held off until the middle of dinner, and came crashing through as it was wont to do, noise and drama and pyrotechnics that lit up the room. "I have missed these storms! It never crashes like this in England." I breathed it in. "That smell!"

"I did try to live in England myself," the colonel said. "My wife was desperate to go back, but I'd never lived there, you see."

"It was the same for me," I exclaimed, leaning forward. "I was in Nainital until I was fifteen."

He coughed. "I never went back for school. My parents were working people, you know. But my wife came out in the nineties to find a husband and found me." He laughed a little. I was warming to him as he grew more inebriated. "But she never loved India. It was too hot, too dry, no bluebells. All the complaints. We went back after our sons were born, but I did not care for the damp and the cold." He shuddered.

"What brought you back, then?"

"Oh, my wife died, I'm afraid, just before the war. I wanted to get out of England before they conscripted me."

Tanveer, at the head of the table, went quite still. "You did not serve?"

"No, I came here. That was service enough, ha!"

"I spent the war in France," Tanveer said. His hand with its jewels rested motionless on the table. "Are you aware that Sikhs made up twenty percent of the British forces?"

"Is that right? Impressive."

"Indeed. Especially when one considers that Sikhs only make up two percent of the Indian population." His eyes held a dangerous glitter, and I found myself sitting up straighter. "In fact, a good many of those 'cells' you are so concerned with are made up of veterans of the war, men who were promised an independent India if they would serve. And yet, here we are, these eight years later and not only has that promise been rescinded, but martial law has been invoked, and punishments are humiliating and extreme." His eyes burned. "And I need not mention the massacre at Amritsar."

"An unfortunate incident, indeed. No one was happy about that, Singh."

"Someone was."

"Look, man, I know. I know." He slammed his hands on the table. "But you'll shoot yourself in your own foot if you don't calm the locals. They'll come after you next." He pointed at me. "Her."

Tanveer stood. "This conversation is over. Shafi will see you to your chambers." He held out a hand toward me. "Lady Turner?"

Blinking at the sudden turn of events, I stood. "Of course. Good night, Colonel."

—69—

Tanveer walked so quickly, I had to hurry behind him, my little heels clicking on the tiles. Once we left the dining room, the noise of the storm was even louder, but only the corridor was lit with lanterns at regular intervals. Tanveer did not let go of my hand as he strode through one corridor, and then to another, which was only lit by a single lantern at the foot of a staircase. He turned there, and pulled me behind him, up and up, and up.

At the top, another lantern burned nearby a door, one I recognized as a twin to my own. We were heading for the tower opposite mine, which housed his bedroom.

My heart suddenly pounded in my ears. "Tanveer," I said.

He halted, and I felt the fury pulsing from his limbs. He broke away and paced for a moment, back and forth, back and forth beneath the shelter of the corridor. Just beyond, on the open balcony, the rain poured in wild splendor. "They're all so bloody arrogant," he said finally, hands on his hips. "How can they still believe they'll hold on to their power?"

"I don't think they do," I said mildly. "They know their time is nearly finished here."

He measured me. "Do you believe that?"

"Of course I do."

"Because I have brainwashed you."

"No," I countered. "Because you've taught me. And because I've been observing for years. The old ways are crumbling."

"So they are."

I leaned on the wall, hands behind me. "And it reminds you that I am a daughter of the empire," I said with some despair.

He sighed. "Yes." He shook his head, but suddenly seemed overcome with strong emotion.

I waited.

He moved toward me, drew my hands out from behind me. "And no. It does seem there should be room for the intimate and the personal as well as the political."

"It does," I whispered.

He lifted my hands to his lips and kissed my fingers. Pent-up emotion swelled through my chest, up through my throat, and I could not hold back a wash of tears. I bowed my head, trying to hide them. "I am ever weeping with you."

"I do not mind it." He kissed my wrists, my inner arm. The lantern glistened over his beard and glittered on the jewels of his turban, his rings. "If I were not so manly, I would weep myself."

I laughed, something easing as I flowed closer to him. "Would you?"

He moved my hands to his chest, and covered them with his hands. Our eyes met, and I did not feel I had to look away for fear of revealing the truth of my emotions. "It seems a miracle that you're standing here, with me, tonight. There is color in the world again."

I moved closer and pressed my cheek against his coat. He held me close, his hands on my back, touching bare skin, and then away. And then back, his palm flat against my spine, gliding up and down.

"Sugar in my tea," I said. Against my cheek, his coat was rough and smelled of clove. I rubbed my face against it. Beneath my hands his waist moved infinitesimally. Our thighs brushed.

"I have tried so hard not to think of touching you," he whispered, and brushed his chin over the top of my head. "But tonight, I could think of nothing else." His hand slid down the back of my dress, smoothing over my hips. "This dress is decadent."

I smiled. "It is meant to be."

"Did you wear it on purpose, then?" His hand moved again up the bare flesh of my back, upward to my neck, into my hair, back down.

"To distract the colonel," I said. "From politics."

"Only the colonel?" Hands spreading sparks of light over my back, my hips.

"Not really him at all."

Light moved up through us, leaping from one to the other, setting every cell ablaze. "I'm going to kiss you now, Elsie."

It had been so long. So very, very long, and yet I knew just how our mouths fit together, how precisely we knew to press and tilt, to open and sigh. We moved into his chamber and shut out the rain, and shed all the things keeping our flesh apart. For one blazing second, as we pressed skin to skin, at last, I lifted my head. I touched his face, his beard, his chest, living in this moment, this very one, and then we tumbled into each other, remembering what we had forgotten. And then we were prone and tangled and made love as if we had invented it. When he was buried in me, over me, he lifted his head. "Elsie," he said. "Look at me."

I met his eyes, held him close, and he breathed.

"We are one soul. One heart."

"Yes," I whispered. "One."

And as one being we moved into the place only we could ever occupy, our own land.

~

The rains stopped abruptly toward midnight, and the moon rose, spilling into the room to creep across our bodies, sweaty and naked. "All this hair," I said, teasing, touching his chest with my palm, his shin with my foot, raising my hand to his thick beard. "It is quite thrilling."

"Is it?"

"Yes. When I saw you on the balcony, I very nearly swooned."

"I wanted you to. I saw you out there, reading a letter."

"How wicked!"

His hand moved on my back. "Channan has asked about you a thousand times. I think she might have found some of your letters from when we were young, before I came to London."

"She is not what I expected."

"I know."

A ripple of worry coursed over my heart. "I worry that my relationship with her will change."

He smiled. "Have you known her to say a thing she did not mean?"

I could answer honestly. "No."

"There is more than one way to live in the world," he said. "We war when we insist it should be this or that, when I tell you how to live, or love, or worship. If we make it so that each being is able to choose, the trouble disappears." He snapped his fingers in the air. "Like Nina and Jonathan."

"Hmm. Yes. As it would have been for Rocky and me if he'd lived." I sighed. "I will always miss him. What a lively character."

"You were a bit blind about him, but I agree that he was a cheerful soul. A prat, but cheerful about it." He paused. "It would have saved you a great deal of trouble if you'd been able to marry him."

I nodded, thinking of the loss of Herewich and the extremity of financial trouble that had led to marrying Peter. A bolt of pain shot up my spine.

"What was that?"

"Memory," I said. "Nothing."

His thumb moved over my collarbone. "You were so exhausted when you arrived. Did Peter hurt you?"

"What does it matter now?" I said lightly. "Here I am. He's a broken man and deserves pity, which I only know because I nursed you through your injuries."

His eyes rested on my face. Then he nodded. "We all have things we cannot bear to say."

I kissed him. "Thank you." I pulled the thin blanket over our bodies and settled into the curve of his shoulder. "Will you tell me a story? In Urdu."

And he did, weaving a tale of clever gods and men who outsmarted them, though I do not think either of us made it to the end.

—70—

September 1926
Taos, New Mexico

Dear Elsie,
Please reply to my letters. I know you are angry with Peter, and now with me, but I cannot bear not to know how you are. Please write. Peter has written many times, and I do not know what to tell him. I have not said that I know where you are, but I'm sure he knows. Perhaps you could at least write to him. He's been moved to Kabul at his own request, where he says there is no drinking.

My husband has been poorly this summer. At first we thought it was only the heat (it is very hot in New Mexico at times) but I fear now it might be something worse.

Love,
Mother

October 1926

Dear Elsie,
I will not give up writing to you. I am sure you read my letters even if you do not respond. I beg of you, please forgive me, and let's heal this breach. I feel quite alone without my connection to you, and have we not always shared in each other's lives?

I have been ill with the Indian summer, a recurrence of malaria that surprised me.

My husband is rallying. They think it was a stomach ulcer, and after a few weeks of avoiding the very spicy food he loves, it seems to be healing. I wish you would come visit. The two of you could talk about art all day and night, and we are friends with an entire coterie of artistic people. I have become quite the bohemian.

Tell me what fills your days, what you observe. Have you been to Nainital? How are Tanveer and his wife? Do you see Gurdaya at all? Does she have children?

Do you miss me at all? Please write.

Love,

Mother

November 22, 1926
Talwarpur Palace

Dear Mother,
Of course I miss you. I was just so very, very angry with you for believing Peter's version of events so easily over mine. You didn't even ask which things might be

true, or if I had important reasons. You assumed. You took his part, and worried about your own financial situation rather than worrying about me.

But never mind that. I am very happy in India. I will not be returning to Peter, whether he lives in Kabul or Cairo or the heart of London itself. I have been painting more than I've painted in my life, and with Channan and Tanveer, I feel a sense of home and belonging that has escaped me since William died and we lost Herewich.

I am sorry to hear that you've been ill, and of course I worry. Will Garvey consider relocating to England for the sake of your health? I would think you miss the place, as much as you loved it.

My life is not a conventional one. I did try.

I hope this letter finds both you and Garvey much improved. Let me know where to write to you.

Love,

Elsie

—71—

When I think of that time now, the whole of that fall and winter and spring, it is contained in a globe of golden light, filled with happiness and laughter and making love, painting and building our strange little family, for it was not only Tanveer and me, but Channan, too. Her health improved and I taught her to watercolor. She taught me needlepoint, which I loathed. I worked on their portrait sometimes, and at others, I painted canvas after canvas of a new kind of landscape—sere and rich at once, the combination of shape and harshness and brilliant sky that spoke to me now in a new voice. Tanveer took me to Nainital, and we drove the streets we'd roamed as children. I saw my old house, and his, which the family still owned and rarely visited. We hiked the trail to our pond but found the waterfall had ceased and so it had gone stale, covered with algae.

Gingerly, and then with more vigor, we embraced the new life we'd found, surprisingly, after so much loss and strife. Both of us became more fully ourselves within our intimate connection. I painted. He wrote.

For as long as I live, those nights we slept side by side, entwined, dreaming together, will remain among the best moments of my life.

Gurdaya came to visit with her tumble of children, and stayed for three weeks. Tanveer and I attempted discretion, but in truth, we were so gilded we left pools of light wherever we stepped, and she soon guessed the truth. Once she understood Channan had given her blessing, she accepted it with her usual practicality. "I used to see you sneak into the forest," she said.

But she did warn us to be careful, considering the unrest in the whole of the Punjab that winter. We saw it in the village, too, a fight over an irrigation ditch turning suddenly ugly, a man beaten to death. Accusations of favoritism over the gurdwara, too, and the maharaja's interest in restoring it. He had to hold a durbar to air the complaints after the festival of Guru Nanak Gurpurab, when a Muslim group protested the apparent favoritism of the maharaja giving more attention to Sikh matters than to those of the Muslims or Hindus.

When a rumor surfaced that the maharaja had taken a British mistress, Channan held a festival for the village children, at which she and I worked side by side to dispel the gossip.

The rumbles were everywhere, and I did not leave the grounds of the palace without Tanveer. We insulated ourselves, our little family, in the crumbling old palace.

It was early in January that I realized I'd had no menses for nearly three months. I was certain it could not be a child, not after all these years. I was past thirty and had never been pregnant, not even to lose it.

But the evidence mounted. My breasts grew larger. My hips softened. Some afternoons, I slept for hours on end, lost in a narcotic, dreamless sleep. And then, my belly began to swell, ever so gently. Beneath the loose tunics I wore, it did not show, but I was sure Tanveer would notice sooner or later.

A disaster, which I had foolishly not considered how to plan for.

One night as I padded toward the bed, he stopped me and placed a hand over my belly. "Are you with child?"

I burst into tears. "I don't know how to tell!"

He pulled me to him, and I fell on his shoulder, weeping as if the world would end. "I did not think it possible!" I cried. "It is such a terrible complication."

"Terrible?" He laughed. "I can't think of anything that could bring more joy."

"But what of the villagers, the gossip? Won't it be dangerous?"

He moved his hands over my belly. "No. It must appear to be Channan's child. She will be overjoyed." He paused, hand over my stomach. "I have so longed for a child, Elsie."

I pressed my forehead into his neck. "Our child."

Gently, he spread his fingers, looking, and he whispered, "A baby."

~

The next day we found Channan in her room, sitting in a sunny spot with Topaz on her feet. She looked wan, as often happened, and I hesitated, suddenly afraid this evidence of our congress would be a bridge too far, that she would resent me at last. Tanveer sank next to her, took her hand, kissed her forehead. "We have news."

The blaze of hope on her face was unmistakable. "A child?"

I moved close, and cupped my hands in a semicircle to show the growing mound. She lifted her hand and touched it, just as Tanveer had. She had tears in her eyes as she looked up at me. I pressed my hand over hers. "Our child. All of us."

She kissed my hand. "I have prayed for this."

~

The palace announced the happy news that the maharani was, at long last, going to bear a child. She took to her bed, as if to protect her pregnancy, and I stayed hidden, as well, and draped when I emerged into the palace. Only Sughra was allowed in her rooms, and she alone knew the truth. She had been loyal to Channan since she was a child, and could be trusted with the secret.

Near the end of my confinement, Gurdaya arrived with her midwife and servants who had no connection with the locals and took over the supervision of creating an environment supportive of a new baby.

Kirandeep was born at the end of May, a healthy, robust baby boy. When I had been patched up and cleaned and dressed in fresh clothing, Gurdaya placed him back in my arms. "I will fetch Tanveer."

In the quiet, he looked up at me, as calm as his father, his eyes a rich amber beneath an astonishing thatch of hair. His nose was squished from birth. He took my finger in his tiny hands, and made a soft mooing sound.

My entire being filled with a kind of blaze, a ferocity of love that was larger than the earth, the skies, all of creation, a son born of love and generosity, a being so beautiful I could not imagine how I could even begin to capture him on canvas, a merging of Tanveer and myself, the most miraculous expression of all. "You are perfect," I said.

Tanveer came in quietly and sat on the bed with us. "Look at his tiny fingernails," he whispered, alight with wonder. "And his eyebrows!" He kissed each tiny finger, and Kirandeep regarded him solemnly. "Welcome."

I do not think it would be possible to feel more love than I did in that moment.

"A son," he whispered. "A new generation." He took my hand and kissed my palm. "We are now truly woven into a new being."

"Truly."

His eyes shone. "What a blessing!"

We stayed where we were, admiring every inch of Kirandeep's tiny self, wrapped in a joy that had no equal, not ever in the history of the world.

—72—

June 1927
London

Dear Elsie,
I have not heard from you for many months, but even in the absence of your letters, I must send you my news. My husband has died. His stomach ulcer was instead cancer, and I nursed him until his death two months ago.

I have no means of support, and have returned to London at Peter's urging. He is generously supporting me by buying a house near Russell Square where I know he hopes you will live with me eventually. He has given up drink whilst in Kabul and is a much changed man. He asked that I send this letter to you. Please give him a chance, Elsie. I do fear what will happen to me if you continue to refuse his suit. I truly have no one else. I cannot possibly come to you in India. My health will not allow it, as you must know.

Please come home to England, my dear. I miss you terribly.

Love,

Mother

June 1927
Kabul

Dearest Elsie,

I know I do not deserve even the slightest sliver of your attention, but I hope you will read this letter and allow me to beg forgiveness. I have been a beast, in the truest sense of the word. I am abjectly sorry for the way I treated you in Cairo. No one deserves such treatment, most especially one's beloved wife. I have worshipped you since the first moment I saw your face in that garden. I suppose you were weeping then over hating England, and now you have been able to return to India. I hope you have found some happiness there.

Your mother misses you most desperately. I have put her up in a rather nice house in Bloomsbury, and she has two servants and an allowance I trust will see her through very well. When I return to London, I shall also live there. If you choose to return, I will not ever ask a thing of you, and you will have the entire top floor as your studio. I only want time to make up to you what I stole. I can best do that by showing my altruism around your mother.

I no longer drink spirits. Kabul has cured me of the habit, and I am a much improved version of myself. As you know, it only darkened my moods, and I find it much easier to cope without the influence of gin. If you find it in your heart to forgive your husband, I will not ask another thing. Only come back to England and live with us, your mother and me. It would make her so happy.

Yours, always,

Peter

July 1927
Talwarpur Palace

Dear Mother,
I will not be returning to England. I am grateful to Peter for caring for you so thoughtfully, but our story is more complicated than you will allow.

India is my home. I will not leave it.

Love,

Elsie

—73—

For several months, I drifted in rosy haze. All of us did. Had any being ever been so perfectly rendered as Kirandeep, with his enormous curious eyes and little rosebud mouth, his crop of blackest hair? I could gaze for hours at his perfect tiny toes, the yawning toothlessness of his mouth, the rolls of fat on his arms and legs. We were all besotted, Tanveer, Channan, and I. No child had ever been so showered with love.

Outside the palace walls, however, life continued its relentless roar. Small skirmishes among villagers, divided by allegiance to their faiths, broke out constantly that hot summer. Men gathered in the palace and engaged in deep and sometimes fierce discussions of how best to move forward in light of the promised reforms of the government, which had not materialized quickly enough. Gandhi's writings, urging simplicity, village uplift, and a rejection of materialism were circulated, and even he was concerned with the rising conflict between religions. Tanveer shared the writings with both the hidden radicals agitating for violence, and with me, so I would understand what they were debating, what was on his mind.

But as a new mother, I could not connect to that world of strife. I planted flowers on my balcony and tended my son, and Channan and I grew as close as sisters.

Our lack of vigilance would be our downfall.

Villagers often came and went through the palace gates, a fact we all took for granted. The gatekeeper, a man named Banta, thoroughly vetted anyone on their way in, and saw to it that they made their way out, but late in September, he was trampled by a buffalo. His position was filled by another man named Rashid, whom I barely noticed except to be saddened by the sudden death of Banta.

We had grown comfortable. Careless.

~

One hot September afternoon, Channan had retired from the heat, and I sat in the shaded courtyard with Kirandeep in his cradle, protected from mosquitos by netting. We were positioned close to the cooling wall, covered with rushes woven with vetiver, and the fountain. I sipped mint tea and read a novel I'd just received in the post. My feet were hot in the sunshine, and periodically, I dipped them in the fountain. The air was utterly still.

Which meant I heard the shout and outcry long before they reached the gate. Tanveer appeared at the door. "Take Kirandeep upstairs," he said urgently, "and stay there until I find you."

I grabbed my sleeping child, who barely stirred in the soporific heat, and raced up to my chamber, where I laid him in a basket and drew the netting around him again, then went to the balcony to see what I could.

It was very little, though I could hear shouting and a repeated cry in Punjabi.

We stayed in the room until evening, when Tanveer finally appeared. "It is safe enough now," he said. He looked weary, his feet dusty from his trek to and from the village. I poured him a glass of water from a pitcher, and he drank it down.

"I must go to Lahore. One of the most respected men in the village has been arrested, almost certainly to bring my cooperation with the demands of the British, and I must get him out."

"Of course."

He touched my hair. "There is a great deal of anger over this arrest. I've added a man to the gate, and offered incentives to calm the anger, but—" Kirandeep had been watching him with his sober, calm eyes, and cooed at his father. Tanveer eased instantly, and took the weighty softness of Kirandeep out of my arms.

In Hindustani he said, "What say you, little tiger? Have you wisdom for me in this matter?"

Kirandeep pursed his lips and made a soft whoo, his fingers waving.

"I will take that under advisement." He kissed his head, and Kirandeep grabbed great handfuls of beard. Laughing, I helped disentangle them.

"Strong grip," he said, and then seriously cupped a hand to my face. "They want someone to pay for this arrest, and they are furious with the British. I fear that anger will turn in your direction. Stay within the walls, and be wary."

A ripple of warning burned through my gut. "Must you go?" I asked, even though I knew there was no one else who could carry the gravitas he would need. "Never mind. Be safe."

"Stay with Channan in her chambers, and I will ask Shafi to stay nearby your doors. I shall only be a few days. I'll come back as quickly as possible, and once they have Anand back, the village will settle."

I nodded. He took us into his arms, and I leaned in, smelling his neck, his solid chest, and my son in the other arm, and everything that mattered was there, in that space of moments.

—74—

Channan and I played ludo and grazed on samosas. The day had been hot, but now a cool wind blew into her rooms, lifting the airy curtains, bringing a scent of jasmine and dung smoke. Channan held Kirandeep in the crook of her arm. He gurgled and cooed, moving hands and feet as if to test their range, and we laughed when he caught sight of his fingers and startled. When he tired and grew fussy, I took him and offered my breast, where he settled, gulping noisily until he found a rhythm. He made a low sound of humming contentment, his fingers gripping the edge of my scarf.

"If I were a painter," Channan said, "I would paint your portrait just now, the two of you."

Awash in deep contentment, I smiled, brushing my hand over his soft hair. I would paint it from this direction, the edge of my arm, the flesh of my breast, the rosebud shape of his tiny mouth. Why had there not been more paintings done of such moments, from the eyes of the painter, the mother? "I would paint this." I touched his cheek, brushed his tiny eyelashes.

"You must."

From outside came a sound of shouting, loud enough that Kirandeep unlatched, his arms flying out. It so startled him that he let out a cry. "Sughra," I said, "look and see if you can tell what's happening." I pulled Kirandeep closer, covering myself. Through the open windows, we heard more voices, much closer than they should have been. "What is it? Can you see?"

"It is villagers, memsahib," she said with knotted hands. "They're in the courtyard."

"What?" I settled Kirandeep in Channan's arms and hurried over. Below, in the main courtyard, spilled a dozen men, spreading out in different directions. Their cries were in Punjabi, but I heard a word I knew, *firangi*: *foreigner*. "What are they shouting?"

"I would not want to say."

"Please say. It is important."

Channan said behind me, "'Firangi chudail.'" She clutched the baby to her shoulder. "Concubine. And witch." Her wounded face did not show emotion easily, but I could see the terror in her eyes.

"They want me."

Shafi came into the room. "Memsahib, come with me." He gave a directive to Sughra in Punjabi, and Channan cried out in protest. "No! I will stay with Elsie!"

He gave me a slight shake of the head, and with a chill, I realized what he wanted. "Channan-ji," I said, "stay with the baby. You'll be safer without me."

"No. I am afraid!"

Shafi said, "I will come right back. You are safe here."

I gave her a quick hug. "Do not worry. There are men to protect you."

She made a moaning noise. "There were men to protect me before." She gripped my arm. "Do not leave me."

I looked over my shoulder. "Can you take all of us together?"

He was not happy, but made a quick gesture for us to follow. Outside, there was a roar, and we hurried behind him. The hairs on my body stood up as we rounded a corridor that overlooked the courtyard and I saw three men knocking over pots and small tables, yelling, their fever stoked by each other. They did not see us.

Shafi led us down, down, down into a dark hallway, and opened a heavy door. Within was a small bed and a window high on the wall.

"Is this a dungeon?"

He shrugged. "It will be safe."

We curled next to each other as he left us, drawing our shawls around us in the cold room. At the top of the stairs, I heard a door being locked, and a little panic fluttered in my throat. I hoped that if the mob killed everyone, Tanveer would know how to get us out.

~

We heard little, although every so often, a shout rang out, or a loud noise. I couldn't tell if the fight was intensifying or they were being driven back. Channan shivered next to me, but eventually fell asleep in my lap. I couldn't imagine what horrors she was reliving.

My back against the cold wall, my son sleeping in my arms, I wondered what triggered cruelty in humans. Why brutalize a young woman? Why drag away an old man and throw him in prison? Why did rooms like this one exist?

Darkness fell. I nestled Kirandeep into a space by the wall at Channan's back so that he wouldn't fall, and stretched out on the floor to doze. In that half-awake state, I thought I saw a fire flickering over the walls. I heard a tiger roar in the distance, no doubt agitated by the smoke and shouting.

My imagination tortured me with visions of what might happen if they found us. I did not fear for my son so much, as I thought even a mob would spare a baby, especially the maharaja's son.

But I saw Channan dragged away. I saw myself, captured by the angry villagers and—what? What punishment would befit the harlot foreign mistress of the maharaja? Did they burn women at the stake here? Drag them to their deaths? Stone them? The possibilities were endless for women who did not behave.

But I would die myself rather than allow anything to happen to Channan.

Lying there on the hard floor, praying to any entity that might listen, I begged for safety for all of us, and I offered the very thing I knew I had to deliver: I would have to leave. The pain of the knowledge flayed my very skin from my body.

In the dark, in the cold, with Channan safely asleep next to the cradled body of my son, I let my sorrow howl into the room so that I could be strong for what would come next. For the safety of my beloveds, I would endure whatever was required.

~

I didn't know how long we'd been there when I heard the door above unlock, and footsteps coming down the stairs. Shafi appeared at the door. "It is safe now, memsahib. You may all come with me."

We followed him without speaking into the gray dawn. As we walked along the corridor overlooking the courtyard, I looked down to see the destruction of anger—overturned furniture and savagely uprooted plants. I smelled smoke, but saw no evidence of it. "Did something burn?"

He nodded darkly, and gestured. "The ruins were set on fire."

A thin line of smoke rose from the rubble, and Channan made a sound. I took her hand. "All is well, sister."

We ate parathas and yogurt Sughra brought. I fed and changed Kirandeep, and we all fell into a restless slumber. Shafi stood guard, and the gates had been locked, but none of us would rest until Tanveer returned.

At last he rode into the gates, rushing to find us in Channan's chambers.

That night, while Kirandeep slept, we made love with sacred intent. I pressed into memory the taste of his tears, the fierce clasp of his arms around me. In the darkness, with rain falling beyond the rooms, I lay against his chest and wept with such gravity I thought the river might carry us away. When I was at last spent, I whispered into his neck. "Why give us this deep love when we are forced to part again and again and again. What is the point of all this heartbreak?"

"It is the space between heartbreaks," he said. "How many are so lucky as to know this connection we share? It is rare and true." He brushed my cheek. "We shall not be physically together, but that does not divide"—he swallowed, paused—"us. Our souls."

I thought of all the days and months and years ahead of me, empty of his company. "I will miss you all the time, every day."

"As I will." He twined our fingers together. "Distance will not change us, what we share. It is eternal."

I didn't want eternity. I wanted now, but there was nothing to be done. As long as I stayed in the palace, the people I loved here would be in danger. I could not take Kirandeep away from the world he deserved, from his place and his father, so I would go alone.

Exiled.

On the morning of my departure, I nursed my son one last time, the two of us alone. I sang him a song from my childhood, about fairies and bluebells. He cooed at me, and I nibbled his fingers and forced myself to give him only joy in this moment. He smiled at me, gazing upward with love. I knew he would search for me in the days and weeks to come, crying for his mother, for my arms.

I also knew that he would be easily comforted by his other mother, who had not been able to bear a child in her own body, but had given me the gift of a child from mine.

When it came time, I nestled his soft, hefty body into her arms. She pressed her face into my shoulder, and I held her close. "Thank you," I said. "I love you."

"I shall miss you every day of my life."

At last, I embraced Tanveer, fiercely. "One soul," he whispered.

"One soul."

I managed to leave without breaking down, and traveled to the train station with stoic dignity.

But on the train to Bombay, I wept so continuously that a porter brought me a towel and supplied me with chai and cakes I could not consume. Where once my heart had been torn from one side, it was now torn in three, and it did not matter that I knew I would survive. I also knew the wounds would not heal.

How could they?

A TERRIBLE NIGHT, PART TWO

Autumn 1940
London

—75—

The first bomb landed so close by that the house shook, and even on the stairs as I was running to Mother's side, dust shook out of the ceiling. The cats ran with me, and I dropped them in the box I kept for them, lined with a towel, the flaps closed but not tight. It seemed to make them feel safer. I carried the box into Mother's room and checked on her, but it was hard to hear her breathing over the noise of the guns and engines. They were right overhead, too many, too loud, and I ducked when a bomb exploded not far away.

Mother's breath was ragged. I held her hand. "I'm here, Mother. Don't be afraid." I turned off the light and sat on the bed with her, singing in the dark.

A plane flew close overhead, droning, and chillingly the sound of a bomb falling, falling—

It landed hard and close, sending a shock wave that knocked me down and blew out the windows in the room. I rolled into a crouch with my hands over my head as plaster fell from the ceiling and glass rained down on me, the floor, the bed. A bright light flashed in the windows, and I realized the house across the street had taken a direct hit and was on fire. I stood and shook the glass from my clothing, and checked to make sure nothing heavy had fallen on Mother. Glass covered the bed, but nothing else, and I said, "Don't worry. It's okay. We'll get you downstairs and make sure you're—"

Her eyes were open. "Mother?" I brushed dirt off her face, plucked an errant piece of wood from her shoulder. "Can you hear me?"

She could not. She would not hear anyone again. A howl went through my heart, and I took her limp hand, pressed it to my cheek.

Another droning engine circled, and a wind blew through the shattered window, fire flickering. Sirens roared, and a sudden percussion made me duck again. What should I do?

Mother had passed to a place where bombs no longer mattered, but I still lived in a body. Taking the cats with me, I ran to the cellar, where at least there was some kind of protection.

Alone with Bastet and her kitten as the battle raged overhead, I did the only thing I could think of. I wrote a letter to Tanveer.

~

To my surprise, I fell asleep on the sofa with a cat and kitten curled up on my belly. When I stirred, it was dark, but there were no sounds of a battle overhead. I must have missed the all clear. "Come on, little ones," I said, tucking them back into the box. "Let's get out of here."

Upstairs, I could hear cries and shouts, and when I looked out, there were crews working on the house across the street. I felt remarkably calm. Focused. Leaving the cats by the door, I went upstairs to look into Mother's room, but she lay exactly as she had. I leaned on the threshold, winded for a moment, trying to think of what to do. There would be no one to call until morning. The idea of staying here with her dead body was untenable.

I crossed the floor and tugged the blankets over her shoulders.

I would go to Nina's.

First, I headed up to my studio for my bag of watercolors and pencils.

A lamp cast a yellow glow onto the wooden floor at the top of the stairs, and I could see a faint flicker from the fire across the street, which I didn't question until I came into my studio and realized the blackout curtains were open, glass on the floor here, too, and canvases blown over.

I didn't see Peter until I picked up the painting I'd done of angry Demeter. He sat in the armchair, flipping through a sketchbook. He'd clearly been doing it for quite some time. A discarded number were flung across the floor, carelessly tossed into the water on the floor. "Peter, what are you doing? These are my things. You're not allowed to touch them." I grabbed one off the wet floor, trying to shake it off, and realized it was turpentine that had spilled in the blast. The jug lay on its side on the floor. "This is dangerous," I said, glancing at the fire across the street. "Even a spark will—"

"Burn it all down?" He was bleary-eyed with drink. He tossed the sketchbook in his hands aside. "Why would I care? What do I even have to live for?"

I didn't need the bag. I would buy new paints. I turned for the door, trying not to move too quickly, give him reason to flip. He grabbed me by the arm before I could get there, and I squeaked.

Calm. Calm. "Peter, you don't want this. You are grieving." I turned toward him, rather than away. "You don't want death, you want love."

"Maybe." He bent to kiss me, and I let him, smiling when he lifted his head.

I stepped backward, freeing myself from his grip, thinking to get closer to the door, and pulled my sweater off over my head. "You want to make love. Let's leave this mess and do that."

He scoffed. "I'm not an idiot." He held up a cigarette lighter as a threat. "Stay where you are."

My skin condensed in terror, and I backed against the wall, trying to think of something to bargain with as he moved toward the door and closed it. "Your mother is dead. I saw her. She's dead and you'll leave me." He picked up another sketchbook, flung it on the floor, kicked it into the pile. The turpentine had not spilled. He'd poured it out deliberately. "You're just going to go right back to India, and leave me here to rot."

"Peter—"

He held up a hand. "No. Here is what I remembered tonight." He held up a vial. "We have cyanide. I have yours, too. We can take them together, and I'll leave your paintings alone, or you can refuse and I'll burn it all down, and you'll still die. Burned up by your paintings. Rather poetic."

I heard Tanveer's voice in my mind: *You must live*. A sense of perfect, cold calm filled me.

In my peripheral vision, I scanned the room for anything that might serve me. The table was covered with nails and a hammer, but could I reach it in time? Would it be enough of a weapon?

I needed to distract him. "Did you know that my mother's husband didn't die in America?"

He scowled. "Why would I care?"

"She came back to England to get me to come home."

"So? It worked."

I shook out my sweater, and put my arms through the sleeves, in preparation for pulling it back over my head. "That's not why I came home."

He lost interest in the conversation. In one swift motion, I pulled the sweater over my head and reached for the hammer all at the same time. I slipped a little on the turpentine and water, but righted myself and then drove forward with the hammer, aiming for his knees. It landed, and he screamed in fury and pain, the lighter flying out of his hand. It fell on the floor and I kicked it toward the door.

Peter roared and looped one arm around my throat from behind, using his other hand to try to open my mouth to shove the cyanide inside. I bit him as hard as I could, and as he jerked away, I rammed my elbow into his ribs. He grunted, and I scrambled away, diving for the lighter.

I grabbed it, intending to throw it on to the landing. Before I could, I heard the unmistakable sound of a falling bomb and turned to see an incendiary fly through the open window. It landed on the chair, and instantly, flames exploded. Peter, standing in a pool of turpentine, screamed as his clothes caught fire. He staggered toward me.

I ran for my life. Down the stairs, grabbing the box of cats, and out the door into the night. I ran until I could no longer breathe, and then I walked, Bastet and her kitten jostling in the box, but silent, as if they understood I could not take one more distraction. I walked to Nina's, and when she let me in, I fell into her arms. "Peter's dead. My mother is dead. I need to go home."

"Oh, darling, come in. Come in. I've got you."

VICTORIA TERMINUS

December 1940

—76—

TELEGRAM

TO: TANVEER SINGH, TALWARPUR PALACE
FROM: ELSIE TURNER, ABOARD SS EASTERN STAR
MOTHER AND PETER DEAD STOP ARRIVING BOMBAY SATURDAY. STOP DECEMBER 14 STOP VICTORIA TERMINUS STOP PLEASE ADVISE. STOP
ELSIE

TO: ELSIE TURNER, SS EASTERN STAR
FROM: TANVEER SINGH
WILL MEET YOU VICTORIA TERMINUS. STOP
LOVE TANVEER

I stood on deck in a cold wind, watching Bombay approach on the horizon. My body felt hollow after the long journey on dangerous seas, but the sight of the city blew a wind of possibility through me.

At last. Again.

My meager belongings fit into a single bag, my shoes ill-fitting since it had been impossible to find a new pair before I left.

Jonathan had used his connections to secure the passage, and I traveled with a ragtag group of passengers, all of us war weary and escaping the madness of London, many Indians, of course, but a good many British as well. We were a subdued lot, grateful for the modest meals, the quiet. No sirens, no bombs, just the soothing swoosh of water against the walls of the ship, murmured conversations.

The weeks at sea gave me time to grieve. The house had burned to the ground. Mother and Peter were both found within, the fire blamed on incendiaries. Jonathan and Nina took care of the arrangements for Peter's body.

Of course I had handled Mother myself, arranging for her interment next to my father and brother at Herewich, but I found I could not bear to remain in England one more week. She was gone and would not care if I attended her funeral.

On those long empty days on the open sea, I tried to collect myself, reassemble the jumbled jigsaw of my life. The piece I struggled most to fit was the betrayal of my mother, and perhaps even more, the way she'd held the secret from me for so many years. It was difficult to forgive.

And yet—would I do such a thing to protect my child? Her motives were ill-advised, but I knew in my deepest soul that she'd done everything for love of me. That was something I could understand. And truly, I would miss her the rest of my days.

Finally, I gave myself room to grieve Channan, who had slipped away a few weeks before my mother. Tanveer's letter had arrived only days before I left.

November 13, 1940
Talwarpur Palace
[In Urdu]

Dearest Elsie,

I attempted a phone call to deliver this news more personally, but there was no answer. I shall worry until I receive another letter.

It is with a heavy heart that I must bring you the news of Channan's passing. She slipped away painlessly overnight. I know you share my feelings that she was one of the finest humans to have lived in this world, and my grief is deep tonight. My only consolation is that she is at last free of the prison of her body. Kirandeep has vowed we will honor her by taking her portrait (the lovely miniature you made of her) to the Paris opera one day. Perhaps you shall be able to make that pilgrimage with us when better days have arrived.

None of us would be who we are without her grace, and the world is a poorer place tonight. I am a better man for having known her.

I also miss you deeply, meri jaan. Please write and let me know you are well.

Tanveer

Once more, I carried my meager belongings down the gangway, a small basket and my ancient carpetbag. The terminus was a familiar wild cacophony of noise and color and humanity. As I waded into the crowd, I felt the carapace around me suddenly split and fall way, leaving a revitalized version of myself, both fresh and raw, a woman ready to—once again—begin anew. My spirit expanded, warmed my skin. I smelled fish and sweat and cardamom, and was jostled along, bumped and knocked, and I did not mind. Not one bit.

Home. The only home I'd ever wanted, filled with the humans I peered through the crowds for a glimpse of. Turbans of many styles and colors caught my eye, but none of them crowned the man I wanted to see.

And then, at last, he was there, looking anxiously over the crowd. He wore a pale-gray suit, his hair covered by a dastaar in a very similar color, and he looked dapper and modern and entirely himself.

Next to him was a youth, lean and tall, with a face so like his father's I was transported back in time.

Kirandeep.

My breath left me, and for a long moment, I could not move, overcome by a tidal wave built of thousands of hours—ten thousand!—of longing that I had compressed and pushed away, knowing I had done the best thing for him. For my son.

But seeing him, I feared I might dissolve into the intense love that filled me. He was standing there, right there. Alive and loved and well.

He spied me first, and pointed. Urgently, Tanveer pushed through the bodies toward me, and hurtled into the space. It would not do for us to embrace in public, but he took my fingers and kissed them fervently. "You're alive," he said. His beard had small threads of silver in it. "You're alive."

I brought his hands to my lips, and as ever, tears filled my eyes, spilled over. He smelled of himself, and I turned my cheek to his hands. "I am alive."

Our eyes locked, and it was as it ever had been, the river of our connection flowing from me to him and him to me in a weaving of deepest union the same as always.

In the basket, Bastet mewed. Tanveer said, "What's this?"

"I couldn't leave her."

He laughed, that enormous sound that made people turn to look. Then he turned to Kirandeep. "He wanted to be here to greet you. Channan spoke of your return with great longing."

At last I allowed myself to fill my soul on Kirandeep's face—the straight brows, the dark eyes, Tanveer's particular nose. "I am so happy to see you again," I said. "I have not seen you since you were a small baby."

He bowed. "My mother said to tell you she loves you, and she will always be grateful for the gift you gave her."

Our agreement had ever been that he would never know I was his physical mother, and that would continue, but the words unleashed the emotion I had been desperately trying to rein in. My tears spilled. "She loved you like the sun," I said, and took his hands. "One day, perhaps we will all take her to the opera."

He nodded.

Tanveer touched my back lightly, and we walked to the car. When Kirandeep was settled within, with the cats, which he took on his lap with great curiosity, Tanveer held me back. Clasping my hand tightly, he cupped my face. He seemed to struggle for words, but in the end, his thumb simply brushed my cheekbone, my eye, while the other hand held my hand so tightly our fingers might have melted together.

The recognition of the moment suddenly overwhelmed me, and I bent my head into his coat.

"You must never leave us again," he whispered. "Promise."

"Never." I lifted my gaze. "Never, never, never."

—77—

In the darkness of the roof of Talwarpur Palace, Tanveer and I stood beneath a January sky and looked at the stars. The Milky Way ran in her river, and we pointed out constellations to one another. Venus burned brightest. I leaned into Tanveer's back. His arms looped around my torso, and I rested my hands on them.

"We must never let the world part us again, Elsie. Do you promise?"

"I promise."

"Our work matters, it does. And we have been born in difficult times, but I have come to believe that our individual lives, our loves and hopes and dreams, are just as important. What is the point of all those politics and even books and art, without the individual?"

I thought of the homes destroyed by bombs in London, a kitchen fallen away, the memories lost in the rooms at Herewich, the sketchbooks and paintings lost in the fire of Peter's despair. I thought of the lovers parted by war and strife all around us, even in this very moment.

And, too, I thought of my tears whenever I saw him again after a long stretch, tears of longing and relief and hope. I thought of winding his hair for him when he was so broken. I thought of painting a hundred styles during the years at Slade, seeking the truth of my own heart, and my conviction, always, that this thing between us mattered.

He rested his chin on my hair. "Perhaps it is time we marry at last."

"Will Kirandeep mind?"

"He will not. Channan prepared him."

My throat tightened. "Of course she did."

"Shall we marry, then, meri jaan?"

In the distance, a tiger roared—warning or complaint or perhaps only a comment. I was transported to another night, so long ago, when we'd spied the tiger over the wall. I had fantasized a tiger from a storybook, one who would whisk me into a world of wonder. Instead, when we saw her in the garden, I'd glimpsed her true nature—freer and wilder than I could even comprehend, and the sight of her dead body on that wagon had shown me true sorrow.

So many days had passed since then, some gilded, some wretched. Such a long, hard path to stand here with Tanveer, not in victory or even peace, but relief. The hours had left marks on my body, on his. How much had it cost us, both of us, to create and hold this connection? How could such a thing, a single union, matter so much in the wildness of the world?

And yet, somehow it did. Somehow, it mattered that we had endured all of it, coming back together again and again and again. I could not say that my love for this particular, singular man had brought more joy than grief into my life. It had not.

But this holy quiet, even with all the shattering, was the truest thing I'd ever known.

"We shall marry," I said.

He bent and kissed my ear. "At last."

ACKNOWLEDGMENTS

There are just some books that show up in a writer's life and insist they will be written. This one followed me around for almost four years, and when Elsie started inserting herself into *The Last Letter of Rachel Ellsworth*, I realized she really did want to tell her story.

The first person I have to thank is my agent Meg Ruley, who might have had a private eyebrow raised when I pitched an epic historical novel when I've mainly been writing contemporary women's fiction, but never batted an eye in my direction. The same goes for my editor, Nancy Holmes, who cheered me on, and my dev editor Charlotte Herscher, who recently fell back into my life after a long time away. (The publishing world is small, friends. Be a good sport all the time.)

Thanks to my pals from our Deadline group for cheering me on while I wrote a book that challenged, thrilled, and terrified me in equal measures. I don't know how I did this job without you all in my corner—Jamie Beck / Harper Ross, Priscilla Oliveras, Virginia Kantra, Amy Tally, Sally Kilpatrick. I especially appreciate Sonali Dev's willingness to help me brainstorm ideas, discuss the tangle of Indian and British history and colonialism, and especially the light-bulb reveal of Urdu script, which ended up forming such a huge portion of the storyline.

I am deeply grateful to writers Meeta Kaur and Navdeep Singh Dillion for offering such careful feedback on the Sikh angles of the book. All errors and misalignments are on me.

I don't know how I'd write books without my medical consultant, a.k.a. my sister Cathy Stroo, nurse extraordinaire, who has helped me imagine and create dozens of illnesses and injuries over the years. She assisted with many scenarios in this book, particularly Mother and Tanveer, delving into some dark research to help me understand what happened to the soldiers in those brutal trenches.

Two books triggered my deep interest into Sikh practice and culture. One I found "by happenstance" (is anything ever really a coincidence?) at the San Francisco Airport, *The Light We Give*, by Simran Jeet Singh. The simple, clear explanation of Sikhi moved me deeply. The other is the very powerful *Thousands of Heroes Have Arisen*, by Sukwinder Singh Bassi, a collection of letters from Sikh soldiers written during the Great War.

A book of this nature takes a tremendous amount of research. For more on many different subjects, please visit my website at www.barbaraoneal.com.

As ever, I am most grateful to you, dear reader. Without you, this circle of story would not be complete. Please know that I read every word you write back to me with great love. Thank you for being part of my world. I treasure you.

ABOUT THE AUTHOR

Photo © 2009 Blue Fox Photography

Barbara O'Neal is the *Washington Post*, *Wall Street Journal*, *USA Today*, and Amazon Charts bestselling author of twenty novels of women's fiction, including the #1 Amazon Charts bestseller *When We Believed in Mermaids*, as well as *The Last Letter of Rachel Ellsworth*, *Memories of the Lost*, *This Place of Wonder*, and *The Starfish Sisters*. Her award-winning books have been published in more than two dozen countries. She lives on the wild Oregon Coast with her husband, a British endurance athlete who vows he'll never lose his accent. For more information, visit www.barbaraoneal.com.